T0196509

# OPERATION: MOUNT MCKINLEY

## JEFFERY SEALING

iUniverse, Inc.
New York   Bloomington

# Operation: Mount McKinley

iUniverse books may be ordered through booksellers or by contacting:

iUniverse
1663 Liberty Drive
Bloomington, IN 47403
www.iuniverse.com
1-800-Authors (1-800-288-4677)

ISBN: 978-1-4502-5806-7 (sc)
ISBN: 978-1-4502-5807-4 (ebook)

Printed in the United States of America

iUniverse rev. date: 09/15/2010

# Dedication

To all those who have never given up on something. For those that have given up on something, take another crack at it!

To Emmett, James, Bonnie, Ruth, Leslie, Molly, Dion, Jim "Lunatic" Grohdotksi. To those who live in my memory: Andrea, Cassandra, C.J., Lonnie, Chuck, Frank V., Willie K., Maureen and others.

To my two very special family members Horace Sealing TMC (RET), USN, SS-395 and my uncle AFCM, (RET) USN, George Sealing on Eternal Patrol.

To my mother's new friend Dolly and her other golf buddies.

"The word impossible, Mr. Booth, is only found in a dictionary of fools." Maximillian Schell from Walt Disney Pictures, The Black Hole ©1982.

# Chapter 1

The sun was rising on the submarine base located at Pearl Harbor, Hawaii. At the submarine piers, one lonely submarine was moored to pier 12. The cobalt blue waters of the Pacific Ocean began to lap up against the hull of the ship. On the boarding way from the pier to the makeshift quarterdeck, located on the lower part of the conning tower, a vinyl sign hung down. On the sign, in bold, blue letters, was the name of the submarine, USS SEASIDE HEIGHTS, SSN-747. The ship was one of the last two of the LOS ANGELES class fast attack submarines built before funding ran out in fiscal year 2005. The ship was only seven years old.

On this particular day, the 0400 to 0800 watch had just begun. At 0545 hours, the command duty officer, serving as the Officer of the Deck, walked about the conning tower. He had a cup of coffee in his left hand as he looked toward the rising sun. The sun started out as a small orange ball, but steadily grew larger and brighter every minute. The heat grew exponentially along with the humidity. Only a small breeze ruffled the flags flying off the bow and stern ends of the ship. The weapons officer finished off his cup of coffee and tossed the empty cup into the trashcan at the quarterdeck.

A car suddenly appeared on the dock. To the Command Duty Officer, Commander Andrew Hinton-Smith, Weapons Officer of SSN-747, this was nothing new at this hour of the morning. The car came to a stop at the boarding way to SSN-747. The doors opened and both the commanding officer and the executive officer of SSN-747 stepped out of the car. They both put on their caps and the car drove off. Both the commanding officer and the executive officer stopped at the top of the boarding way to salute the flags and then the officer of the deck.

"Request permission to come aboard, Commander Hinton-Smith," they asked, almost in unison.

"Permission granted, sirs," replied Andrew, returning both of their salutes.

The Petty Officer Of the Watch, HM2 Stacey Plotss, had just finished waking up the crew. She saluted both the commanding officer and the executive officer as they passed by her station on the quarterdeck. She then pushed a small button on the panel to her right.

Gong, gong, gong, gong, went the ship's electronic bells as she grabbed the small microphone on the quarterdeck.

"Commanding officer, SEASIDE HEIGHTS, arriving," she announced to the ship. This was followed by one gong.

As the sun continued to climb higher into the sky, so too, did the temperature. When the diving officer relieved the weapons officer, Andrew went to the wardroom to get another cup of coffee before going on his weapons department tour. As he was leaving the wardroom, Andrew bumped into the ship's Personnel Officer, Ensign Theodore Ross.

"Weapons officer, here are your advancement exam results," he said, handing Andrew the sealed envelope.

Andrew took the envelope and noticed that not only was it still sealed on the back of the envelope, but also, the top of the envelope was undamaged.

"You didn't open up the envelope?" asked Andrew suspiciously since almost all command sealed envelopes were opened when they arrived to the person they were addressed prior to delivery.

"No, I don't have a need to know everything. Besides, the skipper has the master copy in his safe," said Theodore, smiling.

"I suppose you're right," said Andrew, putting the envelope into his right, front pants pocket.

As Andrew went towards the forward torpedo room, Ensign Ross entered the wardroom just as the commanding officer and executive officer did. The ship's Commanding Officer, Commander Lou Staggs, looked at Theodore. The ship's Executive Officer, Lieutenant Commander Rob Bertsen closed the door to the wardroom, which he had just entered. Theodore looked around and locked the door through which he had just entered. Lou spoke first.

"Did you see the weapons officer?" he asked.

"Yes, sir, just now and I handed him his advancement exam results," replied Theodore.

"Did he ask why the envelope wasn't opened?" asked Rob.

"Yes, sir and I responded with answer #3 of what we had rehearsed, sir."

"Was Andrew convinced?" asked Rob.

"Yes, sir, I believe he was. He made no indications to me that he was suspicious of what I had said."

"Good answer, Ensign Ross," commented Lou.

"Thank you, sirs,"

"Dismissed," said Lou.

"Yes, sirs,"

Andrew had finally arrived at the forward torpedo room and found the entire weapons department crew assembled for the morning muster. TM1 (SS) Shawn Dailey stepped forward from the ranks with a printout, handing it to Andrew.

"Good morning, sir. Weapons department crew accounted for and ready for inspection!" he yelled, saluting Andrew.

"Very well."

Andrew returned the salute, taking the printout from Shawn. This printout was the same today as it had been in the days, weeks and months prior. He then looked over his crew and then over at the open, torpedo tube doors. He walked over to them and looked inside; empty.

Removing his flashlight from his left, front pants pocket he turned it on. He shone the tiny beam of light inside the empty tubes; all clear. He looked over at the brightly painted, non-working, exercise shots with which he and his crew had practiced with during the last deployment.

"Close the torpedo tube doors," said Andrew.

"Aye, sir," replied Shawn, closing and securing each torpedo tube door.

"Dismissed, go about your duties," he announced to his department.

Andrew went to the amidships torpedo room. He looked over the empty tubes there on both port and starboard sides. Shawn was following Andrew around with a clipboard in hand, taking notes whenever Andrew pointed at something or said something to Shawn.

They entered the aft torpedo room and discovered water inside of tube number seven. After Shawn had closed and secured the aft torpedo tubes, they went to the armory. The armory was small enough that it only took a few minutes to inspect the few small arms that were in the various lockers. The ammunition was stored in another part of the armory and the seals were still intact on all of the boxes.

The next stop was the forward vertical launch tube system compartment. Each vertical launch tube had its own sight glass on the side of the compartment to see if there was a missile inside. When the inspection was completed there, he and Shawn went into the ship's combat control center, which housed the AEGIS series IV combat computers.

Shawn turned on all the combat systems one by one. He then pushed the "TEST" button on each section to check for faults or alarms. The only alarm that showed up was for "Water in Torpedo Tube 7." Since the submarine had never fired her weapons, the AEGIS IV system was still considered new. The only time the combat computers were updated was about once a month when a new security virus update or other program came from the manufacturer. With this part of the inspection completed, Shawn turned off the computers and they both left the compartment.

Their final stop on the inspection tour was to inventory all of the counter-measures. They entered the small compartment below the bridge where the 68 counter-measures were located. Andrew let Shawn count the counter-measures first. After Shawn had written down the totals, Andrew recounted them. He came up with the same number of counter-measures: 34 passive and 34 active counter-measures used primarily for confusing torpedoes.

They left the compartment where these things were located and headed towards the weapons department office. They arrived at the weapons department office and they both went inside. Shawn closed the doors behind them and sat down at a small desk in the far corner. Andrew decided to sit down at the desk reserved for the weapons officer. Shawn looked over this notes before speaking.

"Sir, what do you want to do about torpedo tube seven?" asked Shawn.

"Put in a maintenance report. Are the outer doors closed?"

"Yes, sir, in accordance with naval regulations, except during time of war, the torpedo tubes on all submarines in port must be closed."

"You're right, TM1. Are the inner doors closed?"

"Yes, sir."

"In the maintenance report, put a request in there about checking the outer door alignment and request that the seals be checked for damage or debris."

"Yes, sir. Anything else, sir?" asked Shawn, writing down what was being said.

"No, I'll be in my quarters."

"Yes, sir."

Andrew went to the quarters that both he and the Chief Engineer, Lieutenant Commander Bill Ellsworthy, shared. Andrew knocked first. Receiving no answer, he opened the door and entered the room. Andrew then shut the door and walked over to the small desk that was in the room. He reached up and turned on the small light. After sitting down in the chair at the desk, he removed the envelope from his right, front pants pocket. He put the envelope down on the desktop and stared at the thing for a little while.

After several minutes, he finally summoned enough courage to actually open the letter. He picked up the letter and put his right pinky finger underneath the right side of the back flap. Once the letter had been opened, he removed its contents. He then tossed the empty envelope aside on the upper left corner of the desktop.

He grabbed his reading glasses out of his upper, right shirt pocket and put them on to read the letter. He stopped reading the letter after the end of the first paragraph. The words in that first paragraph hit him like a stone in the side of his head. "We regret to inform you that, although you passed both the written and verbal parts of the Captain's Exam, you did not have enough total points in the Engineering section of the test on Reactor Operations. The minimum number of total points required for advancement was set at 200. Your maximum total points were 189. Therefore, you have been awarded 15 Passed but Not Advanced (PNA) points towards the next Captain's Exam cycle."

Andrew folded up the envelope and tossed it into the trashcan next to the desk. He then crumpled up the letter and stuffed it into his left, front pants pocket for later disposal. Andrew then reached up and shut off the light over the desk so that he could sit in the dark. He reached a decision that he would retire.

He left his quarters and headed back towards the aft torpedo room. As he came to the bottom of a ladder, he bumped into the command master chief. This person also served as the chief of the boat and career counselor. NCCM (SW/AW/SS) Lyle Stennings looked up at Andrew and smiled.

"Good afternoon, Commander Hinton-Smith," said Lyle.

"Good afternoon, master chief. What do I have to do to retire?" asked Andrew, almost without blinking.

"Put in a letter of resignation and fill out some paperwork in my office," answered the master chief, looking concerned.

"Do you have time today to fill out the paperwork?"

"See me in my office at 1500 hours."

"1500 hours it is then."

"By the way, I just checked aboard two new torpedoman's mates."

"Wonderful. I do hope that someone has shown them a bunk."

"Ensign Ross is taking care of that right now. That letter of resignation should, although it's not required, state the reason or reasons why you're giving up your commission."

"I'll keep that in mind. Now, if you will excuse me, I have a leaky torpedo tube to attend to."

After Andrew had arrived at the aft torpedo room and closed the hatch behind him, he opened up torpedo tube seven and some water came out. It merely poured itself into the bilges of the aft torpedo room. Andrew went to the wardroom and had lunch before returning to his quarters to type up his letter of resignation.

At 1500 hours, with his neatly typed-up letter of resignation, Andrew went to the master chief's office. He knocked on the door and waited for the master chief to open the door before entering. The master chief showed him a chair and took the letter. The master chief looked over the letter and gave Andrew some forms to fill out. When the master chief had finished reading the letter, he set it down on his desktop.

"Twenty-one years is a long time, commander," said Lyle.

"Well, master chief, after four times trying to make captain, I'm reasonably certain that this mustang isn't going any further up the chain of command," replied Andrew dryly.

"That's wrong, sir, and you know it. Mike Boorda was a mustang and he was made the Chief of Naval Operations in the 1990's."

"He also committed suicide, master chief."

"Good point."

"Any special hurry on these forms?" asked Andrew, looking down at them.

"The sooner the better. You live off ship right?"

"Yes."

"Well, until you're completely processed out of the navy, you might have to report to Officer Transient Personnel Unit here at Pearl."

"That's fine and thank you."

"No, thank you for your service, commander. I also wanted to let you know that Boggs and Dailey finally turned in their Limited Duty Officer Program packets last week because of you."

"I'm surprised that they brought those packets to you after I signed them."

"Why?"

"They see the constant ridicule that I sometimes get from the Annapolis officers. I warned them that they would get the same treatment if, or when, they get made into officers through the various LDO programs they put in for," Andrew said as he left the master chief's office before the master chief could say another word.

After Andrew left the master chief's office, he headed back to his quarters. When he entered his quarters, he saw all the lights were turned on and he could hear water running in the shower they shared. Andrew knew that the Chief Engineer, Lieutenant Commander Bill Ellsworthy was home.

"CHENG, it's me," announced Andrew as he closed the door.

"Okay Andrew, I'll be out in just a minute."

"All right, no hurry."

Andrew took off his shoes and socks as well as the upper part of his uniform. He reached over and opened up the door to his locker. Inside of this locker, he kept all his uniforms neatly pressed and smartly hanging. He hung up his uniform top inside of this locker and closed the door. The water stopped running and the shower curtain opened. The chief engineer began drying himself off with the towel that he had hanging on the outside of the shower.

"Hey, I saw the folded up envelope. What ship did you get?" asked Bill.

"No ship, no advancement," replied Andrew, nonchalantly.

"That's just wrong. You're more qualified than most of the officers on board this ship including, I might add, myself."

"I'm deficient in reactor operations, Bill."

"Not much you can do about that one, Andrew. Did the captain ever sign off on your Form SF-24 for a Secret Clearance?"

"I gave the captain that paperwork about a week after I arrived on board."

"That's been about three years now, hasn't it? How many ships are you qualified to operate on anyway?"

"Five classes of surface ships, this class of fast attack submarines and, in the simulators, the SEAWOLF class fast attack submarines."

"What are you going to do now?"

"I put in my letter of resignation today. I'm eligible for retirement."

"Has the master chief done your retirement pay calculations yet?"

"No, not yet. I just gave him the letter today."

"Well, whatever you decide to do, good luck, sir," said Bill, shaking Andrew's right hand.

"Thank you, Bill."

Andrew waited until after the captain and the executive officer had departed the ship before he left in his civilian clothes. He departed the quarterdeck and walked to the end of the pier. He occasionally glanced over his shoulder to see if anyone was following him. He continued walking after he arrived at the end of the pier to the base shuttle bus stop. A few minutes later, the base shuttle picked him up and took him to the main gate. He walked out the main gate to the navy exchange, still glancing around to see if anyone was following him.

There, at the pre-arranged time and place, was Andrew's spouse. Andrew had to make sure that no one saw him with his spouse together; especially someone from the ship. He looked around one last time, smiled and stepped into the car. Andrew's spouse was a young, muscular, Native American. This Native American was also a professional bodybuilder. He had high cheekbones and long, straight, coal black hair that was mid shoulder in length.

Once they were home and the doors were all locked, they could be themselves: happy, carefree, loving. After dinner, they walked down the beach, holding hands, for a short ways before returning home. When they returned home and the doors were locked once again, Andrew's spouse finally spoke to him.

"Did you hear back on the advancement exam?" asked Gary "Two-Feathers" Smith.

"Yes. No advancement, no command."

"I'm sorry. You've worked so hard in the last few years to get your own command."

"That's okay. I already put in for retirement today."

"That's wonderful. Where are we going to live after you retire?"

"I thought we would move back to New Mexico because of your father. If memory serves me correctly, he isn't doing well is he?"

"Funny you should mention that, I talked to mom today. He's doing about the same."

"Okay. What happened with your last competition?"

"I received the official results today in the mail. I took first in my weight class, third in the division I was in and seventh overall."

"Wonderful."

"And, I received a check for $5,000.00, minus taxes."

"That's even better. Let's pay the car off."

"I'll make sure to do that first thing in the morning. Right now, it's time for bed."

Andrew woke up early the next morning. Andrew had woken up from a terrible nightmare. A nightmare that consisted of being denied retirement and included getting command of his own ship. He slipped quietly out of bed so as not to prematurely wake up Gary. Andrew stepped into the shower and by the time he stepped out of the shower, Gary was awake and fixing breakfast.

When breakfast was over and the dishes were done, Gary drove Andrew to the navy exchange. They both waited there a few minutes as they both looked around for anyone watching them. They kissed each other goodbye and Andrew walked in the main gate and caught the shuttle bus to pier 12.

Upon his arrival to the ship, the ship's Master-At-Arms, MACS (SW/AW) Ron Boesters, greeted him. Ron smiled and looked right at Andrew.

"Good morning, weapons officer. I arrested one of the newest crewmembers to your department last night."

"What the hell did he do? Moon the captain?" asked Andrew, smiling.

"Very funny, commander. Well, sometime last night, after you left, but before sunset had fully set in, he tied his diver's flag on the stern end of the ship, put on his diving gear and went over the side."

"Did he say why he went midnight diving?"

"Yes, he said he was going to check out a leak on the number seven torpedo tube."

"I am having trouble with that tube's outer door. Did you know that I submitted a ship's maintenance activity report to get it looked at?"

"Yes, I have a copy of that report for the case file."

"Did he say who authorized his little excursion?"

"He said you did. I couldn't get a hold of you on either the pager or the cell phone."

"That's because the captain of this ship has not ever paid the bills to activate them. Did you try my home phone?"

"I thought it would be better not to disturb you at home. I wanted to speak with you privately about this matter."

"Very well. May I see him and did you read him his rights?"

"Yes, you may see him and, yes, I read him his rights."

As they passed by the quarterdeck on their way to the ship's brig, Andrew pulled the Petty Officer Of the Watch, BM2 Chris Connors, aside. Andrew whispered something into his ear. BM2 Connors nodded and Andrew continued down the ladders to the lower, forward portion of compartment number 2. Senior Chief Boesters opened the first door on the ship's brig.

When Andrew and the senior chief entered the cell, TMSN Bart Bradley stood up. Andrew couldn't figure out why he couldn't salute them as was customary when an officer enters the room. Andrew looked down seeing Bart's leg irons and handcuffs. Andrew looked at his watch and noticed that it was almost past breakfast time.

"Have you been fed Mr. Bradley?" asked Andrew.

"No, sir, I have not had breakfast."

"Senior chief, do you have something against feeding prisoners? Do you realize that you are violating naval regulations that require you to feed the prisoners in your custody? I'll write you up for that one myself," said Andrew through clinched teeth.

"There's no need to write me up. I will go get him a breakfast tray, commander."

"Thank you," said Andrew.

The senior chief left, locking the door to the brig cell behind him. When Andrew was sure that the senior chief was gone, he looked at Mr. Bradley. Mr. Bradley was a young, lanky, blond-haired kid, fresh from torpedoman's mate school. He was small, about five foot seven inches tall and Andrew wondered how he was able to get through boot camp. Andrew figured that Mr. Bradley weighed about 100 pounds/ 50-kilograms with wet clothes on.

"Are you a certified diver, Mr. Bradley?" asked Andrew.

"Yes, sir, Class 2 Open water. I have a copy of my certificate in my bunk locker and I think that there is a copy of it my service record, I hope," replied Bart.

"Did anyone see you dive off the side of the ship?"

"No, sir. I took my gear to the aft torpedo room and stowed it there. I then checked with the duty reactor person, duty sonar person and duty engineering to see if they were doing anything."

"Sounds like you were taking precautions. Was the word passed that there were divers over the side?"

"Yes, sir."

"What did you do next?"

"I had the duty weapons department person, TM3 Sanchez open the interior door to the torpedo tube. I then crawled into it."

"Did you work out some sort of signals?"

"Yes, sir. I took my small diving hammer with me as a means to communicate."

"Okay. When you're brought before the captain today, tell the truth; can you do that?"

"Yes, sir."

"Also, if they ask, you want a special court-martial."

"Yes, sir. Who is going to be my legal counsel?"

"Lt. Gambousia at the sub base here. You see, she and the captain don't get along with each other very well."

"Thank you, sir."

"Did you enjoy the view while you were down there?"

"Yes, sir. This ship is more impressive underwater than above. I also found damage that was most likely done by another ship's propeller blades. There is damage to the outer door and the door's facing. That is probably why it leaks."

"Thank you. The senior chief is back. Do not talk to anyone about this issue."

"Yes, sir."

The cell door to the brig opened and the senior chief entered carrying a breakfast tray. Andrew stood up and faced the senior chief. As they left the brig cell, Andrew turned to look at the senior chief.

"Do you have his diving gear?" asked Andrew.

"Yes, his gear is in my office."

"What time is he going before the captain?"

"1045, commander."

"Senior chief, if you have lied to me, there will be hell to pay."

Andrew went to his department meeting. Shawn handed him the same stack of paperwork with one exception. The morning report showed the one department member who was in the brig. Andrew did a quick inspection of his department personnel noting only minor deficiencies. He stood in front of them for a minute to gather his thoughts.

"TM3 Sanchez, see me in the weapons department office after this muster," said Andrew.

"Yes, sir," replied TM3 Sanchez.

"Carry on," announced Andrew.

TM3 Sanchez followed Andrew and Shawn into the weapons department office. When the door was shut, there came a knock on the door. Andrew opened the door and took a piece of paper from BM2 Connors. After BM2 Connors departed, Shawn looked up and down the passageway. Then Shawn closed the door to the office.

"TM3 Sanchez, did TMSN Bradley really swim out of the torpedo tube?" asked Andrew.

"Yes, sir. Even with all his gear on, he isn't much larger than a HARPOON or TOMAHAWK. In fact, he had room to spare," said Sanchez.

"Did he tell you that I gave him permission to be swimming around the ship?"

"Yes, sir. However, since no one could get a hold of you, I figured you authorized it and forgot to tell me."

"Very good answer, Mr. Sanchez. Shawn, please prepare Mr. Bradley's Navy Achievement Medal paperwork," said Andrew.

"Okay," said Shawn, turning on the office computer with a confused look on his face.

"Mr. Sanchez, go about your normal duties. Do not talk to anyone about this matter."

"Yes, sir."

After Mr. Sanchez had left the office, Andrew turned to Shawn.

"Shawn, I want you to find the date of the last time we pulled out of port."

"You mean on our last deployment?"

"Yes."

"That's easy, it was December 28th."

"Thank you. I'll be in the captain's cabin or wherever this hearing is going to take place."

"Yes, sir and good luck."

Andrew arrived outside the captain's cabin. He looked at Mr. Bradley and then at the senior chief. Andrew noticed that MA2 Evelyn Delware was present as well as the Reactor Officer, Damian Furth. Damian looked at Andrew and smiled. Soon, the chief engineer joined them. The door to the captain's cabin opened and the executive officer appeared.

"The prisoner will enter along with the other officers for this special board of inquiry," said Rob.

Andrew looked over at the chief engineer.

"Bill, was it my imagination, or did Rob not even blink his eyes?" asked Andrew.

"It wasn't your imagination," replied Bill.

Everyone entered the captain's cabin. No one said a word as they soon went to another location, the wardroom. Once everyone was inside the wardroom, senior chief Boesters had MA2 Delware post herself outside the wardroom entrance door as a guard. The reactor officer motioned for everyone to take seats. The senior chief moved Bart to a position in front of the commanding officer, the executive officer and the reactor officer. Andrew stood beside Bart as the senior chief sat down in a chair behind them.

The commanding officer had just closed Bart's service record and put down his pen. Andrew saw Lou pull out a small tape recorder from his upper, left shirt pocket. Lou placed this tape recorder on the table in front of him and pushed the RECORD button before speaking.

"These proceedings are going to be recorded. Does the prisoner have departmental representation?" asked Lou.

"Yes, sir, I do have departmental representation," replied Bart, nervously.

"Who is the departmental representative?" asked Lou as if he were reading a pre-written script.

"I am, sir," answered Andrew.

"For the record, state your name, rank or title, current duty station and social security number," said Lou.

"Andrew Arthur Hinton-Smith, Commander, United States Navy, Weapons Officer USS SEASIDE HEIGHTS, SSN-747. Social security number 741-29-0016."

"Very well. Will the prisoner state their name, rank or title, current duty station and social security number."

"Bart Anthony Bradley, Torpedoman's Mate Seaman, USS SEASIDE HEIGHTS, SSN-747. Social security number 989-60-9998."

"Very well. Will the prisoner and his departmental representative step outside into the passageway," said Lou.

Andrew and Bart walked outside and stood in the passageway. After about fifteen minutes, the door opened. The reactor officer appeared this time and escorted them both back inside the wardroom again. Andrew and Bart stopped in front of Lou.

"Mr. Bradley, this group of the most senior ranking officers of the USS SEASIDE HEIGHTS, SSN-747, are going to start asking questions of both you and your departmental representative," said Lou, pausing before continuing.

"Mr. Bradley, did you come before this special board of inquiry to lie to or deceive us?" asked Lou.

"No, sirs."

"Did you, Commander Hinton-Smith, come here to lie to or deceive us?" asked Rob.

"No, sirs."

"This is a fact finding special board of inquiry. We will not argue whether or not Mr. Bradley was given an order or the validity of that order," said Lou.

There was a brief pause before Lou looked at Bart.

"Mr. Bradley, do you know why you were arrested?" asked Rob.

"Yes, sir," replied Bart a little less nervously.

"Do you realize that if you are found guilty of the offense for which you were arrested for, you could be reduced in rank to E-1, given a dishonorable discharge and serve time in a military prison?" asked Lou.

"Yes, sir, I am aware of those facts."

"Mr. Bradley, were you read your rights when you were arrested?" asked Damian.

"Yes, sir."

"The prisoner will now be seated with his department representative," said Rob.

Andrew and Bart sat down to the right of Lou, Rob and Damian.

"This board calls forth Master-At-Arms, Senior Chief Petty Officer (SW/AW) Ron Boesters to the front," said Damian.

Ron approached and stood in front of the officers.

"Did you, senior chief, come before this special board of inquiry to lie to or deceive us?" asked Lou.

"No, sirs," responded Ron, confidently.

"When you arrested Mr. Bradley, did you read him his rights?" asked Rob.

"Yes, sir, as required by naval regulations," replied Ron.

"Did you physically see Mr. Bradley go over the side of the ship, jump off the pier or any other type of activity that would constitute the basis for your arresting him?" asked Damian.

"No, sir. I only saw Mr. Bradley exit the water by the aft torpedo tubes."

"So, you assumed, then, that he went into the water the same way you saw him exit the water?" asked Lou.

"Yes, sir. I did assume that was the case."

"Has the prisoner made any statements to you?" asked Damian.

"Not since I read him his rights."

"Very well; dismissed," said Rob.

"Will the prisoner and his department representative approach," said Lou.

Andrew and Bart stood before the board once again. Andrew, in his head anyways, was beginning to wonder if Ron had bugged the cell. Then it dawned on Andrew, Ron or one of his cronies, was probably close by the cell and overheard some of the conversation. This person could have reported anything they heard to the board. To Andrew, this clearly violated Bart's rights.

"Mr. Bradley, according to your service record, you finished fifth in your class at 'A' school and you have no Page 13 entries for disciplinary issues," said Lou.

"Yes, sir, that is a correct statement," replied Bart, swallowing hard.

"You are also a Class 2, Open water diver, correct?" asked Lou again.

"Yes, sir, that is also a correct statement."

"What is your story, Mr. Bradley?" asked Damian.

As Bart recounted what had happened to him the night before and earlier this morning, Andrew thought things were going a little too easy. In fact, Andrew was thinking that maybe Lou, Rob and Damian were all clairvoyant.

"It is almost lunchtime. Damian, have MA2 Delware take the prisoner back to the brig and make sure that the prisoner is fed in accordance with naval regulation 1899," said Lou, looking right at Andrew.

"Yes, sir."

Damian brought MA2 Delware into the wardroom. She took Bart away and when the door was shut, Lou stood up.

"Commander Hinton-Smith, I have never improperly hazarded a vessel under my command including this one. We will reconvene at 1300 hours."

"I never said anything about improperly hazarding a vessel, captain," said Andrew, suspiciously.

"But you were thinking it, weren't you?"

"Yes, the thought had crossed my mind."

At 1300 hours, Andrew and the other officers assembled back outside the wardroom in the small passageway. Bart showed up a few minutes later with Ron and Evelyn in tow. The door to the wardroom opened and the reactor officer lead everyone inside. Both Andrew and Bart stood before Lou, Rob and Damian. Ron took a seat to the left of Damian.

"Mr. Bradley, before we pass judgment on your actions, do you wish to say anything further on your behalf?" asked Lou.

"No, sir. I will accept whatever punishment is given out by this special board of inquiry," replied Bart.

"Do you wish to add anything, Commander Hinton-Smith?" asked Rob.

"No, sir," replied Andrew, looking at a spot on the bulkhead behind Damian.

"It is the finding of this special board of inquiry that the accused is not guilty of the crime for which he was arrested for due to lack of clear and convincing evidence and some procedural errors made by Senior Chief Boesters," said Lou.

"Thank you, sirs," said Bart with much relief in his voice.

"XO, have the ship's personnel officer remove these proceedings from his service record. Have the arrest record expunged," said Lou pushing the STOP button on the tape recorder.

"Yes, sir," replied Rob.

As Bart was lead away by Ron and Evelyn, Andrew was leaving as well. However, he was stopped by Rob who whispered into his right ear.

"You had better sharpen up your skills on the Iranian navy," he said and let Andrew go.

Rob shut the door to the wardroom as Lou pushed the EJECT button on the tape recorder. The officers all started laughing because there was no cassette tape in the recorder.

# Chapter 2

For the next few weeks, Lou and Rob had the entire ship going through emergency drills of all sorts. After each drill was an evaluation and suggestions as to how to improve for the next time. The crew was a little on edge because they were aware that the ship was still battle ready and deployable. There were reports in both the military and civilian news that, once again, Iran was threatening to attack Israel with a deadly missile attack. Although most of the senior officers ignored these reports, the reports were having a drastic affect on the enlisted personnel.

One day, after a particularly hard session of emergency drills, Lou sent for Lyle. Lyle took care of some paperwork and then went to the captain's cabin. He knocked on the door.

"Come in, Lyle," said Lou from behind the door.

Lyle entered and saluted both Lou and Rob. Rob reached over and shut off the TV news program that had yet another report on the ranting and raving of the leader of Iran. Lyle was aware that over the last few months, Lou and Rob had been in meetings with their boss, the Commanding Officer of Submarine Squadron 22, Captain Mel Henning. Until now, Lyle had never been privileged to the content of those meetings.

"At ease, master chief," said Lou.

"Yes, sir," said Lyle, relaxing a little.

"Master chief, myself and Rob have just come from yet another meeting with our boss," started Lou, but the master chief interrupted him.

"What did Captain Henning have to say, sir?" asked Lyle.

"Master chief, I cannot tell you what Captain Henning said, you understand that, right?" asked Lou.

"Yes, sir. I thought I might ask anyway."

"I handed Commander Hinton-Smith's letter of resignation to Captain Henning. He told me to tell you that Commander Hinton-Smith must stay in the Navy at least a few more years."

"Is the chain of command invoking the war clause?" asked Lyle.

"Who said anything about war, master chief?" asked Rob, defensively.

"That's the latest rumor, XO."

"It will stay a rumor for now. You have your orders; dismissed," said Rob, curtly.

When the master chief had left, the XO locked the door. Rob turned back around to face Lou.

"You told the master chief a lot, sir," said Rob.

"Rob, I have the actual officer advancement exam results here in the safe. Commander Hinton-Smith was promoted to the rank of Captain. This advancement, however, is contingent upon him completing a highly experimental and dangerous war game exercise," said Lou.

"How come he was given a PNA letter then?" asked Rob.

"That letter was mailed directly from Captain Henning's office. The hope was he would stick around for another year or so. It appears that this plan has backfired."

"Let me guess, we cannot tell Commander Hinton-Smith about his promotion either?"

"That's right. By the way, our boss is coming aboard after 1400 hours today to talk to Commander Hinton-Smith. Our boss does not want us around."

"I understand, sir."

"Did you know that I have a spy in Commander Hinton-Smith's department?"

"No, sir, I wasn't aware of that issue. Who is it?"

"TM1 Dailey. He has been keeping tabs on Commander Hinton-Smith for me since he came aboard. Shawn reports to me directly, giving me daily reports."

"So, the Navy has been looking at Commander Hinton-Smith for awhile then?"

"For the past seven years. Ever since he entered Limited Duty Officer School and entered the submarine community. Did you know that Commander Hinton-Smith has two submarine simulation games on his office computer?" said Lou as he started staring at the bulkhead in front of him.

"I wasn't aware of it, sir."

Lou continued staring blankly at the bulkhead in front of him as he continued talking.

"In those simulation games, he has scored successfully against the enemy at inflicting better than 80 percent damage to their attacking forces. He's intelligent and resourceful."

"I have noticed that, sir. I have also observed that Commander Hinton-Smith seems to command respect with not only his department personnel, but other department personnel as well."

"Yes, he does command respect wherever he goes. Instead of ordering people to do things, all he has to do is ask. Have you noticed that even during the emergency drills, he rarely gives any orders?"

"I've noticed that, sir."

"Were you aware that Commander Hinton-Smith is married to another male?"

"I thought that the military's policy is 'Don't ask, don't tell.'"

"That was a ploy to appease the civilians. Commander Hinton-Smith's secret clearance was approved about nine months after he put in for it."

"How come you didn't tell him or have it put into his service record?"

"The Navy thought it was better to see how a homosexual functions and interacts with others before giving a homosexual command of a ship full of young men."

"Obviously, his sexual orientation and preference hasn't affected him one bit, sir."

"Correct. The poor Naval Investigative Service agent that was sent out to complete the background check interviewed Commander Hinton-Smith's better half, I believe is the term. The NIS agent was absolutely terrified of the man."

"Why?"

"His better half is a professional, Native American, bodybuilder by the name of Gary 'Two-Feathers' Smith."

The XO was about to speak when Lou stood up and turned to face his bunk. Lou began speaking again before the XO could say anything.

"Commander Hinton-Smith never hid his sexual orientation or preference away from anyone. If you want proof, look in his service record at his marriage certificate. The best place to hide something is out in the open."

"That's true. What's so special about his marriage certificate?"

"It's from the State of New Mexico where their marriage law says a marriage is a civil contract between two persons. Commander Hinton-Smith took advantage of this loophole before it was closed off during legislative year 2006."

"I see."

"Did you know that it took Shawn about nine months to find out where

Commander Hinton-Smith lived? Commander Hinton-Smith would meet his better half at different locations and at different times."

"Commander Hinton-Smith is definitely not stupid, sir."

"You're right about that one. Well, we had better get out of here. Let's go play some golf, shall we?"

"Sounds good to me, sir."

"XO, I sure hope that the Navy knows what they are doing," said Lou.

Meanwhile, in Captain Henning's office, Captain Henning was looking across his desk at a lone civilian. This civilian was a defense department contractor who was contracted through Boeing to make parts and equipment for the HARPOON anti-ship missile. As the civilian finished looking over the stack of feedback reports from Commander Hinton-Smith and his missile crews, he closed up his notebook and put it into his lap.

The forms, containing some interesting feedback that Mr. Bruce Harvard wanted more clarification on of Commander Hinton-Smith's feedback reports, was just one part of the larger picture. Mr. Harvard put the notebook away inside his zip-up, folding briefcase. Mr. Harvard was also going to check out the weapons systems, on the HARPOON side, to see how functional the weapons systems were.

"Are you sure you want to talk to Commander Hinton-Smith?" asked Mel.

"Yes, I do want to talk to him for the last time. People like him, Captain Henning, give people like me ideas. We in turn create jobs for people like yourself when you retire and our stockholders become very rich people," said Mr. Harvard.

"Well, you'll get your chance to meet him in just a few minutes. My duty driver will be in shortly to take us to the ship. Make sure that you have your DOD ID on you," said Mel.

"Right here," said Bruce, showing the lanyard at the end of which was a DOD ID.

A few minutes later, Captain Henning and Bruce arrived on the pier. As they drove down the pier, Mel and Bruce both saw a car pass them, going the opposite direction. Mel hoped that Lou and Rob were inside that car. Finally, the car stopped and Mel and Bruce exited the vehicle. They both walked up the boarding way to the quarterdeck.

"Officer of the Deck, request permission to come aboard," said Mel, saluting MTC Carl Snowden.

"Permission granted, sir, but you just missed the skipper," he replied, returning the salute.

"I know. I planned my visit that way chief. This is Mr. Bruce Harvard, he is a DOD contractor with appropriate security clearances," said Mel, pointing at Bruce.

"Can I see your identification, Mr. Harvard?" asked Carl.

"Sure," replied Bruce, showing Carl the DOD ID.

"Welcome aboard, sir," said Carl.

"Thank you," replied Bruce.

The Petty Officer Of the Watch, STS1 (SW/AW/SS) Gladis Harpose pushed the button on the quarterdeck to announce people. The ship's electronic bells sounded. Gong, gong, gong, gong. She pressed the button on the microphone.

"Commanding Officer, Submarine Squadron 22, arriving," she said and pressed the button again; gong.

"Chief, do you know where Commander Hinton-Smith is?" asked Mel.

"Yes, sir, forward torpedo room," replied Carl.

"Thank you."

Mel and Bruce wound their way down ladders and passageways until they reached the forward torpedo room. They entered just as TMSN Bradley, Commander Hinton-Smith, TMSN Lori Sanders and TM3 Nick Sanchez were restowing the MK-48, ADCAP series IV and the MK-50 Heavyweight, ADCAP series II torpedoes that were the exercise shots for drills. These weapons had been accidentally dropped onto the deck. Once the exercise shots were secured to the port bulkhead, TMSN Sanders saw Mel.

"Attention on deck!" she yelled.

Everyone came to attention.

"Carry-on. Commander Hinton-Smith, may we speak to you?" asked Mel, pointing to Bruce.

"Well, Captain Henning, I'm a little busy cleaning up this mess in my torpedo room," replied Andrew a little disgustedly.

"Here, let me help you, Commander Hinton-Smith. I've been waiting three years to speak to you," said Bruce, putting his zip-up briefcase on a rail along the port bulkhead. He then took off his suit jacket and tie and unbuttoned his top shirt button.

"Commander, I will be in your office looking over your training and maintenance records," said Mel, leaving the torpedo room.

"Yes, sir."

With much struggling and straining by all involved, the HARPOON and TOMAHAWK exercise shots were secured to the starboard bulkhead. Once Andrew had double-checked to make sure that the latches were properly secured, Bruce shook Andrew's right hand. Bruce then grabbed his zip-up briefcase and opened it up. He reached inside and grabbed the notebook with the questions written on it.

"Well, Mr. Civilian, what can I do for you?" asked Andrew, cleaning off his uniform.

"My name is Bruce Harvard. I'm a missile design engineer and a DOD contractor. My company makes most of the parts for these HARPOONs," said Bruce, tapping the HARPOON exercise shot with his right index finger.

"Mr. Harvard, do you work for Boeing?" asked TM3 Nick Sanchez.

"Yes, I do, Mr. Sanchez," replied Bruce, looking at Nick's uniform.

"Can I ask you a question then?"

"Go ahead, Mr. Sanchez," said Bruce.

"An Army buddy of mine told me they have the HARPOON. Is that true?"

"Yes. Boeing made a special land mobile launcher for Department of the Army. This was so that Army coastal commands could protect the shores from invasion. In fact, their HARPOON is the same as the one you have aboard this ship," replied Bruce.

"Thank you," said Nick.

"Mr. Hinton-Smith, I have a few questions for you from my design technicians," said Bruce, pulling a pen from one of the notebook pockets.

"Are any of these questions related to security matters?" asked Andrew.

"No, in fact, most of these questions are just general in nature. My technicians want some clarifications on some of the feedback reports you and your missile crew sent to me."

"Alright. Nick, tell Shawn to let the department go for the weekend. Begin the weekend watch rotation. Let Shawn know that if he has any questions, he can find me in the forward torpedo room."

"Yes, sir," replied Nick as he and the others left the torpedo room.

Andrew made sure that the hatch to the torpedo room was secured before he turned back around to face Bruce.

"Alright, what do you want to know?" asked Andrew.

"This is a 688 class of ship, right?" asked Bruce.

"It's a 688-Improved."

"688-I? That means you have the AEGIS III-D installed?"

"AEGIS IV."

"AEGIS IV? That is excellent. How do you think making a HARPOON six inches longer will make it go farther?"

"My Missile Technicians and myself have calculated that six inches more in length will allow another two pounds or one kilogram of fuel. That extra bit of fuel could theoretically give the missile an estimated 10 nautical miles more."

"I see. Do you have a vertical launch system?"

"Yes."

"Have the weapons ever been fired?"

"No."

"Okay, that answers all the questions I have for you. Could you direct me to where I might find MT1 Boggs and MT2 Bliss?"

"Sure, I'll take you there myself."

"Thank you."

Andrew located the two Missile Technicians in the vertical launch tube compartment. After Andrew showed Bruce inside the compartment, he smiled at MT1 Boggs.

"MT1 Boggs, MT2 Bliss, when Bruce is done with you, show him to my office."

"Yes, sir."

Andrew left the compartment and headed towards his office. As he came down a ladder well, he bumped into Lyle. Lyle smiled at Andrew and started to fumble through his stack of paperwork. He finally found the paperwork he was looking for. He handed Andrew the piece of paper with his retirement pay calculations. Andrew took the paper and started looking it over.

"Commander, I just completed the retirement pay calculations for you. I might suggest staying in for at least another three years or more," said Lyle.

"Why should I stay in for another three or more years, master chief?" asked Andrew.

"Because, you came on active duty after January 1, 1980. Your retirement is calculated at 40 percent of your base pay for your three highest pay years," replied Lyle, thinking fast.

"My three highest pay years? What happens after I reach 30 years of service in, say, the inactive reserves?"

"Your three highest pay years, according to your pay record are E-6, O-3E and 0-5. Once you reach 30 years of service, you will be able to get the full 50 percent retirement."

"I'll think about what you said, master chief. Now, if you will excuse me, Captain Henning is in my office."

"Yes, sir," said Lyle.

Lyle hurried off towards his office and then to the quarterdeck. When Lyle was off the ship and at the end of the pier, he pulled his cell phone out of his left, windbreaker jacket pocket. He opened it up and called Lou. The phone on the other end only rang once before it was answered.

"Yes?" asked Lou.

"Paperwork was delivered just as we rehearsed," said Lyle, still a little nervous that Andrew might have been onto him.

"Very good. Is Captain Henning still aboard?"

"Yes, sir."

"I'll see you tomorrow morning."

"Good-bye, sir."

Meanwhile, Andrew was just entering his office. Shawn stood up as Captain Henning was closing the book on the training levels of the weapons department personnel. Mel handed the book to Shawn who put it up on a nearby shelf.

"Did the master chief find you?" asked Mel.

"Yes, sir. He handed me my retirement pay calculations."

"Good. I'll see to it that your maintenance report receives prompt attention by the submarine intermediate maintenance activity."

"Thank you, sir."

"You're welcome. Do you have any dinner plans for tonight?" asked Mel, looking at his watch, which read 1845 hours.

"No, sir, I have no dinner plans that I am aware of, yet."

"Good. Dinner is on me since I kept you so late and we can talk about your letter of resignation I received the other day."

"Yes, sir."

"Meet me at the Seven Seas restaurant. I made reservations for 2000 hours. Bring Gary along, I'm looking forward to meeting him."

"Yes, sir."

Andrew continued to smile at Mel as he was leaving. When the office door had shut, MT1 Boggs knocked on the door. Shawn opened up the door and saw Mel still standing in the passageway. Mel turned back towards the civilian who was beaming with excitement.

"This ships' weapons systems are fully operational. The weapons controls need three upgrades for launching missiles and tracking them. I have those at my hotel room. The sonar system needs two upgrades. I have one of the two upgrades at my hotel room and I can order the other one," said Bruce.

"Good. See to it that Commander Hinton-Smith here gets those weapons and sonar upgrades within the next 72 hours. Until 2000 hours, commander; don't be late," said Mel.

"Yes, sir."

Captain Henning left the ship and called the Commander of Submarine Forces for the Pacific Fleet, Rear Admiral Upper Half Sandra Milton, from his cell phone. The phone at the other end of the call rang only once before being answered by Sandra.

"Mel, speak to me," she said, dispensing with the usual formalities.

"Ship's material readiness is better than expected. The civilian told me that he had all but one of the upgrades for the weapons and sonar systems."

"Good. I'll inform Pacific Fleet of such. Any major material problems and did you get Commander Hinton-Smith to retract his letter of resignation yet?"

"The ship has one badly leaking torpedo tube, number seven and I'll be discussing the letter of resignation with Andrew tonight."

"I can give you a 48 to 72 hour window on getting Commander Hinton-Smith to retract his letter; after that, the show is off forever. Does the ship have to be dry-docked for the repair on the torpedo tube door?"

"Yes, about four days minimum."

"She will get her four days in dry-dock, but she has to be ready within 15 days after the repairs are completed or the show is off."

"Dry-dock time is going to be a problem admiral."

"Why is the dry-dock time going to be a problem?" she asked.

"There are only three dry-docks here at the sub base that are capable of handling a nuclear powered submarine. One is down for major repairs and the other two already have ships in them."

Admiral Milton thought quickly before coming up with a plan to solve Mel's problem.

"I'll make arrangements for the dry-dock to come to her okay?'

"Thank you, that will speed up the repairs."

"I'll make arrangements for the meeting with Mr. Devonshire, Vice Admirals Bond and Williams. I'll call you later on this week with the details. The ball is in your court."

"Yes, ma'am, I understand; good-bye."

Meanwhile, back aboard the ship, Andrew had showered and changed into his dress up type civilian clothes. He stopped by his office to call Gary. He opened the door to his office and saw Shawn sitting there at his desk doing some paperwork. Shawn looked up to see Andrew standing there.

"Shawn, could you get me an outside line?" asked Andrew.

"Already done, sir," said Shawn, handing the receiver to Andrew.

Andrew looked at Shawn a little suspiciously before placing his right hand over the receiver's mouthpiece.

"How did you get my home phone number?"

"Captain Henning gave it to me, sir," replied Shawn, lying through his teeth. Shawn knew that Commander Staggs had given him Andrew's home phone number.

"Oh, that was mighty nice of him."

Andrew put the receiver to his left ear.

"Hello?" asked Andrew.

"What's going on?" asked Gary.

"We've been invited to dinner with my boss."

"Commander Staggs?"

"No, Captain Henning. He wants both of us to meet him in about an hour at a place called the Seven Seas restaurant. Dress appropriately."

"Where should we meet?"

"At the end of the pier."

"I'll be there in 15 minutes."

Andrew left the ship; Gary showed up at the end of the pier and picked Andrew up. After picking Andrew up, they drove towards the restaurant. Andrew looked at Gary before looking out the passenger side window. He drew in a deep breath before speaking.

"Captain Henning knows about you and I," said Andrew.

"How did he find out?" asked Gary, who already knew the answer; NIS investigation.

"I don't know, but I intend on finding out. Did you know that Captain Henning gave my home phone number to TM1 Dailey?"

"No, I wasn't aware of such things," said Gary, lying through his teeth again. Gary had to give the NIS agent Andrew's home phone so that the NIS investigator could conduct the security check interview on Gary.

They drove the rest of the way in silence. They arrived at the restaurant around 1950 hours. Gary parked the car and after Andrew shut his door, Gary locked the car up. They entered the front entryway of the restaurant and were greeted immediately by a hostess. She looked and soon started to gawk at Gary.

"You must be Mel Henning's party," she squeaked.

"Yes," replied Andrew.

"Right this way," she stammered.

They walked down a short passageway to an elevator. The hostess pushed a button on the small brass control panel and the elevator began its descent to the main restaurant floor. When the elevator car had cleared the main entryway, both Andrew and Gary could see fish and the last rays of sunlight penetrated through what appeared to Andrew to be a Plexiglas™ tube. Andrew looked around in amazement.

"How far down are we going?" asked Gary to the hostess.

"30 feet or about 10 meters," she replied.

"30 feet? That means there is about 400 pounds per square inch or about 200 kilopascals of pressure."

"441 pounds per square inch or 200.45 kilopascals. Don't worry, this Plexiglas™ tube and the surrounding roof over the restaurant is stronger than your submarine hull; in relative size."

The doors to the elevator soon opened and she showed them to a table in the back where Mel was already waiting. Mel saw immediately why the naval investigative service investigator was so terrified of Gary. Gary was young

25

and muscular. In fact, his muscles were not very well hidden by what he was wearing. Mel stood up and greeted them with handshakes and then pointed to their chairs.

Once they had taken their seats, Gary and Andrew noticed that the menu was a floating hologram. The hologram was coming from a small black box that was situated in the center of the table. Mel spoke first.

"Would either of you care for drinks before dinner?" asked Mel.

"I'll take a white Russian," said Gary.

"Okay. How about you, commander?"

"I'll take a Scotch and seven with Johnnie Walker® Gold Label."

"Very well."

Mel placed their drink orders along with his own drink order. He typed their order into the automated drink order taker at the table. As Andrew looked over the menu, he noticed that the prices were very high. Gary looked over the menu and decided on live lobster with a baked potato. Gary looked up in time to see the underside of a large hammerhead shark pass above the table. He continued to stare off into the distance at the dark blue water. Mel caught onto this as the drinks arrived.

"Mr. Henning, what is that dark blue water area out there?" asked Gary, pointing out the window.

"Please, you can call me Mel. You may have to call me Mr. Henning if I make rear admiral lower half, but until then, you can call me Mel. To answer your question, that dark blue water is the trench between Oahu and Maui Islands. It's about 7,500 feet deep. If you're in the navy, that makes it about 1,250 fathoms."

"That's neat," remarked Gary.

"Does everyone know what they want for dinner?" asked Mel.

Everyone nodded in affirmation. Mel typed their dinner orders into the keyboard, which was located under the table. This was the same keyboard that he had used to place their drink orders. Gary chose the live lobster with a baked potato with everything on it. Andrew chose the octopus. The dinner computer immediately returned a flag on Gary's order. Mel looked at the drop down menu, which listed the live lobster at "Market Price." This listing gave many options. Mel looked up at Gary.

"Gary, the chef wants to know the answer to these questions. How big of a live lobster do you want?"

"What are my choices?"

"One pound, one and a half pounds, two pounds, two and a half pounds, three pounds, three and a half pounds or four pounds plus."

"Four pounds plus."

"Okay. Now, the chef wants to know if you want to see the diver go catch your dinner."

"You're kidding, right?"

"No, you see that woman standing over there on that platform in the purple wetsuit? She's going to go get some live lobsters for you to chose from," said Mel, pointing to his left.

"Okay. Excuse me, Andrew," said Gary as he left the table.

After Gary had left the table, Mel turned towards Andrew.

"You've got yourself a good man there, Andrew. Now I see why the NIS investigator was so terrified of him. His arms look like they could break boards," said Mel.

"The Naval Investigative Service has interviewed him?" asked Andrew.

"Yes. Andrew, it was all part of the security requirements for granting you your Secret clearance. The NIS agent made Gary sign a piece of paper that stated he could not talk to you about the interview unless I did."

"Do I have my security clearance?"

"Yes."

"So, I've been watched for at least six years then?"

"Yes. NIS was told to keep tabs on you as part of a great experiment. Part of that experiment was to see if being a homosexual would affect your command abilities. Since there are no signs of your command ability being affected, you have moved to the next level of the experiment."

"I'm a naval officer guinea pig, then, for some dark government agenda?"

"If you want to call it that, commander. I can't tell you all the details, because even I don't know them. However, sometime later this week, or next week, you're going to have a meeting with Vice Admirals Bonds and Williams and there will probably be a couple of civilians there."

"Okay. Answer me this question, are we going to war with Iran?"

"I don't know. Have you brushed up on the Iranian Navy?"

"Yes, sir, I have brushed up on their naval capabilities."

"I received your letter of resignation from Commander Staggs the other day. I'm going to ask you, professionally, of course, to rescind that letter."

"Can I think about it, Captain Henning?" said Andrew, finishing off his drink.

"Sure, I can give you say 72 hours, fair enough?"

"Fair enough, sir."

A hostess pushing a cart to their table interrupted them. On this cart was what appeared to be a large glass aquarium. Andrew looked at the contents of the aquarium and then at the hostess.

"Who ordered the octopus?" she asked with an accent.

"I did," Andrew replied.

"Which one do you want?" she asked.

"That one in the far left corner," said Andrew, pointing at an octopus in the far left corner of the aquarium.

She put on gloves and grabbed a plate from under the cart. She reached into the aquarium and viciously pulled the octopus out of the aquarium. She then threw it onto the plate where it landed with a splat. After she left, Gary returned.

"The diver told me I got Lobster Bitin' Bob," said Gary happily.

"Really, why did the diver call the lobster by that name?" asked Mel.

"The diver told me that lobster has bitten her three times this week."

They all ate dinner in silence. Mel paid the bill and Andrew and Gary took a cab back home. Andrew woke up at his usual time the next morning and ate breakfast. Gary had awakened at the same time as Andrew and dressed quickly. Gary headed out the door right after breakfast to go get their car from the restaurant parking lot. Gary returned a little while later and took Andrew to work.

Andrew went to the department office and began his day. He went about his normal duties. Around lunchtime, after a fire drill in his aft torpedo room, of all places, he went to the wardroom. He ate lunch and after lunch he bumped into Lou.

"Commander Hinton-Smith, good to see you today. I gave Captain Henning your letter of resignation the other day," said Lou.

"Yes, sir, he mentioned that fact to me last night at dinner. I suppose you didn't have any knowledge of that meeting, did you?" asked Andrew.

"No, I had no knowledge of your meeting with our boss. Did you have a good conversation?"

"Yes, sir, we did have a wonderful conversation."

"Oh, I thought I would let you know your security clearance finally came through. Ensign Ross is putting an updated Page 1 into your service record right now."

"Thank you, sir."

Andrew and Lou departed. Andrew went back to the weapons department office to check the duty watch roster. Andrew found out that he and the reactor officer were going to be on duty with each other on the 28th of the month. He put the duty watch roster back into his office desk drawer. Shawn entered the office.

"Commander, I sent that maintenance report off ship yesterday morning on the torpedo tube like you asked."

"Good work. Congratulations on submitting your Limited Duty Officer packet; good luck," said Andrew, shaking Shawn's left hand.

"Thank you, sir. By the way, TMSN Bradley has a question for you, sir."

"Well, where is he?'

"Outside the office."

Andrew sighed a little as he stepped outside of the office and into the passageway. Shawn didn't bother to close the door to the office as Andrew found TMSN Bradley standing at attention. Mr. Bradley was holding his cover in his hands and nervously twisted it around in circles.

"I understand that you wanted to talk to me, Mr. Bradley?" asked Andrew.

"Yes, sir. Please forgive me if I insult you when I ask this question, but, some of the crew, commander, have referred to you as a mustang. Is that because of the kind of car you drive or the size of your penis, sir?" asked Bart.

Shawn started laughing hysterically. Andrew pursed his lips together and turned to face Shawn. He tried to control his own urge to laugh until it was more appropriate.

"It's a valid question, Mr. Dailey," said Andrew almost ready to laugh out loud.

"So, sir, let me get out of here," he said, closing the door to the office and going down the passageway. He was still laughing.

"Mr. Bradley, why don't we take a walk and I will explain to you why I am referred to as a mustang."

# Chapter 3

The sun was rising at sea for the crew aboard the USS SEA SAW, MD-1. The crew was just waking up and getting their day started. Outside the ship, the calm, Cobalt blue waters of the central Pacific lapped up against the hull. The USS SEA SAW was a combined engineering effort by the United States Navy and the civilian military sealift command.

The ship was a 200,000-ton behemoth that was powered by two nuclear reactors geared to four massive propellers. She was capable of lifting an injured ship completely out of the water, provided that the ship didn't exceed 16,000 tons, and taking the ship home. A floating, mobile dry-dock facility or city as some of the crew called her.

The officer of the deck had just been relieved by the ship's Commanding Officer, Captain Jon Paulik. He was looking over the ship's current status on a viewing screen that was attached to the left arm of his captain's chair on the bridge. He was also looking at any other ships that were out here with him. He found only one.

The USS SEA SAW's current position placed her 1,062 nautical miles southeast of the Hawaiian Island chain. The ship was traveling at a speed of 10 knots on a course of 030. The computer estimated another six weeks at sea before the ship would arrive in San Diego where it was home ported for the time being. He turned off the viewing screen as the ship's Executive Officer, Captain Mary Hanson, approached.

"Good morning, Captain Paulik," she said, sipping her coffee.

"Good morning, XO. XO, what kind of a yahoo is out here, over a thousand nautical miles from any sort of land in a 30 foot/10 meter sailboat?" asked Jon.

"Someone who has an excellent navigation system, sir," she replied, trying to understand where the question had come from.

"I guess so. Any message traffic for us today?"

"None yet, sir. Radio did receive the normal message traffic, but nothing directed at us, specifically, that I know of, sir."

"Well, I'm going to get myself a cup of coffee. I'll return shortly."

"Very well, sir."

Captain Paulik went to the wardroom and poured himself a cup of coffee. He put cream and sugar into the coffee and stirred it up. He returned to the bridge and had to put on his sunglasses. The glare off the nearly calm water from the mid-morning sunshine was almost blinding. As he took his seat on the bridge and started drinking his coffee, the XO left the bridge to begin her daily inspection of the ship. A few minutes after the XO left the bridge, the ship's radio room called.

"Radio, bridge," said RMCS (SW/AW) Ramsey.

Captain Paulik put his cup of coffee down on the bridge window ledge. He then reached up for the button on the box that was above his chair. He pushed the button into the box.

"Bridge, aye," said Jon.

"We've received a priority message," said the senior chief.

"Bring the message to the bridge, senior chief," said Jon, yawning.

"Aye, sir."

A few minutes later, Senior Chief Ramsey arrived with the message. Captain Paulik pulled out his reading glasses from his upper left, front shirt pocket and read the message. After he finished reading the message, he put the message down in his lap. He then reached for his viewing screen. After making sure that the small keyboard was attached to it, he adjusted the view screen several times so that he could read it clearly.

Jon typed in the location of the Pearl Harbor Submarine Base and asked the computer to calculate the distance and time required to get there. The computer came up with an estimated 120 hours travel time to the submarine base. The computer automatically defaulted to a preset repair time of 48 hours. Jon looked back up at Ramsey.

"Take this reply down," said Jon.

Senior Chief Ramsey took out a pen from his left, shirt pocket and prepared to take down the reply. He then removed a small stenographer's pad from inside of the clipboard that he carried with him.

"To Commander, Submarine Forces Pacific Fleet. 1. Will be glad to help, but understand that this command, due to our engineering limitations, cannot arrive at the submarine base, Pearl Harbor, Hawaii, before 120 hours from the date and time of transmission of this reply. 2. Could cut time down by going through the Pacific Naval Gunfire Support Range, which is off-limits to this command. 3. Can do the required repairs in 13 hours, not the requested 12 hours due to ballast pump configuration."

"Anything else, sir?"

"Send that off priority with today's date and time stamp on it."

"Yes, sir."

After the senior chief had left the bridge, Jon walked over to the chart table where Quartermaster Third Class Petty Officer James was on duty. He had just finished writing his log entry and looked up from the chart table.

"Good morning, captain, what can I do for you, sir?" he asked.

"Plot me a course to the Pearl Harbor sub base without going through the Naval Gunfire Support Range."

"Aye, sir," he responded as he turned on his computer and started punching in the ship's desired location. In a few minutes, the computer had charted a course to the requested destination.

"Recommend coming to new course 004 and increase speed to flank," said James.

"Will do and keep the bridge informed of any course changes."

"Aye, sir."

Jon left the chart table area and returned to the bridge.

"Helm," Jon announced.

"Helm, aye," responded BMSN Craig.

"Come to new course 004."

"Aye, sir. Using left standard rudder, coming to new course 004."

"Lee helm."

"Lee helm, aye," responded BMSA Greg.

"Increase speed to flank."

"Flank speed, aye, sir."

Meanwhile, Rear Admiral Upper Half Sandra Milton was in her office on a conference call with Vice Admirals Bonds and Williams. She was doing her best to stall them as long as she could, but time was running out for her. Just then, her secretary stepped into the threshold of the door. He pointed at the phone and held up his right index finger. She knew that was the sign for an important call on Line 1.

"Who is it?" she mouthed to him.

The secretary responded with a back and forth motion with both the right index and middle fingers up. She nodded and he left the room.

"I hate to be rude, sirs, but I have an outside call coming in from Captain Henning. I'll have to put both of you on hold," she said, placing them both on hold before either of them could protest. She then punched Line 1.

"Mel, what the hell is going on? I've got both of THEM on a conference call," she stammered.

"I just received word from Commander Hinton-Smith personally. He has reconsidered his resignation. He mentioned something about the retirement pay calculations were unsuitable for him," said Mel, choosing his words carefully.

"I'll bet he found those calculations unsuitable because that's what I told Master Chief Stennings to come up with."

"Well, it worked. Commander Hinton-Smith has rescinded his resignation letter."

"Thank you, I'll call you back."

"Okay."

Mel hung up and when he did, she pushed the button for the conference call to resume. When she went to speak, Vice Admiral Bonds spoke first rather irritably.

"Damn woman, why were we on hold for so long?!" he said.

"Terribly sorry, sir. It was an important outside call from Captain Henning," she said, holding her tongue.

"What did Mel have to say?" asked Vice Admiral Ken Williams.

"He wanted to let me know that Commander Hinton-Smith has rescinded his letter of resignation."

"Good work, admiral. There may yet be a third star for you," said Vice Admiral John Bonds.

"Thank you, sir."

"Have Commander Hinton-Smith report to my office first thing Monday morning in his dress whites. Tell him to prepare for a possible two day stay and you will accompany him, is that clear?" asked John.

"Yes, sir, that is very clear. Am I to be in my dress whites?"

"Yes. I will call Naval Military Personnel Center in the morning and tell Section 28 to lose Commander Hinton-Smith's retirement paperwork," said John.

"I'll call Commander Hinton-Smith personally and inform him of your orders."

"Thank you, Sandra. I'll put the finishing touches on the rules of engagement for the war game. I'm looking forward to meeting Commander Hinton-Smith," said Ken.

"Good-bye, sirs," she said, ending the call.

Meanwhile, in the radio communications center for the navy at Pearl Harbor, the priority message was received. The duty radioman, RMSN Seines, waited for the computer to decode the message. He took the message to the command duty officer's office. The Command Duty Officer was CW01

Stagermen. RMSN Seines found the office door open slightly, so he knocked on the door.

"Enter," said CWO1 Stagermen.

"Priority message, sir," he said handing the message to Mr. Stagermen.

"Thank you; dismissed," said Mr. Stagermen. He started reading the message as Seines shut the door completely.

After Mr. Stagermen had read the message, he reached for the phone. He had Rear Admiral Upper Half Sandra Milton's cell phone number pre-programmed into the speed dial. He pushed the pre-programmed number on the speed dial and her cell phone started ringing. She answered after the second ring.

"Admiral, this is the command duty officer for Radio Communications Station Pearl Harbor. Per your instructions, I am notifying you that I have received a priority message from the USS SEA SAW," he said.

"Excellent warrant, what does the message say?"

"Begging the admiral's pardon, in accordance with Naval Security Regulation 126, I cannot tell you the contents of a message that is rated priority or above on an unsecured line."

"Damn naval security regulations. Very well, I will be in there in 45 minutes."

"Good-bye," he said, hanging up the phone.

Forty-five minutes later, Rear Admiral Upper Half Sandra Milton arrived at the Radio Communications Station, Pearl Harbor. She walked across the quarterdeck and straight to the command duty officer's office. She was still in her uniform of the day. She knocked on his door and entered the office.

He stood up and saluted her, she returned his salute as he handed her the message. She read the message over and began staring at the bulkhead behind the warrant. After a few minutes, she started to stare at him.

"This message is nine hours old according to the date and time stamp on the top line. Warrant, call ships tracking and find out where the USS SEA SAW is currently located," she said.

"Yes, admiral."

CWO1 Stagermen picked up the receiver and dialed a restricted, military phone number. Naval Ships Tracking Center was located in Patuxent River, Maryland. The facility was buried almost completely underground. Only the vast antennae array and armed guards patrolling the property gave any indication as to what was there.

The facility was further security protected by a high, chain link fence with Microwire® across the top. The rest of the facility was built out of several feet of concrete and reinforced steel. The facility knew the location of every naval ship on the active duty ship roster.

The phone was ringing on the desk of a lower level room. The Command Duty Officer, Lieutenant Junior Grade Harry Hoffman, currently occupied the room. He looked at the Caller ID® and noticed it said, "RADIOCOMSTATPEARL." He reached over and picked up the receiver.

"Good evening, Naval Ships Tracking Center, Command Duty Officer, LTJG Hoffman speaking, how can I help you?" he said in one breath.

"A good evening to you Lieutenant Hoffman. This is CW01 Stagermen the CDO at Radio Communications Station, Pearl Harbor, Hawaii. Could you give me the status of the USS SEA SAW, MD-1?"

"One moment," replied LTJG Hoffman as he reached over and opened up the blinds in his office so he could see the status board. He located the USS SEA SAW easily.

"CW01 Stagermen, the USS SEA SAW is approximately 950 nautical miles southeast of the Hawaiian Island chain. She changed course from 030 to 004 and increased her speed to 16 knots at approximately 0915 hours your time, sir."

"Thank you, LTJG Hoffman," said Stagermen, writing down the information onto a piece of paper and handing it to Sandra.

"Is there anything else I can do for you warrant?" he asked.

"No, mission was accomplished; good-bye," said Stagermen, hanging up the phone.

After Sandra had looked over the ship's current status, she put the status sheet down on top of the message.

"Call the Commander-in-Chief of Pacific Fleet Forces," she said.

"Yes, admiral."

Mr. Stagermen called Vice Admiral John Bonds' main office number. The duty secretary that answered the phone there transferred Stagermen to the vice admiral's cell phone. He was in Washington, D.C. trying to get a special project completed for the navy. However, Senator James Arthar a Republican from the State of Idaho was stalling the project in the Senate Armed Forces Committee. Vice Admiral Bonds' cell phone started ringing. He took his cell phone out of his shirt pocket and saw who was calling. He smiled as he looked at the Senator.

"Please excuse me, Your Honor. I have some important business to take care of, it shouldn't take too long," said John.

"Of course. I'll be waiting," replied the Senator.

John left the table and went to a quiet corner of the restaurant.

"This is Vice Admiral Bonds, who the hell is this?!"

"Rear Admiral Milton, sir," she said irritably.

"Damn woman, this had better be important. I'm having dinner with Senator Arthar of the Senate Armed Forces Committee."

"Well, then, I will make my request quick. I need your permission for the USS SEA SAW to transit the Pacific Naval Gunfire Support Range enroute to the Pearl Harbor Sub Base. Allowing her to transit the PNGFS range will cut down on the repair time by about 72 hours."

"Permission granted, but she has to run IFF until she is out of the area."

"Thank you, sir," she said, hanging up the phone.

During the phone conversation, Stagermen had taken steps to write down a reply to the message. He opened up a stenographer's notepad and reached across the desk to the penholder and grabbed a pen. He looked up at Sandra.

"Ready to take down a message?" she asked.

"Yes, admiral," he replied.

"To Commanding Officer USS SEA SAW, MD-1. 1. Permission has been granted, per verbal authorization of the C-In-C Pac Flt Forces, to transit the PNGFS range. 2. C-In-C Pac Flt Forces orders you to run IFF until you have cleared the PNGFS range."

"Anything else, admiral?"

"Make sure that message gets off as soon as possible and make sure that both Vice Admiral Bonds and Vice Admiral Williams are in the info line."

"Yes, admiral."

"Good-night," said Sandra, leaving Stagermen's office.

The message was sent off on the next outgoing batch of priority messages. The message was received aboard the USS SEA SAW four hours later. The duty radio operator downloaded and decoded the message. He then called the bridge. The time on the clock in the radio room read 0240 hours, Hawaii Standard Time.

"Radio, bridge," said RMSN La Count.

The Duty Bridge Officer, Stevedore Savage answered the call.

"Bridge, aye," he said.

"Priority message received."

"Bridge, aye. I will note the message in my logbook and tell the captain in the morning."

"Radio, aye."

Stevedore Savage stayed on the bridge until he was relieved the next morning by Captain Paulik. Mr. Savage told Jon about the message. Jon went through the previous night's log entries and verified the information. Jon then reached up above his captain's chair and pushed the button on the box.

"Bridge, Radio," said Jon.

"Radio, aye," answered Senior Chief Ramsey.

"Bring me that priority message from last night to the bridge."

"Radio, aye."

A few minutes later, Senior Chief Ramsey entered the bridge. He went to Jon's chair and handed him the message. As Jon read the message, Ramsey prepared for Jon's reply by withdrawing his pen and pulling out his notepad. Jon pulled up the viewing screen and keyboard and began typing in the course adjustment. The computer recomputed the estimated time of arrival, which was reduced by an estimated 74 hours. Jon looked up at Ramsey.

"Take down this reply."

"Ready, sir."

"1. Will comply with C-In-C Pac Flt Forces verbal authorization to transit the PNGFS range. 2. Estimated time of arrival will now be Thursday morning between 0300 and 0400 hours, Hawaii Standard Time, at the estimated early morning high tide. 3. Have SIMA repair personnel waiting on the pier for repairs to begin when we have the USS SEASIDE HEIGHTS, SSN-747 out of the water. 4. USS SEASIDE HEIGHTS, SSN-747 will have to be classified as DSRA-2 for an estimated 24 hours."

"Anything else, sir?"

"Send that off priority. Info the C-In-C Pac Flt Forces, Commander, Submarine Forces Pacific Fleet, Commanding Officer Submarine Intermediate Maintenance Activity, Commander of Submarine Squadron 22 and the Commanding Officer of the USS SEASIDE HEIGHTS, SSN-747."

"Yes, sir," replied Ramsey, leaving the bridge.

"Bridge, Operations," said Jon.

"Operations, aye," said the voice.

"Activate IFF until further notice," he said.

"Operations, aye."

Jon switched channels to the chart table.

"Bridge, Navigation," said Jon.

"Navigation, aye," said the voice.

"Permission has been granted to transit the PNGFS Range. Plot me a new course to Pearl Harbor."

"Navigation, aye,"

A few minutes later, Navigation called back.

"Navigation, Bridge," said the voice.

"Bridge, aye," said Jon.

"Recommend new course 355."

"Bridge, aye. Helm, come to new course 355."

"Helm, aye. Left standard rudder coming to new course 355."

The message was sent off. A copy of the message arrived aboard the USS SEASIDE HEIGHTS late that night. After being downloaded and decoded, the message was placed into the captain's In-box along with the other messages received for the ship in the radio room.

The next morning, after reading all of the messages, Commander Staggs called an all officers meeting in the wardroom. The meeting began as soon as all the officers had arrived. Commander Staggs began with reading the priority message. It was a sunny Friday, about mid-morning.

"First lieutenant, have Deck Department ready to loosen all lines when the USS SEA SAW comes alongside," said Lou.

"Yes, sir. My department will be ready," she replied.

The ship's First Lieutenant was Lieutenant Junior Grade Lisa Aiken.

"Commander Hinton-Smith, it appears that your leaky outer door of torpedo tube 7 is going to get fixed after all," said Lou sarcastically.

"I noticed that, sir. Perhaps SIMA personnel were bored and wanted something to do," replied Andrew smiling.

"Everyone has their orders; dismissed," said Lou.

All the officers left the wardroom to prepare for the temporary dry-docking of the ship. Andrew called his department together and told them what was going to happen. He issued everyone their orders for things to get done in a certain order. When he dismissed his department, he went to the weapons control room to check on the progress of the upgrades.

He entered the compartment to find FT3 Tyler Combs pulling another compact disc out of the weapons computer and putting it back into a sleeve inside of a large folder like object. He looked up to see Andrew standing there.

"Good morning, commander, " he said.

"How are the upgrades coming along?"

"Slow, sir. I found that there are 11 discs per upgrade for a total of 44 discs. I just finished loading up disc 18 and I'm rebooting the system."

"Keep up the good work. Any reports from Sonar yet?"

"No, sir, but he's got it easier than me. If these discs weren't filled to the maximum amount of space, the upgrading might go faster."

"Well, keep up the good work. I'll go check on Sonar."

Andrew left the weapons control room, walked across the deserted bridge to the Sonar Suite. He found STSSN Jon Costillo pulling out a disc from the sonar computer and rebooting the system. Andrew tapped on the doorframe.

"Good morning, commander," he said, smiling.

"Good morning to you as well. How are the upgrades coming along?"

"I should be done by dinner time, sir."

"Good. Are the upgrades difficult?"

"No, although each upgrade is 13 discs long, the discs aren't full. I've also noticed that the upgrades are for background noises and protocols."

"Keep it up and when you get done, give Weapons Control a hand if he needs one."

"Yes, sir.'

Andrew returned to the weapons department office and began reviewing the procedures for repairs on the torpedo tube exterior door. He let his mind wander for a few minutes and finally came to the conclusion that all this was all very suspicious. As he put the procedure manual back up on the small bookshelf in the office, TMSN Bradley entered the office.

TMSN Bradley sat down where Shawn normally sat and took out a notepad from the top left drawer of the desk. He put the notepad on top of the desk and then pulled out a pen from the blotter that was on the desk. He then went about shuffling around paperwork on the desktop and filing it away. He had just sat back down when the phone rang.

"Good afternoon, USS SEASIDE HEIGHTS Weapons Department, TMSN Bradley, how can I help you?" he said.

"TMSN Bradley, this is the Commander of Submarine Forces Pacific Fleet," she started to say.

"That would make you Rear Admiral Upper Half Sandra Milton, then."

"That's correct. Is Commander Hinton-Smith there?"

"Yes, admiral, one moment please," he said, handing the receiver to Andrew.

"Yes, Admiral Milton, what can I do for you?" asked Andrew.

"Andrew, I'm glad that you decided to rethink your letter of resignation and retirement. I assure you that you will not be disappointed."

"Why, thank you, admiral."

"When we get through talking, put Mr. Bradley back on the phone. I want to talk to him."

"Sure admiral, not a problem."

"Andrew, I will be picking you up Monday morning at 0100 hours. Be prepared for a possible overnight stay in San Diego."

"Yes, admiral."

"Be in your dress whites when I pick you up."

"Yes, admiral. What's going on?"

"You're going to have a private, informal meeting with myself, Vice Admiral Bonds, Vice Admiral Williams and Admiral Simon. There are going to be some civilians there as well."

"Mother of God, what did I do?!"

"Nothing. In fact, you were chosen by the admirals, myself included, as being the best candidate for a unique proposition."

"Thank you for thinking so highly of me, admiral."

"There are a lot of others, close by, that think very highly of you as well. Be ready on Monday morning."

"I'll be ready, admiral," said Andrew as he handed the receiver back to Bradley. "She wants to talk to you," said Andrew as he left the office.

"Yes, admiral, what can I do for you?" asked Bradley, nervously.

"Has Commander Hinton-Smith left the office, yet?"

"Yes, admiral."

"Good. How long have you been aboard the ship?"

"About three weeks, admiral."

"Good. What do you think of your department head?"

"He's very intelligent and resourceful. He knows the rulebook forward and backwards and he even steps in to help when needed."

"Hypothetically speaking, if you could serve with Commander Hinton-Smith again, would you?"

"You mean at another command that he is in charge of?"

"Yes."

"Yes, I would serve with him again, admiral."

"Good answer. Now, I'm going to give you an order."

"Yes, admiral, I'm listening."

"You are not to discuss this phone call with anyone for any reason unless I give you permission."

"Yes, admiral, I understand my order."

"Good-bye, Mr. Bradley," she said, hanging up the phone.

A few minutes later, she called Lou on his cell phone.

"Yes, admiral, what can I do for you?" he asked.

"I'm going to be taking Commander Hinton-Smith with me on Monday. He may not be back until Wednesday."

"I understand, admiral."

"The experiment has moved to Phase 3."

"Understood, admiral."

Lou hung up the phone and went back to doing his paperwork. Phase 3 of the highly experimental exercise, started many years ago by the military's top psychologists, was entering the danger zone. If the experiment failed on Monday, years of dedicated observations would be for nothing. However, if Monday went well, which Lou knew it probably would, the exercise would be moved to the next level: a war game exercise called The Ultimate Command Challenge.

Andrew arrived at the pre-designated place and Gary picked him up. Andrew had his dress white uniform with him along with the accompanying dress white shoes and white cover. They went home and Gary fixed dinner while Andrew put up his uniform. After dinner, Andrew packed up a small overnight bag and grabbed an extra working uniform. Gary looked at him and smiled.

"Going on one of those special operations you've told me about?" asked Gary as he started massaging Andrew's shoulders and neck.

"Yes and I find it highly suspicious, too."

"Do you think the military is up to something?"

"Yes, I do, and I'm going to find out what's going on Monday."

"I know you will."

Gary turned off the bedroom lights and gave Andrew a full body massage.

# Chapter 4

0100 hours Monday morning came too soon for Andrew. He was standing outside of his apartment when the admiral and her duty driver showed up. He walked to the curb as the duty driver exited the car. The petty officer first class opened the passenger-side, rear door for Andrew. Andrew stepped inside and saw Sandra.

After the door was shut, Andrew looked at Sandra. He then took off his cover and placed it into the seat between the two of them. The duty driver stepped inside the car and pulled away from the curb.

"It's too damned early in the morning, admiral," said Andrew, yawning and putting his overnight bag into his lap.

"I know, however it is a necessity. Besides, I don't think you'll turn down the offer."

"What makes you think I won't turn down the offer?"

"I've got two months of pay riding on your acceptance of the offer and another month's pay if you succeed."

"Admiral, that's a lot of money," said Andrew, yawning again.

She smiled as the car began to pull up to the front gate of the naval air station. After the shore patrol petty officer had checked their ID's, he motioned for them to go through the gates. In a few minutes, the car stopped in front of a plane. The duty driver stepped out of the car and opened up both passenger-side car doors.

Andrew stepped out onto the tarmac, straightened up his uniform and put on his cover. He then grabbed his overnight bag and walked towards the plane with Sandra walking on his left side. When they arrived at the plane, the pilot saluted both of them. Andrew returned the pilots' salute.

"Good morning, Admiral Milton, good morning Commander Hinton-Smith. If you will step aboard, I will get us out of here," he said to both of them.

They both stepped inside the plane. The pilot closed the main door and locked it down. The pilot then stepped into the cockpit, closed the door and started up the engines. Andrew buckled up this seatbelt and put his overnight bag under his seat. He then took off his cover and placed it into his lap. As the plane began to taxi, Sandra spoke to him.

"Try to get some sleep," she said.

"Yes, admiral, I will try," he replied, closing his eyes as the wheels of the plane left the runway.

When Andrew opened his eyes again, Sandra was standing in front of him. She was holding a cup of coffee and a choice of many different flavors of breakfast bars. Andrew yawned, took the coffee and one of the berry flavored breakfast bars.

"Where are we now?" asked Andrew, sipping his coffee and looking out the tiny window at nothing but the Cobalt blue waters of the Pacific Ocean.

"We are on final approach to the San Diego Naval Air Station. Drink your coffee quick, the pilot told me it's going to get a little rough on landing."

"Wonderful," Andrew replied as he finished off his coffee as quickly as he could and literally choking down his breakfast bar.

The pilot did his best to avoid the turbulence they encountered, but it wasn't effective. The small plane was tossed and bounced around very roughly. Andrew thought they were possibly flying through a typhoon. When the plane did land, both Andrew and Sandra tried to regain their composure as best they could. The plane taxied for a few minutes before the engines shut down. The pilot opened the cockpit door and then opened the main door.

"Sorry about that, admiral, we caught the Santa Anna Winds," he said apologetically as he made sure that the small ladder had locked into place.

"That's a good thing to know, I thought we had flown through a Category 1 typhoon."

They exited the plane and were greeted by the duty driver for Vice Admiral Bonds. Andrew and Sandra stepped into the car after exchanging salutes with the duty driver. Once the doors were shut and the duty driver drove off the tarmac, the rest of the trip to the headquarters of the Supreme Allied Commander of Pacific Fleet Forces, whether sea, air or land, was in silence. The car stopped at the front entrance to the building.

The front of the building was decorated with all sorts of military hardware. Andrew could see that there were old tanks, howitzers, anti-aircraft guns and a large anchor, probably from a World War II aircraft carrier. This massive anchor, painted a bright white, was on top of the large, black granite plaque in the center of the front entrance.

The plaque was brass in color with the symbol of the United States Navy in the center surrounded by the symbols of the United States Marine Corps, United States Army, the United States Air Force and the Coast Guard. There was writing on the plaque that surrounded all the symbols. It said WELCOME TO THE HEADQUARTERS OF THE SUPREME ALLIED COMMANDER OF PACIFIC FLEET FORCES.

Still trembling a little bit from the rough landing, Andrew exited the opposite side of the car from Sandra. He had put on his cover and had just grabbed his overnight bag when a master chief petty officer approached them. This master chief saluted all of them as they stood at the front of the car.

Andrew looked at the master chief's uniform and saw that there was an extra star over the center of his gold rocker as it was called. The extra star indicated that he was the Pacific Fleet Force Master Chief. The symbol in the center of the rocker and the three chevrons designated him an Airframes Master Chief Petty Officer.

"I'll take your bag Commander Hinton-Smith. Hotel arrangements have already been made for you," said Force Master Chief Rollins.

"Thank you, Force Master Chief Rollins, right?" asked Andrew, handing over his overnight bag and returning his salute.

"Yes, commander, you're correct. Right this way, admiral; commander," he said, escorting them up the small flight of stair steps and into the 5-story building.

The entrance doors were doublewide and opened automatically. When Sandra entered the quarterdeck area, everyone came to attention. She requested permission to cross the quarterdeck. When she was given permission, Andrew stepped onto the quarterdeck and looked around the immediate area.

He could see that the entryway carpet was an exact replica of the granite plaque outside. To the right and left sides of the quarterdeck podium were 3 brass shells from a Mark 76, 3-inch by 38-caliber deck gun. These shells were tied together with an equal length of ship's mooring line. On the top of each of the shells were finely polished wooden "bullets". Andrew was most impressed by this display.

"Request permission to cross the quarterdeck?" said Andrew, saluting the Cryptologic Technician second-class petty officer behind the podium.

"Permission granted, sir," she said, returning his salute.

Andrew soon joined Sandra and they walked down a long hallway to an elevator. Sandra pushed the "UP" button and the doors opened. They stepped into the elevator and she pushed the button for the 3rd floor. The doors closed and soon they reopened on the 3rd floor. They exited the elevator and walked down another long hallway to their left. When this hallway ended, Sandra opened the large, shiny, wooden doors to reveal an office. The secretary, a senior chief petty officer, looked up and then stood up. He saluted both of them.

"Is this Commander Hinton-Smith, admiral?" he asked, looking at Andrew.

"Affirmative," she replied as she returned his salute.

The senior chief turned around and knocked, heavily, three times, on the set of wooden, double doors just behind and slightly to the right of his desk.

"Admiral Milton, they want to talk to you first. Commander Hinton-Smith will have to wait out here," said the senior chief.

"I understand," she replied, quietly, as she entered through the doors.

When the second door had closed, Andrew thought he could hear the heavy click of a high-security lock securing into place.

"Commander, feel free to help yourself to coffee and breakfast items. You can leave your cover on my desk; it will be alright," said the senior chief, pointing to a small coffee bar on the far bulkhead from his desk.

"Thank you, senior chief," said Andrew, removing his cover and setting it down on the man's desk.

Andrew soon helped himself to two croissants, four Twinkies® and one donut along with two cups of coffee. When he had finished off the second cup of coffee, he tossed the empty coffee cup into the trashcan next to the coffee bar. Andrew then sat down in the chair next to the coffee bar that faced the two wooden doors that Sandra had entered earlier. He sat there and began the waiting process.

Meanwhile, the day was just starting for the crew of SSN-747. Lou was already up and going on his inspections. He checked all of the departments, including weapons department, during the absence of Andrew. When he had finished his inspections, he headed for the wardroom. He entered the wardroom and sat down in the first available chair after pouring himself a cup of coffee. Lou was awaiting the supposed arrival of Rear Admiral Lower Half Sam Livingston.

Rear Admiral Lower Half Sam Livingston was the commanding officer of the Submarine Intermediate Maintenance Activity at the Pearl Harbor sub base. The door to the wardroom opened and SSN-747's command chaplain entered. The chaplain had told Lou that he had an extreme dislike for Commander Hinton-Smith for being a homosexual. Lou looked up into the face of Lieutenant Junior Grade Mark Sullivan.

"Is there anything I can do for you, spiritually speaking, of course, Lou?" asked Mark.

"Pray for Commander Hinton-Smith, Mark," replied Lou without blinking an eye and staring almost straight through Mark to the bulkhead behind him.

"I will not pray for a homosexual, sir," announced Mark, rather disgustedly.

"Then, I want you to think about the sermon you gave all of us on this ship on the 26th of June of this year," said Lou.

"First Corinthians 13; I will start praying, sir," replied Mark.

"Thank you," said Lou as Mark left the wardroom.

Meanwhile, the large wooden doors had opened and Sandra appeared there. She looked at Andrew.

"Come on in, Andrew," she said.

He stood up and walked into the office. Andrew saw that Sandra had placed herself at a chair that was to the far left of Vice Admiral John Bonds. Andrew looked at the arrangement of the rest of the persons in the room.

To Andrew's left was Vice Admiral Ken Williams and in the left center position was Admiral Ray Simon. Andrew looked to his right and saw the civilians. Andrew then saw one lone chair sitting up against the bulkhead to his right. Admiral Ray Simon spoke first as he shook Andrew's left hand.

"Good morning, commander. Admiral Milton, here, says the flight was a little rough," said Ray smiling.

"Yes, sir, the flight was a little rough right at the end. The pilot mentioned something about the Santa Anna Winds being the culprit," replied Andrew, now highly suspicious of this whole situation.

"Sorry about your flight. Since this is an informal meeting, you can call all of us by our first names," said Ray.

"Thank you, Ray. How come we need medical?" asked Andrew, seeing the female captain sitting in the far right corner that he couldn't see earlier. She was in her dress white uniform, as well, with her staff officer insignia of the caduceus.

"I'll explain in a minute, Andrew. I believe you know the two vice admirals here, don't you?" asked Ray, pointing to them.

"Yes I do. Ken, its been about five years since we last served together, hasn't it?"

"Yes, it has been about five years. The last time we served together was for the commissioning of the last NORMANDY class cruiser," replied Ken.

"It's good to see you, Commander Hinton-Smith," said John.

"You too, John."

Ray moved towards the civilians next. All three of them stood up and introduced themselves. The first civilian was an older gentleman who worked with Raytheon Corporation. He shook Andrew's left hand. Next to him was a large, black briefcase.

"Commander Hinton-Smith, I'm Bob Devonshire of Raytheon Corporation. It's a privilege to finally meet you. I have many questions that my design engineers wanted me to ask you," he said, smiling.

"Raytheon Corporation? Manufacturers of the TOMAHAWK cruise missile?"

"Yes. I believe the military lists the TOMAHAWK cruise missile as a BGM-109, with the L series being the most current version available," said Bob as he sat down.

The next person to stand up was a man whom Andrew guessed to be right about his own age. He was clean cut and dressed in a black suit. He shook Andrew's right hand.

"Commander Hinton-Smith, it's a pleasure to finally meet you. I have questions, too, that need to be answered. My name is Roy Bevins. I work in the submarine design and engineering section of the General Electric Boat Division," said Roy.

"Your company designed and built a lot of the U.S. Navy's submarines."

"That's correct. From the first prototype submarine in the 1870's to the current nuclear powered submarines. We even sold a custom design nuclear powered submarine to a civilian a few years ago."

"What civilian needs their own nuclear powered submarine?"

"Mr. Dell of Dell Computer Corporation," he responded as he sat down.

The last civilian to stand up was a young man. Andrew guessed his age at maybe his late 20's. He was dressed in business casual attire. His hair was long and dirty blond in color. He stood up and had to push some of his hair out of his face, placing it over his ears. He shook Andrew's right hand and Andrew could detect that the man was very nervous. Next to this person was a large, black briefcase.

"Commander Hinton-Smith, my name is David Eggins. I'm the CEO and chief design engineer of Advanced Concepts, Inc.," he said, having a hard time saying the word commander.

"Glad to meet you, sir."

"Thank you."

The civilians had sat down as Andrew turned to face the admirals and the captain.

"Will the civilians please leave the room? We have military business to discuss that doesn't concern you," said Ray.

Ray's secretary opened the doors to the room. The civilians left and the doors shut once again with a loud thump.

"Andrew, did you get the latest advancement exam results?" asked Ray.

"Yes, Ray, I did receive my advancement results. I was not advanced," replied Andrew.

"That letter was sent to you, per my orders, directly from Captain Henning's office. The thought was that you might stick around a little while longer," said Ray, looking for some kind of reaction to the statement; Andrew never responded. Ray continued on as if nothing that he had said meant anything to Andrew.

"Well, I put in my retirement paperwork and a letter of resignation shortly after I read the letter."

"Which, I understand from Admiral Milton, here, you have rescinded that letter. Is that correct?"

"Yes, I have rescinded my letter of resignation."

"Smart move, Andrew. Captain Bonner, here, and her staff have had you under observation for many years. I will now turn this meeting over to her. Please have a seat," said Ray, pointing at the lone chair in the room.

"Thank you, Ray," said Andrew, sitting down in the chair.

Captain Bonner spent the next hour explaining the entire plan that the top navy psychologists had come up with for him. She explained how his email had been periodically monitored; his mail to his various apartments and houses had been periodically monitored. She explained the whole plan all the way up to the point of monitoring him at his current command. When she was done talking, she looked at Andrew.

"Do you have any questions for me right now?" she asked as she pulled out her pen from her uniform top left pocket and a small notepad from her right uniform pocket.

"Well, I hope that I haven't disappointed the navy's medical personnel," said Andrew, rather sarcastically.

"No. You've got to understand that the psychological community has been trying to find a test subject, from the GLBT community as it is called, that could make it past phase 3 of the testing platform."

"And I'm it, right?"

"Yes and there is much more to this testing. We've interviewed not only your current command department personnel, but your previous commands department personnel."

"What did you find out during these interviews?"

"You treated everyone fairly, with respect and with no prejudices. We also found out you never, um, what's the term one interviewee used…"

"Played around with the young males, captain."

"Thank you, yes. Since no one has made it past phase 3, yet, we won't know the answers to certain questions and theories until after phase 3 is completed. The U.S. Navy wants to be sure that if they turn over a submarine full of young males to a commanding officer that is a known homosexual, that there won't be any embarrassing sexual impropriety allegations."

"Good thinking, captain."

"Well, I have to get back to Bethesda. Admiral Simon, would you please let me know what Commander Hinton-Smith's decision is?"

"Of course, Captain Bonner. I will call you personally on your cell phone," replied Ray as she left the room.

When the doors had closed, Andrew noticed that Ray had opened up a small version of a service record. He and the other admirals were looking it over. Andrew knew, instinctively, that this service record was probably his. Ray spoke first.

"I'm not going to ask you about your platform qualifications. We can all plainly see what the platform qualifications are. What we want to know is, are you willing to take on a war game exercise entitled the Ultimate Command Challenge?" asked Ray.

"Whom am I being put up against?"

"The best that the surface fleet has to offer on the Pacific Ocean and a few top submarine commanders," replied Sandra.

"Okay, you've got my attention."

"The plan's outline, complete with rules of engagement, are waiting for you at your hotel room. Let me know what your decision is," said Ken.

"I will read the outline and get back to you on my decision, Ken."

"Don't worry, John and Ken, Andrew will take the challenge," said Sandra, almost salivating about how she was going to spend the money.

"Thanks for the vote of confidence, Sandra," said Andrew.

"You're welcome, Andrew. Ray, what is for lunch?" she asked.

"Lunch will be catered. After lunch, the civilians will have their chance to talk to you about your feedback reports," said John smiling.

"Thanks, John. Ray, since I will be staying here overnight, could I please call my command to let them know?" asked Andrew.

"I'll call Commander Staggs personally."

"Thank you, Ray, that is very kind of you."

Ray sent the civilians to lunch, telling them to return after 1300 hours. The catered lunch was much better than the breakfast Andrew had had earlier. Although Andrew was starting to feel a little tired, the excitement kept Andrew focused and energized. When lunch was completed and the dishes cleared away, all the admirals left the room. As Vice Admiral Bonds was walking past Andrew, he stopped and looked at Andrew right in the face.

"Commander, what do you think is the most important part of the order of battle?"

"Number 3; taking out oil refineries, oil storage areas, bridges, railroads, armories and power generation facilities, to name a few on that target list," replied Andrew.

"Why?"

"If the enemy can't see you coming, can't rearm, repair or refuel their war machine, then they're pretty much done in the first hours of an attack. The enemy can only fight for so long without being resupplied."

"What about back-up power?"

"Diesel generators can only run, at best, 72 hours before running out of fuel. If you have already hit the fuel storage areas and the accesses to them, there's no fuel; the generator dies after it burns up the last drop of fuel."

"Good point, commander."

He left the room as the civilians returned. Each one of them took out a notepad from their various briefcases and some other forms. Andrew surmised that some of those forms were probably the feedback reports he and his crew had submitted over the last several years. Andrew sat down in the lone chair and prepared for the questioning. It was Mr. Devonshire who started the questioning.

"Commander Hinton-Smith, in one of your feedback reports to Naval Sea Systems Command, you stated that the current Block IV, TOMAHAWK Tactical Anti-Ship Missile is too small?"

"Yes, that missile is too small for some applications," replied Andrew.

"Care to elaborate on that statement?" Mr. Devonshire asked as he prepared to take notes.

"A U.S. Air Force B-52H series Stratofortress carries a 1,000 kilogram or 2,000 pound payload on their TOMAHAWK's. Why can't I carry that same firepower as a surface ship or submarine?"

"Why would you need that kind of firepower?"

"I can cripple a ship the size of a Soviet KIEV Class Aircraft carrier at about 85,000 to 100,000 tons full combat load with one missile. However, if I should have to attack some of these VLCC and ULCC civilian ships at more than 140,000 tons, one missile may not do it much damage unless the ship isn't carrying any cargo."

"I see."

"Here's another reason for a larger payload, more diversity of attacking targets. If I should have to try and hit a hardened, defensive enemy target, such as a bunker buried in the bottom of a building or a heavily reinforced concrete and steel power turbine building, the 500 kilogram or 1,000 pound payload is simply ineffective."

"Doesn't the military have bunker busters for that purpose?"

"Yes and sometimes they are totally ineffective on a hardened target. When those bunker busters are dropped off target by so much as a few feet, they're wasted. With a cruise missile, I can park that missile right at the front door of the building, so to speak."

"That's true. Aren't you afraid your hydraulic systems will be overloaded by the increased payload, assuming that we could modify the TOMAHAWK to do such a thing?"

"No. The Mil-Spec on the hydraulic system, from Mechanicsburg, Pennsylvania states that the system has to be able to handle a weight of 1.5 times its current rating of 3,000 kilograms or 6,000 pounds. There's no way that a missile could overload the system."

"Why not use a tactical warhead?"

"Are you referring to the 250 kiloton, tactical, low-yield, nuclear warhead designate TN-250 for the TOMAHAWK Land Assault Missile or TLAM?"

"Yes."

"It is against Geneva Convention rules, which this country signed and has to abide by, to use tactical nuclear warheads against civilians in any capacity. Tactical nuclear weapons can only be used against military targets and only when authorized by the President of the United States."

"I have no further questions," said Mr. Devonshire as he continued writing things down.

Andrew looked at all the civilians in the room. They were all taking notes, writing fast and furiously. It was the CEO of Advanced Concepts, Inc. that spoke next. Andrew could tell the young man was still very nervous.

"Commander Hinton-Smith," he asked nervously.

"Yes. But you can call me Andrew if you want," Andrew replied, trying to ease the man's nervousness.

"Thank you. I also received your feedback reports from Naval Sea Systems Command via the Naval Weapons Systems Command. Naval Weapons Systems Command's engineers are under the impression that what you want aboard a submarine is impossible."

"Let me guess, NWSC gave the feedback reports to your company to see what you could do with the ideas, right?"

"Yes, Andrew. However, my company was given permission by NWSC as you call them to begin the research into the idea."

"Relax David, you've sold me on your company and yourself. What can I do to answer your engineering or other questions?"

"I understand that submarines already have countermeasures aboard. The admirals had to explain their function to me because I didn't have a clue as to what a countermeasure did."

"David, I appreciate your honesty. Honesty will get you a long way to getting what you want. However, those feedback reports you have were submitted by two of my most intelligent and gifted missile technicians," replied Andrew.

"Okay. I just wanted to know why either you or them felt it was a good idea to have an underwater version of what one of the admirals referred to as a PATRIOT Anti-Missile defense system?"

The other civilians started to chuckle at their fellow countryman. Andrew didn't like this at all.

"It's a valid question, Mr. Devonshire and Mr. Bevins," said Andrew.

"Sorry," said Mr. Bevins.

"Sorry," said Mr. Devonshire.

"David, once I launch either a HARPOON Anti-Ship Missile or a TOMAHAWK Anti-Ship/TLAM Missile from either my torpedo or my vertical launch tubes, the missile breaks the surface. When the missile breaks the surface, the enemy will know right where I am. The enemy will then fire missiles at me."

"I see that makes more sense."

"Those missiles will be carrying either a torpedo or a depth charge. A torpedo or depth charge-carrying-missile is something that a submarine has no defense against unless I can shoot down that missile before it can deliver its payload," explained Andrew as he noticed that David was both writing and drawing almost at the same time.

"Are you referring to what one of the admirals called an Anti-Submarine Rocket?"

"Yes. The navy calls the system an ASROC."

"What is the maximum depth that a depth charge can reach?"

"200 meters or about 600 feet. The torpedo can reach about 600 meters or about 1,900 feet before it is crushed by the water pressure."

"What about an ASROC?" asked David, having a little trouble pronouncing the word ASROC.

"Everything within one kilometer or 6/10th's of a mile of where the ASROC enters the water will be destroyed. At three kilometers or about 1.5 nautical miles, a submarine's hull can be severely damaged. The ASROC is pre-programmed to enter the water a short time after launch and proceed to a depth of 250 meters or about 750 feet and detonate. However, if the ASROC is lucky enough to hit the submarine's hull, it has a contact fuse detonator; boom!"

"In other words, you don't have to be very close to your target, then?"

"That's correct."

"I don't have any more questions for Andrew."

The only civilian that hadn't asked Andrew any questions was Mr. Bevins. He had been watching Andrew the whole time. Mr. Bevins took, from Andrew's point of view, lots of notes. Andrew stared at Mr. Bevins for a while before Mr. Bevins put down his notepad and pen. Mr. Bevins then cleared his throat.

"Commander, why do you think it's a necessity for an attack sub to dive to 1,000 meters or about 3,000 feet? Do you realize what kind of pressure is on the hull at that depth?"

"Yes, Mr. Bevins, I do know what the pressure is at that depth. It is 44,100 PSI or about 22,000 Kilopascals. It's something that someone in the Soviet fast attack sub world knows about and capitalized on."

"Just how do you know that a Soviet fast attack sub can dive that deep?" asked Roy, defensively.

"Three years ago, while I was stationed aboard the USS ORCA, a SEAWOLF class fast attack nuclear sub, we were at test depth monitoring two newly outfitted Soviet fast attack subs as they came out of the Vladivostok Naval Yards."

"Where you able to identify their classes?"

"Yes. There was one AKULA-II Improved and one ALPHA class."

"You do realize that their hulls are made almost exclusively of Titanium, right?"

"Yes, I'm aware of their building materials. It also gives a really nice return on active sonar. These two subs made the U.S. Navy laughing stock by simply diving underneath us at test depth by 200 meters and staying there for more than 45 minutes."

"I'll look into that issue. One more question, why would it be an advantage for an attack sub to have twin propellers?"

"If the sub is detected, the sub could easily be mistaken for a DELTA IV class SSBN, a TYPHOON class SSBN, or any of the other various countries out there that have twin propeller propulsion plants."

"True. I don't have any further questions."

The admirals returned a short time after the questioning had ended. Andrew started to leave when Sandra stopped him. Andrew turned to face her and she winked her right eye at him.

"Ray wants to make sure you get to your hotel safely," said Sandra.

"Please, lead the way, Sandra," replied Andrew, taking the hint.

Sandra didn't say too much to Andrew on the way to his hotel. Andrew stepped out of Sandra's rental car and walked into the hotel's front lobby. He was asked for ID by the front desk staff and then given a key to his room. He arrived at his room, 1414 and turned on the lights.

He saw, on the bed, a large manila envelope with his name on it. He sat down on the side of the bed and grabbed the envelope. He ripped it open to find a spiral notebook inside. Andrew readjusted the pillows so he could begin reading. He then took off his dress white uniform and hung it up in the small closet at the entrance to the room.

As Andrew read each page of the "Ultimate Command Challenge" war game exercise, he wondered how the crew would react to him being in charge. Suddenly, the phone, which was next to the bed on the nightstand, began to ring. Andrew knew only a few people would know his exact whereabouts. He picked up the receiver and placed it to his right ear.

"Hello?" asked Andrew.

"Its Ray, Andrew. Did you get the package?" asked Ray, excitedly.

"Yes, I did. What's the matter, don't trust Master Chief Rollins?"

"He's a good man, I trust him. Well, what do you think of the proposal?"

"I'll let you know in the morning, Ray."

"Fair enough. Be downstairs at 0730 hours. My duty driver will pick you up out front of the hotel."

"See you in the morning, Ray."

Andrew hung up the phone and continued reading late into the night. When he finished off the proposal, he set the alarm on his cell phone. He fell asleep immediately after turning off the lights. The alarm went off, by Andrew's calculations, what only seemed like a few hours later. He stepped out of bed, shaved and showered. He put on his uniform, grabbed a quick bite to eat in the hotel's lobby and waited for the duty driver to pick him up with his overnight bag.

The duty driver dropped Andrew off at the front entrance to the building. After Andrew had cleared the quarterdeck, he went to the elevator. He stepped off at the 3rd floor and walked into the outer office. The senior chief opened the double doors where a civilian in business attire met Andrew. The man was smiling and shook Andrew's right hand, vigorously.

"You must be Commander Hinton-Smith," the man said, enthusiastically.

"Yes, I am. Sir, do you have an ID?" Andrew asked.

"Why, yes, I do," the man replied, reaching into his back, right rear, pants pocket.

The man produced a government issued photo identification. Andrew looked at the ID and saw the letters across the top; "THE UNITED STATES SENATE." Andrew scanned over the ID to see the man was Senator James Arthar of Idaho and he was registered as a Republican. The ID also stated that Mr. Arthar was an assistant chairman to the Senate Armed Forces Committee. Andrew looked over the senator's left shoulder. All the admirals were staring at Andrew with their mouths agape and their faces the same white color as their uniforms.

"I'm terribly sorry, Your Honor. Can't be too careful these days. What can I do for you?" asked Andrew as the senator put his ID back into his right, rear pants pocket.

"The admirals here tell me that you would know what a Project 855 ship is."

"Your Honor, the Project 855 ship is the current 22 ship ARLEIGH BURKE Class destroyer. If you look over Admiral Simon's head, you will see a picture of one of those ships."

"What about a Project 955 class of ship?"

"Your Honor, a Project 955 is the current 26 ship NORMANDY class cruiser. If you look over Vice Admiral John Bonds' right shoulder, you will find a picture of one of those ships."

"What about a Project 21 class of ship?"

"Your Honor, a Project 21 class of ships is the current 12 ship out of 20 ship SEAWOLF class nuclear powered fast attack submarine. If you look over my right shoulder, you will find a picture of, I believe, the USS SEAWOLF, SSN-21."

"Thank you, Commander Hinton-Smith," the senator said as he turned to face the admirals who were all smiling by this point. "Admiral Simon, a most impressive submarine commander. You will be hearing from me shortly, I assure you; good-bye."

When the senator had left the office, Vice Admiral Bonds spoke first.

"Jesus H. Christ, did you have to ask the man for his ID?" he thundered.

"Yes, Vice Admiral Bonds, I did have to ask him for his ID. He knew me, but I didn't know him. He could have been a potential terrorist, sir."

"John, sit down, it's okay. Well Andrew, what did you think of our proposal?" asked Ray.

"I accept your proposal. However, I want it made crystal clear to the enemy fleet they must adhere strictly to the rules of engagement. If they don't, all bets are off."

"That's fair enough, Andrew. I will ensure that everyone, including you, abides by the rules of engagement. You also understand that this is a live fire exercise right?"

"I do realize and understand the complexity of this proposal as you call it being a live fire exercise."

"Okay. Myself and the other admirals here will put the finishing touches on the exercise. I will make sure that your ship is properly armed as well. My pilot will fly you and Sandra back tonight."

"Thank you, Ray," said Andrew as he and Sandra left the office.

A few minutes after they had left, Ray stepped outside of his office to talk to his secretary. The senior chief stood up.

"Have you sent off all those messages from this morning, yet?"

"No, sir. I was waiting on the one about the commander's decision. If he said yes, then I was going to send all the messages off at once."

"Well, the answer is yes. Will you also add, in bold, capital letters, the words 'strictly adhere to the rules of engagement or face severe penalties' in paragraph 3?"

"Yes, admiral."

"Good. After lunch, prepare to take down more messages for the remainder of the day."

"Yes, admiral."

# Chapter 5

Andrew arrived back to the Pearl Harbor Naval Air Station late that Tuesday night. Sandra's duty driver took Andrew home and dropped him off before returning the admiral to her home. After a quick dinner with Gary, Andrew went to bed. He woke up the next morning at his usual time and had breakfast. He tossed his dress white uniform and associated gear in the car. As Gary drove Andrew to the pier where the ship was located, Andrew spoke.

"Be prepared for some unusual happenings in the next few months."

"Okay. Does this have something to do with your trip you went on?"

"Yes. I'm still suspicious of the military's motives, but I never could turn down a challenge," said Andrew as he stepped out of the car with his dress white uniform.

Gary drove off and returned home to prepare for his day at work. Once Andrew was aboard SSN-747, he went straight to his quarters. He opened the door and found the chief engineer shaving. Andrew immediately opened up his personal locker and put his dress white uniform and associated gear into the locker. Andrew then closed the door to his locker as the chief engineer finished wiping off his face. The chief engineer then put on some aftershave and looked at Andrew.

"Well, did you enjoy your trip?" asked Bill, with some sarcasm in his voice and an almost evil smile on his face.

"Yes, the admirals were awfully nice to me. I met some civilians and a senator. I'm betting some of those civilians probably think that myself and some of my department personnel are lunatics."

"Which senator did you meet?"

"Senator James Arthar, a Republican from Idaho according to his ID."

Andrew went on to tell the informative short story about the ID incident. They both laughed when Andrew was done telling the story. Bill, however, suddenly put on a straight and serious face.

"Scuttlebutt is, we're going to war soon. Did they say with whom?" asked Bill, prodding Andrew for any scrap of information.

"Bill, the admirals didn't say anything to me about going to war with anyone. I will tell you, however, be prepared for some unusual war game exercises."

"Okay, is it Iran that we will be fighting?"

"I just told you, I don't know. Besides, we could blow the entire Iranian navy out of the water in a matter of hours."

"Yeah, I guess we could."

The ship's announcing system came to life. Gong, gong, gong, gong, gong, gong went the announcing bells.

"Commanding Officer, Submarine Intermediate Maintenance Activity, arriving," gong.

"There will be an all officers meeting in the wardroom in 10 minutes."

Andrew and Bill looked at each other rather oddly. They went to the wardroom and sat down at one of the tables. After everyone was seated, Lou went into the briefing. Andrew saw Rear Admiral Lower Half Sam Livingston sitting to the left of Lou. Sam's eyes were almost riveted to Andrew. The briefing seemed like it lasted only a few minutes before Lou looked right at Andrew and spoke.

"Commander Hinton-Smith, you are not needed for the rest of this briefing. I will need a complete weapons inventory status on my desk by 1600 hours today," said Lou.

"Does this complete inventory require small arms munitions?" asked Andrew, rather perplexed by the order.

"No, primary weapons only."

"Yes, sir," said Andrew as he stood up and left the briefing.

The briefing continued without Andrew. He went to his office and found Shawn doing some filing and processing some reports. Shawn looked up to see Andrew as Andrew shut the office door. Andrew looked around the office and found, on the back of the door, one clipboard. The clipboard contained the weapons department's current status. Andrew looked over the status sheet and then looked at the date on the sheet; it was today.

"Shawn, the captain gets his copy of the weapons inventory and departmental status every morning, right?" asked Andrew.

"Yes, commander, he does. Every morning at 0800 hours, even on weekends and holidays. Now, it's a totally different matter whether or not he reads those reports," replied Shawn.

"You're right. Please print up another copy of the weapons inventory list."

"Yes, sir," replied Shawn as he printed up another copy of the report.

When the printer was done printing, Shawn tore off the sheet containing the report. He handed the report to Andrew. Andrew looked the report over, pulled out a pen from the desk blotter and signed the report. As Andrew looked over the departmental readiness portion of the report, he noticed that TMSN Bradley was on the sick list until the next morning.

"Shawn, why is Mr. Bradley on the sick in quarters list?" asked Andrew.

"I don't know. All I know for sure is, he reported, the morning you left, to sickbay with a problem. The medical officer placed him on the sick in quarters list for 48 hours."

"Very well. Make sure that he is at departmental quarters which will be held at 0300 hours."

"Yes, sir."

Andrew left the department office and headed towards the captain's cabin. He knocked on the door. Lou opened the door and Andrew handed Lou the report. Lou took the report and looked it over briefly. Andrew started to turn around to leave when Lou stopped him.

"We have nothing but exercise shots aboard? What happened to our primary weapons?" asked Lou.

"We off loaded our weapons, captain, at Diego Garcia, to the USS THERMITE, AE-30."

"That's right, because we were supposed to go into the shipyards for a short-term yard period. I forgot, Commander Hinton-Smith, sorry."

"Not a problem, sir. Is there anything else I can do for you?"

"Have your personnel ready to transfer those exercise shots to Admiral Livingston's personnel between 0900 and 1100 hours," said Lou, setting the report down on his desktop.

"Yes, sir. Sir, is there something wrong with our exercise shots?"

"No, the SIMA personnel would like to perform the 60M-1R maintenance check while they have the opportunity," said Lou, lying through his teeth. Lou knew it was in preparation for the full weapons on load for the war game.

"Yes, sir. I completely understand the maintenance issue; a dirty weapon will get you killed."

"Quite correct; dismissed," said Lou, smiling.

Lou shut the door to his cabin. Andrew walked off towards the weapons control room. When he arrived there, he didn't find anyone in there. He then walked over to the fire control system and turned on both the fire and launch control computers.

Once the computers had powered up, Andrew saw the message box pop up. "NO NEW SOFTWARE UPDATES REQUIRED." The last time Andrew saw that message box it said that the system was behind by many updates. Andrew turned off both computers as he left the compartment.

Andrew continued walking towards the weapons department office and found Shawn doing more paperwork on the computer. Andrew shut the door and took down a small, green, 3-ring binder from the bookshelf. The binder contained all the required preventative maintenance checks for the weapons department. He opened up the binder to find out who was the current PMS coordinator; TM2 (SS) Heather Doenitz.

"Shawn, where is Heather?"

"I believe that she is in the Countermeasures room, sir, performing a maintenance check."

"Thank you."

Andrew left the office and went down into the very belly of the ship. The countermeasures room was small and cramped. He looked into and around the compartment before finding what he was looking for. He saw a large, muscular shadow moving around inside. TM2 (SS) Doenitz was one of a handful of female bodybuilders that the U.S. Navy had. She participated in various physical fitness events. She had won several certificates, awards and at least three medals. Andrew knocked on the compartment hatch door.

"Who's there?" she asked in a rather husky voice.

"Commander Hinton-Smith."

"Please come in, sir."

Andrew entered the small compartment and found Heather. She was putting one of the passive countermeasure decoys back into its storage space. She then closed the small flap over the launch tube. She secured the flap and turned around to face Andrew. Her sleeves were rolled up her forearms and she was sweating.

"What can I do for you, sir?" she asked.

"When is the 60M-1R PMS check due on our exercise shots?"

"March of 2014 I believe, sir."

"That's funny. SIMA wants us to off load our exercise shots in the morning so that they can perform that check now."

"What time tomorrow morning, sir?" she asked, rather alarmed.

"Between 0900 and 1100 hours. Will doing this 60M-1R check early affect the PMS maintenance scheduling?"

"No, sir, doing the check early will not affect the PMS schedules. By SIMA doing the check for us, the next time the check comes due would be five years from this month and year."

"Okay. Get yourself a team together tonight for the off load."

"Yes, sir."

"Another thing, Heather, would you teach our new crewmembers how to manually open the torpedo tube outer doors and fire a torpedo manually?"

"Yes, sir."

"Quarters will be at 0300 hours; try to get some sleep."

"Yes, sir."

Andrew left the compartment and returned to the office. When he opened the door, Shawn handed him the phone receiver.

"Who is it, Shawn?"

"SACPACFLT, sir."

Andrew put the receiver to his left ear.

"Yes, Admiral Simon, what can I do for you, sir?"

"Would it be okay with you if I sent that civilian, David Eggins, out to your ship? He has some further questions for those missile technicians of yours."

"Sure, Admiral Simon. I'll make arrangements for Mr. Eggins to get a base pass. How long will he be aboard, sir?"

"He claims he only needs two days. He's supposed to be arriving tomorrow morning."

"I'll be waiting for him, sir. Good-bye admiral," said Andrew as he hung up the phone.

"Shawn, call the naval station pass office and find out how a DOD contractor can get on the base."

"Yes, sir."

Andrew sat down in the chair at his desk in the office. Shawn soon hung up the phone after talking with the base pass office personnel. Shawn handed Andrew the list of things that were required. Andrew reviewed the list and called the ship's security officer to notify him of the DOD contractor that was coming aboard. The ship's security officer asked Andrew a series of questions that were easily answered with a yes or no. When the conversation had ended, Andrew hung up the phone.

"Tell everyone to try and get some amount of sleep. It is going to be a long day for all of us. Please notify me when Mr. Eggins arrives aboard."

"Yes, sir."

Since Andrew was the command duty officer, he spent the night aboard the ship. He made sure that everyone, regardless of their department, was able to get some sort of rest before the dry-docking commenced. At precisely 0300 hours, the officer of the deck woke up the crew.

Andrew went to the quarterdeck and saw the USS SEA SAW, MD-1 turning herself around in the bay. He also noticed that the usual tugs were not there to assist her. In another 20 minutes, divers were seen going over the side. They dragged with them a long, large communications cable for giving precise directions to the ship's stevedore.

The captain and the executive officer arrived a little while later. Andrew greeted them and they relieved Andrew of his duties as the command duty officer. Lou was looking behind himself at the pier. Some of the shore personnel were on the pier ready to loosen up the mooring lines, power connections and other items.

Periodically, a ship wide announcement was made about divers being over the side. Lou could see the SIMA personnel were waiting on the pier as well. Lou looked forward of the ship and saw a rare spectacle in the navy; a massive ship submerging herself.

The USS SEA SAW started moving herself forward. As she moved forward, she constantly adjusted her position with directions from the divers stationed along the underside of SSN-747. Soon, the massive ship was completely submerged. At 0340 hours SSN-747 was jarred hard.

When this happened, the mooring lines and other shore connections were loosened. Slowly, SSN-747 was lifted higher and higher out of the water. Andrew had gone below to brief his crew when the ship's announcing system came to life.

"Attention, all hands, this is the captain speaking. For anyone who has never seen a ship of any kind in dry-dock, feel free to take a look at both ships from the pier. This is a rare opportunity to see this; that is all," said Lou.

Meanwhile, at the Naval Weapons Station for Pearl Harbor, the commanding officer had arrived to begin his day. Captain Juan Perez began driving through the massive warehouse area that was partially above and partially below ground, in a small golf cart. He carried with him an electronic clipboard showing his current weapons inventory. He started with driving up and down the aisles marked for small arms.

He found the boxes and boxes of 7.62MM NATO rounds, .50BMG rounds, and 20MM machine gun rounds. There were also the 20MM cannon rounds for the Close In Range Weapons systems called CIWS. He then drove up and down the aisles with old boxes of .30 caliber machine gun rounds, 9MM NATO rounds, .45ACP rounds, 5.56MM NATO rounds and even some old .38Special rounds. He had armor piercing, armor piercing incendiary, incendiary and full metal jacket rounds.

He then drove to the warehouses filled with hand grenades, shotguns, rifles, and machine guns. He checked the several levels of rounds for these weapons and then drove towards the surface fleet arms. He drove for a few minutes before arriving at a particular warehouse where he had to use a special code on the box to get into the place. Once the doors had opened and he drove his golf cart inside, the doors closed behind him and the lights came on.

He started driving up and down aisles and aisles of HARPOON anti-ship missiles and TOMAHAWK anti-ship and land assault missiles for surface ships. He then drove up and down aisles of Mark 48, ADCAP IV series torpedoes for launching from surface ships or aircraft, Mark 50, ADCAP II series torpedoes for launching from surface ships or aircraft.

The next aisles he came to contained the ASROC's, old SEA LANCE's and even some old Mark 66 Depth Charges. These depth charges were capable of being launched from a destroyer, cruiser or frigate as well as any aircraft that the U.S. Navy had at the time. He looked around at the inventory of his surface launched Mark 79 mines for anti-submarine operations.

After he finished off this part of the inventory, he left that warehouse and went next door to the other warehouse. This warehouse housed the weapons for submarines.

He entered this warehouse like the other one and drove up and down empty aisles. These aisles were silent and empty of their cargo with the exception of the last row of weapons for submarines. These other empty aisles were to house the newest version of the submarine launched anti-ship missile the HARPOON designated as an UGM-84F series.

There was another set of empty aisles that were to have housed both the anti-ship version and land assault missile versions of the TOMAHAWK cruise missile. This missile was designated as an UBGM-109L series. Next to those aisles were supposed to be Mark 50, ADCAP II series submarine launched torpedoes. They were empty. Only the last two aisles actually had anything in them.

One aisle had 12 Mark 48, ADCAP IV series submarine launched torpedoes in case of an emergency. The navy ordered removal of all other submarine launched torpedoes from service many months ago. Captain Perez was still waiting for the promised replacement ordnance to arrive. To date, the replacement ordnance had never arrived.

The final aisle contained a mixture of active and passive countermeasures, Underwater Unmanned Vehicles or UUM's as they were called and some underwater mines designated as UM-28's. These mines were launched from submarines many nautical miles away from their intended target. They allowed a submarine to carryout offensive mine laying operations without ever coming under enemy fire.

Having completed his inventory inspection, Captain Perez left this warehouse and was heading back to his office when another vehicle pulled up alongside his golf cart. The Duty Driver for the naval weapons station, RM2 Simms, rolled down the passenger side window. Juan looked up at the window as he stopped his golf cart. The Command Duty Officer, Commander Jenkins, looked down at Juan.

"Good morning, commander, what brings you out here?" asked Juan.

"We received a priority message early this morning from Vice Admiral Bonds," said Commander Jenkins.

"What did the good admiral have to say?"

"We are to fully combat load out SSN-747 for a live fire war game exercise that is to take place in the Pacific NGFS range in the next few days. We are also to combat load out all surface vessels with whatever we have on the list he sent on the message."

"Thank you, commander. I'll be in my office in about 45 minutes to relieve you," said Juan as his blood started boiling.

"Yes, sir," replied Commander Jenkins as he rolled up his window and the car drove off.

Captain Perez handed the completed inventory to his administrative assistant when he arrived back at his office. Once he had relieved Commander Jenkins, Captain Perez stepped into his office and turned on his computer. After the computer had powered up completely, he accessed his military email and checked to see that the current inventory list had been uploaded from this morning's inspection. He saw that the upload was completed and turned off the computer. He then stepped out into his outer office and found his administrative assistant typing up some letters and messages.

"Would you please call Admiral Milton for me?" asked Juan.

"Yes, Juan."

Juan entered his office and waited for his phone to start ringing. Line 4 started to ring almost immediately. Juan picked up the receiver and placed it to his left ear as he pushed the flashing lighted button on the phone. He was relieved to find Admiral Milton was at the other end and not some call screener.

"Juan, this is Sandra, is everything all right?" she asked.

"No, Sandra. I cannot comply with Vice Admiral Bonds' request for a full combat load out of SSN-747. If I call and try to tell him that, I will most likely lose my temper and tell him to do things that are not humanly possible, anatomically speaking."

"I understand. What exactly is the problem?"

"All of the newest and greatest submarine launched weapons are sitting aboard a military sealift command ship in the Los Angeles harbor because some bureaucrat in Washington, D.C. won't let the weapons get underway."

"Okay, I'll see what I can do."

"Thank you, admiral. I have nothing but pity for the poor bastard who replaces me in four months."

"I can believe that, Juan. Let me make some phone calls and have a couple more cups of coffee, it will help relax you."

"Good-bye, admiral."

A few minutes later, after Juan had finished off the first pot of coffee, his phone started ringing. Juan picked up the phone and found out it was Sandra calling.

"Juan, I just got off the phone with Vice Admiral Bonds. He says he will try and do his best to get you your sub launched weapons," she said nicely.

Little did Juan realize or know that Vice Admiral Bonds was listening in on the phone call. Sandra had received Vice Admiral Bonds' assurance that he would keep quiet if she could make a conference call. Bonds agreed, keeping a notepad and pen handy to take notes.

"I'm glad the vice admiral saw things from my point of view, Sandra," said Juan.

"However, the vice admiral would like to know why or how you don't have the sub launched weapons in your possession."

"Well, when the U.S. invaded Iraq in early 2003, I received a priority message to deplete all stocks of on hand weapons by the then chief of naval operations."

"Do you recall what the message number was, Juan?"

"Yes. It was NAVWEPSMSG0845031220031100ZULU."

"Okay, go on," Sandra was praying that the vice admiral was taking notes.

"I then received another message in October of 2003 from the then secretary of the navy and then secretary of defense to prepare for return to the manufacturer all Mark 48, ADCAP IV series sub launched torpedoes, all UGM-84's and all UBGM-109's."

"What message number was that one?"

"NAVWEPSMSG1050101920031800ZULU."

"Okay. Did you follow your orders?"

"Yes, admiral, I did follow my orders. A civilian military sealift command ship, instead of an AE or an AOE, arrived a few days later and took my sub launched weapons from me."

"Go on Juan, what happened next?"

"NAVWEPSMSG1345021020041900ZULU told me that by June of 2004, I would be fully restocked on all the latest and greatest sub launched weapons. In the message, paragraph 2 clearly stated that the Mark 48, ADCAP IV series sub launched torpedoes were due to be made obsolete as the Mark 50, ADCAP II series sub launched torpedoes were being delivered. I was originally thinking that the manufacturer of these new torpedoes screwed up royally somewhere along the way until I received a later message."

"I understand."

"At no time, admiral, was there a recall on any of the weapons for the surface fleet; just the sub launched weapons."

"Did you follow up on that message?"

"Yes, admiral, I did send a follow up message. It seems that in August of 2004, Congress had some sort of budget crisis. My weapons, to this day, some 26 months later, are sitting in the Los Angeles harbor."

"Can you outfit the surface fleet?"

"Yes, admiral. My current inventory would allow me to fully combat load out three complete battle groups minus their submarine escorts."

"Do you have any Mark 48, ADCAP IV series sub launched torpedoes in your inventory?"

"I do, however, I cannot issue them."

"Why not?"

"NAVWEPSMSG1645010120040700ZULU states clearly in paragraph 1 that no Mark 48, ADCAP IV series sub launched torpedoes with stock number 4M 1001-00-106-5445 shall be issued to a submarine. This stock numbered item is, or has been, obsoleted by Naval Weapons Systems Command."

"I understand. Do you have the name of the military sealift command ship that has your weapons?"

"The EL HOMBRE."

"While I have you on the phone, do you have any UM-26 Alphas?"

"No. I have about 150 UM-28 Alphas because they carry a larger payload of explosives. I also have about 12, Mark 66-D series depth charges with the new hydrogen payload."

"Excellent; thank you for your time."

"Good-bye admiral," said Juan as he hung up the phone.

Sandra waited a few minutes before speaking.

"Did you take notes, John?" she asked.

"Yes, I did, Sandra. That third star is looking better all the time."

"Thank you, John."

"I'll see what I can do to get Juan his weapons for this live fire exercise."

"Good-bye John."

Meanwhile, SSN-747 had been put back into the water. With a new torpedo tube door installed, the leak check watches began. The USS SEA SAW, after pulling out from underneath SSN-747, turned around and anchored herself a few hundred meters/yards from SSN-747. The USS SEA SAW was keeping a watch on SSN-747 in case the repair job didn't hold. Captain Paulik was sitting on the bridge of MD-1, looking at the setting sun. He then reached up and used the box above his chair.

"Bridge, navigation," said Jon.

"Navigation, aye," replied the female voice.

"When are the next high tides due?"

"There's a minor high tide tonight at 2140 hours. The next major high tide is not until 0249 hours tomorrow morning, sir."

"Bridge, aye."

Jon reset the channel selector switch.

"Bridge, main control," he said.

"Main control, aye," said the female voice.

"Set your sea and anchor detail at 2100 hours for getting underway at 2140 hours."

"Main control, aye."

Jon released the button and turned to face the duty boatswain's mate of the watch.

"Have deck department personnel assembled to set the sea and anchor detail at 2100 hours."

"Aye, sir," he responded.

Meanwhile, aboard SSN-747, Commander Hinton-Smith had stationed a weapons department person in the aft torpedo room. The first person on watch, checking for leaks, was TMSN Bradley. TM2 (SS) Doenitz had come up with a watch rotation list for the next 24 hours. As the rest of the weapons department personnel were either in their bunks asleep or on watch at the quarterdeck, Andrew stopped by the aft torpedo room before going home.

"It's not leaking yet, commander," said Bart.

"It probably won't until the ship goes diving."

"You're right, commander."

"Mr. Bradley, make sure that your diving gear is in good working order before we get underway for this war game exercise."

"Yes, sir."

"When are you going to get relieved?"

"In about 30 minutes, commander, by TM2 (SS) Doenitz."

"Okay. You don't have to answer this question, but why were you sick in quarters while I was gone?"

"Medical personnel told me I had blue balls, sir."

"Well, quit jacking off so much and you won't get blue balls again."

"Aye, sir."

Andrew left the compartment and headed towards the quarterdeck. As he went up a ladder, he bumped into one of the youngest members of the crew, BMSN Oliver Franz. Oliver was usually at the diving command station when the ship set sail. Oliver saw Andrew and nodded his head at Andrew.

"Good evening, Commander Hinton-Smith; going home, sir?" he asked.

"Yeah, I will be going home shortly."

"Good night, then, sir."

"Good night to you, too. By the way, did you ever get your master helmsman qualifications?"

"Yes, sir. The diving officer quizzed me on the basics and the captain asked me some of the advanced questions."

"What is the crush depth of this ship?"

"For the 688 Improved class nuclear powered fast attack submarine, crush depth is 1,850 feet or about 617 meters."

"How long can we operate at that depth?"

"Six minutes, sir. However, hull damage may occur in as little as three minutes and damage to the pressure hull can shorten that time even more."

"Good answers."

"Any other questions that I can answer for you, sir?"

"No. Good night and good-bye."

"Yes, sir."

# Chapter 6

The sun was rising on the buildings that housed Advanced Concepts, Inc. David Eggins was getting ready to start his day. He walked into his main office and poured himself a cup of coffee. He then entered his inner office, setting down the notebooks that he had been carrying. After taking a few sips of his coffee, he picked up the phone.

He dialed his research and development department. Finding no one there, he left a message for them to come pick-up the notebooks. He then dialed a phone number known only to him. The phone rang many times before someone answered.

"Good morning and thank you for calling Lockheed Martin-Marietta Missile Defense Systems Command, this is Ginger, how can I help you?"

"Good morning, Ginger, this is David Eggins of Advanced Concepts, Inc. Is Sally Ratherton available?"

"One moment please."

David was put on hold for a few minutes before Sally's voice snapped him back to attention.

"David, so good to hear your voice. I understand from our classmate, Alethia Van Gilder, that you own your own company now. Was what I heard just a rumor?"

"Not a rumor Sally, I do own my own company. I'm the CEO of Advanced Concepts, Inc. Look, the reason why I called was to obtain some information on your Patriot Anti-Missile Defense System."

"Well, unless you're a governmental entity with a need-to-know, I cannot supply you with any restricted information. I can only give you general information."

"Believe it or not, I'm a new defense contractor for the navy and I need to know how your system works."

"Congratulations on getting one of those coveted government contracts. Do you have an FSCM number?"

"Is that my Federal Supply Code to Manufacturer number?"

"Yes, that's the number."

"Oh, my FSCM number is 12G818."

"Okay, what do you want to know about my system?"

"How does the thing work, exactly?"

"Basically, the Patriot Anti-Missile Defense System is a land-mobile, multiple missile launcher. The missile itself is a short range heat seeker."

"Great. Could I possibly get, for research purposes only, a non-working model of this thing? My research and development department needs to get measurements."

"Okay. I'll talk to my supervisors about your request. Where's your company located?"

"In a small California town in the middle of the San Rafael Swell."

"Leave your shipping address with Ginger. Perhaps we can get together next month. I'm supposed to be at a symposium in San Diego on the 20th."

"Sounds great, looking forward to seeing you; good-bye."

"Good-bye, David."

Sally transferred David back to Ginger. David gave Ginger his company's shipping address. As David hung up the phone, the head of his research and development staff arrived. She picked up the notebooks and was leaving the inner office when David stopped her.

"Rachel, if we're lucky, we'll have a non-working model of that Patriot Anti-Missile Defense System like you requested."

"Wonderful, however, I still don't know exactly what it is."

"Oh, I found out that the missile is basically a short range heat seeker. All we have to do is make it waterproof and capable of being fired from a submerged submarine."

"Do we know what the maximum depth is that the missile might be fired from?"

"125 feet or about 40 meters and at a speed of no more than 3 knots. Those are the maximum parameters for launching missiles from a submerged submarine."

"Okay, what about the missile decoy?"

"The same stats, however, could we try and make it so that when the submarine launches the decoy, that there is a delay before it breaks the surface?"

"You mean, so that the launching submarine is clear of the area and can safely fire its missiles?"

"Yes."

"Already programmed that into the computer simulations. Is there anything else?"

"Don't go into production until you have good, constant computer simulations and I sign off on it."

"Yes, sir."

Meanwhile, in Washington D.C., Senator Arthar had completed another grueling committee meeting over the budget for the next fiscal year. The next fiscal year, which was still months away, had money destined for the Navy. In the request, among other items, were more cruise missiles, better pay and more ships. Although the committee had approved much of the budget, they were at an impasse over the weapons issues. During one of the breaks, the senator called the department of the navy and was put through to the Chief of Naval Operations, Admiral Theodore Rosin.

"Yes Senator Arthar, what can I do for you?" asked Theodore, looking across his desk at Admiral Simon.

"Could I possibly observe a live fire naval weapons exercise in which HARPOON's and TOMAHAWK's are being used among other weapons?"

"I believe that there is a live fire exercise planned for the Pacific Naval Gun Fire Support Range in the next few days. Could you find some time in your busy schedule to fly to Honolulu?"

"I think that I can get there by Saturday, admiral."

"Good, I will arrange for transportation to SSN-747. Have a good day, Your Honor," he said, hanging up the phone.

Meanwhile, the National Oceanic and Atmospheric Administration, based in Honolulu, Hawaii, was keeping a keen eye on a tropical depression that was still many days out from Hawaii. The tropical depression, during the night, had strengthened into a tropical storm that was gaining in intensity. Although the satellite images showed no cyclonic activity, the tropical storm was given a name anyway; Kendra. At 40 knot sustained winds, Tropical Storm Kendra could easily develop into a Category 1 Typhoon.

As the printout completed printing off the printer at the night person's duty desk, he grabbed the printout. He then headed for the director's office on the 4th floor. He approached the door, which read "Director of Pacific Typhoon Watches", and knocked before entering. The director looked up.

"Good morning, Bob, what has happened since I left last night?" asked the director, drinking his coffee.

"Where do you want me to start, sir?" asked Bob.

"North Pacific."

"The North Pacific is quiet with the exception of a storm situated approximately 90 nautical miles North Northwest of Midway Island. We have alerted air traffic control to reroute Trans-Pacific flights around the storm and we have issued small craft warnings. We have also alerted cruise ships and the like to avoid the area."

"Good. What about the South Pacific?"

"A tropical depression that was picked up on weather satellites last evening in GPS Grid Square 1827, achieved tropical storm status a few minutes ago with sustained 40 knot winds," said Bob, handing the director the latest information on Tropical Storm Kendra.

The director looked over the printout and then set it down on his desktop.

"So, we have a new tropical storm named Kendra, that could develop into a Category 1 typhoon. Is there any evidence of cyclonic activity?"

"No, sir, not at this time. However, the seas are building in front of her and she appears to be producing dangerous up and down drafts along with dangerous lightning."

"Alert air traffic control to divert Trans-Pacific flights coming into Honolulu from the South Pacific areas. Issue a small craft advisory to the out lining areas ahead of Kendra."

"Will do, what about the military?"

"The navy and coast guard are probably already aware of it; no need to concern yourself with them."

"Okay. I'll alert air traffic control right away."

"Bob, where is GPS grid square 1827?"

"It is approximately 370 nautical miles to the southwest of our current position on a bearing of 250 degrees."

"Where is Tropical Storm Kendra at, exactly?"

"As of 15 minutes ago, she was approximately 365 nautical miles southwest of here on a bearing of 240 degrees with sustained 40 knot winds."

"Do we have speed and course?"

"Yes, sir. Kendra is on a course of 040 degrees at a speed of approximately 12 knots."

"Very well. Keep an eye on Kendra for any signs of cyclonic activity. Notify me immediately if Kendra gains enough strength for Category 1 typhoon status."

"Yes, sir."

"Anything else I should know about?"

"No, sir. All other areas are normal for this time of the year."

Meanwhile, several Aerographer's Mates aboard the USS CARL VINSON, CVN-70, were keeping an eye on Tropical Storm Kendra as well.

Color weather radar images were showing red indicators in several regions of the tropical storm. The on duty Aerographer's Mate was Master Chief Smith, who reviewed the weather images and called the captain.

"Yes, master chief, what can I do for you?" asked the captain.

"Sir, Tropical Storm Kendra is gaining strength. I project that if she stays on her present course and maintains her present speed, she'll hit the NGFS range right in the middle of the exercise that we're suppose to monitor."

"So, what you want me to do is tell the CNO to call off this war game exercise for a storm, right?"

"For safety's sake, yes, I would advise that the navy do just that, sir."

"I understand your concern, master chief. Why don't you bring your projections and weather charts to my in-port cabin so we can discuss the matter."

"Yes, sir."

A few minutes later, the master chief arrived at the captain's in-port cabin. He knocked on the door and then entered. He saluted the captain and handed him the weather reports and the master chief's own projections. The captain looked over the reports and the master chief's projections. Soon, the captain put down the reports, images and projections. He said nothing to the master chief except for a curt nod of the captain's head to indicate for the master chief to follow him.

They left the captain's in-port cabin and walked up many levels of stairs. When they reached the 08 level, which housed the bridge and navigation, they entered the bridge. The place was nearly deserted; only occupied by a few boatswains' mates who were shining up the brass fixtures in there. The master chief followed the captain into the chart room. When they entered the chart room, a fresh from "A"- School Quartermaster jumped up from behind his large chart table and saluted the captain. The captain returned his salute and turned towards the master chief.

"Fresh from 'A'- School, master chief?" asked the captain.

"Yes, sir, I believe he is fresh from 'A'- School. He arrived aboard last week," replied the master chief, thinking quickly.

"Figures, what's your name, son?" asked the captain.

"QMSN Sanchez, sir!" he yelled in return, causing the captain to duck involuntarily.

"Well QMSN Sanchez, would you pull out your charts of the NFGS range?"

"Sir, yes, sir!" he yelled again as he pulled out four rolls of charts and set them down on the chart table.

"Sir, is there anything else I can do for you, sir?!" QMSN Sanchez yelled again.

"Yes, there is, go get yourself a cup of decaf coffee and don't come back for a few hours, okay?"

"Sir, yes, sir!" he yelled again as he left the chart room, shutting the door.

The captain drummed the fingers of his right hand on the chart table for about a minute before speaking.

"Jesus Christ, master chief, where the hell did the recruiters find this guy?"

"I believe he comes from New Port Richey, Florida. His father and grandfather were both Marine Corps officers," replied the master chief.

"That fucking explains it right there. So, where is Tropical Storm Kendra going to enter the NGFS range?" asked the captain.

The master chief found the chart with a full showing of GPS Grid Square 1727. The master chief then found a grease pencil that was red in color and drew a star in the southwest quadrant of the square. He then drew a dotted line through the grid square to the northeast quadrant of the grid square. The dotted line indicated a course of 040 degrees.

"Assuming, captain, that Kendra maintains her course and speed, I estimate that she will hit the NGFS range 48 to 72 hours after the exercise begins."

The captain studied the map and course as plotted. There wasn't anything of value in the NFGS range except for the missile range.

"It looks as though Kendra will pass directly through the NGFS range which includes the Malikai Missile Test Range Island."

"Yes, sir."

"What are your primary concerns?"

"The dangerous lightning could create problems for communications, radar and planes, sir. The other concern is the large seas that will be encountered. You know, sir, that this ship suffered damage to her hull from a typhoon in 1994."

"Yes, you're right," replied the captain as he reached for the phone.

He dialed "0" for the switchboard and was transferred to the quarterdeck.

"Quarterdeck, GMG3 Franks, how can I help you?" he asked.

"This is the captain, patch me through to SACPACFLT."

"Yes, sir."

A few minutes later, Admiral Simon's voice came on the line.

"Yes, captain, what can I do for you?" asked Ray.

"My Aerographer's Mate master chief thinks we need to call off this exercise, for safety reasons, because of Tropical Storm Kendra."

"Could you please provide me with the reasoning behind this request?"

For the next few minutes, the captain told the admiral about the storm. He went on to explain the master chief's recommendations. After a brief exchange of words, the captain hung up the phone. The master chief looked at the captain before speaking.

"Let me guess, SACPACFLT thought I was a lunatic," said the master chief.

"No. He said he would check your recommendations and calculations with his own Meteorological Officer, Captain Schwartz. He also told me to tell you good job and to keep an eye on this storm. If this storm makes typhoon status, notify me at once."

"Aye, sir. I will begin an in-port storm watch immediately," replied the master chief, looking a little perplexed.

They both stepped out of the chart room onto the starboard wing of the bridge. They were greeted with a slightly strong breeze and some minor whitecaps out in the bay could be seen. The storm was several days away and, already, the winds had picked up. The captain looked back at the master chief.

"You have your orders," said the captain.

"Aye, sir."

SACPACFLT confirmed the USS CARL VINSON's master chief's projections. SACPACFLT then called the USS SEASIDE HEIGHTS who was taking on her full combat load. Commander Hinton-Smith was very busy supervising the loading of the torpedo and vertical launch tubes. Once this was done, he went on to supervise the storing of the torpedoes, HARPOON's and TOMAHAWK's in their various storage areas. When the last HARPOON had been stowed away in its storage rack location, Commander Hinton-Smith took the phone call.

"Sorry about keeping you on hold for so long, admiral, what can I do for you?" asked Andrew.

"I know you're busy, so this won't take long. There's a high probability that Tropical Storm Kendra may become Category 1 Typhoon Kendra. She may hit right in the middle of the exercise. Do you want me to call this exercise off?"

"No, sir. Do you think that our enemy would call off an attack because of some bad weather, sir?"

"You're right. By the way, Senator James Arthar is going to be coming aboard during this exercise. He wants to see some naval action."

"I understand, sir and I will brief the crew. Could you send me the weather data?"

"Sure thing; good-bye."

"Good-bye, sir," replied Andrew as he handed the receiver back to Shawn.

Andrew left the ship that night with a strong breeze in his face. When he arrived home, Gary had already turned on the Weather Information TV channel for Honolulu. The TV was showing Tropical Storm Kendra and a proposed route that she might take to get to Hawaii.

If the storm made typhoon classification, the islands of Oahu and Maui would have to be evacuated. As Gary started packing things into crates for the eventual evacuation, Andrew touched Gary on his left shoulder. Gary turned around to face him.

"Don't worry about me, Gary. If this tropical storm makes typhoon status, go to the designated shelter immediately. I'll be alright," said Andrew, smiling.

"Oh, I know you'll be alright because you'll be underwater," replied Gary, laughing.

Both Gary and Andrew watched the computer simulations of what directions the storm/typhoon could go. They watched as the TV showed evacuation routes out of their area to higher ground and the typhoon shelters. Gary left briefly to refuel their car. He returned to start loading some of the crates into the car. The crates that were going into the car contained all sorts of important personal documents. One of the crates contained cash for emergencies such as this. When Gary had packed up the last crate into their car, they both went to bed.

Meanwhile, during the night, at about 0400 hours, Hawaii Standard Time, NOAA personnel were watching Tropical Storm Kendra gain strength. By 0430 hours, Hawaii Standard Time, Tropical Storm Kendra was pushing 60-knot winds in front of her. The dangerous lightning had increased and Kendra had the starting of cyclonic activity; an "eye" was forming.

At 0500 hours, Hawaii Standard Time, the "eye" was almost fully formed. Satellite shots showed the small "eye." The "eye" was only a few nautical miles in diameter, but the "eye" was definitely there. The satellites recorded 65-knot sustained winds with some gusts reaching 75+ knots. Seas were building in front of Kendra as well as inside of Kendra's range.

Surface winds were driving the seas to 10 to 14 foot/ 3 to 5 meter swells. The lightning was getting worse in both intensity and the number of strikes. The NOAA Agency, in 2004, had developed a 4.0 Lightning Strike Scale. The number of lightning strikes for Typhoon Kendra was averaging between 3.2 and 3.8 on this 4.0 LSS scale.

Meanwhile, the duty aerographer's mate, AG1 Sampson, was on duty in the USS CARL VINSON's weather center. He went outside of the ship's weather center to get some fresh air and looked at the dark, blood red sky.

There were a few scattered clouds and a stiff breeze was hitting him in the face.

He quickly stepped back inside the weather center. He then started watching the newly formed typhoon on multiple screens. He was intently watching the screens when the master chief walked into the weather center. AG1 Sampson turned around to face him.

"Good morning, master chief. Tropical Storm Kendra has been reclassified as Typhoon Kendra, Category 1," said AG1 Sampson.

"When did this occur?" asked the master chief.

"At about 0510 hours, master chief."

"That means the Coast Guard will be sending out their typhoon hunter planes soon."

"Yes, sir."

"That also means all navy ships that can get underway must get underway if they can."

"Yes, master chief, that is correct too."

"What are her stats?"

"65-knot sustained winds with wind gusts reaching 75+ knots. 10 to 14 foot/ 3 to 5 meter seas being driven by the 65-knot surface winds. The satellites have seen an occasional 20-foot/ 7-meter wave. Small craft advisories are in effect."

"Is she still producing dangerous lightning?"

"Yes, master chief, she still is."

"Well, let me go tell the captain."

Meanwhile, Andrew was waking up to a stiff breeze and a dark, blood red sky. As he finished off breakfast, he took his cup of coffee with him outside onto the small patio and heard something. He turned his head to see, off in the distance, above the tops of the billowing palm trees that surrounded his apartment and to his left, were four turbo-prop planes.

He watched them fly by as they headed out to sea. Andrew knew that Kendra was now a typhoon. Gary stepped outside onto the same small patio and saw the back end of one of the typhoon hunter planes. Andrew finished off his cup of coffee and handed the empty cup to Gary.

"When you drop me off today at the pier, go to the designated typhoon shelter immediately," said Andrew sternly.

"Okay."

Gary drove Andrew to the pier and dropped him off. Gary then headed immediately to the designated shelter.

Already, Andrew could feel the ship rocking gently at the pier. Andrew looked over his right shoulder towards the open sea to see dark thunderheads. They were billowing, angry looking, black thunderheads. Andrew estimated that they must have been 50,000 feet/ 16,667 meters or more in height at their tops. As he boarded the ship, he went to the captain's cabin where he found both the captain and the executive officer were packing up their bags. They left the captain's cabin and Lou looked at Andrew.

"Don't sink my boat and have a nice trip," said Lou.

"I would call this whole thing off, if I were you," said Rob.

"I think I will let the crew decide that one, sir," replied Andrew, confidently.

Andrew saw the captain and the executive officer off. They saluted Andrew from the pier as they walked towards the end of the pier. They were picked up by their wives and were soon heading towards their designated evacuation centers. Andrew turned around and ran into the Command Master Chief.

"Master chief, muster the ship's crew on the pier. I need to ask them a question and then provide them with some information," said Andrew.

"Aye, sir."

It took almost 30 minutes to get the entire ship's crew mustered on the pier. Once everyone was on the pier, Andrew spoke. He had to almost yell to be heard above the stiffening breeze.

"There's a Category 1 Typhoon headed this way. It will strike the NGFS range about 24 to 48 hours into this exercise. If there is anyone who wants me to call off this exercise because of this typhoon, speak now," yelled Andrew above the breeze; no hands went up.

"Okay. If there is anyone who does not want to go on this exercise, speak now!" yelled Andrew again.

"I don't want to serve under your command, sir," announced the command chaplain.

"I understand, chaplain. There's the end of the pier and have a nice day," said Andrew, saluting him as he walked off.

"Is there anyone from the state of Idaho aboard?" asked Andrew. He then saw seven hands go up.

"I'll need to speak with you seven after this muster. For the rest of the crew, I was informed by SACPACFLT that Senator James Arthar, a Republican from the state of Idaho, is coming aboard as an observer. Treat him with respect, he's an assistant chairman of the Senate Armed Forces Committee and signs your checks with tax payer dollars."

There was a roar of laughter; Andrew laughed with them as well. Andrew then turned and faced the master chief.

"Master chief, crew the ship. Set the sea and anchor detail. We get underway at 1300 hours with or without the senator aboard," said Andrew.

"Aye, sir. Crew the ship!" yelled Lyle.

The crew, with the exception of the seven petty officers from Idaho, boarded the ship. The seven petty officers gathered around Andrew.

"All I ask of you seven petty officers is, treat the man with some respect. Address him as Your Honor, Senator or Sir. Finally, if you decide to tell him about a problem, at least give him some solutions so that he can take those solutions back to Washington, D.C. That's all I have to say."

The seven petty officers walked up the gangway. The whole crew began to make preparations for getting underway. As Andrew walked aboard, the master chief met him.

"Permission to speak freely, sir?" asked Lyle.

"Permission granted. Mind taking a walk?" asked Andrew in return.

They both started walking as Lyle spoke.

"I thought what the Chaplain did was wrong. Everyone knows what you are, but you treat everyone you have ever met as an equal. That man could never do it, sir."

"Why, thank you, Lyle, I appreciate the candid observation."

"If you ever get command of your own boat, consider me your first choice as chief of the boat, sir."

"I'll keep that in mind, Lyle. Continue with your duties."

"Aye, sir."

Andrew began going through his part of the underway check-off list. Now, as the commanding officer, he was looking at the large, long list. He was about half way through the check-off list when TM2 (SS) Heather Doenitz arrived on the bridge. He looked up and saw the look of concern on her face. He set the check-off list down on the chart table as she approached.

"May I have a word or two with you, captain?" she asked nervously.

"Sure, Heather, what's on your mind?"

"The new TMSN we have aboard, Mr. Bradley, is he attached to anyone that you know of, sir?" she asked.

"No. I don't believe he has a wife or a girlfriend that I know of, Heather."

"Is he one of you, sir? If he is, I understand."

"No. I'm pretty good at detecting that issue."

"Thank you, sir," she said as she left the bridge.

Andrew returned to his underway check-off list. He turned around and Lyle handed him the departmental underway check-off lists. He reviewed them and put them into his underway check-off list. Lyle looked up at Andrew.

"Is there anything I can do for you, sir?" he asked.

"All officer's meeting in the wardroom when or if the senator arrives."

"Aye, sir. Is there anything else?"

"Tell our Religious Programming Specialists to pray hard."

"Aye, sir."

Meanwhile, Senator Arthar was doing his best not to vomit on the rough ride into the Honolulu International Airport. It was the roughest landing he had ever experienced when landing at this airport. When the plane landed and had taxied up to the gate, he made sure he exited the plane as quickly as possible.

He went to the baggage claim area and claimed his baggage. He then stepped outside into the sun and stiff breeze. The duty driver for Rear Admiral Upper Half Sandra Milton soon met him.

The Radioman Senior Chief Petty Officer picked up the senator's luggage. He put the luggage into the trunk of the car and shook the senator's right hand. The senior chief then opened the left, rear passenger door so James could get inside. After closing the door, the senior chief drove off. James started talking to the senior chief.

"That was one rough landing," said James.

"I understand, Your Honor. There is a Category 1 typhoon headed our way."

"I know. It's all over the news. Supposed to be one of the worst typhoons to hit Hawaii in over 50 years."

The senior chief drove on to the naval base. Once they were on the pier, the senior chief helped James aboard. Andrew met the senator on the bridge. They shook left hands as Andrew took James' luggage.

"Welcome aboard, senator. I will have you properly gonged aboard. If you will ever be so kind as to follow the master chief, here, he will show you your quarters. You're also invited to the all officer's meeting in the wardroom."

"Thank you, captain."

Gong, gong. Gong, gong. Gong, gong went the ship's electronic bells.

"Senator James Arthar, arriving," gong.

The seas were continuing to build as Andrew went over his battle plan for the exercise with the remaining officers. When the tugs showed up, Andrew gave the order to get underway. When the ship had cleared the pier, James came up to the bridge and stood behind Andrew.

He said nothing, merely looking around at the view. The bow of the submarine was diving heavily into some of the waves as the tugs left the submarine's side. Andrew spoke first to James.

"Senator, I already informed the crew that they could speak their minds to you without fear of retaliation or retribution. I also told the seven petty officers from Idaho that they could speak to you as well."

"Thank you, captain. I already met with the seven petty officers and they gave me a large list of things to fix, with options. You know, captain, you have a great deal of respect amongst the crew."

"Thank you, Your Honor."

Suddenly, without warning, the sub was struck broadside on the starboard side by one of the white cap waves in the bay. The salt spray and water nearly drenched the senator. The sub came back up out of the wave and continued on its course.

"I might suggest, Your Honor, that you go below and get some rain gear on before returning to the bridge."

"Will do, captain."

An hour and half later, the USS SEASIDE HEIGHTS, had cleared the last shallow water warning marker. As the ship was preparing to dive, a tiny life raft was floating aimlessly in the large swells near the NGFS range. Aboard this life raft were four teenagers; one male, badly burned and still deaf from the explosion. Only a few hours ago, they were fishing on one of the teen's father's 70-foot/23-meter yacht, when a bolt of lightning came from nowhere. This bolt struck the engine compartment.

The yacht was turned into fiberglass and wooden splinters in a matter of seconds. The teenagers were all thrown overboard. Thankfully, the life raft had surfaced, fully inflated and upright. They all climbed aboard the life raft and put on the life vests, inflating them immediately.

So far, almost eight hours after the explosion, only two of the teenagers had partial hearing back. They all silently agreed that this would be one fishing trip that they would never forget. The three not so badly injured teens rowed in silence towards what they thought was the way to land. As they rowed, they were praying to be found soon.

# Chapter 7

At 1545 hours, Hawaii Time, the USS SEASIDE HEIGHTS slipped under the building seas. When the conning tower was cleared, Andrew closed the hatches and took off his rain gear. He looked at the men and women present on the bridge. He drew in a long breath, letting it out slowly.

"Diving officer, make your depth 600 feet/200 meters. Maintain course and speed," he said.

"Aye, sir. Helm, maintain course 195 degrees and current speed of 8 knots. Ten degree down angle on the diving planes make your depth 600 feet/200 meters," said the Diving Officer Lieutenant Junior Grade Katherine Bates.

"Yes, ma'am," replied BMSN Franz.

The conning tower disappeared as a large swell crashed over the top of the periscope. Once the ship had reached her ordered depth, Andrew began looking over the charts of the NGFS range. He was looking for whatever advantage he could find to "win" this exercise. This exercise was far more complicated than any of those that he had faced while in the submarine simulation games at sub school or any of those on his computer.

One of the charts showed their current position as entering GPS Grid Square 1727. He looked at the other chart of GPS Grid Square 1728. Both charts showed the exercise area was fairly shallow at no more than 200 fathoms. Only one area, a trench, was over 400 fathoms deep.

The chart showing GPS Grid Square 1728, showed the two primary and one secondary TOMAHAWK missile launch points. Andrew looked over the rest of the charts and then grabbed the microphone for the 1MC, as it was called, to make an announcement to the crew. There was a short announcing tone before Andrew spoke.

"Ladies and gentlemen, this is the captain. I will now tell you that within the hour, we will be engaging the enemy. The U.S. Navy's best minds have come up with this war game exercise to test this ship to it's fullest potential."

Andrew paused before continuing.

"They know that this ship has never fired her weapons systems and that I am incompetent at commanding this or any other vessel. They also estimated that this vessel has only 28 minutes of survivability once the enemy has located us."

Andrew paused once again before continuing.

"All I ask is that you do your jobs and that you do them to the best of your abilities. That is all," said Andrew as he put the microphone back up into its cradle.

In the forward torpedo room, TMSN Bart Bradley and TM2 (SS) Heather Doenitz were checking their equipment and making sure that the right weapons were in the right tubes. While they were checking over their equipment, the senator stepped into the torpedo room, closing the hatch behind him.

He then took out a pen from his left shirt pocket and began taking notes on what he saw inside of the torpedo room. The notes were being recorded on a yellow style legal pad. When he had finished taking his notes, he put his pen back into his left shirt pocket and shook their hands.

"Hello, I'm Senator Arthar. You must be the semi-professional female bodybuilder that Ray told me about," said James.

"Yes, Your Honor, I am," Heather replied.

"Most impressive, Madam. Where are you from?"

"Oklahoma, Your Honor."

"Your senator is right above me at the Sherman building in Washington, D.C. When I get back, I will tell her that I saw you."

"Thank you, Your Honor."

He turned from her to face TMSN Bradley and smiled.

"You must be Mr. Bradley, the diver. I heard from Ray that you went diving in port. Is that right?"

"Yes, Your Honor, I did go diving in port and got into some serious trouble over it to boot," replied Bart.

"Well, it looks like you survived your punishment. Where are you from?"

"Wyoming, Your Honor."

"Your senator is across the hall from me. I will tell him I saw you when I return."

"Thank you, Your Honor."

"If you will excuse me, I'm going to go get us some coffee," said Heather as she left the compartment.

"So, Mr. Bradley, what can you tell me about these weapons in here? Are these just exercise shots?" asked James, pointing at the torpedoes with his right hand as he pulled out his pen, preparing to take notes.

"No, Your Honor. Those are Mark 50, ADCAP Series II torpedoes."

"I see. What kind of explosive do they carry?"

"A 1,000 pound/454 kilogram, PBXN-409 explosive payload, Your Honor."

"I see. What are these?" he asked, pointing to and resting his left hand on a HARPOON.

"That, Your Honor, is a HARPOON anti-ship missile. In fact, tubes 3 and 4 are loaded with HARPOON's."

"What kind of explosive charge does it carry?"

"A 500 pound/250 kilogram, PBXN-109 series explosive payload with a contact fuse. The payload is reverse cone shaped for maximum blast effect. The HARPOON can travel at about twice the speed of sound."

"Most impressive. What are these missiles?" he asked, pointing at one of the TOMAHAWK anti-ship missiles with his right hand.

"That, Your Honor, is a TOMAHAWK anti-ship cruise missile. We call them a TASM. If you move your hand towards the nose of the canister, you can feel a single notch."

The senator reached, with his right hand, inside of the canister. His fingers found a single notch on the nosecone of the TASM.

"Incredible. What about these missiles?" he said, pointing at the TOMAHAWK Land Assault Missile version.

"That, Your Honor, is a TOMAHAWK land assault cruise missile. We call them TLAM's. If you feel the nose of the canister, you will find two notches."

"I trust you on that one. Can you fire these missiles from torpedo tubes?"

"Yes, Your Honor, we can fire these missiles from a torpedo tube provided that we are not more than 125 feet/42 meters deep and that we are not doing more than 3 knots."

"Most impressive, Mr. Bradley."

Heather returned with two cups of coffee. The senator excused himself and started moving aft. He arrived at the weapons control room. He entered the space and stood quietly in the back. He was intently watching what was going on and taking notes. He heard a beeping noise and saw one of the female

Missile Technicians reach up with her left hand and silence the noise. She then grabbed the phone and called the forward torpedo room.

"Weapons Control, Forward Torpedo Room," said MT1 Joan Boggs.

"Forward Torpedo Room, aye," replied Bart.

"Flood the tubes."

"Aye."

In the forward torpedo room, all four torpedo tubes were flooded. When the pressure was equalized inside the tubes, Heather and Bart hand cranked open the outer doors. The indicators inside of the weapons control room turned green. MT1 Boggs then called Andrew.

"Weapons Control, Conn," she said.

Andrew reached up above him in the chart room and grabbed the receiver there.

"Conn, aye," he replied.

"Phase 1 has been completed."

"Conn, aye. Proceed with Phase 2."

"Weapons Control, aye."

The senator watched as MT2 Cindy Lance and MT1 Jordane Bliss began programming the TLAM's attack coordinates. When the final coordinates were programmed into the last TLAM, MT1 Boggs called Andrew. In all, 45 minutes had expired in programming the missiles.

"Weapons Control, Conn," she said.

"Conn, aye," said Andrew.

"TLAM's programmed."

"Conn, aye. What are the flight times of the missiles?"

"Depending on which launching area we are able to launch from, about 4 to 12 minutes."

"Very well. Flood vertical launch tubes 5, 6, 7, 8, 9 and 10."

"Weapons Control, aye."

Water filled the vertical launch tubes. When the VLS tubes were flooded, that pressure was equalized. When the green indicators showed up on the launch boards, MT1 Boggs called Andrew back again.

"Weapons Control, Conn," she said.

"Conn, aye."

"VLS tubes 5, 6, 7, 8, 9, and 10 flooded and pressure equalized."

"Conn, aye. Prepare countermeasures to be deployed in pairs, both shallow and deep."

"Weapons Control, aye."

MT1 Bliss programmed the countermeasures. When she was done, she nodded at MT1 Boggs that the programming was completed.

"Weapons Control, Conn, countermeasures programmed," she said.

"Conn, aye. Set the torpedoes and UM-28's to detonate at 900 yards/300 meters from their targets. Program the HARPOON's and TASM's to self-destruct at one nautical mile from their target."

"Weapons Control, aye."

The weapons were programmed with their instructions. When the programming had been completed, another 45 minutes had elapsed.

"Weapons Control, Conn. Weapons have been programmed."

"Conn, aye."

Andrew reached up and switched channels.

"Conn, Aft Torpedo Room."

"Aft Torpedo Room, aye," replied TM1 (SS) Shawn Dailey.

"Any leaks yet?"

"Negative, sir. The repair job appears to be holding."

"Initiate Phase 4."

"Aye, sir."

The aft torpedo tubes were flooded. Once the pressure was equalized, Shawn and TM3 Sanchez manually opened up the torpedo tube outer doors. Green indicators showed up on the weapons control boards. MT1 Boggs called Andrew.

"Weapons Control, Conn," she said.

"Conn, aye."

"We're ready to shoot, sir."

"Conn, aye. Diving officer, come to new course 210 and decrease speed to 3 knots," said Andrew.

"Aye, sir. Helm, come to new course 210, decrease speed to 3 knots," she said.

"Helm, aye. Coming to new course 210, decreasing speed to 3 knots."

As the ship slowed down, the senator continued moving aft. He briefly stopped by the bridge and looked at everyone. He was getting ready to leave, when the Reactor Officer, Commander Damian Furth, who was also the executive officer, made a loud announcement to the bridge crew.

"For the remainder of this exercise, I am locking myself in the reactor compartment," he said as he walked off the bridge.

"Very well, Commander Furth. Lyle, have the Chief Engineer report to the bridge," said Andrew scratching his head.

"Aye, sir."

Senator Arthar walked over to the chart table. He could see the various charts of the NGFS range among other features on the charts. He put up his pen and notepad and looked at Andrew. Andrew smiled and looked back at James.

"What can I do for you, Your Honor?" asked Andrew.

"Nothing, but can I help in any way?"

"No, Your Honor. This is all part of the test. Why don't you go over to sonar, perhaps they have found some whales or dolphins for us to chase."

"Okay."

James moved across the bridge to the sonar suite as it was called. He found STS2 (SS) Elaine Hudson and STSSN Jon Costillo in the suite. They were intently watching their soundboards. James looked up at the three soundboards.

The forward sonar soundboard showed lots of noise from the surface from Typhoon Kendra that was entering the area. The amidships sonar soundboard showed only ambient background noises like fish, whales, dolphins, etc. The aft sonar soundboard showed nothing but the slight propeller noise of the ship itself. James watched as STSSN Costillo reached for the phone.

"Sonar, Conn," he said.

"Conn, aye," replied Andrew.

"Are there any friendly ships in this exercise and should we be worried about helicopters?"

"There are two friendly ships out here. One NIMITZ Class Nuclear Powered Aircraft Carrier. Probably the USS CARL VINSON."

"Aye, sir,"

"One OHIO Class SSBN, probably the USS TEXAS."

"Aye, sir."

"All other ships are enemy combatants. I don't think with the current weather conditions, anyone will be flying helicopters or planes. That would be a dangerous gamble."

"Sonar, aye," he said, putting the phone back into its cradle.

They both kind of ignored the senator and went back to watching their scopes and soundboards. James merely took some notes and was preparing to leave when Jon gave James the headphones.

"Have a listen, Your Honor," said Jon as he handed the headphones to James.

"Thank you."

James put the headphones on and was amazed at what he could hear. Even at the depth the ship was at, he could hear thunder from the surface, ocean mammals and even a noise that sounded like peep, peep. He gave the headphones back to Jon.

"What did you think, Your Honor?"

"I thought it sounded great, except for that peep, peep noise. That was a little annoying."

Jon put the headphones back on and heard the high-pitched peep, peep noise that James had heard. He immediately recognized that noise as high frequency sonar emissions. He picked up the phone and called the bridge.

"Sonar, Conn," he said.

"Conn, aye," said Andrew.

"High frequency sonar being emitted."

"Bearing?"

"110."

"Range?"

"25,500 yards/8,500 meters and closing at 8 knots. Probably the enemy, sir. The high frequency sonar emissions are consistent with a LOS ANGELES Class Fast Attack Nuclear Powered Submarine."

"Conn, aye. What is her depth?"

"Same thermal layer as us, but shallower."

"Conn, aye."

As the ship continued on its course, STS2 (SS) Hudson detected the propellers of the surface ship that was in the area. She listened for about two minutes before determining exactly what the propeller noise was emanating from; a NORMANDY class cruiser. The ship was definitely anti-submarine capable as well as anti-ship and anti-aircraft capable. She knew it was one dangerous customer as she reached for the phone this time.

"Sonar, Conn," she said.

"Conn, aye," said Andrew.

"Surface contact."

"Bearing?"

"240."

"Distance?"

"30,000 yards/10,000 meters and closing at 9 knots. She's a NORMANDY Class Cruiser, sir."

"Conn, aye. Are there any biologics out here with us?"

"Yes, sir, off of our starboard beam."

"Conn, out."

Andrew looked over the charts. He knew that the ship above had either finished laying mines in the shallow water that could be used as a short cut to the TLAM launch areas or was working with the sub to triangulate Andrew's position. Andrew looked at the ridge they were running alongside.

The ridge was partially coral reef with lots of sunken ships. The other part of the reef was made of hardened lava flows from centuries ago. Some of the ships were wooden and some were metal. The reef make-up consisted of several freighters, cargo carriers and an old supertanker among other items scattered along the bottom.

There were fisherman's nets and some sunken fishing boats. There was also a WWII Japanese I-Class submarine along with some destroyers. Andrew noted that the bottom was of sufficient density that if it was kicked up by something, like explosions or propellers, it was sonar opaque.

"Conn, Sonar," said Andrew.

"Sonar, aye," replied Elaine.

"How far to the bottom?"

"The bottom varies, but it averages 925 feet/308 meters."

"Conn, out."

Andrew weighed his options. He was counting on two things. One, that the surface ship was probably having a difficult time distinguishing them from the bottom of the sea. Second, that both captains were probably over confident. He also knew that the ships would have to slow down to properly detect Andrew. He looked over at Lyle.

"Lyle, pass the word for silent running," said Andrew.

"Aye, sir. Rigging for silent running."

Andrew decided to go ahead with another plan as he looked over the charts one last time. The charts showed the shallow water short cut to the TLAM launch areas. Andrew figured that this area was probably mined already. Or, if it weren't mined, then the enemy would have placed sonar buoys in the area to detect Andrew coming. Once detected, Andrew saw he had almost no room to maneuver.

He then saw a deep trench that would allow him access to the TLAM launch areas by a roundabout way. He also figured that there would be a sub waiting for them in there as well. He would have to draw that sub out to him.

"Diving officer, decrease speed to 1 knot, come to new course 250 and decrease depth to 125 feet/42 meters."

"Diving officer, aye. Helm, come to new course 250 and decrease speed to 1 knot. Ten degree up angle on the dive planes, make your depth 125 feet/42 meters," said Katherine.

"Helm, aye," said Franz.

"Conn, Weapons Control," said Andrew.

"Weapons Control, aye," said MT1 Boggs.

"Reprogram tubes 7 and 8 with a time delay of 25 minutes. Set them for 900 feet/300 meters."

"Weapons Control, aye."

Lyle came over to where Andrew was standing. He waited until Andrew was finished talking to QM2 Traci Walker. Andrew turned around to face Lyle.

"Sir, the other ship will run right over those mines," said Lyle.

"Yes, I know. I am hoping that in the ensuing confusion, I can fire tubes 1 and 2, getting the surface ship before she can detect us or the torpedoes."

"I see. You are indeed very creative, sir."

As the ship quietly slipped through the thermal layer she was in into the thermal layer above her, tubes 7 and 8 were fired. The surface ship was monitoring all noise bands. Indeed the cruiser's sonar crew was having great difficulty distinguishing between the sea floor and the shape of SSN-747. The sea floor, being littered with multiple shipwrecks, made the sonar crews' job even harder. The surface ship was closing in on SSN-747 so intently, that they never saw the tiny life raft.

The teens were yelling and waving frantically towards the cruiser, to no avail. They splashed the water with their oars. Still, the NORMANDY Class cruiser continued on its mission. Within minutes, the cruiser was almost out of sight.

The whitewater wake created by her propellers soon vanished in the swells. The teens went back to rowing. Little did they realize that, although the seas were continuing to build, SSN-747's sonar crew had picked up their splashing.

"Sonar, Conn," said Jon in a whisper.

"Conn, aye," replied Andrew in a whisper.

"Asymmetric surface disturbance bearing 104."

"Distance?"

"About 18,800 yards/6,267 meters. The noise seems to be coming from inboard and aft of that cruiser."

"Conn, aye. Let me know when either you or the sonar computer come up with an answer."

"Sonar, aye."

The diving officer spoke to Andrew.

"Could it be side-scan sonar?" she asked.

"Possibly, but I would think our sonar crew would have been able to detect the low frequency pulses."

"Just a suggestion, sir," she said.

"And a very good suggestion, Katherine. It shows me that you have some advanced critical thinking skills."

The surface vessel started to slow down. Her gun crews were readying a barrage of depth charges. The depth charges were set in pairs at different depths. 70 feet/23 meters was the first pair. The second pair was set for 250 feet/83 meters. The third pair was set for 350 feet/117 meters. The fourth pair was set for 450 feet/150 meters and the final pair was set for 600 feet/200 meters.

The ship started a fast run in a zigzag pattern. As the depth charges were finished being armed, the ship picked up as much speed as was safe in the building seas. The waves were 4 to 6 feet/2 to 2.5 meters in height. The gun crews took cover inside the port side entrance on the main deck. The depth charges were ready to hit the water.

Meanwhile, SSN-747's Chief Engineer, Bill Ellsworthy, had arrived on the bridge. He walked over to where Andrew was standing and cleared his throat.

"I got here as soon as I heard what happened," said Bill.

"Thank you, Bill. For the remainder of this exercise, you're going to be the XO."

"Aye, sir. I suspected as much, Captain Hinton-Smith. I've already turned the engine room over to MMC Orphus."

"Very well."

The sonar crew picked up the cruiser's bizarre zigzag pattern and sudden increase in speed.

"Sonar, Conn," said Elaine.

"Conn, aye," replied Andrew.

"NORMANDY Class cruiser has increased speed and is zigzagging, sir."

"Distance?"

"11,500 yards/3,833 meters and closing."

"Conn, aye. Pass the word to prepare for depth charges."

"Aye, sir."

As the cruiser continued closing in, the sonar crew aboard SSN-747 finally received their answer from the sonar computer. The printout sheet said, "Non-Biological Asymmetric Noise." The next line read, "Suggestions: Life Raft, Surf or Side-Scan Sonar Equipment not previously recorded." Jon tore off the printout and took it to Andrew. Andrew reviewed it carefully and gave the report to the XO. He read it and shook his head in disbelief.

"Thank you, Jon; dismissed," said Andrew.

"Captain, who in the hell is out here in a life raft with a typhoon bearing down on this area?" asked Bill.

"I don't know, XO, it might be a decoy. We go to the surface to check it out; boom!"

"Game over," said Bill.

"That's right. Any suggestions?"

Before anyone could answer, sonar called.

"Sonar, Conn."

"Conn, aye."

"Surface splashes in the direction of the cruiser."

"Conn, aye. You do know what those splashes are?"

"Depth charges, sir."

"Conn, aye."

Andrew, Bill and the rest of the crew heard the explosions from the depth charges. The first pair of explosions were clear whereas the others were muted until they couldn't be heard at all except by sonar. Andrew picked up the phone.

"Conn, Sonar," said Andrew.

"Sonar, aye."

"What were the depths on those explosions?"

"First explosions were at 70 feet/23 meters."

"Go ahead and give me the rest of them."

"Aye, sir. The second pair was at 250 feet/83 meters, third pair at 350 feet/117 meters, fourth pair at 450 feet/150 meters and the final pair at 600 feet/200 meters."

"Are there any more HF sonar soundings?"

"No, sir."

Bill looked at Andrew rather inquisitively.

"They're echo ranging us, XO."

Before Andrew could speak again, two muted explosions were picked up by both weapons control and sonar.

"Weapons Control, Conn. Tubes 7 and 8 have reached their target."

"Conn, aye. Fire tubes 1 and 2!" yelled Andrew.

"Weapons Control, aye, firing tubes 1 and 2."

"Sonar, Conn. We confirm tubes 7 and 8 have destroyed that target. The units from tubes 1 and 2 are running normally."

"Conn, aye. Now we wait, XO, to see if the surface cruiser detected us."

"Aye, sir," replied Bill.

The cruiser had closed in so intently that they never detected the torpedoes being fired. The cruiser began another zigzag pattern of dropping depth charges. As the explosions were counted by sonar, the surface, just aft and to the port side of the cruiser, suddenly exploded. The game was over for the cruiser.

The wall of water was seen by the teens. They once again beat the water frantically, hoping that the cruiser, which was heading somewhat their way, would see them. When the noise level had dropped down some, the sonar crew aboard SSN-747 again picked up the teens splashing.

"Sonar, Conn."

"Conn, aye."

"Tubes 1 and 2 have reached their target. I don't think the other ship heard our torpedoes until it was too late. I detected no countermeasures or evasive maneuvers."

"Conn, aye. Are there any other contacts?"

"Yes, sir. That asymmetric surface disturbance has returned. Bearing 106, speed 1 knot. About 8,500 yards/2,833 meters."

"Conn, aye. How many depth charges were dropped?"

"60, sir."

"Where are the cruiser and sub located?"

"They are heading out of the area at high speed on a course of 010 degrees."

"Conn, aye. Conn, Weapons Control."

"Weapons Control, aye."

"Reload tubes 1 and 2 with torpedoes, but do not flood the tubes."

"Weapons Control, aye."

"Reload tube 7 with a TLAM and tube 8 with a TASM."

"Weapons Control, aye."

"By the way, do we have any unmanned underwater vehicles aboard?"

"Negative, sir."

"Conn, aye."

Meanwhile, in GPS Grid Square 1728, Typhoon Kendra was gaining strength and preparing to transit the rest of the NGFS range. Aboard the USS CARL VINSON, the Aerographer's Mates inside of the weather center watched as Kendra's sustained winds reached 85 knots. Wind gusts were reaching 100 knots. She was now officially a Category 2 typhoon.

Heavy sheets of rain were falling and lightning was causing many problems for both radar and communications operators. The other NORMANDY Class cruiser was just aft and to the port side of the carrier. Another SSN was accompanying the other cruiser. Both ships were in the area of the aircraft carrier.

The USS TEXAS was monitoring both of the other subs left in the game making sure that no one cheated. At least one of the other SSN's left in the game was down deep into the trench not far away and rigged for silent running. This made keeping tabs on her difficult.

Waves, being driven by the wind, were reaching heights of more than 25 feet/8 meters. The carrier was riding out the storm as best she could. The cruiser decided to pull out in front of the carrier and turn to the carrier's starboard side. This put the cruiser on a southeasterly course towards the borders of GPS Grid Squares 1727 and 1728. With nearly blinding, wind driven rain and fierce lightning, detecting a submarine or incoming missile was especially challenging.

Meanwhile, as the seas continued to build, the life raft was being tossed around violently. As they rowed, they had to bail out the life raft every so often. They also decided that no one would find them. They all said a prayer for one another and went back to rowing and bailing. The wind was becoming stronger and the waves were becoming larger.

Meanwhile, many nautical miles away, milling around the outer boundaries of the TLAM launch areas, an ARLEIGH BURKE Class destroyer was being tossed around by 12 to 16 foot/4 to 5.1 meter waves. Lightning was wreaking havoc on the radar systems and sonar was having trouble keeping a track on the SSN that was down deep in the trench.

Both ships were being handicapped. So far, the SSN could only hear the propellers of the destroyer, the carrier and the SSBN. The surface disturbances made detection of any other ships difficult, especially at long-range, for the sonar crews.

The destroyer captain knew that his part of the exercise was to make sure that no TOMAHAWK's were launched. The captain knew that if any TOMAHAWK cruise missiles were launched, the game was over. He was hoping that the typhoon would keep Andrew from launching missiles. The ship was on high alert status since both the cruiser and her protective sub were "destroyed" earlier. The sun was setting on turbid waters and howling wind.

Meanwhile, Andrew had finished off dinner and went back to the bridge. As he entered the bridge, Bill stopped him for a status report. It was Andrew who spoke first.

"Is it night time up there, XO?" asked Andrew, pointing up towards the surface.

"Yes. Why don't we go up for a look see on that disturbance?"

"Can't risk it, Bill. If there is another ship up there that we haven't detected yet and she's running radar, we would have missiles raining down on us."

"Yeah, I guess you're right. So, what do we do?"

"Make circles around this anomaly at 5,000 yard/1,667 meter to 10,000 yard/3,333 meter intervals in a zigzag pattern. Alternate the distances and zigzag patterns every 15 minutes. Do not go below this thermal layer."

"Aye, sir. Is there anything else?"

"Tell sonar to keep on that disturbance, but be ever vigilant for the enemy. At 0545 hours, come to 60 feet/20 meters and prepare ECW."

"Aye, sir."

"Good-night."

Meanwhile, the Coast Guard had made the decision to call off the search and rescue efforts because of Typhoon Kendra. Since only a few small fragments of the yacht had been found floating in the water near the NGFS range, a sense of loss was felt by all rescuers. The parents of all the teens involved felt a sense of loss as well. All the Coast Guard Cutters were being recalled except for one.

Coast Guard Cutter ALBINO, CGC-1022 was to be left on station near the NGFS range in case the teens were found after all. The captain of the cutter was riding out the storm, but the lightning was creating problems for his ship as well. He was ordered to stay on station until further notice or if the seas suddenly reached 30 feet/10 meters or more.

# Chapter 8

It was shortly before 0300 hours in the morning, when the sonar personnel detected the NORMANDY class cruiser. They also detected the LOS ANGELES class SSN with her and another, very weak, set of sound noises. The sonar personnel assumed them to be the OHIO class SSBN. Once the sonar personnel had steady tracks on all the ships, they alerted the officer of the deck. Sonar personnel on the night staff consisted of STS3 (SS) Dave Davidson and STS1 (SS/SW/AW) Ken Karlsen. Both were highly dedicated personnel to their jobs.

"Conn, Sonar," said Dave.

The officer of the deck, CW02 Melissa Andrews, answered.

"Conn, aye," she said.

"Surface contact bearing 295. NORMANDY class cruiser, speed of 5 knots and closing."

"Course and distance?" she asked making her entries into the logbook.

"Course 120 at about 50,500 yards."

"Any other contacts?"

"Two submerged contacts. One LOS ANGELES class SSN and, I believe, in the background, was the propeller noise of an OHIO class SSBN."

"Bearings and courses?"

"Same as the cruiser's, but the SSN and the SSBN are at different depths."

"What depths?"

"The SSN is at 450 feet/150 meters, speed of 5 knots and about the same distance as the cruiser. The SSBN is at 200 feet/67 meters, speed of 4 knots and slightly further behind the cruiser."

"Conn, aye."

Andrew was waking up as the sun was preparing to rise. The first light rays were waking up the teens. They took time out from bailing and rowing to eat some breakfast. After breakfast, they went back to bailing and rowing. As the one teen girl looked around, she could see nothing but rain and waves. There was a thick fog bank surrounding them as well. Her wet matted brunette hair brushed against her face as she started to cry.

When Andrew had finished breakfast, he went to the bridge. He did a quick turnover with Melissa. When the turnover was completed, he noted that the ship was doing a complete change of the watch. When the turnover was completed on the bridge, Andrew noted that BMSN Franz was at the helm now. Bill entered the bridge a short time later and looked over the log entries. It was Andrew who picked up the phone.

"Conn, Weapons Control," he said.

"Weapons Control, aye," replied FT1 Tom Allison.

"Assign Tube 3 to the surface target."

"Weapons Control, aye."

A few minutes later, FT1 Allison called Andrew back.

"Weapons Control, Conn, Tube 3 has been assigned to the surface target."

"Conn, aye. XO, get me Mr. Bradley and have him meet me with his diving gear in the forward escape trunk."

"Aye, sir,"

Andrew walked to the Electronic Countermeasures Room. He found Electronic Warfare Technician Senior Chief Petty Officer Harold Williams at the controls. EWCS (SS/SW/AW) Williams looked up as Andrew knocked on the bulkhead frame.

"Good morning, sir, what can I do for you?" he asked.

"I'm going to be putting up the periscope in a few minutes. I need to know who's out here."

"Aye, sir. My equipment will be ready."

Andrew left the room and continued back aft. He made a stop by Radio. He found the Communications Officer, CWO2 Melissa Andrews, RM2 William Deforrest and RMSN Jill Peters in the room. He knocked on the bulkhead frame. It was CWO2 Andrews that turned around to face him.

"Good morning again, sir," she said.

"Good morning again to you, warrant. In a few minutes, I'll be coming shallow. I want a weather report and that's it."

"Aye, sir. I will need at least two minutes to get that report though, sir."

"I think I can give you at least three minutes. I seriously doubt, with all the lightning and wave activity, the enemy could get a good fix on us."

"We'll be ready, sir."

Andrew returned to the bridge. He walked in on the XO talking to the duty quartermaster. Andrew waited until they were finished talking. Andrew handed the XO a set of keys.

"XO, find Senator Arthar. He's about to see a live fire of a missile," said Andrew, handing the XO the keys.

"Yes, sir. Andy, what are these for?" asked Bill.

"Go to the armory and get me a noisemaker. The last four digits of the stock number should be 1628. Bring the noisemaker to me in the forward escape trunk."

"Aye, sir."

Andrew turned to face the diving officer.

"Diving officer, make your depth 30 feet/10 meters, slow down to 1 knot and come to new course 106."

"Aye, sir. Helm, come to new course 106, decrease speed to 1 knot, come to 30 feet/10 meters."

"Helm, aye."

The ship slowed down and began rising slowly towards the surface. As the ship reached 30 feet/10 meters, it started rocking slightly from the wave action above it. As Andrew verified that the ship was at the correct depth, course and speed, he looked at the seawater temperature: 78 degrees Fahrenheit/25 degrees Celsius. Andrew walked over to the periscope and unsecured the ring.

"Master chief, pass the word, we're coming shallow."

"Aye, sir."

Andrew raised the periscope up. He saw almost nothing but black clouds coming in from the west. Waves were crashing over the periscope and there appeared to be a low-lying fog bank to the east. Andrew could see rain and very heavy lightning. He kept the periscope up for about three and half minutes before lowering it, resecuring the ring. It was ECW that called first.

"ECW, Conn," said EW1 (SS/SW/AW) Lou Edwards.

"Conn, aye."

"Two hits on the periscope. One at bearing 295 and one at bearing 020."

"Conn, aye. Good job ECW."

Radio called next.

"Radio, Conn," said Melissa.

"Conn, aye."

"Kendra's a category 2 typhoon. That's all I could get on such short notice."

"Conn, aye. Thank you warrant, good job as well."

A short time later the senator arrived on the bridge.

"Senator, stand over at the periscope. We're about to launch a missile," said Andrew.

"Alright!" said the senator, obviously excited about the prospect of seeing a real missile launched.

The diving officer showed the senator where to stand and prepared the periscope for deployment. When the senator was in the correct position, Andrew met the XO. The XO gave Andrew back his keys, which Andrew put back into his left, front pants pocket.

"Mr. Bradley is waiting inside the forward escape trunk," said Bill.

"Thank you, XO. I'll go brief him and return."

Andrew walked forward to the forward escape trunk. He found Bart inside the opening of the escape trunk. He was attaching the noisemaker to himself. Andrew knocked on the opening.

"Are you ready to go?" asked Andrew as pleasantly as he could.

"Yes, sir. Just give me your orders, sir."

"I'm going to ask you to do this mission. If, after what I have told you, you want to say no, that's fine with me."

"What is it you want me to do, sir?"

"Sonar has reported an intermittent surface contact at bearing 106. The computer thinks it is a life raft. We've already eliminated surf, biologics and side scan sonar not previously recorded."

"Okay, go on, sir."

"Currently we are about 300 yards from this disturbance's last known location. I want you to go see what is causing this disturbance."

"What's the weather like up there?"

"Low clouds, fog, and heavy rain. It would also appear that fierce lightning is in the area; be careful. I don't know about winds, but there are 6 to 8 foot/2 to 2.7 meter swells."

"Okay. Bearing 106 at or about 300 yards," said Bart, calibrating his compass that was attached to his left forearm.

"I'm going to be launching a HARPOON at a surface target after you leave the ship. If everything goes right, I'll be back to pick you up in about two hours. I'll repressurize the escape trunk and open it; just swim inside."

"Okay. What is the water temperature?"

"About 78 degrees Fahrenheit/25 degrees Celsius. Listen to me, if you find something up there, use the noisemaker to let me know where you're located."

"Aye, sir. I accept your mission voluntarily."

"You might just get a Commendation Medal out of this. Now, when you're all suited up and ready to go, just tap on the bulkhead with the hammer inside the trunk."

"Aye, sir."

Andrew closed the hatch, securing it tightly. When the hatch was secured, Andrew called the bridge.

"Forward Escape Trunk, Conn, all engines stop, XO."

"Aye, sir. All engines stop," replied Bill.

The ship coasted to a stop. When Bart was ready, Andrew heard the tap, tap, tap on the hatch from the hammer. Andrew pressed a button that was located to the right of the hatch, flooding the escape trunk. After the trunk was completely flooded and the pressure equalized, the trunk's hatch opened automatically.

Bart swam free of the ship and towards the surface. Andrew watched as the indicator on the right side of the hatch showed that the trunk's top hatch was closed. The next indicators showed that the pumps were pumping out the water from the escape trunk. He then proceeded towards the bridge.

"Diving officer, make your depth 50 feet/16 meters, set the engines for 3 knots and come to new course 130."

"Aye, sir."

As Bart looked down into the water, he saw the ship turn on her own axis and disappear into the depths. He made it to the surface and took a look around him. The weather conditions were worse than what he expected. There was wind, heavy rain and lightning. He could hardly see through the fog bank that was being driven by the wind and wave action.

He looked down at his compass. The needle was pointing towards a bearing of about 106 degrees. He began swimming with the waves and looking around as much as he could. As he crested yet another wave, he saw something in the trough of the wave that made him nearly swallow his breathing tube: a life raft. He quickly started swimming towards it catching the back end of the life raft as it started to rise with another wave.

Meanwhile, Andrew had completed the preparations for launching the HARPOON. He called sonar to confirm that the cruiser was still coming towards him. Andrew then walked over to where the senator was standing and unsecured the ring around the periscope. The periscope was now ready to be raised.

"Your Honor, when I tell you to, push the button on the right side of the periscope handles that says RAISE."

"Okay," replied James.

"Conn, Sonar," said Andrew into the phone.

"Sonar, aye."

"Surface contacts?"

"Two, sir. One bearing 020 and one bearing 295."

"Submerged contacts?"

"Two, sir. One bearing 290, SSN and one bearing 285, SSBN."

"Good. Distance and speed of the surface contact?"

"NORMANDY class cruiser bearing 295, speed 5 knots, distance 38,500 yards and closing."

"Good. Weapons Control, Conn."

"Weapons Control, aye."

"Assign tubes 5 and 6 to the SSN."

"Weapons Control, aye."

"Senator, the cruiser probably won't be able to detect our missile launch nor will that ship be able to get a good bearing lock on us for a response shoot. This is due mainly to the deteriorating weather conditions up there."

Andrew waited until this information looked as if it had settled into the senator's brain before continuing.

"If you will, Your Honor, raise the periscope and while looking through the periscope, turn it until the digital compass reads 295."

It took the senator a few seconds to find the numbers 295 on the digital compass. When he finally found the numbers, all he could see was ocean and waves crashing over the periscope obscuring his view for a few seconds. He spoke.

"The digital compass reads 295."

"Good. Fire tube 3."

The missile was launched out of the torpedo tube. In a few seconds, it broke the surface and dropped its protective case. The tail fire from the missile lit up the sky. Bart and the teens both saw the missile launch.

Andrew was right, the other ship wasn't able to detect the missile right away, but it was able to detect it a few seconds before it self-destructed. In those few seconds, the ship, before being ruled "dead", fired four ASROC's. The SSN fired on the same bearing as the alleged HARPOON launch.

Andrew, knowing that a possible retaliatory strike could be launched, took evasive actions. He changed course and speed several times. He dropped countermeasures, both active and passive. He set those countermeasures both deep and shallow.

He then went to the bottom of the area just inside the entrance to the trench. He waited for the reports from sonar. So far, none of the torpedoes nor missiles had reached anywhere near him. The closest was over three nautical miles away on a bearing of 180. This was far outside the "kill" perimeters set by the exercise.

Andrew fired tubes 5 and 6 at the SSN. He dropped countermeasures both, active and passive. He set them deep and shallow and then changed courses and speeds once again. SSN-747 now sat just a mere 10 feet/3 meters off the bottom. Muted explosions were detected by sonar as tubes 5 and 6 reached their target; Bart had just boarded the life raft.

He saw the badly injured male teen with bandages wrapped around his forearms, legs and the left side of his face. The wounds, due to the exposure to saltwater, had begun to fester and leak fluids. Bart was helped aboard the life raft and began removing his diving gear. The female teen with the black, matted hair was the first person Bart saw, so he spoke to her.

"Which one of you is the captain?" asked Bart trying to be heard over the wind and waves.

Bart looked at the area they all were pointing towards. It was the injured male teen. Bart looked down at him and saluted him.

"Captain, I'm Torpedoman's Mate Seaman Bart Bradley of the United States Navy Warship 747; help is on the way!" he said loudly.

The teen merely nodded his head as best he could.

"I'll summon some help," said Bart as he detached the noisemaker from his diving gear belt.

Bart read the directions that were posted on the side of the noisemaker. He removed the tabs at both ends of the noisemaker and carefully dropped it into the water. The noisemaker started bubbling and popping as saltwater entered the holes. The noisemaker stayed on the surface for a short time and then disappeared under a wave.

Bart started looking around at the 10-man life raft. He started going through the equipment in the life raft. He was looking for the life raft's sea anchor hoping that he would find it soon. He located it inside of the small shelter. Bart grabbed the sea anchor and read the directions on how to deploy it.

He unstrapped it from its holder and removed the straps from the casing it was being held inside of. He then unfurled the sea anchor. The sea anchor resembled a large parachute and had about 100 feet/33 meters of heavy cord tied to it. Bart secured one end of the cord to the life raft and tossed the sea anchor over the side.

The sea anchor settled into the water and soon it pulled the life raft onto a steady course. Bart looked down at his compass and saw a course of 113. Bart then assisted in bailing the life raft out, waiting for the submarine to surface at any minute.

Down below, the sonar crew had new troubles to deal with after all of those explosions and countermeasures that had been dropped. The bottom had been kicked up very badly. The cloud that was soon overtaking them turned out to be sonar opaque.

The sonar crew was having trouble telling if anyone was out there with them. The sonar crew soon lost track of the noisemaker within the cloud. Andrew called sonar to see what was going on out there.

"Conn, Sonar," said Andrew.

"Sonar, aye," replied STS2 (SS/SW) Florence Garbo.

"Any noises out there?"

"I can't hear a damn thing, sir. The bottom has been kicked up. The cloud that is overtaking us is sonar opaque."

"Did you detect anything before the cloud moved over us?"

"Yes, sir, a noisemaker in the water bearing 113 at or about 8,000 yards/2,667 meters."

"Conn, aye. Diving officer, we will wait here another minute. Then, come to new course 113. Set the engines for 1 knot and come to periscope depth."

"Aye, sir," she replied.

As the ship slowly cleared the cloud, the sonar crew couldn't hear anything at first. Then, slowly, off in the distance, the propellers of the Coast Guard Cutter could be heard. As the ship reached up towards the surface, the sonar crew picked up the surface disturbance. They also picked up thunder and other surface disturbances.

"Sonar, Conn."

"Conn, aye."

"Two surface contacts. One at bearing 113; that same surface disturbance we detected earlier and one at bearing 020."

"What is the surface contact at bearing 020?"

"I think it's a Coast Guard Cutter, sir."

"Distance?"

"47,850 yards/15,950 meters."

"Conn, aye."

Andrew looked at all of his available options. He knew that putting up the periscope would pose little problem for them. The waves would hide the periscope and the low cloud cover, coupled with the heavy rain, would make detecting the periscope difficult. Andrew stepped up to the periscope and looked over at the diving officer.

"We're just passing 100 feet/33 meters, sir, on our way to 60 feet/20 meters," she said.

"Very well. XO, if you need to ventilate to recharge the HP air system, now would be the time."

"Aye, sir."

Bill made preparations to snorkel when Andrew gave the word. When the ship reached 60 feet/20 meters, Andrew raised the periscope up. Although the waves were obscuring the tiny life raft, Andrew set the magnification to the maximum level. As Andrew turned the periscope all the way around, ECW detected three hits on the periscope.

ECW personnel went to work on the hits right away to see if they could determine whom the hits had come from. Before long, ECW personnel had determined who two of the three hits were. The third hit was far too weak for a positive identification.

"ECW, Conn," said the senior chief.

"Conn, aye," replied Andrew still looking through the periscope.

"three hits, sir. One bearing 020, distance 45,850 yards/15,283 meters, it is a Coast Guard Cutter. According to our charts, she should be CGC-1022, USS ALBINO."

"What about the second hit?"

"Bearing 270, distance 55,550 yards/18,517 meters, NIMITZ Class nuclear powered aircraft carrier."

"What about the third hit?"

"Too weak to tell, sir."

"Bearing and distance?"

"Bearing 299 at or about 60,000 yards/20,000 meters."

"What do you think produced the hit?"

"Signal frequency is consistent with cruisers, fast frigates, and destroyers, sir."

"Conn, aye. Conn, Weapons Control."

"Weapons Control, aye," replied FT2 Tom Allison.

"Assign tubes 7 and 8 with a weapon waypoint of 315. Have their seekers go active at 45,000 yards/15,000 meters."

"Weapons Control, aye."

Andrew was looking through the periscope when the life raft appeared. Andrew had to back off the magnification setting so that a correct distance could be calculated. When the periscope was reduced to normal magnification, Andrew could tell that the ship was very close to the life raft. In fact, he could see TMSN Bradley bailing out water and waving his right hand. Andrew motioned for the XO to step up to the periscope to see for himself what was up there. The XO looked through the periscope and his jaw dropped open.

"Holy shit, sir!" said Bill.

"My sentiments exactly, XO. Diving officer, emergency surface the ship!"

"Aye, sir, emergency surface."

The submarine exploded out of a wave. Once the sub was on the top, it started rocking violently side to side as well as up and down in the heavy swells. As Andrew lowered the periscope, he turned to the master chief.

"Master chief, muster the rescue and assistance detail in the conning tower with full heavy weather gear."

"Aye, sir."

Andrew turned to face Bill as members of the crew assigned to the rescue and assistance detail went up the ladder into the conning tower.

"Bill, shut the hatch behind me and turn on the pumps. Alert the medical officer to prepare for civilian injured personnel with unknown injuries."

"Aye, sir."

Andrew entered the conning tower and closed the hatch behind him. He checked everyone's gear before opening the top hatch to the outside. The ship dove into a wave that nearly flooded the conning tower. The pumps worked effortlessly to dewater the space.

Soon, the life raft was tied up to the sub temporarily. The injured teens were helped aboard and put into the conning tower. When the last teen was aboard and being taken below for a medical exam, Bart was coming aboard the sub. Bart had released the life raft and punctured several holes in it with his diver's knife to sink it. Suddenly, without warning, a large wave smashed broadside into the sub inundating the conning tower.

Andrew held his breath as he grabbed Bart's left ankle. Andrew turned as much as he could as the wave fought furiously to take both of them to Davy Jones' Locker. Andrew could only turn so far. Then he heard a loud pop coming from somewhere behind him.

As the wave subsided, Andrew could now feel the pain from his right shoulder. Andrew was trying to close the top hatch with his left arm, while gagging on saltwater, when another wave smashed it shut for him. He was now pinned against the top of the ladder and the bottom of the hatch. The pain level was beginning to rise.

Andrew used his left arm to hold the hatch down as one of the crewmembers secured it tight. When the pumps had emptied out the space, Andrew saw four scared teens looking back at him. It was the female teen with the black matted down hair that spoke to him.

"Captain Hinton-Smith, on behalf of my captain, request permission to come aboard," she said.

"Permission granted," said Andrew through clinched teeth.

Soon, the conning tower hatch was opened. One at a time, the crewmembers and Andrew went down the ladder. Andrew realized that he couldn't use his right arm at all. The arm hung there limp at his side.

He figured that the arm had been torn out of its socket. Andrew nearly fell down the ladder and into the arms of Bill. Once Andrew saw that the teens and Mr. Bradley were being taken care of, Andrew turned to Bill.

"XO, have Radio put me on a civilian channel to the Coast Guard Cutter," said Andrew, about to pass out from the pain.

"That violates the rules, Paragraph 98, Section A; we lose," replied Bill.

"True, however, in this instance, we have to transmit on a civilian frequency. The Coast Guard does not monitor, nor are they allowed to transmit on, military frequencies except during time of war or as directed by competent naval authority."

"You're right, sir. I'll have Radio redeploy the radio masts immediately."

"Thank you, get me to sickbay."

"Aye, sir."

Andrew, with a little help from Bill, made it to the sickbay. He entered the sickbay and looked around to make sure that everyone was being taken care of properly. He went to all four of the tiny exam rooms. He saw that the last exam room held the female he had talked to earlier. She looked up at him.

"Yes, XO, what can I do for you?" asked Andrew, anticipating that she was going to ask a question.

"Did we see a ballistic missile launch earlier?"

"No. That was an anti-ship missile called a HARPOON. I launched it from one of my torpedo tubes."

"Thank you for answering my question, sir. I thought that perhaps World War III had started and we fired first."

It was the medical officer, CW01 Rob Bertsen, who met Andrew. Rob took one look at Andrew's right arm and knew Andrew had dislocated his right shoulder. Andrew spoke first.

"What is your opinion of these teens and Mr. Bradley?"

"The teens have minor dehydration. One has burns and a possible infection. They all need to be in a soundproof room for at least 72 hours. Mr. Bradley almost drowned."

"Very well. Can you be ready to transport these kids to a Coast Guard Cutter within the hour?"

"Yes, sir."

"Prepare them for transport to a Coast Guard Cutter."

"What about your shoulder, sir?"

"I'll deal with it later. There's nothing in the rulebook that says I have to use both arms. XO, help me to Radio."

"Aye, sir."

Bill helped Andrew to the Radio Room. When Andrew arrived, he was sweating. The pain was almost blinding, but he managed to see through it anyway. CW02 Andrews handed Andrew the microphone. Bill was holding up Andrew as the sub rocked side to side and up and down violently. Andrew pressed the "TRANSMIT" button.

"Coast Guard Cutter 1022, this is the warship 747; come in please," said Andrew, gasping for breath.

Andrew waited a few seconds before repeating himself.

"Coast Guard Cutter 1022, this is the warship 747; come in please. We are declaring an emergency."

"Warship 747, this is the Coast Guard Cutter 1022, are you declaring an emergency?"

"Affirmative, Cutter 1022. I have four injured civilian personnel that need immediate transport to a more suitable medical facility. Please alter your course to 030 and maintain your speed. We will rendezvous with you within the hour."

"Warship 747, this is Cutter 1022, we will alter course and maintain speed."

"Thank you, Cutter 1022."

Andrew left the radio room and stepped onto the bridge. His arm was throbbing now. He looked up at Bill.

"Diving officer, come to new course 030. Make your depth 100 feet/33 meters, engines ahead to flank."

"Aye, sir."

# Chapter 9

"Bill, I had to have the cutter make the course change to keep us within the GPS grid square and in the game," said Andrew, confidently.

"Very ingenious, Andrew."

"I'm going to medical now to have my shoulder set. How much longer do we have before the game is over?"

"About 16 hours."

"Good. Have the quartermaster plot a high-speed, zigzag run to the secondary TLAM launch area."

"Aye, sir."

"Also, every fifth and eleventh turns that we make, drop countermeasures, both passive and active; just in case."

"Aye, sir."

"Vary the depths at which we operate at during the run. On the countermeasures, deploy them both deep and shallow."

"Aye, sir."

"The bridge is yours, XO," said Andrew as he left the bridge.

"Aye, sir."

A few hours later, Andrew was back on the bridge. Once the Coast Guard Cutter was located, the sub surfaced immediately. The teens were transferred and the sub slipped under the building seas once again. Fifteen minutes later, two TASM's broke the surface and headed for the destroyer. The aircraft carrier had the advantage of being able to detect the missile launches immediately. This was due to the fact that the carrier's radar systems were sitting about 298 feet/100 meters above the water.

Aboard the carrier, the Combat Information Center began tracking the missiles. The combat personnel noted that the missiles' trajectory path seemed to indicate that the destroyer was their intended target. After determining that the missiles were indeed headed for the destroyer, the duty Combat Officer, Lieutenant Commander Bergman, called the bridge.

"Combat, Bridge," he said.

"Bridge, aye," replied the officer-of-the-deck.

"Two inbound TASM's bearing 025."

"Course?"

"355."

"Armed?"

"Not yet. Their trajectory path seems to indicate that the destroyer is the most likely target, sir."

"Bridge, aye."

The officer-of-the-deck did a quick look into the radarscope on the bridge. He noted the missiles' position and apparent trajectory path. The missiles did indeed seem to be heading towards the destroyer. He looked back up and then back down into the scope. He then looked back up, looking out the bridge windows. The wipers were going back and forth.

Heavy rainsqualls and high winds were the norm for the day. Lightning was dancing all around the ship as well as the ocean surrounding the ship. Low clouds and heavy seas would make detecting an incoming, sea-skimming missile almost impossible. He wanted to fire off a quick warning message to the destroyer, but the rules of this war game prohibited any type of warning messages. The officer-of-the-deck stood rigid.

"Helm, come to new course 120."

"Helm, aye, coming to new course 120."

The aircraft carrier turned onto its new course leaving a wide gap between them and the incoming missiles. Far too late, the destroyer detected the missiles.

"Combat, Bridge. Two TASM's bearing 025!" the man yelled.

Once the missiles had self-destructed, the captain put down his binoculars. He then turned towards his executive officer.

"Weren't you the one, XO, that told me he would never launch missiles in this kind of weather?" asked the captain, sarcastically.

"Yes, sir. I was confident that the weather, combined with the high winds, would prevent him from launching missiles."

"Well, I think you're wrong on that one. Better hope and pray that the SSN finds him."

"Aye, sir."

"Head for home, helm," said the captain.

"Aye, sir."

Aboard the SSN, the sonar crew was zeroing in on a loud sound source. Frantically wanting to identify the sound source as the "enemy" SSN, the sonar crew discovered that the sub had chased down another countermeasure. The duty sonar technician picked up the phone and called the captain.

"Sonar, Conn," the man said.

"Conn, aye," replied the captain, with both the diving officer standing to his right and the executive officer standing to his left.

"We chased down another countermeasure, sir."

"Conn, aye," said the captain, his fury growing.

It was the XO who spoke first.

"Very cunning enemy captain we have, eh, sir?"

"Very cunning indeed, XO. We've just chased down our ninth countermeasure and still he eludes us. Well, I think I know exactly where he is going."

"You do, sir?" asked the diving officer.

"The secondary TLAM launch point. Diving officer, make your depth 70 feet/23 meters, increase speed to flank, course 340."

"But, sir, that will give away our position to the enemy captain," said the XO, cautiously.

"I don't think that the enemy captain is terribly worried about that issue."

"You're probably right, sir."

"Get me the weapons officer."

"Aye, sir," said the XO as he left the bridge.

The weapons officer arrived a few minutes later on the bridge. She looked at the captain who had the charts out for the GPS grid square they were inside of: 1728. The captain had taken a red grease pencil and marked a circle around the secondary launch area. She noticed that there were a lot of little white "X's" in many different spots on the chart. Each of the white "X's" was inside the red circle of the TLAM launch area. When the captain was finished marking up the charts, he looked up at the weapons officer.

"You wanted to see me, sir?" she asked.

"Yes. How many pieces of ordnance can we fire and keep track of at one time?"

"Twelve, sir."

"Good. Load all the torpedo tubes with torpedoes and when I say fire, launch all of them on these weapon waypoints," he said, pointing at all the little white "X's."

"Aye, sir," she replied, taking notes on the waypoints.

"Diving officer, when we reach the 25,000 yard/8,333 meter mark, go to test depth and slow down to 3 knots."

"Aye, sir."

SSN-747's radio crew had picked up the updated typhoon report. The wind speeds were well above acceptable tolerances by the U.S. Navy. The heavy seas and rain were worse than before. By all accounts, no missile launches were possible. When Andrew had read the report, he set it down on the chart table. The XO picked up the report, scanned over it and put it back down on the chart table.

"What are we going to do, skipper? The wind speeds are well above normal," said the XO.

"So are the seas. However, the manufacturer says that these missiles are all weather launch and flight capable."

"You're not going to test that theory, are you?" asked the XO, nervously.

"I sure am."

Meanwhile, at the Malikai Missile Test Island Range bunker, rain was obscuring the entire test range. A navy SEAL detachment group was monitoring the end of their war game. Inside the bunker, they waited for an update on the "enemy" missile attack.

The most recent update on the war game came from the aircraft carrier. When the printer was finished printing the report, the SEAL detachment commanding officer tore it off the printer. He read the report and gave it to the other SEAL team members to read.

"If this report is true, then what, sir?" asked an ensign of the team who operated the radar equipment.

"Ensign, I would prepare for incoming missiles within the next three hours," said the commanding officer.

"I'll man my radar sets, then, sir," said the ensign as he left the room.

Meanwhile, aboard the pursuing SSN, the XO walked over to the captain and looked at him. Without looking up, the captain could tell something was on the XO's mind.

"Something on your mind, XO?" asked the captain, still looking down at the chart table and the charts.

"Skipper, if the 'enemy' captain goes to one of the primary TLAM launch points, we won't be able to get him in time. How can you be so sure that the 'enemy' will go to the secondary TLAM launch point?"

"Simple. The two primary TLAM launch points can only be accessed by going through one of four shallow water approaches and transit points. It would make detecting her, even at extreme range, very easy. She would be a sitting duck."

"I see. If I were her skipper, sir, I would go to the secondary TLAM launch point because I might assume that you would have mined the approaches and transit points."

"Very good critical thinking skills, XO. You're correct in that assumption."

"Sonar, Conn."

The captain looked up and grabbed the telephone receiver.

"Conn, aye."

"30,500 yards/10,167 meters and closing."

"Conn, aye," he replied as he put the receiver back into the cradle.

Meanwhile, SSN-747 was closing in on the secondary TLAM launch point. In another hour and forty-five minutes, SSN-747 would launch her missiles at the Malikai Island Missile Test Range targets. Andrew was going through the compartments one by one to see that they were ready. As he was about to leave the sonar suite, the duty sonar technician, STS1 (SW/AW/SS) Harpose stopped him.

"Sir, can I speak to you, professionally?" she asked.

"Permission granted," replied Andrew.

"We've come so far, sir. Since we have not been able to locate and track the other SSN out here, we could be in for a surprise, sir."

"Good thinking, STS1. I will keep that in mind."

"Thank you, sir."

Andrew left that compartment and headed for the weapons control room. When he arrived, he found MT2 Cindy Lance and MT1 Joan Boggs at the controls. They looked up at Andrew and smiled.

"Are the TLAM's ready, MT1?" asked Andrew.

"My birds are ready, just tell me when, sir," replied MT1 Boggs.

"Set a 90 minute timer. When the timer goes off, launch."

"Aye, sir," she said, setting a small timer on her console. "And, sir, the weather is not going to stop my birds."

Andrew left the compartment and went to the bridge. When he arrived on the bridge, he noted their course and speed. He met the XO and they started looking over the charts of the TLAM launch area. Most of the area was almost flat, filled with numerous shipwrecks. Andrew looked to the western side of the area and saw a deep trench. The trench was deep enough to hide a sub and it was close enough to the TLAM launch area to be effective.

"XO, I think that the enemy may have set a trap for us."

"Okay, how do we counter this alleged trap?"

"By firing four torpedoes into the trench area at these points," replied Andrew as he put four red "X's" on different spots on the charts.

"I see, you figure that the other SSN is probably rigged for silent running then, eh?"

"Yes and if the 'enemy' SSN is rigged for silent running, she could be ready to ambush us."

Andrew reached up and grabbed the receiver.

"Conn, Weapons Control."

"Weapons Control, aye."

"Load tubes 1 through 4 with torpedoes. Set tube 1 with a weapon waypoint of 185. Set all torpedoes with a pre-set of arming at 900 yards/300 meters."

"Aye, sir."

"Set tube 2 for a waypoint of 225."

"Aye, sir."

"Set tube 3 for a waypoint of 265."

"Aye, sir."

"Set tube 4 for a waypoint of 305."

"Aye, sir."

"How much longer before we can fire our missiles, XO?"

"About another 45 minutes."

"Good. Conn, Weapons Control."

"Weapons Control, aye."

"Have the torpedoes self-destruct at 20,000 yards/6,667 meters."

"Aye, sir."

Meanwhile, the "enemy" SSN had reached its goal. As the sub slipped down to test depth at flank speed, SSN-747's sonar crew briefly picked up the cavitation of the propeller. The sonar crew listened to the noise, but could not positively identify the noise. As the other sub made it to test depth, her captain made the ship ready for a fight.

"XO, rig this sub for silent running and ready all tubes to fire on my command," said the captain.

"Aye, sir."

Aboard SSN-747, the sonar operator gave up on the noise. He was about to leave his post for a few minutes to get a cup of coffee when Andrew called.

"Conn, Sonar."

"Sonar, aye."

"Any contacts?"

"A brief contact that sounded like the cavitation of a propeller at 25,500 yards/8,500 meters."

"How long ago?"

"About 10 minutes."

"Depth?"

"400 feet/133 meters heading down to the next thermal layer at 1,300 feet/433 meters."

"Bearing and duration of noise?"

"Bearing 270 and the noise lasted about 26 seconds before I lost it to the surface disturbances."

"Conn, aye."

Andrew looked down at the charts. The bearing mark that sonar had given him was out in the trench. After thinking about it for a few minutes, Andrew called weapons control.

"Conn, Weapons Control," said Andrew.

"Weapons Control, aye."

"Reprogram tubes 1 and 2 with waypoints of 265 and 275."

"Aye, sir."

"When the reprogramming is complete, launch tubes 1 through 4."

"Aye, sir."

A few minutes later, all the forward tubes were fired. As the torpedoes headed towards the trench seeking out a target, Andrew fired his missiles. A few minutes after he launched his missiles, Andrew left the area at high-speed. Along the way, he dropped all of his remaining countermeasures at the torpedoes pursuing him. When the last torpedo was evaded, Andrew went to the sonar suite to see how many torpedoes were fired at him.

"How many torpedoes were fired at us?" asked Andrew, rather disgustedly.

"Twelve, sir," replied STSSN Costillo.

"Christ, that captain was really pissed off," said Andrew as he left the sonar suite.

The cruise missiles had been detected on radar. The ensign operating the radar sets saw them appear on the center radar sets' screen. He looked down and saw six of them appear on the screen. They were flying in a "V" formation. He quickly called the commanding officer.

"Captain, six birds inbound!" he yelled.

"Bearing?"

"350!"

"Time to impact?"

"Four minutes 18 seconds."

All the SEAL team members picked up their binoculars. They all turned their attention downrange where the missiles were to impact. The captain looked down at the weather station's readings; 115-knot surface winds, heavy rains and severe lightning. The missiles impacted on the island. Six bright flashes of light were seen, followed by the ground shaking slightly. As they all put down their binoculars, the ensign looked up at the captain.

"Game's over, sir."

"So it would appear, ensign. We have to ride out this typhoon and await better weather to see if the satellite shots show the missiles' impact points were where they were suppose to be."

As SSN-747 proceeded towards homeport, they were suddenly diverted to another location. Once the sub arrived at this other location, a Board of Inquiry was convened. This Board of Inquiry was to determine the effects of the war game. When Andrew arrived aboard the bridge of the USS CARL VINSON, he was greeted by all the participants of the war game. It was the captain of the CARL VINSON that noticed Andrew's injury.

"Good Lord, man, do you need medical help? I'm currently underway with a full surgical staff aboard," said the captain, rather concerned.

"Thank you, captain, for your concern. I'm fine as long as I keep taking the painkillers that my medical officer has given me. Request permission to come aboard," said Andrew, saluting with his left hand.

"Permission granted to come aboard, captain. If you run out of painkillers or if you need any other medical help, you let me know."

"Thank you, sir."

Andrew looked around and saw Rear Admiral Upper Half Sandra Milton mixed in with some commanders and a captain. Andrew assumed that the captain was probably the commanding officer of the SSBN that was monitoring the war game. Captain Mel Henning was present as well. They all left the bridge as one group and headed down many flights of stairs to the wardroom. When they all had arrived at the wardroom, Sandra pulled Andrew aside.

"They called this Board of Inquiry because they lost," she said smiling.

"I figured that they were pretty upset with me," he replied.

Suddenly a large, broad-shouldered commander came through the doorway and pointed a finger, the size of a small piece of sausage, at Andrew.

"You! You had me chasing my tail around in circles after countermeasures!" he snapped as he went back into the wardroom.

"Sorry," replied Andrew as he realized that it was this angry man who had fired all those torpedoes at him. Andrew entered the wardroom.

Upon entering the wardroom, Andrew saw Vice Admiral Bonds and Vice Admiral Williams. Just to Williams' left was Admiral Ray Simon. Sandra walked passed Andrew and stood beside Captain Henning. They all pointed at a lone chair in the middle of the room. Andrew walked over to it, saluted them all and remained standing after they returned his salute and sat down.

"Before we make this exercise valid or invalid, this board has some questions for you," said Ray, who was trying hard to conceal his excitement for Andrew.

"I understand, Admiral Simon," said Andrew.

"Please, sit down," said Vice Admiral Bonds, pointing to the chair.

"Yes, sir," said Andrew, sitting down.

"Sorry to see you injured, Commander Hinton-Smith; is it serious?" asked Vice Admiral Bonds.

"No, sir. A little painful, but well worth it for saving a shipmate's life."

"Indeed. How many missiles did you fire?" asked Ray.

"Nine, sir."

"What types?"

"Six TLAM's, two TASM's and one HARPOON, sir."

"Do you know if your missiles actually hit their targets?" asked Vice Admiral Bonds.

"No, sir, I do not know for a fact that my missiles hit their targets. All my fire control personnel told me was that the missiles had reached their targets. I figured with this typhoon, it might be a few days before we know."

"Well, I have a preliminary report from the SEAL team that was in the bunker at the missile range. Their report seems to indicate that your missiles did, indeed, hit their targets. However, you're right, satellite shots won't be available for another week," replied Bonds.

"How many countermeasures did you use?" asked Captain Henning.

"All 64, sir."

"Good Lord, man. Admiral Simon, may I be excused to send a message to Captain Perez of the Naval Weapons Station Pearl Harbor to replenish SSN-747's countermeasures?" asked Mel.

"Permission granted," replied Ray as Mel left the room.

"Commander Hinton-Smith, you made a radio transmission on a civilian frequency. That is a violation of the rules, why did you do this blatant act?" asked Sandra.

"I picked up four civilian teenagers in a life raft. I gave them medical attention and provided them shelter as required by International Maritime Law, even during a war game exercise. In fact, Admiral Milton, I thought the life raft was a clever decoy to bring me to the surface and end the war game quickly."

"But you discovered that it wasn't a decoy, was it?"

"No, admiral, it wasn't a decoy. I had to transmit on a civilian frequency to the Coast Guard Cutter that was on patrol of the NGFS range."

"Why?" asked Ken.

"Naval Regulations specifically prohibit the Coast Guard from monitoring or transmitting on military frequencies except during time of war. I know of only two exceptions to this rule."

"What are those known exceptions?" asked John.

"One, for joint law enforcement operations with the military, the

Commandant of the Coast Guard may authorize Coast Guard units to monitor and broadcast on military frequencies."

"And the other?"

"Transmission and monitoring may be ordered or directed by competent naval authority."

"Naval Regulation 165, Paragraph A. Were you aware that the Coast Guard Cutter was outside of the NGFS range?" asked Ken.

"The Coast Guard Cutter was inside of GPS Grid Square 1727 by one nautical mile. I ordered her commanding officer to alter her course to keep me in the game."

"We are going to verify your statement commander," said Ken.

"I expect you to, sir."

"Admiral Simon, if you will allow me, I will call the Coast Guard station at Pearl Harbor to verify this alleged statement," said Sandra, standing up and getting ready to leave the room.

"Permission granted, Sandra," said Ray.

A minute later, Captain Henning returned. He took his seat where he had been sitting earlier to the right of Vice Admiral Bonds. The room was silent with the exception of the noise from the flight deck and the engine room. A few minutes later, Sandra returned. Andrew looked up at her and she was smiling once again.

"Admiral Simon, I have confirmed Commander Hinton-Smith's statement. I spoke personally with the commanding officer of Coast Guard Cutter 1022."

"What did her captain have to say?" asked Mel.

"That a person radioed his ship identifying themselves as the warship 747 and had declared an emergency."

"Go on, Admiral Milton," said Ray.

"This designation of warship 747, which Captain Hinton-Smith used or ordered used, is the correct military identification for USS SEASIDE HEIGHTS. He also told me that this person on his radio ordered his ship to alter course to 030. This course alteration kept SSN-747 about one nautical mile inside of the stated GPS Grid Square on its northeast corner."

"Thank you, Admiral Milton. You seem to be very thorough," said Ray.

"I thought you would expect it of me, sir."

"And you're right."

"Am I done, sirs?" asked Andrew, nonchalantly.

"Yes, for the time being. You are to return to your ship, maintain radio silence all the way back to Pearl Harbor. You will be berthing at Pier 5," said Ken.

"Aye, sir."

A few minutes later, Andrew arrived back aboard SSN-747. When the conning tower hatch was secured, Andrew looked over at the officer-of-the-deck, CW02 Andrews.

"Warrant, set incoming and outgoing transmission condition Echo. Only our repeater will be active," said Andrew.

"Aye, sir," she replied.

"Diving Officer, make your depth 150 feet/50 meters, course 010, set engines ahead to 15 knots."

"Aye, sir."

"The bridge is yours, XO. I'll be in my quarters."

"Aye, sir. Andy, I think they're pissed off because they lost."

SSN-747 slipped under the water and headed for homeport in silence.

# Chapter 10

The ship pulled into the pier just as dusk was beginning. Soon, large floodlights came and illuminated the pier. The ship was secured to the pier by early evening. Once the ship was secured to the pier, Andrew had the topside watch set. The crew was happy that the Hawaiian Islands had been spared the brunt of the typhoon. The pier personnel soon departed. As Andrew finished off the post underway check off list, Bill came up to Andrew.

"The reactor is about to be shutdown. In port watches and duty rotation has been implemented," said Bill.

"Thank you. Are we on shore power or ship's power?"

"We're on shore power, sir. I waited until the connections were made before I told the reactor officer to shutdown."

The ship's announcing system sounded.

"Prepare to shift from ship's power to shore power in five minutes. Place all electronic and electrical equipment in standby."

The lights flickered a little bit on the bridge.

"Any sign of the skipper or XO?" asked Andrew.

"No, sir. It would appear that you're still in charge."

"Very well. I'm going to make a quick phone call and probably go home."

"Sounds good. How's the shoulder holding up?"

"Hurts very badly and it is time to take another painkiller."

"Good luck, sir."

After making his phone call, Andrew decided to stay aboard the ship. He ate dinner in the wardroom and stopped by the enlisted dining facility to inspect the place. Once the inspection was completed, he went back to his quarters. The painkiller that he had taken earlier was taking effect. As Andrew lay down in his bunk, the phone started ringing. He reached over to pick up the receiver.

"Hello?" asked Andrew.

"Skipper, this is the command duty officer. I received several phone calls. One from Captain Perez, he will be here in the morning for weapons replacement. One from Admiral Livingston, he says that he is through with your exercise shots and will return them on Wednesday."

"Okay, I'll let my personnel know."

"And finally, the Commander of Submarine Forces Pacific Fleet Forces is due to arrive any minute now and she has a guest with her."

"Oh, crap, thank you."

Andrew hung up the phone and called the weapons office; TM2 (SS) Doenitz answered.

"Heather, this is Andrew. Prepare for weapons on load in the morning. Also, prepare for the return of our exercise shots on Wednesday."

"Aye, sir; anything else?"

"Who's on watch with you in weapons?"

She listed off several names. Andrew chose two of them.

"Heather, have the duty master-at-arms escort TM3 Sanchez and FT3 Combs to my quarters."

"Yes, sir."

Andrew, with a little help from Nick and Tyler, was able to get dressed. He then began to walk towards the wardroom. When he entered the wardroom, he found the command duty officer, CWO2 Andrews, seated at a table. He walked over to where she was seated and looked down at her. She looked up.

"What can I do for you, skipper?" she asked.

"Any other problems or changes in personnel since we last talked?"

"TMSN Bradley has been returned to duty, sir."

"That's good news."

"The admiral let me know that she does not want to be gonged aboard, sir."

"Very well. Go to the quarterdeck and inform them to escort the admiral and her guest to the wardroom."

"Yes, sir."

The admiral arrived a few minutes later, carrying a large bag over her left shoulder. The command duty officer found out her guest was a civilian, Gary. As they all walked towards the wardroom, Heather came out of the weapons office and almost ran straight into Gary. She stepped back and looked into Gary's face before clearing her throat.

"Sorry, sir. Admiral on deck!" she yelled.

There were a few seamen and a few seamen apprentice's in the passageway at the time. They all popped to attention.

"Carry on," said Sandra.

"Excuse me, sir. Are you Gary 'Two-Feathers' Smith?"

"Yes, I am. You must be Heather Doenitz. Andrew has told me a lot about you. Perhaps we should workout someday," said Gary.

"I would appreciate that greatly," said Heather.

Gary had started to move off down the passageway, when Heather stopped Sandra.

"Admiral, permission to speak freely?"

"Granted."

"That's one FINE man, admiral. You definitely have great taste in men."

"Why, thank you."

Sandra caught up with Gary and they continued on until they arrived at the entrance to the wardroom. Sandra opened the door and walked inside. She saw Melissa and Andrew sitting at a table on the far side of the wardroom. Sandra walked over to the table and set the large bag down on the tabletop. She opened it up and withdrew a stack of photos. She then dropped those photos in front of Andrew.

Andrew looked at the photos. Each photo was grid squared, at the top and bottom of the photos were the words "Department of Defense Photo. NOT FOR PUBLIC RELEASE." The sides of the photos were labeled "Classified." Andrew looked over the last photo, set it down on the tabletop and smiled.

The photos showed six impact craters. Where the impact craters were located, Andrew could see collateral damage to surrounding structures. Overall, it appeared that the cruise missiles, without receiving any further instructions from the ship, had hit their intended targets. Smoke could be seen from the impact craters; frozen in time in each photo.

"How did you get these pictures, admiral?" asked Andrew.

"I had one of my computer personnel hijack the satellite transmission from the Special Forces unit to Ken."

"I see. Do you think he knows?"

"Not yet, I wanted you to be one of the first to see your handiwork."

"Thank you, admiral."

"My pleasure. CDO leave us alone and I was never here with a guest. Do you understand me?"

"Yes, admiral, I understand you completely."

Sandra waited until after the door was shut. Then she searched the galley, the scullery and the passageway. When she didn't see anyone, she returned to the wardroom and locked the door. Sandra smiled before speaking to Andrew.

"Thanks to you, I won the bet," she said, beaming.

"Why, you're welcome, admiral. However, my missile technicians that programmed those missiles are the reason why you won the bet."

"Please, pass my compliments and congratulations along to them."

"Will do."

"The coast is clear."

After a brief, passionate kiss, Gary backed away from Andrew. He saw Andrew's arm in a sling.

"It's good to see you," said Gary.

"Good to see you, too," said Andrew.

"How does your arm feel?"

"It hurts and the painkillers are doing a number on me."

"While I was in the shelter, there was a sad story about some teens missing at sea. Mysteriously, those teens showed up in Honolulu before the full force of the typhoon hit. You wouldn't know anything about that, would you?"

"Yes, I was responsible for that mystery as you call it. International Law ordered me to provide assistance," said Andrew, trying to smile through the pain.

"By the way, captain, why are you still aboard?" asked Sandra.

"Naval Regulation 75, Paragraph A. When the commanding officer has not met the ship nor contacted the ship in any form, the acting commanding officer remains in charge until contact can be made or established."

"I see. Well, this exercise is officially over in the morning. I think Commander Staggs will be aboard tomorrow."

"Very well, admiral."

"Well, time for us to go, Gary," said Sandra.

"I'll see you tomorrow night then, sweetheart."

The admiral and Gary left the ship. Andrew went back to his quarters and went to bed. The next morning, after he heard the announcements for the ship and crew, he got dressed. Since getting dressed was a somewhat painful experience for him, he took a painkiller. He then walked to the wardroom and had breakfast. After breakfast, he went to his department quarters and inspected his personnel. When the inspection was completed, he made his announcements.

"I need to see MT1 Boggs and MT2 Lance in my office. Mr. Bradley, glad to see you back to duty. I need to see you in my office as well."

"Yes, sir."

"Dismissed."

The ship's electronic announcing bells sounded. Gong, gong. Gong, gong.

"Commanding Officer, Submarine Squadron 22 arriving," gong.

There was a brief silence before the ship's electronic bells sounded again.

Gong, gong. Gong, gong. Gong, gong.

"U.S. Commander-in-chief Pacific Fleet Forces, arriving," gong.

Gong, gong. Gong, gong. Gong, gong.

"Supreme Allied Commander Pacific Fleet Forces, arriving," gong.

Gong, gong. Gong, gong. Gong, gong.

"Commander Submarine Forces Pacific Fleet, arriving," gong.

"Captain Hinton-Smith, contact the quarterdeck."

"Before I leave here, MT1 Boggs and MT2 Lance, your missiles did indeed hit their targets. However, DO NOT let anyone know you know that information, yet."

"Yes!" said MT1 Boggs, triumphantly.

Gong, gong. Gong, gong.

"Commander, Judge Advocate General's Office, Pearl Harbor, arriving," gong.

Andrew picked up the phone that was in the weapons office and called the quarterdeck. The petty-officer-of-the-watch instructed Andrew to report to the wardroom. Andrew hung up the phone and dismissed the personnel that were in the office. The painkillers were starting to take effect. He was moving slowly towards the wardroom. As he stepped around the corner, he saw the wall of brass.

"*Holy crap, what did I do?!*" thought Andrew as he walked the gauntlet of admirals and captains. As he walked by Sandra, she mouthed some words to him.

"Act surprised," she mouthed and smiled at Andrew as he nodded his head slightly.

He arrived at the entrance to the wardroom and knocked on the door. The door opened and a voice that Andrew did not recognize, told him to enter. When Andrew entered the wardroom, he saw the person that belonged to the voice. The man held the rank of captain with Special Forces insignia. Andrew continued walking into the wardroom.

He saw a lone chair at one of the tables in the middle of the room. He stood behind the chair as the admirals and captains filed into the room. As the top three ranking admirals took their seats, Andrew saw the large, brass bell. Next to the bell was a wooden hammer that was to Andrew's left. Admiral Simon struck the bell several times in groups of two followed by a single strike.

The other ranking officers took up positions to Andrew's left and right. The JAG officer, Captain Ral Nagupe, was seated to Andrew's immediate right. Captain Nagupe leaned over and whispered that he was there to defend Andrew. Andrew nodded his head up and down as the Special Forces captain closed and locked the wardroom door as he sat down in the back of the room.

"This Special Board of Inquiry is now in session. Have a seat Commander Hinton-Smith," said Ray, pointing to the lone chair.

Andrew remained standing and whispered something into Captain Nagupe's left ear. Captain Nagupe nodded his head up and down and spoke to the admirals.

"Objection, Admiral Simon, with all due respect to your rank, sir. Commander Hinton-Smith is still this ship's acting commanding officer. I would appreciate it if you would refer to Commander Hinton-Smith as Captain Hinton-Smith," said Ral, almost out of breath.

"What do you base this assumption on, Captain Nagupe?" asked Vice Admiral Williams, sternly.

"The commanding officer of this vessel failed to make contact in any known form with Captain Hinton-Smith here. Also, the commanding officer of this vessel made no efforts to relieve Captain Hinton-Smith here in accordance with Naval Regulation 75, Paragraph A."

"Very well, objection noted. Captain Hinton-Smith, will you please have a seat? Are you happy, Ral?" asked Admiral Simon, rather irritably.

"Yes, sir, I am happy with the decision you have made, sir," said Ral.

"Good. This board has determined that you, Captain Hinton-Smith, may have violated the conditions of this exercise in several ways. One, you violated known safety protocols on missile launches. How do you plead?" asked Ray.

"Guilty as charged," replied Andrew.

"Very well. Ral, is such the case?"

"Yes and no," said Ral, confidently.

Ral, at this time, removed a set of photos from his briefcase. He set the photos in front of the admirals and captains. They all looked at the photos and soon the photos were handed to Andrew. Although Andrew had already seen the photos, he acted as surprised as he could be. He then set the photos down on the tabletop.

"I say good shooting, Admiral Simon. May I keep these photos? MT1 Boggs and MT2 Lance will be really proud of these craters," said Andrew.

"You may keep those photos," said Ray.

"Thank you, but I will need a second set of the photos for MT2 Lance."

"I'll make sure that MT2 Lance gets a copy of the photos. Is that okay, Captain Hinton-Smith?" asked Sandra.

"Yes, admiral, that will be acceptable."

"Admiral Simon, Vice Admirals Williams and Bonds, Rear Admiral Upper Half Milton, Captain Henning. I read over the war game rules and looked at the results. I also received and reviewed Captain Henning's confidential reports from certain crewmembers about the exercise."

"What were your findings?" asked John.

"Although you worded the exercise so that some things were deplorable in it, Captain Hinton-Smith did achieve the goals of the exercise. This is despite the handicaps that you placed upon him."

"He was out of time set by the rules," said Ken.

"There was, in accordance with your rules, no time set. The only time limit that was in writing was when the exercise should end. This time was arbitrarily set at 1900 hours."

"Captain Hinton-Smith was still out of time, Captain Nagupe," said Ken, sternly.

"No, admiral, Captain Hinton-Smith was not out of time. As long as the missiles impacted on the Malikai Missile Test Range Island by 1900 hours, Captain Hinton-Smith would win. According to the Special Forces captain monitoring the war game, the missiles impacted just before 1705 hours."

"Captain Nagupe, since we did set the time and he was beyond that time, Captain Hinton-Smith loses," said John as if it mattered.

"Well, if he was out of time, then, admirals, why didn't you specify the time zone? I have a report that there was some heavy amounts of money riding on this war game."

"You're right, we did not specify the time zone. That was our mistake. Now, let's move on to the fact that he violated known, military safety rules in regards to missile launches," said Ray.

"Let's ask Captain Hinton-Smith if he thinks he violated the safety rules," said Ral.

"I will admit that the weather conditions were above acceptable military norms. However, I did not order MT1 Boggs or MT2 Lance to fire the missiles. I asked them, prior to the launch and after giving them the current weather report, if they wanted to abort," said Andrew.

"And what was their response?" asked Ral.

"MT1 Boggs said words to the effect of 'my birds are ready to fly.' MT2 Lance was in agreement."

A few smiles went across a couple of the faces looking at Andrew.

"So, it would appear that you gave your crew a chance to say no. By saying no, your crew would be able to not perform a task without fear of retaliation; is that correct?" asked Ral.

"That is correct, Captain Nagupe. Only during an emergency should I have to give orders. If you start giving orders, you kill any opportunity for the crew to work together towards the goal. Besides, don't give an order unless you're willing to follow that order, sirs."

"Words well spoken, Captain Hinton-Smith. Did you give the order to get underway?" asked Sandra.

"I did only after I had briefed the crew on what the weather reports currently showed and what the weather reports predicted. I even gave the crew a chance not to get underway if they so chose. As I recall, several crewmembers did leave."

"Yes and I thought that was another deplorable act, admirals," said Ral.

"Your objection is so noted, Captain Nagupe," said Ray in a flat tone of voice.

"You stated earlier that MT1 Boggs launched the missiles. Did she say no, at first?" asked Ral.

"Why don't you ask her yourself, Captain Nagupe? I think she is in the Fire Control Center at extension 6624," replied Andrew.

"Admirals and Captains, I would like to call MT1 Boggs, MT2 Lance and the Chief Engineer Lieutenant Commander Bill Ellsworthy as witnesses for Captain Hinton-Smith," said Ral.

"Agreed. There will be a 15 minute recess," said Ray as he banged the bell with the hammer.

Andrew disappeared to his quarters to take another painkiller. He then stopped by the Enlisted Dining Facility to get a cup of coffee. He returned to the wardroom where he saw MT1 Boggs, MT2 Lance and Lieutenant Commander Ellsworthy waiting in the passageway. As Andrew walked passed Bill, Bill leaned towards Andrew's left ear and whispered.

"I'm going to kick those admirals in the balls, sir," he said.

"Thank you, XO. I appreciate that very much at this point."

"You're welcome."

Andrew knocked on the door. The door opened and he stepped inside. When the door was shut, Andrew took his seat. Admiral Simon banged the bell and then put the hammer down.

"This Special Board of Inquiry is back in session. Captain Hinton-Smith, please have a seat in the chair to your right. Captain Nagupe, are you ready to call your first witness?" asked Ray.

"I am, sir. I would like to call MT1 Boggs," said Ral.

"Very well. Captain Franks, would you please call MT1 Boggs in here?" asked Ray, pointing his right index finger at the Special Forces captain.

A few seconds later, MT1 Boggs, dressed in her working uniform, entered the wardroom. As he stood beside Captain Nagupe, she spoke to him.

"Captain, if these admirals think that they can intimidate me, they had better think again," she said.

"So noted," replied Ral.

She took her seat. Vice Admiral Williams was taking notes. Vice Admiral Bonds was staring straight at her and Admiral Simon was looking over her Enlisted Service Record before he closed it and began speaking to her.

"MT1 Boggs, did you tell your commanding officer, Captain Hinton-Smith, words to the effect of 'my birds are ready to fly'?"

"Yes, sir, I did."

"Were you aware that at the time of the missile launch, weather conditions were above acceptable military safety limits?" asked Ray.

"Yes, sir, I was aware of the weather conditions. I am also aware that the military sometimes sets the safety threshold artificially low."

"Then, you were also aware that a missile malfunction would have destroyed the ship?" asked Sandra.

"Yes, madam, I was aware of such an occurrence; they are rare. Besides, what better time for an enemy attack than poor weather conditions; don't you agree, Admiral Milton?" asked MT1 Boggs to Sandra.

"I do agree," said Ken.

"What are the capabilities of the TLAM that you launched?" asked John.

"Admiral Bonds, the TLAM is an all weather, all purpose, multiple platform, in-flight programmable missile. It has a military designation of UBGM-109 and can travel up to 600 nautical miles with an attached booster."

She paused before continuing with her answer.

"It carries a 1,000 pound/500 kilogram PBXN-409 series explosive warhead at speeds just under Mach 1. It can also carry a TN-250, 250 kiloton, low yield, tactical nuclear warhead to a distance of 1,400 nautical miles making it an Intermediate Range Ballistic Missile or IRBM."

"Do you think your missiles hit their targets, MT1?" asked Sandra as she pulled out the photos and prepared to give them to MT1 Boggs.

"Yes, admiral, my missiles hit their targets; they don't miss," she said, confidently.

"You're right, they did hit their targets," said Sandra as Joan looked over the photos.

"May I keep these, admiral?"

"They are yours."

"We have no further questions for you MT1; you're dismissed," said Ray.

"Thank you," she replied, standing up and leaving the room with her photos and wearing a proud smile on her face.

The next person to enter the room was MT2 Lance. She took her seat and waited for the questioning to begin. Admiral Simon started the questioning.

"MT2 Lance, did you have any doubts as to the launching of the missiles, given the current weather conditions at the time of launch?" asked Ray.

"Objection, calls for speculation on the part of the witness," said Ral, loudly.

"Whether or not it is speculation, I want an answer to the question," said Ray.

"MT2 Lance, you do not have to answer the question if you don't want to answer," said Ral.

"I will answer the question, Captain Nagupe. Yes, I had a few reservations about the missile launch. However, Captain Hinton-Smith gave myself, MTC Snowden and MT1 Boggs the chance to abort."

"Did you abort?" asked Ken.

"No, we did not abort. We launched."

"Were you coerced into the launch?" asked Ken.

"No, Vice Admiral Williams, I was not coerced into the launch. The decision to launch was reached by all concerned. Captain Hinton-Smith has always evoked cooperation with everyone he commands. I realize that, to some of you sitting here in this room, that is a contradiction in terms for the military."

"So noted," said Ray.

"Were you aware of the dangers at the time of launch?" asked Sandra.

"Yes, Admiral Milton, I was aware that if the missile failed to launch completely, it would sink the ship. If the protective casing didn't fall away correctly, the ship would be hit and sunk. There were other problems that I was aware of as well. However, there was the minimum 7-second trough to wave ratio required for launch."

For the first time, Captain Henning spoke.

"What do you know about the UGM-84F series missile?" asked Mel.

"Captain Henning, the UGM-84F series missile is the sub-launched version of the HARPOON anti-ship missile," she started off and paused before continuing her answer.

"The HARPOON is a sea-skimming, anti-ship missile carrying a 500 pound/250 kilogram explosive warhead with a contact fuse. The HARPOON can destroy a target up to about 30,000 tons. If the target is larger than 30,000 tons, the HARPOON will cripple the target. The missile travels at speeds under Mach 1 and, due to its small cross-section on radar, is almost impossible to detect the HARPOON before impact."

"Can it be used against other targets besides ships?" asked Mel.

"Yes, sir. The HARPOON can be used against large, land targets."

"What would you consider a large, land target?" asked Ray.

"A large office building, oil refinery, oil storage tanks, power generating facility, armory or other hardened targets."

"Can the HARPOON carry a nuclear warhead?" asked Ken.

"Yes, Vice Admiral Williams, the HARPOON can carry a TN-150, 150-kiloton, low yield, tactical nuclear warhead which is designed to airburst over its intended target at or about 3,000 feet/1,000 meters for maximum blast effect."

"Thank you, MT2 Lance," said John.

"No further questions; dismissed," said Ray.

"Thank you, sirs and madam," she said as she left with her own set of photos given to her by Captain Franks.

"We do not need to talk to Lieutenant Commander Ellsworthy," said Ray.

"It would appear, sirs, that despite your misgivings you may have had about the validity of the exercise, the exercise is valid."

"So noted. This Special Board of Inquiry is adjourned," said Ray as he banged the bell one time and set the hammer down.

The rest of the afternoon was a blur to Andrew. As he was leaving the ship, he saluted the flags fore and aft. When he had reached the bottom of the gangway and stepped onto the pier, he heard the ship's electronic bells sound. The four gongs were followed by a solemn announcement.

"SEASIDE HEIGHTS departing," followed by the single gong that seemed to echo eerily down the pier.

As Andrew was getting ready for bed that night, Gary looked at him strangely.

"Did something happen today on the ship?" asked Gary.

"Yes, something did happen. I heard myself being gonged off the ship, just like in my nightmares."

# Chapter 11

The sun was rising on the Washington State coastline just like it had for many millennia. Today, three trucks were entering the coastline area. The first truck was carrying a film crew, the head of Boeing's Military Hardware Division Mr. Frank Foster and Bruce Harvard. Just behind them in the large, semi truck, were the two experimental HARPOON's that had been built for today's test fire. The third truck carried a heavily armed security detachment. All three trucks turned off the main road and onto a small paved road. The driver of the first truck stepped out of the vehicle and walked towards a locked gate. He used a key to unlock the padlock and a keycard to disarm the security system.

The trucks all passed a sign that warned that only authorized personnel should be in the area and that the missile test range was a dangerous place to be. As the last truck turned down this road, a member of the security detachment made the final turn towards the remote missile launch area for the Boeing Corporation.

The first and third trucks stopped at a small building just before the clearing that was the missile launch area. The people in the first truck stepped out. The filming crew went immediately to their respective positions with their cameras. They began setting up their equipment to record the launch. As the sun began climbing higher in the sky, the cloud cover was more visible. Thick, black clouds that were carrying rain to the Pacific Northwest area were obscuring the missile test range.

The second truck with a female driver went down the road to the end. At the end of the road was a large clearing. She turned the semi truck around so that the missile launcher was pointed out to sea. Leaving the engine to idle, the driver then pressed two buttons inside the cab of the semi.

The first button activated the hydraulic systems that raised the missiles to a pre-set firing angle of 65 degrees. The second button locked the missile blast deflector plating into place. When this was completed, the driver shut off the engine and left the truck. The security force escorted her towards the small building as they continued deploying around the area.

Mr. Foster stepped outside into the morning chill along with Bruce. Both men could see their breath every time they exhaled. Both were bundled up for the cold, wet weather. Bruce took out a set of keys and a keycard as they both approached the small building. Bruce used his keycard to deactivate the security system and the keys to unlock the door locks and padlocks on the door. Once they were inside, both men took off their jackets.

Bruce hung up both of their jackets on the back of the door. Mr. Foster immediately noticed that the building was very warm. He looked at the thermometer mounted on the far wall from where he was standing. The thermometer read 82 degrees Fahrenheit/28 degrees Celsius. Bruce was busy talking to the recovery and salvage ship as Mr. Foster drank his coffee.

"Base to Recovery 1, come in please," said Bruce.

Soon the radio crackled to life.

"Base, this is Recovery 1, we are on station," said the voice.

"Recovery 1, I will launch at 0630 and 0715 hours."

"Recovery 1, aye. Bruce got a case of beer bet against you that your birds splash before they reach their targets."

"No go, my birds are armed and ready. Are the dummies ready?"

"In position at 95 nautical miles bearing 200 and at 115 nautical miles bearing 305, per your instructions."

"Thank you; 15 minutes to launch."

Bruce turned around to face Mr. Foster. Mr. Foster was looking at the radar screen. The little arm was going around and around in circles showing nothing but surface clutter from the rain falling. Finally, Mr. Foster spoke.

"For God's sake, man, it's 0615 hours. You know, I hope this missile launch is successful because I usually don't get out of bed before 0900 hours," said Frank.

"The launch will be successful and if the filming crew is on their toes, you'll be able to see the results first hand."

"Why is it so damn hot in here?" asked Frank, switching subjects.

"The radio, radar and computer equipment is constantly running. They all produce large amounts of heat."

"Those HARPOON's are just test missiles right?" asked Frank, looking downrange.

"No, sir, those HARPOON's are the real thing. They are both armed and ready."

"My God, man, what if one of those missiles crashes!?"

"Don't worry, I've programmed the missiles to self-destruct if they don't reach their targets, if there is any kind of malfunction, or if they completely run out of fuel."

"Do you know that each of those 'modified' missiles cost the taxpayers about 2.5 million dollars? And you're going to destroy them? You're insane, aren't you?"

"That's right and when the testing today is seen as a success, Boeing will have another decade, perhaps more, of government contracts. Besides, don't you overcharge the government for the missiles, anyway?"

"Well, yes. We manufacture the missile for about $900,000 and sell it to the government for about $1.4 million. By the way, wasn't Mr. Bevins supposed to be here?" asked Frank, trying to change the subject once again.

"Yes. However, if he doesn't show up, he will be sent film of the shoot. I have told Ray, our Security Chief out here, to let Mr. Bevins onto the test range if he shows up."

"Very well."

"Why don't you watch the radar screen for a little while and finish off your coffee?"

There came a knock at the door. Bruce walked over to the door and opened it up. Ray informed Bruce that the security detachment was in place. Bruce told Ray to be ready for the first missile launch at 0630 hours, quickly followed at 0715 hours by the second launch. Bruce returned to the Fire Control Station and opened up the switch cover.

Inside there were many switches and button type indicators. The switch box was equipped with enough switches and indicators so that up to four HARPOON's could be launched at any one time. Bruce activated the first and third row of switches and button type indicators. The first indicators to come on were white backlit with the words "PRE LAUNCH."

There came another knock at the door. Bruce answered the door. The woman standing at the door said something to Bruce. When she had left, Bruce pressed the yellow indicator buttons on the Fire Control Panel.

The yellow indicator buttons were labeled "WARNING MISSILE LAUNCH!" As Bruce looked through the smoke colored glass downrange, he could see the flashing warning lights. Flashing yellow and orange lights lighted up the range. The sun was now a little higher in the sky. The clouds were starting to dissipate. Frank came over to where Bruce was standing.

"What type of targets are out there?" asked Frank, pointing out to sea.

"We have some old navy supply ships out there of about 18,000 tons.

When those HARPOON's hit them, there won't be much left," replied Bruce.

Roy Bevins had arrived and was being escorted by Ray to the building. There came another knock at the door. Frank greeted Roy and showed him where Bruce was standing.

"Mr. Bevins just arrived," said Frank.

"Did you show him in?" asked Bruce.

"Yes, I did."

Bruce turned around to see Roy. Roy had a beaming smile on his face and a cup of coffee in his right hand. Bruce walked over to him and they shook hands.

"Glad you could make it," said Bruce.

"Thank you. You have great security up here."

"Thank you."

"When is the launch?"

"First one is at 0630 hours. The second at 0715 hours; I'll make you a copy of the film."

"Sounds great. By the way, even with the six inch extension, there's still two inches of room left in the torpedo tubes."

"That's great news. I was afraid you would tell me it wouldn't fit."

Both men laughed. Bruce looked up at the clock; 0625 hours. He turned on the TV monitors. Bruce informed the recovery and salvage ship to be ready. As 0630 hours approached, Bruce pushed the amber colored indicator button labeled "MISSILE LAUNCH EMINENT!" Bruce looked downrange to see both flashing and strobing red and yellow lights. Bruce looked up at the clock; 0630 hours. He pushed the red indicator button labeled "FIRE!"

A second later the top left missile launcher tube exploded. The missile leaped into the cloudy sky, locking its flight fins into place first. A split-second later, the stabilizer fins locked into place. A bright orange ball of fire erupted from the back of the missile. Smoke wafted over the missile range and down on the security personnel.

Bruce, Roy and Frank were watching the missile's flight. Bruce had mounted a small, high resolution, TV camera inside of the nosecones of each missile. The pictures showed the missile was flying true on a heading of 200. The speed was a constant 575 knots/662 miles per hour.

Bruce turned around to see the radar tracking the missile, labeled X-1. Roy and Frank watched as the missile, just barely 7 feet/2.3 meters off the surface of the ocean, blasted towards its target. Suddenly, a shape appeared in the camera's field of view. A ship of some kind was in the missile's flight path.

"Bruce, are there supposed to be other ships out there on the missile range?" asked Frank, a little concerned.

"There might be some fishing trawlers out there, why?" asked Bruce.

"I think your missile is going to hit one of them!" yelled Roy, rather loudly.

"No, watch what the missile does. I just updated the software for these two special missiles. I wanted to make sure the software upgrades worked before releasing them to the military," said Bruce, starting to chuckle.

"I sure hope your software upgrade works. If it doesn't, there won't be anything left of that tiny thing," said Frank.

Roy, Bruce and Frank watched as the missile continued closing in on the fishing trawler. At what seemed to be the last second before impact, the missile went up and over the fishing trawler. During this whole time, the missile remained on its heading of 200. Soon, the missile returned to its previous 7-feet/2.3 meter height above the surface of the ocean. The TV monitor soon showed a flashing red warning symbol "TARGET ACQUIRED" which consisted of a set of crosshairs blinking off and on.

The target ship appeared out of the clouds. At 95 nautical miles, the X-1 HARPOON smashed into the target ship amidships, starboard side, near the engine room. The superstructure was ripped off the target ship. The explosion from the impact on the starboard side blew out the port side engine room compartment.

Pieces of target ship's "M" frames were flying into the air along with some leftover cables. They rained back down into the ocean. The cameras aboard the recovery and salvage ship recorded the hit. The target ship heeled over to port and sank to the bottom in over 10,000 feet/3,000 meters of water in a few minutes. As the last bubbles of air escaped from the sinking target ship, the recovery and salvage ship captain called Bruce.

"Recovery 1 to base."

Bruce turned towards the radio transmitter.

"This is base, go ahead Recovery 1."

"Confirmed impact; target ship completely destroyed. She just slipped under the waves."

"Good. Any sign of decreased speed indicating fuel exhaustion?"

"Negative. My instruments showed the missile impacted at full speed. I'll be ready for the next missile launch as I am heading in that direction now."

"Good."

Bruce went through the same launch sequence for the second missile. At 0715 hours, the X-2 HARPOON was launched. When the smoke had cleared away, the female driver went back to the semi-truck. She started up the engine and lowered the missile launcher first. Then she pushed a button that folded up the missile blast deflector plating. She then drove the truck out of the range followed by the security force.

Bruce, Roy and Frank watched as the missile hit the target ship. The ship was so badly damaged that it came apart in three pieces. The amidships section and the aft section heeled over to port and starboard sides, respectively. The forward section took several more minutes before it sank. After the forward section slipped under the waves, they called Bruce.

"Recovery 1 to base."

Bruce picked up the transmitter.

"This is base, go ahead Recovery 1."

"Confirmed impact, target ship destroyed. I think you will like the video footage of this impact better than the other one; more pieces."

"Great, can't wait to see it. Any sign of decreased speed indicating fuel exhaustion?"

"Affirmative. Missile speed at impact was down to 450 knots/520 miles per hour."

"Get me confirmation data on that information please."

"Will do. I am returning to port."

Bruce put the transmitter up and looked at Frank.

"I might recommend, Frank, for safety sake, a maximum flight distance of 110 nautical miles," said Bruce.

"I agree," said Frank.

"Well, I say jolly good tests today, eh, Frank?" said Roy.

"So it would appear. I think I can make the Board of Directors see to it your pet project here is approved by the major shareholders," said Frank.

"Thank you, sir. Roy, have you heard from David, yet?" asked Bruce as Frank was leaving the building, grabbing his jacket on the way out the door.

"Not since last month. Can I give you a ride back to your office?" asked Roy.

"Sure, we can talk along the way," said Bruce grabbing his jacket off the back of the door.

Meanwhile, in New Groton, Connecticut, at the submarine shipyards, the final plans for the newest and stealthiest fast attack sub were being finalized. The new sub with no name and no hull identification number as of yet, was going to be anti-ship, anti-sub and anti-missile capable. The new sub could also act as a backup surveillance craft.

The sub was also going to employ some new technologies, such as sonar absorbent material as well as radar absorbent material. As the engineers looked over the sub's plans, a tired and beleaguered David Eggins stumbled into the meeting room. He was carrying many rolls of design plans. As the faces all turned to face him, he dropped the rolls on the table. His hair covered his face, so he pushed it back over his ears.

"Let me guess, David, no success?" asked Roy Bevins sarcastically.

"No. I have here the anti-missile capability plans, Roy. Tell me, Roy, is it possible to split the sub both length and width wise?" asked David.

"Yes, it is possible. But it would cost an extra $175,000,000 and an extra four months in the shipyards."

"Okay, for that extra time and money, the sub will have an increase of 42% in survivability. A 75% increase in the anti-missile capabilities. I could give you 24 PATRIOT's instead of the current 12 and I can give you 40 missile decoys."

"How do you propose to do all of that?" asked one of the submarine engineers.

"With these design plans," said David as he started dozing off in mid sentence while holding the design plans in his left hand.

Roy walked around the table and took the stack of design plans out of David's left hand. David suddenly fell backwards into the very comfortable, black executive chair. As he snored the day away, the engineers looked over his design plans. They discussed the designs as David continued sleeping. At about 1900 hours, the Chief of Naval Operations, Admiral Theodore Rosen, called Roy. Roy put the admiral on speakerphone for the meeting.

"Roy, the secretary of the navy wants to name the new submarine the USS DIAMONDBACK. He felt the name was fitting because of the peculiar paint scheme on the exterior," said Admiral Rosen.

"Great, I'll get that name on the design plans immediately. What about her hull identification number?"

"S775. The navy will officially call her SSN-75."

"I'll get that name and hull identification number on the design plans right away."

Just then, David started to snore very loudly.

"Roy, I seem to be having a problem with my phone. There are a lot of crackling and static type noises."

"No admiral, that's probably my phone. I'll have one of my phone techs look at it in the morning," said Roy as looked over at and glared down at David's open mouth.

"Who's going to build this sub?" asked the admiral.

"There are five shipyards in the bidding process right now. However, we've had some recent design plan changes that give the sub a 42% increase in survivability and an increase of 75% in her capabilities."

"Sounds good. Pass along my thanks to the design engineer. What's the cost of these alleged changes?"

"About $175,000,000 and four months."

"Ouch, that hurts, but acceptable for the alleged increases. Who are the two lowest shipyard bidders?"

"Perth-Amboy Shipyards at Perth-Amboy, New Jersey; 7.3 billion dollars. The Alameda Naval Shipyards at Alameda, California; 8.0 billion dollars. These cost estimates include the recent design plan changes."

"Who's the highest shipyard bidder?"

"Unfortunately, we are, sir; 17.6 billion dollars."

"I see. What are the two lowest bidder's major problems?"

"Perth-Amboy Shipyards has no covered dry-docks, nor do they have any railroad access. That would make getting the reactors to the new sub almost impossible unless we ship in by barge. They do have four dry-docks capable of handling the tonnage and size of the new sub."

"Good. Do they have any nuclear weld level qualified shipyard workers?"

"Yes. They allegedly have 20 nuclear weld level qualified shipyard workers. Also, all their nuclear level workers are current on their Secret security clearances and qualifications."

"Okay. What about their security threat level?"

"As of last year, Level III-B."

"Minimum level, but acceptable. What's wrong with the Alameda Naval Shipyards?"

"They have excellent railroad access and great security threat level at Level II-A as of last year. However, they cannot get or keep enough nuclear weld level qualified shipyard workers because of prior drug convictions of some kind. You know that is part of the Secret security clearance checks."

"Okay, let me get back to you on that one; good-bye."

"Good-bye, admiral."

As they were all leaving the conference room, David was still sleeping in the chair. Roy stopped by his secretary's desk. She looked up after putting the receiver down on the phone.

"Yes, Roy, what can I do for you?"

"When David wakes up, make sure that he gets to his hotel."

"Yes, Roy."

In Washington D.C., the chief of naval operations just finished off a phone call with the secretary of the navy. The secretary of the navy told Admiral Rosen to come up with some options. Admiral Rosen put the phone down and looked up at the calendar on the wall to his right.

In just a few weeks, the USS SEASIDE HEIGHTS would be getting underway for her regular deployment. Admiral Rosen knew he had to have Captain Hinton-Smith's new command ready to go in at least pre-commissioning status. The admiral decided to play one shipyard against the other in a friendly competition of sorts. He picked up the phone and dialed the number for the Alameda Naval Shipyards.

"Good evening and thank you for calling the Alameda Naval Shipyards. This is Captain Togant, how can I help you?" she asked, pleasantly.

"Captain Togant, this is Admiral Rosen. I have a new fast attack sub that is being bid on. Your shipyards came in above the competition that bid 7.3 billion dollars."

"Who said they could build your new sub for 7.3 billion?"

"Perth-Amboy Shipyards."

"What?! Those jokers don't even have railroad access, admiral. At least I have railroad access. How are they supposed to get the sub's reactors delivered?"

"I don't know, but you're a little too pricey for the secretary of the navy and the GAO office," said Admiral Rosen, lying through his teeth.

"Okay, admiral, you're on! I've got railroad access, at least 10 dry-docks to handle a nuclear powered sub, or ship for that matter and I'm superior in security threat level condition. Perth-Amboy is at only Level III-B. I'm proud to say, sir, that, as of last week, my shipyards are at Level II."

"How many of those dry-docks are covered and how many nuclear weld level qualified shipyard workers do you have?"

"I have three covered dry-docks. Am I to assume that you don't want anyone to know about this sub, yet?"

"That's correct."

"I have 120 workers. I'll match Perth-Amboy's price of 7.3 billion."

"Sounds good. If I sent you the plans by the end of the month, could you have the sub ready for pre-commissioning status by March of next year?"

"No, I would need at least 200 shipyard workers to do the sub in that short of time."

"If I could get you another 20 shipyard workers would that help?"

"140? I'll make do with whatever manpower you send me, admiral."

"Sounds good, I'll make it happen; good-bye."

As Captain Togant hung up the phone, she gasped.

*"I'm going to get creamed on this project,"* she said to herself.

She walked out into her outer office and found her night staff working. Of the night staff personnel, she knew only Ramon personally.

"Ramon, get your butt into my office," she said.

Ramon ran into her office and closed the door.

"Ramon, which one of my dry-docks can handle a nuclear powered fast attack sub and the dry-dock has to be covered?"

"What size of fast attack sub?"

"Something along the lines of the current LOS ANGELES or SEAWOLF series. However, this one may be larger and more complex."

"Dry-dock 62. It is covered and it is where we recycled the USS ROBERT E. LEE, SSBN-601, at about 12,000 tons."

"Good. Prep Dry-dock 62 for manufacturing. Get everyone together. I should have the plans by the end of the month."

"Okay," said Ramon as he prepared to leave the office.

"One other thing, Ramon. The sub has to be ready for pre-commissioning status by Admiral Rosen sometime around April of next year," she said lying.

"Ave Maria," he said as he closed the door.

Admiral Rosen, after reviewing the design plans that had been delivered by overnight courier, picked up the phone. He called Captain Togant first. After a brief conversation with her, he called the Perth-Amboy Shipyards. The admiral said that the navy would be using the Alameda Naval Shipyards for security reasons. The shipyard supervisor was not happy, but said he understood. That's when the admiral decided to use his okay, from the secretary of the navy, to make an offer.

"According to the GAO, we pay your people and company a retainer each month in case we have to use your services. Would your workers be willing to work alongside the Alameda workers in assembling the sub?"

"I think they would jump at the opportunity, there's not a whole lot of things going on here at the shipyards currently. Is room and board provided?"

"Room, board, transportation and meals. They are expected to be in Alameda, California for at least 10 months."

The man agreed and Admiral Rosen called Captain Togant back. She was happy at the prospect of more workers. It looked as though the new fast attack sub might get done on schedule. Captain Togant did make the demand for a total of 200 workers. The admiral, although sympathetic to her demand, said she would have to do with what she got.

After the admiral spoke to her, he called Naval Military Personnel Center. The admiral needed to make arrangements for a pre-commissioning unit to be established for the USS DIAMONDBACK, SSN-75. The pre-commissioning unit needed to be established by no later than January of next year. The detailer asked about a crew. The admiral's answer was to establish everything for the sub first. Unknown to the admiral, the ship was to be crewed by a very special group of volunteers.

The next day, the secretary of the navy had an emergency meeting with Admiral Rosen. The secretary of the navy informed Admiral Rosen that USS DIAMONDBACK, SSN-75, was now officially a 'Black Book Project.' The secretary of the navy wanted Admiral Rosen to make security tighter around the USS DIAMONDBACK. The secretary of the navy went on to tell the admiral that he was to have a meeting with Vice Admiral Timms.

The admiral was then told, by the secretary of the navy, that enlisted personnel from the USS SEASIDE HEIGHTS that had taken the advancement exams for Fire Technician Guided Missiles, Torpedoman's Mate, Sonar Technician Sound and Electronic Warfare Technician, among other rates, were to have their advancement exam results listed as "PNA." The admiral was a little puzzled by this and cornered the secretary of the navy about this issue.

"Madam secretary, why must I do this to our dedicated personnel who have worked so hard?" asked Theodore.

"Because Phase IV of the test has been completed and all indicators are go. SSN-75 must have an experienced crew aboard when she sets sail for her first mission," replied Brandi Musche.

"Then, am I to assume that these men and women will be rewarded?"

"Yes, with full back pay and immediate advancement upon reporting to SSN-75."

"How am I to know who is to be PNA'ed off of the USS SEASIDE HEIGHTS?"

"Captain Liza Bonner will be hand delivering the list to you today."

"Yes, madam secretary, I will make sure that everything happens."

Admiral Rosen left Brandi's office and drove back to his office. He discovered that Captain Bonner had already been to his office and had dropped off the list. Admiral Rosen looked over the list and took it with him when he went to Naval Military Personnel Center. The admiral met with Vice Admiral Timms, who was in charge of advancement exam results for the navy. After the meeting was over, Vice Admiral Timms, although mad as hell, followed his orders.

When the advancement exam results arrived aboard the USS SEASIDE HEIGHTS, some of the crewmembers became angry. Others were shocked and stunned by the results. One of the angry crewmembers, TM3 Sanchez, went back to his files on past exam results and looked them over one more time.

This was the fifth time in a row that he was PNA'ed. He compared his results with some of the others that kept track of their results. They soon saw a peculiar pattern of the PNA points as compared to those who were advanced. It appeared to some that if they wanted to be advanced in their rates, they should be on a decommissioning sub. They took the results to Andrew.

Andrew reviewed the information carefully and it all correlated towards decommissioning subs. Andrew did his best to quiet them all down, but was only marginally successful. There was still hatred about this advancement exam results. There were some that felt they shouldn't even bother taking the exams next time. Andrew decided to take this matter to the skipper, Lou.

When Andrew presented this matter to Lou, Lou told him to handle it like a commanding officer should handle the matter. This puzzled Andrew at first and then he realized that something was afoot within the navy. Andrew started to get suspicious of all the alleged tests that were being given to the enlisted crew and only a few selected officers.

After Andrew left the captain's cabin, he went to his office and called Naval Military Personnel Center. He wanted to talk to an old friend of his there. This friend was a Limited Duty Officer just like Andrew and they had been in the same class at Pensacola, Florida. When his friend came on the phone, the friend listened to what Andrew had to say. As his friend was about to answer, he looked up and saw Vice Admiral Timms looking at him through the window of his office.

"I'd like to help, but I can't," he said curtly. He then dropped his voice to almost a whisper.

"This phone is being monitored. All I can tell you is 'Black Book Project;' good-bye Andrew," he said hanging up the phone abruptly.

Andrew hung up his phone. He then turned to Shawn and instructed him to have all personnel, who PNA'ed their tests, to meet with him in the aft torpedo room after the sea and anchor detail secured. The next morning Andrew said good-bye to Gary as the ship deployed.

# Chapter 12

As the USS SEASIDE HEIGHTS slipped under the cobalt blue waters of the Pacific Ocean, the sea and anchor detail was secured. When the normal, at sea watch rotations commenced, Shawn gathered everyone that Andrew had asked for in the aft torpedo room. When the last person joined the gathering, Andrew shut the hatch. The noise from the propeller pushing the sub through the water at more than 20 knots was almost deafening. Andrew then opened the hatch again to speak to Shawn.

"Keep a close eye on who comes near here. If anyone asks what we are doing, its training," said Andrew.

"Training, right, sir," said Shawn closing the hatch behind Andrew.

Andrew gathered everyone in a small circle so he could speak to him or her. He almost had to yell to be heard.

"I called my point of contact at NMPC. I believe he was under duress of some kind when he spoke to me," Andrew started.

"He probably thought we were all crazy, right?" asked FT2 Kim Tarsells.

"No, he said three little words to me and then hung up the phone rather abruptly. I was unable to reestablish contact. He said, 'Black Book Project.' Does anyone here not know what a 'Black Book Project' is?"

No hands went up, so Andrew continued.

"Nothing of what we speak about here leaves this torpedo room. Speak to no one about this meeting. Do your jobs to the best of your abilities and take notes. Make sure that these notes are seen by no one and turn them in to me daily. I will keep them for you until the end of the deployment."

He saw all the heads nodding up and down in agreement.

"Dismissed."

After everyone had left the torpedo room, Andrew opened the hatch. He closed the hatch behind himself and looked at Shawn.

"Did anyone come by?" asked Andrew.

"The XO, sir and I don't think he liked my answer."

"I would be curious to know what is the skeleton crew of an SSN?" asked Andrew to the bulkhead in front of him.

"Did you say something, sir?" asked Shawn who had heard exactly what Andrew had said.

"No, just thinking out loud; dismissed."

In the Arizona desert southwest of Phoenix, the Raytheon Company's Missile Test Range was being modified. Three unique structures were being built on the missile test range to test the capabilities of a new breed of TLAM. The TLAM's were being tested against what was called Building A. Building A was a steel and reinforced concrete structure where the outside walls were a minimum of 24-inches thick. The interior walls were at least 12-inches thick of reinforced concrete.

The second building, called Building B, was built the same, however the walls and the bottom floor of the building were reinforced with 12-inches of cinderblock. The structure was three stories high. Buried 20-feet/6 meters below the bottom floor, was a bunker protected by heavy armor plating. The building's roof was made of reinforced concrete and steel that was 18-inches thick. Each floor was 10-inches thick all the way to the bottom floor. The building was designed to simulate a command/control station disguised as an office building. The TLAM was to impact the roof and go as far down as possible before detonating.

The third structure, called Building C, was a simulated armory or other type of munitions storage area. From the outside, the building almost couldn't be seen because it was partially buried. The armory was covered with 12-inches of sand. Under the sand was 12-inches of broken, steel reinforced concrete. Then the roof of the armory was constructed of 24-inches of reinforced cinderblocks along with 8-inches of armor plating.

The TLAM's were being fitted with a new, special nosecone attachment. This attachment was made of Tungsten Carbide and was designed to collapse down on top of the detonator with about an 8-second delay. It was hoped that the 8-second delay before detonation would allow the TLAM to destroy or, at least cripple, a hardened target. When the last TLAM nosecone "hood" was in place, several assembly workers put the last TLAM into the launch tube.

The semi-truck carrying the missiles left the Raytheon missile plant just before sunrise. The semi-truck, along with a security escort, headed to the missile test range. When the semi-truck arrived, the driver set the missile launcher up and left in the security escort vehicle. At the missile test range command center, Bob Devonshire was watching as the last camera was being set up on the simulated armory.

The camera crew left the building and called the command center. A command center representative took the phone call. After placing the receiver back into its cradle on the phone, the command center commander approached Bob. Bob had just completed his cell phone call and put it up in his left shirt pocket.

"Yes, Darrell, what can I do for you?" asked Bob.

"We are ready for launch. The cameras are in place. For safety sake, you will have to shut off your cell phone."

"I understand; we launch in 10 minutes."

Bob turned off his cell phone completely. He walked over to where the rest of the missile command and control operators were located. On two computer screens at the missile command center were constantly changing pictures and views of the modified TLAM. The workers looked at Bob and started smirking, smiling and then outright laughter. After about five minutes, Bob walked over to where Darrell was located and spoke to him.

"Darrell, what the hell is so funny? Is there something on my tie? Is my fly open on my pants? What?" asked Bob.

"No, not exactly. The nosecone assembly reminds everyone of the head of a penis, sir."

"That figures. How long before the video is recovered?"

"A month at maximum."

"Good. Fire when ready on Building A."

"Yes, sir."

Darrell went through the launch sequence. In five minutes, the first TLAM roared downrange. The missile traveled 115 nautical miles in about three minutes. The TLAM impacted the building at 595 knots/684 miles per hour. The building was completely destroyed. Pieces of the roof and supports were flying downrange for almost a nautical mile. When the dust settled, Bob told Darrell to launch on Building B.

That TLAM took the same three-minute flight time with the same results. When the dust had settled, Bob told Darrel to launch on Building C. That TLAM impacted, but with different results. When the small amount of dust settled, Bob turned to Darrell as he turned his cell phone back on.

"Get me that video footage as soon as you can," said Bob.

"Yes, sir," said Darrell as Bob departed the range.

The secretary of the navy accepted the finalized plans for the new sub. She signed off on them and handed the plans over to Admiral Rosen. He returned to his office and prepared to send them out. He looked over his options for shipping them to Alameda, California and decided on an overnight courier. He even paid the extra fees for either Saturday or Sunday delivery. After the courier had picked up the plans, he called Captain Togant.

"Captain Togant, you need to be in your office on both Saturday and Sunday. The plans should arrive no later than Sunday," said Theodore.

"Yes, admiral, I will be waiting for them."

"One other thing, security has been greatly increased on this project. I hope that the dry-dock is covered."

"It is, sir. How much increased security?"

"Four-fold; good-bye."

As she hung up the phone, Ramon entered her office. He had the dry-dock supervisor and the shipyard workers union representative with him. They all sat down in her office.

"Report, Ramon," she said.

"Dry-dock 62 is ready for manufacturing. These two gentlemen have assured me of that fact."

"I'll have the plans by either tomorrow or Sunday at the latest. Either way, be ready to lay the keel at 0400 hours on Monday morning," said Leslie.

"My dry-dock is ready. What about workdays?" asked the supervisor.

"The new sub has to be ready for dock trials by April of next year," she said.

"Which means what for my dry-dock?"

"24 by 7 ops. By the way, security has been increased four-fold."

"Is the government really going to pay my shipyard union workers for seven days a week?" asked the union representative.

"Yes."

"We need 200 workers. Those 140 we will have are going to get tired real quick," said the union representative.

"We have to use what we get. We get 140 workers, that's it," said Leslie, rather irritably.

"I'll tell the workers to be ready on Monday morning at 0400 hours."

"Dismissed."

Monday morning came almost too soon for the shipyard workers. At 0400 hours, Pacific Standard Time, the keel was laid. After all the shipyard workers were through taking pictures and celebrating, Captain Togant confiscated the photos for security reasons. She told the workers that all the pictures would be returned when the government cleared them.

She locked the cameras and related equipment into her safe in her office. She then opened the logbook for the ship. She entered the date and time the keel was laid for the first official log entry. When the yard workers started moving around in the dry-dock, she went to her office. She called Admiral Rosen.

"Admiral Rosen, we just laid the keel for SSN-75 about three hours ago," said Leslie.

"Excellent. Keep me informed of her progress."

"Yes, admiral."

It took nearly three weeks of sifting through the rubble of the buildings to find the cameras. Once the cameras were located, Darrell sent them immediately to Bob. Bob used his computer to retrieve the video footage after he had plugged into the data and video ports on the outside of the camera's casing. The casing was made of the same indestructible material that aircraft flight recorders were made. When the last minute of video footage from the last missile hit was downloaded into his computer, he sent the cameras to maintenance for repairs and repackaging.

Bob went to work on the video footage. Since it was recorded at normal time and speed, the damage occurred quickly. He took the footage from Building A and had the computer clean it up. When he could see clear images, without sound, he had the computer make a second copy of the images at a slower rate of play.

Bob smiled as he saw, on the slower rate of play images, the warhead completely penetrate the exterior wall. Upon penetrating this wall, broken concrete and some of the steel support beams punctured the missile's fuel tank. The spilling fuel immediately caught fire and quickly engulfed the area in flames. A half second later, the warhead penetrated an interior wall that was 12-inches thick.

This wall was to represent an interior office wall of a disguised command/control center. Bob could see that the penetrater "hood" was collapsing onto the detonator. When the cruise missile's warhead had penetrated this wall, being carried by its own momentum only, it struck the second, corner-to-corner interior wall, detonating.

The explosion leveled the structure. Pieces of broken concrete and steel could be seen flying downrange up to 1km. The backside of the building was blown out. More pieces of concrete, steel and sand were sent flying into the air. There was a wall of flames that came out of the sides and roof of the building.

Bob was impressed with the heavy, collateral damage. It meant that there would be no survivors; target destroyed. Bob quickly made two copies; one for Commander Hinton-Smith and one for the Board of Directors. Bob went to work on Building B's footage next.

The results were the same as for Building A. The warhead went off inside what would have been the lobby area. There was a large shockwave and flames from the burning missile fuel. Bob was impressed that the missile penetrated the roof and went through two more floors before going off. Bob turned his attention to the buried bunker.

He could see the shockwave hit the bunker. There was some smoke and flames inside. However, the bunker appeared to be intact. Bob grabbed his cell phone and called Darrell on his cell phone.

"This is Darrell."

"Darrell, Bob. What was the condition of the bunker in Building B when your team arrived there to retrieve the cameras?"

"Destroyed."

"Equipment?"

"Non-functional."

"In other words, no survivors."

"Yes, Bob. It took my guys four extra days with heavy equipment to clear the rubble out of the collapsed tunnels to get your cameras."

"Thank you, Darrell; good-bye," said Bob, hanging up the phone.

Bob made two copies of this footage as well before going on with cleaning up the final bit of video footage.

Bob put his computer to work cleaning up the images. The images were vastly different. It showed the missile's impact. A few second later, the ground began swelling. The ground continued to swell until it was several times the size of the building square footage wise. The swelling continued for another second or so and then the building collapsed. Bob thought that maybe this swelling of the ground was from an implosion. Bob made two copies of this footage as well. He then called Darrell again before typing up his report and recommendations.

"Yes, Bob, what is now?" asked Darrell.

"What would you estimate the size and depth of the hole is where Building C was standing?"

"About 60 feet/20 meters in depth and 30 feet/10 meters larger than the square footage of the building as made."

"Thank you; good-bye," said Bob as he sent his report and recommendations off to the Board of Directors. He made sure that he included the slower copy video footage so that the Board of Directors could see it for themselves. When this was completed, he went home.

Cruising in the Indian Ocean, the USS SEASIDE HEIGHTS was pulling into the naval base at Diego Garcia. When the sea and anchor detail had been secured, Shawn took the weapons report to the captain who was in his captain's cabin. Earlier in the deployment, Commander Staggs had received one of the weekly reports that indicated Commander Hinton-Smith wanted to see the skeleton crew list for an SSN.

Commander Staggs made a copy of the list that Andrew had asked for and had set the list down, folded into thirds, on his desktop. When Shawn came in to deliver the weekly report along with the current weapons inventory, Commander Staggs looked at Shawn. He then started tapping his left index finger on the folded up piece of paper.

Shawn looked down and saw the folded up piece of paper. The piece of paper was sitting on top of a stack of messages and request forms. Shawn looked up at Lou and nodded his head up and down as he picked up the piece of paper. Shawn left the captain's cabin and returned to the weapons department office. He entered the office and opened the piece of paper up, placing it into the other paperwork. Shawn then went about doing his administrative duties when Andrew entered.

"Did you give the skipper his report?" asked Andrew.

"Yes, sir. I also picked up out return request forms and message traffic," said Shawn.

"Good."

Andrew sat down in his chair at his desk and started going through the paperwork. Andrew got down to the list and looked it over and gasped. He then looked at Shawn.

"How did you get this? It says 'Command Eyes Only'?"

Shawn was about to be found out as the captain's stoolpigeon, so he thought quickly on his answer.

"When I took the weapons department report to the captain, sir, I looked down on his desktop. There was the list you had asked for when we got underway. I made a copy of it and returned it before he knew it was gone," said Shawn, lying and trying to remain calm.

"Good thinking and thank you," said Andrew.

"You're welcome, sir. Will there be anything else?"

"No, go on out on liberty call."

"Yes, sir."

At Boeing's headquarters in Seattle, Washington, Frank was in a deep meeting with the Board of Directors. When the meeting was about over, Frank called Bruce. Bruce's secretary went out into the warehouse that served as research and development labs. The warehouse was small, dank and poorly lighted.

During the winter months, occasional cold drafts would come through, chilling one to the bone. The warehouse used to make and store parts for the B-29 bombers of World War II. Bruce turned off the lights and entered what used to be the warehouse supervisor's office. He closed the door and grabbed the receiver.

"Hello?" asked Bruce.

"Bruce, this is Frank. I'm putting you on conference call with the Board," said Frank.

"Okay."

There was a loud click and then Bruce heard numerous voices. Bruce waited for the questioning to begin.

"How did you get those two HARPOON's?" asked the Chief Security Officer David Reins.

"I called the missile storehouse in Manhattan, Kansas. Asked for them and their launch codes for research purposes."

"How much would one of those modified missiles cost?" asked the Chief Financial Officer Gary Uligopi.

"I don't know. When the missiles were delivered to my research and development facility here in Tacoma, Washington, myself and 8 other dedicated, hand-picked personnel modified the missiles by hand."

"Good Lord, man, you made those missiles by hand?!" exclaimed Karla Dupre.

"Yes madam, we did assemble those missiles by hand. It meant very long and hard hours for some."

"Okay, well, we've all seen the wonderful video footage that you sent to us. The Board of Directors wants to present your modified HARPOON missiles as the HARPOON Block-V to the government. Be watching and listening to the news tomorrow. Also, keep an eye on the stock market," said Karla Dupre.

"Yes, madam."

"I want you to hand over the design plans to the missile makers in Missouri by close of business tomorrow," said Karen Delphian.

"Okay. But my people want something tangible in return for their hard work."

"Thank you, Bruce, that will be all for now," said Frank as he hung up the phone. Bruce hung up the phone and went home himself.

The next morning Bruce watched the press conference on his successful experiments. The press conference showed the rough estimates of the new missile's capabilities for security reasons. There was even some of the video footage of the missile hitting the target ship on the TV.

When the press conference was over, Bruce watched Boeing's stock take off with an opening price of $156.87 a share. This was despite a hard drop in price the day before of more than $10.00 a share. The stock soared to $199.00 a share by the closing bell on Wall Street. This $199.00 a share was the company's fifth largest in Wall Street history.

For Bruce, it meant that the stockholders were very happy with the new product's capabilities. He went to work and gladly handed over the design plans to the Missouri facility. As he was leaving the warehouse, one of the hand picked personnel came up to him.

"Did the Board like our modifications?" he asked.

"Yes, they did. I also made sure that I put in a request for a bonus for all of us who worked on the missile modifications."

"How did that go over?"

"Real well. The stockholders pushed the stock price very high. I believe it was the fifth largest in the company's history."

"Well, I'm looking forward to the bonus; good-night."

The next morning, when Bruce arrived at work, he found all of his staff lined up around a table. At the center of the table was a cake, two sets of multi-colored balloons and lighted candles on the cake. Bruce looked at the writing on the cake. It simply read, "Congratulations-2,400!" That's when Frank stepped forward to shake Bruce's left hand. Frank then set down his briefcase on the tabletop.

"The U.S. Government ordered 2,400 of the new HARPOON's at 1.9 million dollars each. For each one delivered, your team and you will receive increased funding for research and development and bonuses."

"Thank you, Frank."

"It seemed the least that we as the executives could do for your personnel. Here are the first bonus checks," said Frank as he opened up his briefcase.

Frank had everyone who had worked on the project stood around him to get their bonus checks. When the last check was handed out, Frank took a piece of cake with him as he headed off to his usual morning meetings. Bruce and the rest of the staff celebrated. As Frank was leaving, Bruce followed him outside to talk to Frank.

"You said the U.S. Government purchased those missiles. What about the other countries we sell those missiles to?" asked Bruce.

"We are in contract negotiations with those foreign governments. There's a lot of red tape. You're a forward thinking man; someday you'll have my job," said Frank as he stepped into his car and drove off.

"Not on your life," said Bruce to no one. He then went back inside of the warehouse.

In Washington, D.C., the ambassador to the U.N., who represented what little of the Somalian government there was, was waiting to speak to the newly elected female President of the United States. When the person ahead of him had left, the President's press secretary showed the ambassador into the Oval Office. The ambassador and the President shook hands. The President then pointed to a chair to the ambassador's right to sit in. When the ambassador had sat down, the President spoke.

"Back again for your usual request for help Alamir?" she asked.

"Yes. My country can no longer take the warlords shooting it out in the streets and the pirates taking their fair share. The economic U.N. sanctions because of those acts are killing my people."

"We tried to help your country out a few years ago. Your government military forces and the warlord military forces caused many deaths of my military personnel. In fact, your country, I think, enjoys killing U.N. aid workers."

"The number of deaths has been dropping."

"That's because you're running out of bodies."

The ambassador thought about the statement for a minute and then pulled out the last card in the deck.

"My country has many things to offer your country."

"Like what? Sand? Desert?"

"Oil, Madam President. My country, if the U.S. helps, would be willing to sell you our oil for the next five years at or below $75.00 a barrel. If the market prices drop, we will drop our prices to 25% below OPEC prices. The money gained would be used for rebuilding my country. We also offer diamonds, rubies, sapphires, gold, silver and platinum."

"So, what's the take for you?"

"Tourism, Madam President. We have many tourist attractions in my country. Their money would be used to improve ports for ships, build roads, schools and hospitals as well as improving sanitation standards."

"What about those pirates who attack ships?"

"Kill them, Madam President. They are nothing but greedy people who would not hesitate to kill their own if there was any profit in it for them."

"You sound sincere. Can I think about your generous offer?"

"Yes, Madam President and thank you for your time."

"Thank you, ambassador Alamir."

When the ambassador had departed, the President turned on the daily news. Gas prices were at new record highs. $4.999 a gallon for regular unleaded was the norm across the U.S. Diesel fuel was even more expensive, coming in at $5.459 a gallon. Jet fuel, fuel oil and other fuels were at new record highs. She then turned on the business news. Crude oil, from OPEC members, was selling at over $150.00 a barrel. She then turned off the TV and picked up the phone.

The phone started ringing at the other end. It rang a few more times before a familiar voice at the other end answered. The voice was familiar not only to her but most of the rest of the nation. When the person at the other end of the phone saw, on the Caller ID®, who was calling, he swore before picking up the receiver.

"Yes, Madam President, what can I do for you?" he asked.

"I need some advice."

"I'm not sure you want my advice. You know, Iraq didn't go so well for me."

"I know, sir. However, what would you do if a country offered you their oil supplies starting at about 48% below current market prices? Then, lets add to that offer, this same country will be willing, for the next five years anyways, to sell their oil to you at 25% below whatever OPEC is selling their oil for?"

"Is this other country an OPEC member?"

"No."

"What do they want in return?"

"A little law enforcement help."

"I would say go for it. For me, as the manufacturer of fuels, etc., a 48% drop in oil price would mean a 55% drop in the price of a gallon of fuel over the period of a year. With cheaper oil, the price will continue to drop even further. This will probably stimulate the economy in many ways. People will want to travel, etc."

"Thank you for your advice," she said, hanging up the phone.

"And I can maintain my comfortable profit margin of 17 billion dollars," he said to no one.

# Chapter 13

The next few weeks went by quickly for the President. One of the last meetings she had was with the secretary of defense. After a few hours of discussion, a multi-level plan was put together. Since Iraq troops were now home, morale was high among the military personnel. The President wanted a way to take care of the problems with Somalia and do it with style. When the secretary of defense had left, the President went to the last meeting of that week.

The secretary of defense went back to his office. When he arrived, he walked into his private office. He sat down at his desk and opened up his bottom, left hand drawer. He grabbed a file folder that was towards the back and set it down on his desktop. He opened up the file to see when the last intelligence report was written; 05/2006. He read the report and determined only one plan of action would work. He called the secretary of the Air Force.

"Yes, sir, what can I do for you?" he asked.

"How many planes could you spare for continuous bombing for eight to, possibly, 14 days?"

"Seven squadrons of B-52H's, six squadrons of B-1B's and 4four squadrons of B-2's. But, that would mean I would need a place for continuous refueling, repairing and rearming of my aircraft. Do you know where I can do that?"

"Yes, sir, I do. Start pre-staging your equipment and manpower on Diego Garcia," said the defense secretary, trying to hang-up the phone.

"Mr. Secretary, who the hell are we going to bomb for that long?"

"Somalia and possibly Iran," he said, finally hanging up the phone.

The secretary of defense then called the secretary of the Army. She said she could provide as many troops and equipment as needed. She also added that she had some new battlefield equipment that she wanted to try out in a combat zone. The secretary of the Marine Corps said just about the same thing. The secretary of the Navy was only too happy to involve manpower and equipment. The secretary of the defense put the phone down and started typing up the plans for the attack. When the plans were completed, he called the President.

Next came the endless hours of meetings with all the branches of service's secretaries. After many hours of discussion and compromises, the plans were finalized. When the finalized plans were put into a final report, the secretary of the Army spoke first.

"I don't want my troops in the Somalian Desert during the summer. No attacks from the middle part of April through September," she said.

"Agreed. What about November through February?" proposed the secretary of the Air Force.

"November would be fine. That gives me plenty of time to mass troops and equipment," said the secretary of the defense.

"Agreed. Secretary of the Navy, what about your people?" asked the secretary of the Army.

"I can provide six complete aircraft carrier battle groups, five squadrons of submarines, cruise missiles and planes," she said.

"Good. If the President approves of this plan, I will request for continuous bombings, cruise missile attacks and shelling for up to 14 days before our troops move in," said the secretary of defense.

"What is the current intelligence information?" asked the secretary of the Navy.

"Last update was 05/2006, we're on our own on this one. Do we know of any U.S. friendly countries we could use to mass troops and equipment?"

"I believe the French have control of Somalia's neighbors to the south. Perhaps they will allow us to mass our equipment and personnel there," replied the secretary of the Army.

"I also want a plan of action to eliminate those pirates and their base of operations; no survivors. What do you have, Madam Secretary of the Navy, that might be able to do the job?"

"I have a new ship coming off the assembly line in April of next year that will do the job nicely."

"Good. How many cruise missiles do we have, combined?"

"3,814 between myself and the Air Force," replied the secretary of the Navy.

"Plan on using them all. Can the HARPOON be used against a land target?"

"Yes. However, the HARPOON is an anti-ship missile, not a land attack missile. I have TOMAHAWK's for that purpose."

"How many HARPOON's do you have in your inventory?"

"2,300, sir."

"Plan on using all of them as well."

"Yes, sir."

The secretary of defense's cell phone started ringing. He looked at the Caller ID®; the White House. He answered the cell phone. The President wanted to see him at the White House now. He hung up the phone and dismissed everyone. He then drove over to the White House with the battle plans. He entered the Oval Office as the President swung around in her chair. She stood up and dropped a set of photos down on the outer edge of her desk.

"What are those?" she asked, harshly. Since she already knew the answer, she wanted to see if she was going to be lied to.

The secretary of defense picked up the photos, looked through all of them and then set them back down on the desktop.

"The first five photos appear to be Zelzal 3-D missiles."

"What is their official classification?"

"They are officially classified as a medium range ballistic missile, also known as an MRBM."

"Who's got those in their inventory?"

"The North Koreans, Iranians and at least 10 other smaller countries."

"How many do the North Koreans have?"

"500 that we know of, maybe more."

"How many do the Iranians have?"

"Unknown. Perhaps 300+. I have limited intelligence information on them."

"What is its range and payload?"

"Approximately 1,350 nautical miles and it carries a 2,000 pound/1,000 kilogram high explosive payload."

"Could it carry a nuclear warhead?"

"If the Iranians had built a nuclear weapon, it is capable of carrying a 500-kiloton, tactical nuclear warhead. Are you even going to look at the battle plans?"

"Maybe later. Could that missile hit Israel or her neighbors?"

"Yes. In fact, that MRBM could hit Egypt, Eastern Chad, Turkey and Southern Europe among other places."

"Could it hit Somalia?"

"No, out of range. Besides, the Iranians and the Somalians are not exactly friends at this time."

"Okay. What about Diego Garcia?"

"Possibly."

"What about those other photos?"

"Those other photos appear to be Israeli JERICHO-II-D and JERICHO III-A missiles. They carry a 2,000-pound/1,000-kilogram high explosive payload, or they could carry chemical/biological payloads as well. The missiles have a range of between 950 to 1,050 nautical miles making them an IRBM or an Intermediate Range Ballistic Missile."

"Can those JERICHO's carry a nuclear warhead?"

"Yes, the Israeli's do have several 500-kiloton, low yield, tactical nuclear warheads. The Israeli's also have weapons of mass destruction."

"Could the Israeli's park a JERICHO in Tehran?"

"Yes. However, Tehran would be on the very outer range of the JERICHO."

"Worse case scenario. The Iranians launch an all out assault on Israel and Israel is hit VERY BADLY, then what?"

"I feel sorry for the Iranians, poor bastards. Israel wouldn't hesitate to fire everything in their arsenal capable of hitting Iran. Unfortunately, I strongly suspect that the Israeli's would use their nuclear arsenal in return."

"Okay. Can tactical nuclear warheads be used against civilians?"

"No, Madam President, that is against Geneva Convention."

"Thank you; dismissed."

"Yes, Madam."

As the secretary of defense left the Oval Office, he looked around the hallway and shook his head in disbelief. He stepped outside into his car and drove off. When he arrived at his office, his secretary handed him the phone. He looked down at his watch; only an hour had elapsed since he had left the White House.

"Hello?" he asked.

"I just finished scanning over your proposal. Put it into action now."

"Yes, Madam President," he said hanging up the phone.

An hour later, the Iranian ambassador to the embassy in Washington, D.C., was sitting in the Oval Office with the President. She stared at him directly when she spoke. This made the man a little uncomfortable.

"Tell your government leader, Ahmadenijad, that if he fires on Israel with his Zelzal 3-D MRBM's, the consequences could be ugly."

"You know that we, as Iranians, are sworn to destroy Israel at any cost."

"Then consider the words of the Koran 9:11."

"Words well put, Madam President."

"Tell Ahmadenijad that Israel has nuclear weapons and won't hesitate to use them in retaliation. My predecessor talked the Israeli's out of hitting

Baghdad with those nuclear weapons in 1991, but I don't think I could persuade the Israeli's not use them."

"The Israeli's are crazy, not stupid. There are safeguards, right?" he said, faking a smile with a dash of concern in the back of his mind.

"In my country, there are many safeguards on the use of nuclear weapons both tactical and strategic. In Israel, there are only two, the prime minister and General Malik. The world would hardly condone such a retaliation considering the attacker."

"I will let my government leaders know what you have told me. Thank you, Madam President, for inviting me here to express your concerns."

"You're welcome," she said as he left.

In the Indian Ocean, the USS SEASIDE HEIGHTS had received her daily message traffic from the floating wire. Once the outgoing daily message traffic had been transmitted, the floating wire was retrieved. The lengthy process of decoding the messages began. When the last message was decoded, CW02 Andrews began disseminating the messages out to the various departments.

One of those messages was an emergency message to Andrew from the American Red Cross. Commander Staggs was the first one to review the message and initial off on it. He called the Chaplain to have him speak to Andrew about the message.

The Chaplain, who thoroughly hated Andrew to begin with, begrudgingly said he would speak to Andrew about the message. The Chaplain returned to his office with the message and closed the door. He sat down at his desk and called the Weapons Department office first.

"Shawn, this is the Chaplain, is Commander Hinton-Smith there?" he asked as his blood began to boil.

"Negative, sir. He is in Fire Control at 6624."

"Thank you."

The Chaplain called Fire Control next.

"Is Commander Hinton-Smith there?"

"Yes, one moment," said MTC Snowden.

MTC Snowden handed Andrew the receiver.

"Yes, Lieutenant Sullivan, what can I do for you?"

"Come to my office. I received an AMCROSS message for you."

"Yes, sir," said Andrew as he handed MTC Snowden back the receiver.

"Is everything okay, sir?" asked MTC Snowden.

"I think so. You will have to excuse me."

"Yes, sir."

Andrew showed up in the Chaplain's office a few minutes later. Mark handed him the AMCROSS message. Andrew read it and nodded his head. Mark looked at him.

"Was this unexpected, commander?" asked Mark.

"No, it was not unexpected. In fact, it was a distinct possibility that this even could occur while I was deployed. Could I write a reply, Mark?"

"Of course," said Mark, handing Andrew a pen and a message pad.

Andrew wrote something down and handed the pad back to Mark. Mark looked over the reply and handed the reply to his Religious Programming Specialist First-Class Petty Officer Downs. Mark waited until the man had left before speaking.

"I don't like you or your kind very much, however, if there is anything I can do for you, let me know."

"I am unfamiliar with the Native American customs of pre-death and then the actual burial rights thereafter."

"I will try to get you some information, then. What Native American nation is he a member of?"

"The Navajo, I believe."

"I will try and get some information for you then. Have a good day," said Mark.

"Thank you," said Andrew as he left the Chaplain's office.

The next morning, Admiral Rosen called Leslie for an update on SSN-75. After receiving the update, he typed up a set of orders modification to be sent out to the USS SEASIDE HEIGHTS on the next outgoing message transmissions. He then sat back down typing up his orders to start massing ships, weapons and aircraft for the "Law Enforcement" action that had been approved by the Commander-In-Chief herself.

Early the next morning, the USS SEASIDE HEIGHTS extended her floating wire to receive her daily message traffic. When the incoming message traffic was completely downloaded, outgoing messages were transmitted. Once this was completed, the floating wire was retrieved. The USS SEASIDE HEIGHTS continued on her patrol in the middle of the Indian Ocean. The message traffic was decoded and then sent out to the various departments.

The orders modification message went directly to the captain. After he read the message, he handed the message to the XO. He read the message and handed the message back to the captain.

"How the hell does Admiral Rosen think we can do this?" asked the XO.

"I don't know, XO," replied Lou as he looked at the ship's status.

The sub was cruising at 600 feet/200 meters in depth at a speed of 10 knots. The sub's course was 020. The captain called for CW02 Andrews. She arrived with a notepad and pen ready to take down a message. The captain gave her the reply to Admiral Rosen's new orders. When this was completed, he went to the chart room. QM1 Tim Keller was on duty.

"Good morning, skipper, what can I do for you?" he asked.

"How far are we from the country of Somalia?"

"Their coastline or their alleged territorial waters?"

"Their alleged territorial waters."

Tim pulled out a calculator and looked over some charts that he had pulled out earlier during the week. He started punching in numbers and in a few minutes, he had an answer for Lou.

"26 hours at flank speed on a course of 265."

"Thank you."

Lou left the chart room and returned to the bridge. He then reached up and grabbed the receiver.

"Sonar, Conn," he said.

"Sonar, aye," said STSSN Jon Costillo.

"Surface contacts?"

"Eight all together. Six friendly and two unknown's."

"What classifications do you have for the two unknown's?"

"The computer is still chewing on the noises, but I am confident that there is one cargo carrier and one cruise ship up there."

"Sub-surface contacts?"

"Six all together. Three friendly, two NATO and one unknown."

"What classification did you give the unknown?"

"I believe I had brief contact with an AKULA-II Improved, but the computer is still chewing on that noise as well."

"Course and speed?"

"Course 105 at a speed of 12 knots. I had her a depth of 1,000 feet/300 meters."

"Conn, aye."

He switched channels to Radio.

"Radio, Conn."

"Radio, aye," said CW02 Andrews.

"Be prepared to deploy the radio masts when I surface the ship. Get that message I gave to you earlier off immediately."

"Yes, sir."

"Diving officer, surface the ship! Set the engines to three knots when the ship gets to the surface," said Lou as he put up the receiver.

"Aye, sir."

The USS SEASIDE HEIGHTS broke the surface a few minutes later. When the ship's speed had been reduced to three knots, the radio masts were deployed. CW02 Andrews transmitted all messages that had been received up to that point. When the last message had been transmitted, she ordered the radio masts secured. When the radio masts were secured, the ship was ready to dive.

"Diving officer, make your depth 1,275 feet/425 meters. Set a course of 265 at flank speed."

"Aye, sir."

"XO, all officer's meeting in the wardroom right now."

"Aye, sir. Chief of the Boat, you have the Conn."

"Aye, sir," replied the master chief.

The wardroom was full when Andrew arrived. He stood in the back as Lou gave the briefing. When the briefing was completed, Lou pulled Andrew aside.

"You're going to be on watch when we enter their alleged territorial waters; don't get us killed."

"Aye, sir. Then am I to assume that you want the ship rigged for silent running?"

"Extreme silent running. We don't know what their capabilities are."

"Aye, sir."

In Washington D.C., the President was having her second meeting with the Somalian ambassador. This meeting was taking place under heavy security. The President laid down the plans for the Somalian government and what to do with the civilian population. After listening to the plan, the ambassador spoke.

"It would appear that my people have about 13 months before you attack to get into the hills as you called it," he said.

"Yes, I need the time to mass my troops in your southern neighbor's backyard."

"I'm looking forward to seeing your troops once again and to reestablishing my government with good people."

"Like wise," she said as they both left the high security building.

The sun was beginning to rise on the Somalian coast. The port city and capital of Somalia, Mogadishu, was waking up. Fishing trawlers were heading out to sea to catch fish for the markets to sell. There were also several KILO class, diesel/electric submarines heading out to sea for their patrols. These subs, owned by the Somalian government for a number of years, were crewed by men loyal to the five major warlords.

These subs submerged behind the fishing fleet and went in different directions. Today these subs were to be joined by a VICTOR-III SSN. This SSN was purchased with the proceeds from the bounty taken by the pirates who commandeered hapless merchant ships who strayed too close to the Somalian shoreline.

The VICTOR-III was going on her first patrol by herself. Her assigned patrol area was the deeper water off the Somalian coast near the boundary waters with International waters. The SSN cruised on past where the KILO's had submerged before submerging herself to 600 feet/200 meters. Her captain set a new course of 010 at a speed of 10 knots.

Following the VICTOR-III SSN out to sea was another sub that the Somalian government had purchased. Little did anyone know that the Somalian government had purchased a refurbished Delta-IV class SSBN. Again crewed by warlord loyalists, the missile bays had been modified to fire land attack cruise missiles of the first generation from the Soviet Union as well as anti-ship missiles, which were also first generation Soviet Union made.

This older ship had added extra torpedo tubes and more underwater mine capabilities. This was the sub's first training mission in anti-submarine warfare. As the daybreak turned into daylight, the SSBN slipped under the water heading almost due east on a course of 080.

The USS SEASIDE HEIGHTS was still down in the deep depths at flank speed when Andrew came on watch. He looked at where the ship was located. He noticed that, within the hour, the sub would be entering the alleged territorial waters of the country of Somalia. As the minutes ticked by, there were two KILO's on patrol of the drop off point from shallow water to very deep water.

The KILO's were doing about the same speed and since they were making a lot of noise in the water, they missed the USS SEASIDE HEIGHTS pass almost directly underneath them two thermal layers down. It was then that Andrew ordered the sub rigged for extreme silent running and the engines were slowed down to three knots.

At three knots, the USS SEASIDE HEIGHTS was virtually undetectable. Andrew reviewed on the charts where the thermal layers were located. Andrew had the diving officer decrease the depth of the sub slowly so that the sub could rise towards the upper thermal layer silently. The ballast tanks were emptied slightly. When the sub penetrated the first thermal layer at about 450 feet/150 meters, Andrew had the TOW array deployed. When the array was deployed, Andrew started watching the clock tick off the minutes.

STSSN Costillo and STS2 (SS) Elaine Hudson were watching their respective scope displays. STSSN Costillo was assigned to the North Center and Amidships scopes while STS2 (SS) Hudson was assigned to the South Center and TOW array. Nothing but background noise was being picked up until around 1000 hours. STSSN Costillo picked up the propeller noises of the fishing fleet. The noises were faint, which meant the ships were far away. When he was able to determine the correct bearing, course and speed, he called the bridge.

"Conn, Sonar," he said.

Andrew reached up and grabbed the receiver.

"Conn, aye," he replied.

"Three surface contacts, sir. Bearing 350 on a course of 125 at an estimated speed of 7 knots."

"What do you make of them?"

"Fishing trawlers, I believe, sir."

"Keep an eye on them. Keep listening as well; I have a funny feeling that we're being watched. "

"Sonar, aye."

Jon kept track on the fishing fleet until he got off watch. The relief watch monitored the fishing fleet. After dark, the 0000-0400 watch came on shift. The fishing fleet had gone home by then, so the only noises out there for their shift was civilian traffic. STS1 (SS/SW/AW) Ken Karlsen was able to correctly classify a VLCC civilian shift and a cargo carrier of some kind. As he went back to monitoring his North Center, STS1 (SS/SW/AW) Gladis Harpose detected one of the KILO's.

She called the bridge only after she had confirmation from the sonar suite computer. The computer told Gladis that the noise was indeed from a KILO class diesel/electric submarine with a hull identification of SS-808. She listened for a few more minutes to obtain the correct bearing, course and speed. She then called the bridge.

"Conn, Sonar," she said.

"Conn, aye," said the XO who was serving as Officer of the Deck.

"Submerged contact bearing 210, depth 150 feet/50 meters at a speed of 10 knots."

"Course?"

"070, sir."

"Classification?"

"KILO Class, diesel/electric. According to the sonar computer, SS-808."

"Conn, aye. Weapons Control, Conn," said the XO.

"Weapons Control, aye," said FT1 (SS/SW) Kyle Elliot.

"Hostile sub-surface contact, lock a shooting solution into the computer and keep it up-to-date. Place tubes 5 and 6 on stand-by."

"Aye, sir. Did you want me to flood the tubes and open the outer doors?"

"Negative. Warning White, Weapons Tight."

"Aye, sir."

Barely an hour later, the relief watch detected another KILO class diesel/electric sub. The propeller noise was sent through the sonar suite computer. The computer identified the noise as belonging to SS-813. As the day wore on, sonar was keeping track of all six KILO class diesel/electric subs. When the captain had prepared a message about the subs, he broke off contact during the early evening. He headed out into International waters to radio the intelligence report to Admiral Rosen. Little did they know that the sonar crew of the VICTOR-III SSN had momentarily detected their high-speed takeoff.

The sonar operator looked at his scope before he lost the noise in the trench going out into International waters. He looked over the sound recording and made a copy of it on a tape recorder. He took the recording to the bridge. The captain was looking over the charts when the young man arrived. The sonar operator stood to the left of the captain and the Soviet naval officer who was training them all. He set the tape recorder down on the chart table.

"Yes, what is it?" asked the captain.

"Captain, I had brief contact with a submerged, unknown target."

"What type of submerged, unknown target?" asked the captain.

"A high-speed, deep diving one. The unknown target was last on a course of 070 at a speed of I estimate more than 20 knots."

"How long did you have contact?"

"About 36 seconds, sir. I completely lost the noise when the unknown target dove down two thermals below us."

"Did you make a recording of the noise?"

"Yes, I did, sir," he replied as he pressed the PLAY button on the tape recorder so that all could hear the noise.

"Captain, I was in the Soviet navy for over 20 years. That noise belongs to an American LOS ANGELES class nuclear powered fast attack sub," said the Soviet training officer.

"An American, eh? What are they doing inside of our territorial waters?" asked the captain to the Soviet training officer.

"I don't know, but we must surface the ship and radio this information in to your admiral."

"Yes, of course. Are the scopes clear?"

"Yes, sir. With the exception of our own ships, no one else is out here."

"Then surface the ship and deploy the radio masts."

"Yes, captain," replied the duty diving officer.

The sub surfaced and radioed the information in to the admiral. The admiral immediately told the fleet captain of the Somalian navy to send out two KRIVAK-II's and two KIROV's to the area to investigate. The admiral left further instructions that the American sub was not to be harmed in any manner. All the admiral wanted was a good tracking on the intruder. The fleet captain agreed to the admiral's orders and at first light, the four ships left the piers.

# Chapter 14

After delivering the intelligence report to Admiral Rosen, via the chain of command, the USS SEASIDE HEIGHTS slipped back into the depths around 0100 hours. She returned to her patrol area and began her newest patrol. The TOW array was deployed and the waiting game began. The scopes were all clear for hours before the first two ships were detected at long range.

"Conn, Sonar," said STS1 (SS/SW/AW) Gladis Harpose.

"Conn, aye," replied Lou.

"Two surface contacts bearing 245."

"Speed and course?"

"Course 120 at 12 knots."

"Distance?"

"35,500 yards/11,834 meters and closing."

"Classification?"

"Not definitive yet, the computer is still chewing on the noise."

"Best guess, then."

"KRIVAK-II's, sir."

"Conn, aye. Conn, Weapons Control," said Lou.

"Weapons Control, aye," replied MT2 Lance.

"Hostile surface targets bearing 245, speed 12 knots estimated, course 120. Lock a shooting solution into the computer. Place tubes 1 and 2 on standby; warning white, weapons tight."

"Aye, sir."

A few minutes later, the sonar computer confirmed that the propeller noise belonged to a KRIVAK-II. The computer also stated it had detected another set of propeller noises in the same area, but the noise signal was too weak for classification. Gladis notified the captain about the computer's confirmation of the Krivak-II's. As she went back to listening to her scopes, STS3 (SS) Dave Davidson detected the two KIROV's.

"Conn, Sonar," he said.

"Conn, aye," said Lou.

"Two more surface contacts, sir."

"Bearing and course?"

"Bearing 315, course 105."

"Distance and speed?"

"39,500 yards/13,167 meters estimated speed of 10 knots."

"Do you have a definitive classification?"

"Yes, sir, KIROV."

"Conn, aye. Conn, Weapons Control."

"Weapons Control, aye."

"Two more hostile surface targets bearing 315, at an estimated 10 knots of speed on a course of 105. Place tubes 3 and 4 on standby; warning white, weapons tight."

"Aye, sir."

"Lots of activity today, eh, skipper?" commented the XO.

"So it would appear. XO, all officers meeting in the wardroom. The weapons officer will give the briefing."

"Aye, sir."

Fifteen minutes later, Andrew was standing in front of the other officers in the wardroom. Lou stood up and spoke to the officers.

"Commander Hinton-Smith will conduct this briefing. Commander Hinton-Smith," said Lou.

"Thank you, Commander Staggs. The Somalian government appears to have some interesting ships in their arsenal. They appear to have at least six KILO diesel/electric subs. They have at least two KRIVAK-II and two KIROV class surface ships. These surface ships are first and second generation, nuclear powered, ships that are anti-submarine, anti-ship and anti-aircraft capable."

"Are these ships still in the Soviet navy?" asked the 1st Lieutenant LTJG Lisa Aiken.

"No, the ships were pulled from service in 1990 due to their inability of weapons upgrades. The Soviets now have third generation versions of these ships."

"When did these ships see service?" asked CW02 Andrews.

"From 1960 to 1990. They're pre- and post-Vietnam era ships. The KILO subs can only fire 533-millimeter weapons so they are not that much of a threat to us. The ships are also restricted to 533-millimeter weapons.

"Thank you commander; dismissed."

The sonar operators aboard the VICTOR-III were about to enter the trench that marked the alleged territorial waters of Somalia. Once the sub entered the trench, she was unaware that the USS SEASIDE HEIGHTS was in the same trench. The sonar operators aboard the USS SEASIDE HEIGHTS detected the VICTOR-III SSN first. STSN Jon Costillo was on duty in the South Center when he detected the other sub.

The amidships sonar picked up the propeller noise. At first Jon thought it was the SEASIDE HEIGHTS' own propeller noise bouncing off the canyon walls that made up the trench. Jon shook his head a few times and then pressed the "RECORD" button on the recorder in the sonar suite. He then took off his headphones, tapping STS3 (SS) Dave Davidson on his left shoulder. Dave looked up.

"What's up, Jon?"

"I'm going to go get a cup of coffee and see medical. I've set the sonar suite recorder to record the weird propeller noise that amidships sonar has picked up."

"Okay."

A few minutes later, Jon returned to his duty station. He put his headphones back on. He shut the recorder off and went back to listening to the only noise that was out there. Although the noise was very rhythmic, it was louder than earlier which meant it was getting closer. Jon immediately discounted the propeller noise as the USS SEASIDE HEIGHTS because the ship was only doing three knots. At that slow a speed, the noise would be constant. Jon noticed that the noise was also changing in pitch and frequency. It was the forward sonar dome that picked up the distinct noises of the VICTOR-III SSN.

The noise was a thump, whoosh, pop. The noise kept repeating itself. As Jon began his tracking on the noise, he pushed the "RECORD" button once again. Jon closed his eyes and started tapping the deck plates, lightly, to the rhythm of the noise. His mind started going through pictures of subs and surface ships that made that type of noise.

He came up with four possible ships/subs that could make that peculiar propeller noise. As his ears and mind tried to focus on the noise, it started getting more distinct. After only a few minutes, his ears and his mind narrowed the noise down to a sub. This sub was made by the Soviet navy and had a NATO classification of VICTOR-III SSN. Jon opened his eyes and set his headphones down.

On the VICTOR-III SSN, the sonar operator on duty was watching the scopes in the sonar suite. The retired Soviet naval officer, Captain Androv, was watching the scopes as well. The sonar operator, a young Somalian with loyalties to one of the warlords, detected the rhythmic pulsing of the USS SEASIDE HEIGHTS. The noise sounded like the blades of a helicopter. Captain Androv looked down at the operator.

"Mr. Androv, I have a faint, rhythmic noise in the water. It sounds like the blades of a helicopter," said the man.

"Bearing and distance?" asked Androv.

"18,000 meters at a bearing of 180 degrees."

"Speed?"

"Three to five knots. I'm not sure. I wonder if it is our own propeller noise echoing off the canyon walls."

"It could be. I'll have the captain slow down to five knots and I'll have him do a zigzag course to eliminate the possibility of the noise being our own echo. You're recording this noise aren't you?"

"Absolutely, Mr. Androv. But, what good will zigzagging do?"

"If the noise is our own propeller, then the noise should weaken as we turn away from the canyon wall. As we turn towards the canyon wall, the noise should get louder."

"I see."

Androv left the sonar suite and arrived on the bridge. He looked over the charts of the area. He nodded his head up and down before looking up at the captain.

"Captain, might I suggest that you assist your sonar operators by slowing the sub to five knots and do a zigzag course to the other end of the trench."

"Okay, Mr. Androv. Helm, slow down to five knots."

"Aye, sir," was the helmsman's reply.

"Navigation, plot me a zigzag course to the other end of this trench."

"Aye, sir. Helm, come to new course 120."

Aboard the SEASIDE HEIGHTS, Jon lost the noise temporarily. It had either come to a dead stop in the water or it was his imagination. He stopped listening to the noise when the end of his watch arrived. He turned over to STS1 (SS/SW/AW) Gladis Harpose. She received his briefing, smiled at him and plugged in her headphones. The noise would get louder and then softer. As Jon headed to the enlisted dining facility, he ran into Andrew.

"Are you alright, Jon?" asked Andrew.

"I'm going crazy, sir. Too much time in the sonar suite."

"What makes you think you're going crazy?"

"What I am about to tell you, sir, doesn't leave here, okay?"

"Okay, go ahead."

"Somewhere up the trench, I picked up what I first thought was our own propeller noise bouncing off the canyon walls."

"Was the noise our propeller?"

"No, sir. Somewhere up the trench at about 60,000 yards/20,000 meters, I picked up a submerged, manmade noise."

"Did you record the noise?"

"Yes, sir. I plan on having the sonar computer try to correctly identify this noise next time I am on watch."

"What was wrong with this noise that it is driving you allegedly insane?" asked Andrew as another crewmember walked by.

"From all the noises I had to listen to at Sonar 'A' School, the noise was consistent with a Project 671 Soviet Navy sub. NATO gave it a designation of VICTOR-III SSN. I thought those were retired from service, weren't they?"

"Yes, the VICTOR-III series SSN, what you correctly called a Project 671 saw official service from 1967 through 2000. If the Soviets refurbished those subs and sold them to other countries, they could still see service until probably 2020 or 2025."

"Would the Soviets really sell that kind of technology to some foreign country?"

"A distinct possibility. Think about it, the Soviets are cash strapped and someone with money could persuade them to sell such a thing to some unscrupulous countries. If you still feel that you're going insane, please get something to eat and I will personally escort you to the sickbay."

"Thank you, sir."

After dinner, Andrew took Jon to see the medical officer. The medical officer checked Jon's vital signs and then he gave Jon a mild sedative. Jon went to his bunk and soon fell fast asleep. Andrew went to his quarters and went to sleep as well. He knew that he would be officer of the deck on the 0000-0400 watch.

He set his alarm clock and soon it was going off. After he assumed the watch, he went to the sonar suite to see who was on duty with him. He found STS1 (SS/SW/AW) Ken Karlsen in the South Center and STS2 (SS/SW) Florence Garbo in the North Center.

"Ken, have any contacts?" asked Andrew.

"Yes, sir. A couple of the KILO's, one KRIVAK-II and the fishing fleet."

"Anything else that was passed along to you?"

"Yeah, Gladis said that Jon had contact with an unusual noise. I've detected the noise as well. However, it is coming and going."

"When was the last time you heard the noise?"

"About 10 minutes ago. Personally, I think Jon's crazy and it's just our own propeller noise echoing off the canyon walls."

"Let me see the bearing on this mysterious noise."

Ken brought up the noise on the computer screen. Andrew let Ken go across the whole contact area. The noise would get louder and then softer. Andrew looked at the pattern; zigzag. Andrew realized that there was more evidence to support Jon's theory of another sub in the trench with them. He looked down at Ken.

"Ken, begin a track on that noise and consider it hostile."

"Why?"

"If you were picking up what you thought was your own propeller noise, wouldn't you want to zigzag to see if the noise you detected was indeed yours?"

"Yes, I suppose I would plot a zigzag course," replied Ken as he realized the noise could be another sub. Ken put his headphones back on.

"Jon said he made a recording of the noise. Send it through the computer."

"Yes, sir."

Andrew returned to the bridge. He then walked over to where the duty roster was posted to see who the duty chief of the boat was. The duty chief of the boat was RMC (SS/SW) Carly Bennet. He then walked over to the chart room to see who was on duty. He found QM2 Traci Walker on duty.

"QM2, I may need to set this boat down quietly for a while."

"I understand, sir. However, my charts show that almost all of the coastline and shelf here is very rocky and most, not all, of it is beyond crush depth. I'm sorry."

"Are there any flat areas available?"

"One on a course of 345. The area is large enough to let us set down and not too rocky."

"What's the depth?"

"1,700 feet/567 meters."

"Beyond test depth but not crush depth; thank you."

Andrew returned to the bridge. He went about his normal duties. Ken continued to feed the noise into the sonar computer. Ken closed his eyes for a few seconds before the computer started beeping. He opened his eyes and saw the marker that he had put on the noise earlier, flashing. He rubbed his eyes and put his headphones back on. He heard the noise, but now it was much closer and louder. In the background he heard a ting, ting, ting, noise.

He turned around to face the sonar computer because it had positively identified the noise. The printer, attached to the computer, sprang to life, printing a report. Ken tore off the report with his left hand and looked it over. The sonar computer had positively identified the noise as a VICTOR-III SSN. On the next line it read: "Propulsion plant signature is consistent with the STALINGRAD."

Beads of sweat started to form on Ken's upper lip. He went back to his post and started tracking the noise. When he had positively identified the other sub's bearing, course and speed, he called Andrew.

"Sonar, Conn," said Ken.

"Conn, aye," said Andrew.

"VICTOR-III SSN bearing 110. Course 175, speed five knots. She is in the same thermal layer with us, sir."

"Very good, Ken. Is she aware of us?"

"I don't think so, sir. She is continuing on her course without changing anything."

"Good. Helm, come to new course 345 and make your depth 1,700 feet/567 meters. Set us down really gently on that wide open shelf."

"Aye, sir."

The SEASIDE HEIGHTS started turning towards the new course. The duty diving officer angled the sub down slightly and watched the depth gauge readout. When the sub was at about 50 feet/16 meters from the bottom, the duty diving officer leveled off on the dive. Andrew ordered a full stop on the engines. A few second later, the SEASIDE HEIGHTS came to a gentle rest on the flat area. The hull started to groan a little because of the pressure.

Andrew had the duty chief of the boat wake up the captain, the chief of the boat and the XO. Andrew also had the word passed for extreme silent running. He then went to the sonar suite to see where the VICTOR-III SSN was located.

"Ken, where is she?" asked Andrew.

"She's about to pass overhead, sir," he said, nervously, in a whisper.

"Good job."

Soon, the propeller noise ceased. Ken was able to get a good fix on the VICTOR-III SSN. The sub was about 100 feet/33 meters above them. Ken then could only estimate the location as being about 200 feet/67 meters on the aft starboard quarter. He turned to Andrew.

"The STALINGRAD is right above us by about 100 feet/33 meters. I estimate she is about 200 feet/67 meters to our aft, starboard quarter."

"Very good."

By the time Andrew had returned to the bridge, the hull had groaned once again. Andrew saw the skipper, the XO and the chief of the boat. They were all talking in a normal, loud type tone. They were all rubbing their eyes and yawning. Lou was being the loudest of them all, complaining about the early morning wake up among other things. Lou looked over at the depth gauge and his jaw dropped open.

"Lou, Rob, Lyle, keep your voices down to a whisper," said Andrew, harshly.

"This is my bridge and I will talk as loud as I want," Lou replied, rather irritably.

Another groan from the hull echoed throughout the sub.

"It's not your bridge right now. Keep your voices down."

"Is that depth gauge reading right?!" asked Rob, rather alarmed.

"Yes, Rob, the depth gauge is reading correct," replied Andrew.

"Oh Christ! How long have we been at this depth?" asked Rob again, after confirming that the equipment was functioning correctly. The red, digital readout was reading 1,700 feet/567 meters.

"About 45 minutes now. We are not at crush depth, sir," said Andrew.

"Damn close to crush depth. Why are we at this depth and why are we whispering?" asked Lou.

"At or about 0145 hours, sonar detected a VICTOR-III SSN. She's parked 100 feet/33 meters above us at about 200 feet/67 meters to our aft, starboard quarter. I took immediate evasive maneuvers, sir."

"Excellent work, commander, I'll relieve you now," said Lou.

Both subs were playing a deadly game of chicken. After six long hours, the captain of the VICTOR-III SSN moved off down the trench at seven knots. Lou waited another hour after the last noise contact had been lost before coming up to 450 feet/150 meters. Lou carefully left the area being extra careful not to be going fast enough to be detected. When he was in international waters, Lou radioed in the updated naval information.

When the updated Somalian naval information was transmitted, the incoming message traffic was received. CW02 Andrews went to work immediately decoding the messages. When the radio masts were secured, the sub went down to 450 feet/150 meters. The sub cruised along at seven knots. The decoded messages were disseminated to all the departments. There was an additional orders modification message.

The message was clear, "Gain the exact location of the pirate fleet for future ops..." The captain and the XO looked over the message. They called an all officers meeting. Everyone was keenly aware, as it was still fresh in their minds, the fact that the Somalian navy had an older, nuclear powered fast attack sub.

The refurbished Delta-IV SSBN was still on patrol, training her crew in the same area as the VICTOR-III had occupied. The Delta-IV had escaped detection by the SEASIDE HEIGHTS because she had been very deep in the trench and only traveling at five knots. The captain of that sub had decided not to try and train her crew in anti-submarine warfare just yet and instead continued on their assigned patrol route.

The stress level aboard the SEASIDE HEIGHTS had started to affect almost everyone. Arguments broke out among the enlisted and officer crew almost daily. It was while the sub was heading to Diego Garcia for some supplies that an idea struck Andrew. He called Bart into his office.

"You wanted to see me, sir?" he asked nervously.

"Yes. Come in and sit down. Do you remember when I had you go to the surface to check something out during that war game exercise?"

"Yes, sir, I do remember that maneuver."

"Would you be willing to do something like that again?"

"Yes, sir."

"Good. Are there any known dangerous sea life forms that swim in these waters that you know of?"

"Three that I know of, sir. There are seven species of man-eating sharks, two forms of jellyfish to include the Portuguese man-of-war and stingrays."

"Okay; dismissed."

Andrew went to see the captain. After Andrew had outlined his plans, he asked the captain for two special favors. The captain agreed to get Mr. Bradley a chain mail body armor suit and he agreed to let Mr. Bradley be armed as well. When the sub left Diego Garcia, Mr. Bradley received his orders.

Just after dinner, Mr. Bradley began suiting himself up. If all went as planned, the sub would pick him up sometime after daybreak. He would be about three nautical miles outside of the alleged territorial waters of Somalia in international waters. The sub broke the surface just as nightfall began. Only about 6 feet/2 meters of the conning tower was exposed.

Mr. Bradley reported to the conning tower in his full suit. Before exiting the conning tower, to begin drifting with the three knot current through the alleged fishing fleet, Andrew gave Bart a .45 caliber pistol and five magazines. Mr. Bradley was putting on his flippers and put the .45 into one of his waterproof pouches. Andrew spoke to him.

"Mr. Bradley, you're down to your last round in the last magazine, do you know where that round goes?" asked Andrew.

"Right into the back of my mouth, sir."

"Good luck."

Mr. Bradley exited the conning tower and tapped on the hatch. Andrew knew that was the all-clear sign. Andrew exited the conning tower and returned to the bridge.

"Captain, he's clear," said Andrew.

"Aye. Helm, take us down to 600 feet/200 meters. Set a course of 070."

"Aye, sir."

Mr. Bradley drifted with the current through the fishing fleet. All eight of the fishing trawlers looked innocent enough until he passed in-between the forward two trawlers. He started hearing active sonar pings in the water.

He turned his head in the general direction of the two ships. He looked them over carefully and saw that they were not what they appeared to be.

A little before sunrise, Mr. Bradley had been spotted by a rather playful dolphin. The dolphin played around with him for a while and then suddenly left. Bart looked down into the water and saw the reason why.

A fully-grown Portuguese man-of-war was drifting underneath him. He held his breath as it passed just inches below him, undulating its way through the Indian Ocean. He carefully started swimming away from the thing, breathing a little easier with each push of his flippers. Then he heard a noise in the water to his left.

He turned his head around to see the SEASIDE HEIGHTS coming up to the surface. He eagerly swam over to the sub. Andrew greeted him and took down his report. He then made sure that Mr. Bradley was seen by medical and sent to bed.

The information Mr. Bradley gave was correlated with the information they had gained during the night. The active sonar pulses were detected, but the sonar operators could not determine who was using that frequency. It was the captain who called Andrew to the bridge to discuss Bart's report. Lou had highlighted the areas in the report that he didn't understand.

"When Mr. Bradley wakes up, have him explain paragraph 19 of his report," said Lou, handing the report to Andrew.

"Yes, sir."

When Bart had had dinner, he was checking his diving gear in the weapons office, when Andrew entered. Andrew shut the door, gave Bart the .45 and then sat down in the chair at his desk. He turned on his computer and loaded up one of the submarine simulation games. He then chose the button that read, "REFERENCE."

"Bart, the captain is a little confused about this part of your report on the 'different' ships," said Andrew, pointing to the yellow highlighted areas.

"Oh, the two forward ships didn't look like the other fishing trawlers. They were emitting active sonar pings and the masts and bridges didn't look like the ones of the other fishing trawlers."

"Could you identify those two ships if you saw those two alleged fishing trawlers again?"

"Yes, sir."

Andrew turned the computer screen around so that Bart could see it. Andrew then started flipping through pictures of various ships. One by one, they went by Bart's eye. He kept saying, 'No' to all of them. Suddenly, one of the pictures looked like ships he had seen last night. He had Andrew back up the ship pictures one at a time until the destroyer appeared.

"That's it, sir. Minus some of the radar equipment and if you put tarps over the gun and missile mounts, that's it, sir," said Bart, staring at the rotating picture of a KARA class destroyer.

"Thank you and good luck tonight."

"Thank you sir for believing in me."

After Bart had departed the sub, Andrew passed along the information to Lou. Lou asked lots of other questions before putting down this new information on a message pad. The message was due to go out on the next outgoing transmission window in 12 hours.

# Chapter 15

The SEASIDE HEIGHTS found Bart floating face-up in the water. His eyes were glazed over and his hands were holding his crotch. It took several people to get him aboard. Andrew had the team take him to the sickbay immediately. CW01 Bergstrum carefully removed all of Bart's diving equipment. Andrew took the pouch containing the .45 caliber pistol to the armory while the warrant examined Bart.

Andrew unzipped the pouch and pulled out the .45. It was damp and only four magazines came out of the pouch. He set the .45 down on the workbench and saw that the 5th magazine was inserted into the magazine well. Upon further inspection, Andrew found that the slide lock was engaged and the hammer was back.

Andrew picked the .45 up and sniffed it; it had not been fired. After removing the magazine first, he took the slide lock off and pulled the slide back. A single round fell onto the workbench. The door to the armory opened and the only Gunner's Mate Guns, GMG1 Hal Robertson, walked in. Andrew let the slide go.

"Good morning, Commander Hinton-Smith," said Hal.

"Good morning, GMG1 Robertson. Clean and inspect this weapon as if it was exposed to saltwater and discharged," said Andrew, pointing at the .45 on the workbench.

"Aye, sir."

Andrew left the armory and headed back to his office. Along the way, he bumped into Lou.

"Heard your boy wonder got himself hurt up there," said Lou, sarcastically.

"Yes, he did. I think something went terribly wrong."

"Do you have any evidence of this?"

"His .45 was cocked and locked, sir."

"Well, I'll expect a report when you have all of the information."

"Yes, sir."

Andrew continued to his office where he ran into Bill Ellsworthy.

"Hey, how's the kid doing?"

"I don't know, the warrant is still with him. Can you refill his air tanks?"

"Sure. I'll send Chief Orphus to get them."

"Thanks Bill."

"You're welcome, skipper."

Andrew made it to his office. He opened up the door and Shawn greeted him.

"Report to the sickbay, sir, Bart wants to talk to you right now."

"Okay."

Andrew arrived at the sickbay a few minutes later. CW01 Bergstrum took him to see Bart. Bart was in a special room being pumped full of Ringer's Solution and a powerful painkiller. His legs were spread apart with an ice bag on his testicles. Andrew touched Bart's left arm and he opened his eyes.

"Sir, I fucked up. I thought I was a dead man."

"What happened?"

"Just before you all found me floating, I saw a periscope. I didn't swim away in time and the periscope racked me good, sir. My air tanks then hit the periscope."

"Is that why you loaded the .45?"

"Yes, sir. I was going to shoot it out with whomever came to the surface to check out what they had hit."

"I see. Well, next time wear a protective cup."

Bart smiled and tried laughing. As Andrew was leaving, he turned back around.

"Did you see the sub?"

"Yes, sir. It was a humpback."

"You rest easy now. When you're feeling better, I'll show you some pictures of humpback subs and then you can point out the one you thought you saw."

"Yes, sir."

Rob pulled Andrew aside and let him know that the blow to Bart's testicles would heal with time. The warrant wanted to keep Bart in the sickbay for a few days. Andrew headed back to the office to type up his part of the report. After typing up the report, he had Shawn deliver the incomplete report to Lou. When Shawn returned, Andrew had Shawn print up pictures, in black silhouettes only, of all known missile boats. He had Shawn put the pictures into a 3-ring binder, which Andrew took to the sickbay for Bart to look at if he felt up to it.

"HM2 Plotss, please give this binder to Bart when he wakes up again," said Andrew.

"Sure, Commander Hinton-Smith," she replied, taking the binder from Andrew.

"How's he doing?"

"Very good. He needs lots of rest and he may need someone to assist him in his duties for a few weeks."

"I know the perfect person for the job."

"I have no doubt on that one, sir. Have a good day."

Andrew left the sickbay. He found Heather in Fire Control. He talked to her about being Bart's helper when he was released from the sickbay. She eagerly agreed. As Andrew was getting ready to leave Fire Control, the XO found him.

"Skipper needs to talk to you."

"Aye, sir. Where is he?"

"On the bridge."

Andrew went to the bridge. He found Lou standing over by the chart table. When Andrew arrived, he could see charts of the area that Bart had floated through during the night. Lou looked up.

"According to your incomplete report, your boy wonder, we will call him Atlantis Man for now, reported seeing a 'humpback' sub pass underneath him. Is that possible?"

"Yes, sir. The sub would have been shallow if it was at periscope depth. Perhaps only 70-feet/23 meters maximum. The water is very clear at this time of the year around here."

"Alright, lets assume that it is a missile boat. Does he have any idea where he spotted it?"

"I didn't ask him yet, sir, he is still being treated for his injuries."

"Find out, Commander Hinton-Smith. That information could be crucial."

"Yes, sir."

Andrew left the bridge and had lunch in the wardroom. After lunch, he went to the sickbay. Bart was somewhat awake. The drugs were taking effect and he was starting to drool a little. Bart looked up at Andrew and smiled.

"I found the picture and I used a red marking pen to mark it," said Bart slurring some of his words.

"Good man. Do you remember where you saw it?"

"Yes. Check my diving locator; it is yellow. I pushed the "LOCK GPS" button when I saw it."

"I'll do that."

"Thank you, sir," said Bart as he fell asleep, drool hanging out of the right corner of his mouth.

He found Bart's diving gear in the forward torpedo room. He found the yellow diving locator and turned it on. The menu came up and he used the arrow down button until he found the "SAVED GPS LOCATIONS." He selected that choice and then arrowed down to the last entry. The last entry was date and time stamped. He took the locator to the captain.

The captain gave the locator to the duty Quartermaster for a location. Andrew then went to his office, with the binder still in hand. He sat down and opened the binder up and started going through the pictures. A picture, near the bottom of the stack, was marked in red. Andrew opened up the binder completely. The marked picture was an old Soviet missile boat, a Delta-IV SSBN. The phone started ringing.

"Weapons department," said Andrew.

".45 is clean, sir. Ammunition cleaned, wiped down, dry and inspected. Magazines cleaned and inspected as well, sir."

"Good. Make sure you tell Heather that you performed all those PMS checks so that she can put them on her Quarterly PMS Boards."

"Aye, sir."

As soon as Andrew hung up the phone, it rang again.

"Weapons Department," said Andrew.

"The duty Quartermaster used that gadget to find out where that alleged missile boat was located. The location was five nautical miles inside the alleged territorial waters of Somalia."

"That's good news, sir."

"What about that alleged missile boat?"

"Bart marked a silhouette picture of an old Soviet Project 667, NATO ID Delta-IV SSBN."

"What?! Those subs were retired from service in the mid 1990's."

"Yes, sir. Officially, according to the Soviet navy, they were retired in 1998. However, if you refurbished and refueled those old subs, they could still see service for another 20 years."

"Okay. Well, I'll put this new information into the next off-going message transmission."

"Sir, Bart deserves a medal for all of his hard work."

"I'll see what I can do, Commander Hinton-Smith; good-bye."

That night, under the cover of heavy clouds and lightning, the SEASIDE HEIGHTS entered the same trench as before. The sub extended her TOW array and the sub was slowed down to three knots. As the SEASIDE HEIGHTS patrolled the area, the sonar operators were busy trying to track the noises picked up. When Andrew came on watch at 0400 hours, STSSN Costillo was on duty in the North Center. Andrew knew that this was Jon's first late night watch since he had gone to medical earlier in the week. Jon turned around when Andrew walked into the Sonar Suite. Jon took off his headphones.

"Feeling alright, Jon?" asked Andrew.

"Yes, sir. Gladis told me I wasn't crazy. In fact, she handed me the confirmation printout."

"Good. Well, be alert, there might be a Project 667, NATO ID Delta-IV SSBN out here."

"That old, noisy sub will be easy to track, sir," he said putting on his headphones once again.

The SEASIDE HEIGHTS continued her normal patrols. Time soon turned into the fourth day that the alleged Delta-IV SSBN had been failed to be located. The captain and the XO were wondering if maybe the Delta-IV was just a figment of Bart's drugged mind. On day five of the SEASIDE HEIGHTS' patrol, STSSN Costillo picked up the propeller noise of the Delta-IV. He was able to get a good track on her from the North Center and the TOW array.

"Conn, Sonar," he said confidently.

"Conn, aye," said Katherine Bates who was serving as officer-of-the-deck.

"Submerged target bearing 240."

"What do you make of her?"

"A very noisy, Delta-IV SSBN at 1,090 feet/363 meters."

"Course and speed?"

"Course 095 at 10 knots."

Jon turned the noise over to the sonar computer for a positive identification, while Katherine made the log entry. She then drew a line on the charts of the area. The SEASIDE HEIGHTS was in the second thermal layer at 900 feet/300 meters. The Delta-IV was in the third thermal layer. As long as the Delta-IV maintained her course and depth, there would be no problems.

As the SSBN closed in on the SEASIDE HEIGHTS, Katherine began to get nervous. She looked at all the gauges and readouts many times. The SEASIDE HEIGHTS was in the silent running mode. All she could do was wait for the Delta-IV to pass under. The Delta-IV continued closing in on the SEASIDE HEIGHTS and suddenly changed depth. Jon caught this and quickly notified Katherine.

"Conn, Sonar," he said.

"Conn, aye," she said.

"Delta-IV has decreased depth to match ours."

"Conn, aye. Helm, decrease depth by 50 feet/16 meters quietly."

"Helm, aye," replied BM1 (SS) Lords.

The SEASIDE HEIGHTS decreased her depth to 850 feet/283 meters. Katherine had the TOW array brought aboard. Andrew relieved Katherine and received the briefing about the Delta-IV. Andrew looked over the stats on the Delta-IV at almost the same time the sonar computer had positively identified the sub. The Delta-IV was the LENNIN. Jon tore off the printout and took it to Andrew.

Andrew was reviewing the SEASIDE HEIGHTS' current course and speed, when the report was delivered. He reviewed the report and set it down on the chart table. Andrew plotted a course for the SSBN. It was headed towards the port city of Mogadishu. Andrew had a bold plan that called for the best the crew had to offer. Andrew woke up the captain to tell him of his bold plan.

He also had STS1 (SS/SW/AW) Gladis Harpose and STS1 (SS/SW/AW) Ken Karlsen woken up early to man their sonar stations. He then had BMSN Oliver Franz and BM3 Carol Davis placed at the helm. When everyone had taken their positions, he went over the plan.

"Master Helmsman, I want you to match course, depth and speed of that Delta-IV at all times," said Andrew.

"Aye, sir," replied Franz.

"Sonar, I want to make sure that we are at no more than 50 feet/16 meters from that sub at all times. Make sure to stay in her baffles."

"Aye, sir."

The captain finally arrived on the bridge. He saw who was at the helm and who was in sonar. He nodded his head up and down in agreement with the personnel that Andrew had chosen and Lou then relieved Andrew. Lou thought that Andrew's theory of the pirate fleet being near, or in, the port city was sound and worth investigating. Lou followed the sub into the port city.

In the desert of Saudi Arabia, 40 nautical miles southeast of the Gaza Strip city of Rafah, the last Iranian ZelZal-3D missile was being put into place. Hamas personnel were burying the missile cover in the cornfield. They were proud of Ahmadinejad's plan for attacking Israel. As they drove back to Rafah, they smiled at each other. When they arrived in Rafah, they called their contact in Tehran to let them know they had completed their mission.

The person at the other end of the phone put the receiver down. He smiled and lit up a Cuban cigar. He took a few puffs before he picked up the receiver. He dialed a restricted number to the palace. Ahmadenijad answered.

"Yes?" he said in Arabic.

"Mission accomplished," the person said in Arabic.

"Well done, now we wait."

"Yes, sir," he said, hanging up the phone.

Meanwhile, in Washington, D.C., Admiral Rosen was putting the final touches on what was called Operation Mount McKinley. He was putting into action the next phase of the plan. The logistics fleet was to get underway three weeks prior to the rest of the fleet. He had to have supply ships available for the five carrier battle groups he was going to be sending from the west coast. He made ports at Diego Garcia and Yemen as supply bases.

He placed into the orders of Operation Mount McKinley that all hostile targets be eliminated at all costs. If the hostile targets wanted to surrender, unconditionally, they would be taken, crew and all, to Diego Garcia. Diego Garcia would serve as a temporary incarceration facility until the end of the police action. There were only two things that Admiral Rosen was waiting on; the location of the pirate fleet and when the USS DIAMONDBACK would be off the assembly line.

The SEASIDE HEIGHTS, after following the Delta-IV into the port, quickly lost her in all the port activities. Lou settled the SEASIDE HEIGHTS on the bottom of the bay. Lou then had sonar start listening. Within a matter of hours, the VICTOR-III came into port.

An hour or so later, the six KILO's returned. As nightfall approached, the surface fleet returned. Thankfully, the noises of their propellers hid the SEASIDE HEIGHTS' escape to the open sea. Once the SEASIDE HEIGHTS was out to sea, she proceeded immediately to international waters.

On land, in the port city of Mogadishu, Androv went to where the sonar operators slept and found the young sonar operator he was looking for. Androv knocked on the man's bunk. The man rolled over to see Androv standing there. He jumped out of his bunk to face Androv.

"Androv, sir," the man said, standing at attention.

"Relax, son. Do you still have a copy of that propeller noise?"

"Yes, sir. Right here, sir," said the man as he opened up his duffle bag containing several hundred cassette tapes. The man found the tape and gave it to Androv.

"Thank you. I will make sure you get it back," said Androv, taking the tape.

"You may keep it, sir."

"Thank you again."

Androv departed the sub and drove to the Soviet embassy 40 kilometers away. He walked inside and found the courier sitting at his desk. Speaking in Russian, they conversed.

"Send this tape to Red Fleet Command Headquarters Sound Analysis

Unit. Tell them retired Captain Androv wants the noise on this tape analyzed," he said, handing the man the tape.

"Yes, sir. Where do you want the results sent to?"

"Me, aboard the Stalingrad."

"Yes, sir," said the man, putting the tape into a diplomatic pouch.

Three weeks later, Androv received the results to his tape noise. He opened the letter up eagerly. He read it carefully, twice. He then took this letter to the fleet captain. The fleet captain looked it over and handed it back to Androv. The fleet captain looked up at Androv and smiled.

"Who cares if the Americans are in our waters? It is of no concern to me," said the fleet captain.

"If the Americans are trying to stop your pirate operations, that could mean a drop in profits."

"What are you suggesting?"

"The next time your pirate fleet goes after a target, my sub should be there to provide protection."

"Very well. The pirate fleet will be setting sail tomorrow afternoon. There's a cargo ship headed our way with equipment we need. We have the perfect cover. There's going to be a severe thunderstorm in the same area."

"My sub will be ready then."

"Good. I will send both KRIVAK-II's out as well; just in case."

"Good thinking, sir."

The SEASIDE HEIGHTS was about to give up on the pirates. With almost no activity of any kind, with the exception of the fishing fleet, they were getting ready to call the whole show off. Then, that night during the thunderstorm, the SEASIDE HEIGHTS detected the KRIVAK-II's and the VICTOR-III. Sonar alerted the captain that there was a small group of noise contacts making its way towards a cargo carrier. Lou decided on a parallel course so that when the pirates took the ship, they could follow at a safe distance.

The VICTOR-III was preparing to launch an attack on the SEASIDE HEIGHTS. Coldly and methodically, the sub came up behind the SEASIDE HEIGHTS. The captain of the VICTOR-III kept coming closer. The crew, under the guidance of Androv, loaded torpedo tubes 1 and 2. When the tubes had been flooded, the SEASIDE HEIGHTS' sonar crew detected this immediately. STS1 (SS/SW/AW) Ken Karlsen was on duty in the South Center.

"Conn, Sonar," he said.

"Conn, aye," said Lou.

"The VICTOR-III just flooded her tubes."

"Are you sure?"

"Aye, sir. That's what it sounded like to me."

"Conn, aye. Chief of the boat, prepare a full spread of countermeasures."

"Aye, sir."

"Conn, Weapons Control."

"Weapons Control, aye."

"Load tubes 7 and 8. Flood the tubes and open the inner doors."

"Aye, sir. Target, sir?"

"VICTOR-III SSN, dead astern."

"Aye, sir."

The noises were picked up by the VICTOR-III.

"Mr. Androv, they are flooding their tubes," said the sonar operator.

"Have they opened their doors yet?"

"I heard a noise that sounded like a door was opening."

"Keep listening."

"Yes, sir."

The Weapons Officer came up to him.

"Mr. Androv, we must fire now and leave the area at high speed."

"No. Those Type 53, High-Speed torpedoes would run out of fuel before they reached their target."

"How long before we are at minimum range?"

"Ten minutes, sir."

"At eight minutes and 30 seconds, open the outer doors."

"Yes, sir."

"When we have closed to within 1,000 meters/3,000 feet of the Americans, fire."

Lou was looking over his options. Run or fight. Lou was hoping that the VICTOR-III captain would call it off. Andrew walked into the Fire Control Center and saw that torpedo tubes 7 and 8 were loaded, the tubes were flooded and the inner doors were open. The SEASIDE HEIGHTS was about ready to shoot. All that was left was to equalize the pressure in the tubes and open the outer doors. Andrew walked out of Fire Control and went to the bridge.

"Commander Hinton-Smith, what are the torpedo capabilities of the VICTOR-III?" asked Lou.

"Type 53 High-Speed, Type 65 Long-Range, Type 53-65K Wakehomer's and possibly a SHKVAL."

"Thank you."

"You know, sir, our Mark 48, ADCAP III series torpedoes will kill that VICTOR-III."

"Yes, commander, I am aware of that issue. If we have to fire, have your torpedoes, once they have acquired their target, detonate at 300 yards/100 meters from the sub."

"Aye, sir."

Andrew went back into the Fire Control Center. He withdrew his keys from his left, front pants pocket and inserted them into the fire control center main controls. He then inserted another key into the torpedo fire controls and turned it to the left. All the red buttons were illuminated. Andrew systematically disengaged all of the buttons except for tubes 7 and 8. He sat back in his chair as FT2 Tarsells looked over at him.

"An insurance policy, FT2."

"Aye, sir."

The VICTOR-III opened up her outer doors. The SEASIDE HEIGHTS countered. It was now only a matter of time before launch was made. Both Lou and Rob were on the bridge. Lou was waiting for sonar to tell him either that the VICTOR-III had left the area or that her captain had fired on him. It wasn't long before he received the answer he didn't want to hear.

"Conn, Sonar!" yelled STSSN Costillo.

"Conn, aye," said Lou as everyone on the bridge started to sweat.

"Two torpedoes in the water, bearing 180! Type 53, High-Speed!"

"Conn, aye. Chief of the Boat, launch countermeasures and go to evasive maneuvering. Commander Hinton-Smith, fire!"

"Aye, sir."

Andrew pushed the "LAUNCH" buttons for tubes 7 and 8. He then sat back into his chair sweating a little bit, before sonar reported to him. The Type-53's were still incoming despite the countermeasures and evasive maneuvers. However, when the Type 53's went to their active search, one of them found one of the deep, active, countermeasures. It homed in on and destroyed it in a violent explosion. Lou breathed a sigh of relief when sonar reported to him.

"Conn, Sonar," said Jon.

"Conn, aye."

"One of those Type 53's found our deep, active countermeasure."

"Conn, aye"

Aboard the SEASIDE HEIGHTS, everyone could hear the pinging of the other torpedo. This sound was increased when the Mark 48's went to active search. After making many sweeps of the area, the Mark 48's started to double-ping. Andrew watched as their course indicators went from searching 225 through 145 to a steady 199. Andrew watched as the indicators stayed very steady on course 199.

"Conn, Weapons Control. Torpedoes have acquired their target," said Andrew.

"Conn, aye. Commander Hinton-Smith, you know what to do."

"Aye, sir."

When Andrew heard the quadruple pinging of the torpedoes, he knew they were moving in for the kill. Andrew counted to 10 and then pushed both buttons down at the same time. Twin explosions in the water let the VICTOR-III crew know that they had been "killed" by the SEASIDE HEIGHTS.

"Mr. Androv, why did the American torpedoes detonate?" asked the sonar operator.

"That is a sign that they 'Killed' us. They knew those torpedoes would have destroyed us if they had not been detonated."

When the other Type 53, High-Speed had run out of fuel, Lou headed out of the area at high speed towards Diego Garcia. Along the way, Lou typed up the official report that said an "unknown aggressor" had fired on the SEASIDE HEIGHTS and that the sub had fired in self-defense. The enemy was allegedly reported as "killed."

# Chapter 16

The President of the United States was looking over the final plans for Operation Mount McKinley. She set the paper down on her desktop in the Oval Office and looked up at the Commanding General of all ground troops, General Nodez. General Nodez simply stared back at her in silence. She tapped her left fingers on the tabletop. She then looked across the table at Admiral Rosen. He was to be in charge of all naval activity. The general in charge of the Air Force was also in the room. General Orndorf simply looked across the table in silence as well. She stopped tapping her fingers.

"Okay, Admiral Rosen, what, exactly, is going to happen around November the first of this year?" she asked.

"At 0300 hours local time in Somalia, we will start launching the cruise missile part of the attack. We will also be launching anti-ship missiles and torpedoes to eliminate those naval assets that do not surrender."

He paused before continuing.

"I currently have 5,905 cruise missiles in my inventory. I plan on using them all, if need be. I have plans that, three weeks before the attack, the logistics fleet will already be on station. They will provide materials for the five carrier battle groups that will arrive a few days later."

"Sounds very professional, admiral. Please proceed with your plans."

"Yes, madam President."

"Who's next?"

"Madam President, my bombing squadrons will take off two hours earlier than the admiral's attack so as to arrive for another cruise missile attack. This cruise missile attack will be followed by the bombings. By the time the last squadron attacks, the first squadron will be returning to the air," said General Orndorf.

"What bases are you using?" asked the President.

"Guam for the initial strike. Diego Garcia for refueling, rearming and repairing. I plan on totally exhausting my supplies so that I may replenish completely."

"How long will you be able to do continuous bombings without using tactical nuclear warheads?"

"Up to 28 days, Madam President. However, I am told by my flight commanders that there won't be much left of that country in 20 days."

"Good Lord. What about you General Nodez?"

"I'm in charge of all ground forces, both Army and Marine Corps. We will begin using shells and mortars on the warlords and their supporters beginning at around 0800 hours, local time. We will not intentionally target civilians, however, anyone with a weapon in their hands that doesn't surrender will be killed."

"Are we sure about the numbers?"

"Madam President, I planned on having one whole carrier battle group for every one of their ships or subs guaranteed."

"Thank you Admiral Rosen."

"I have 14 planes for every one of theirs."

"Thank you General Orndorf."

"We have them outgunned and out manned by 15 to 1. I planned on using three magazines from each of my rifles if needed."

"Thank you, General Nodez. Is everyone sure that the warlords and their supporters will unconditionally surrender in 20 days?"

"Yes, Madam President, they will unconditionally surrender or else. As General Orndorf stated, there won't be much left of their country."

"General Nodez, when do you plan on going into the country?"

"Four days into the attacks. We've made many improvements since Desert Shield/Desert Storm," said the general.

"Very well. Everyone is dismissed, except for Admiral Rosen."

Everyone left the room except the admiral. The President turned her steel gray eyes to him.

"Is that sub of yours going to be ready?"

"Yes. In fact, that sub will be serving as the sub-launched, cruise missile command post. She will direct all sub-launched cruise missiles."

"Excellent, admiral. I'm looking forward to seeing her in action."

The SEASIDE HEIGHTS made it to her first port of call since leaving Diego Garcia. She pulled into an Australian port and then planned on a stop in Guam. While in Australia, Andrew received his official visit from Vice

Admiral John Bonds. He took Andrew out to dinner. When dinner was about over, John dropped an official envelope onto the tabletop that he had been carrying in his briefcase. He got up to leave and spoke to Andrew.

"When you accept her as your own, she's yours along with a promotion to captain. Don't blow this one," he said.

"Yes, sir," replied Andrew picking up the envelope.

The SEASIDE HEIGHTS departed Australia and headed for Guam. Andrew started reading through the alleged capabilities of the USS DIAMONDBACK. He started looking at the sub's artistic renderings and wondering how the sub would actually look in person. The sub did have a peculiar, diamondback pattern.

Andrew assumed that this was due to the combination of sonar and radar absorbent materials used in the construction of the hull. As he further examined the design plans, he found it odd that the conning tower and associated equipment was to be covered with radar absorbent material. He read the rest of the specifications and decided to accept the position.

The USS DIAMONDBACK was finished three days before the SEASIDE HEIGHTS returned from her deployment. The last of the shipyard workers were cleaning up the bottom and top areas of the dry-dock. In the lights of the dry-dock, there were painters preparing to apply the final coats of radar and sonar absorbent paint. When the shipyard workers had finally left, everyone left but the painters. The dry-dock supervisor turned on the ventilation system and left the painters in there alone.

Captain Togant was suffering severely now from the 7-day workweek. She was asleep in her office, when the dry-dock supervisor knocked on her door. She woke up and walked over to the door. She opened the door up slowly.

"Yes?" she said timidly.

"The USS DIAMONDBACK is complete. The painters are applying the final coats of RAM and SAM. They estimate that the paint should be dry in 24 hours," he said.

"Good. Go home and get some rest," she said, closing the door.

She shut the door. Now that the USS DIAMONDBACK was completed, she could get a whole lot more rest. She picked up her phone and called Admiral Rosen.

"Yes, Captain Togant, what can I do for you?" asked Theodore.

"The USS DIAMONDBACK is complete. However, since she is still a 'Black Book' project, only her commanding officer and crew can commission her."

"A job well done, Captain Togant. Will the ship be ready for dock trials soon?"

"Right on schedule."

"Good. When I have heard from her commanding officer, I will let you know. You sound tired, go home and get some much deserved rest."

"Will do, admiral," she said, hanging up the phone.

A few days later, the USS SEASIDE HEIGHTS returned to homeport from her deployment. After the sub was tied to the pier, shore connections were made. Everyone was then allowed to meet their spouses and kids. Andrew stepped off the sub and walked to the end of the pier. He was getting ready to call Gary when he noticed him standing next to Admiral Milton. Gary waved enthusiastically at Andrew and they met each other. Since a lot of the crew was present on the pier, Andrew did his best to keep the greeting to Gary civil.

"You look really nice, Gary," said Andrew, hardly able to control his excitement.

"Well, thank you and you're a sight for sore eyes," replied Gary, resisting the urge to kiss him.

"Your last letter said you were in a professional weightlifting competition in Venice Beach, California. What happened?"

"Took third place overall; won about $15,000.00."

"Great. I've got my leave approved to go see your dad. Will have to hurry, last flight of the day leaves soon."

Admiral Milton, who had been watching this whole exchange, decided to take matters into her own hands. She turned around to see that the limo had arrived. She opened up the passenger side door on the right and cleared her throat.

"Now, if the bullshit is over, get into the car and kiss him," she said.

Neither Gary nor Andrew wasted any time. They hopped into the limo as the limo driver put Andrew's bags into the trunk. Admiral Milton shut the door. After they had kissed and Andrew was more relaxed, Gary spoke. The limo continued on its way to the Honolulu International Airport.

"Dad never really approved of our relationship. Before he was put on life support, he said that love is truly unconditional; no boundaries. I think it was his way of saying, 'I know.'"

"He was such a kind man even to me. Although, I got the distinct impression that he didn't like me because I was in the military."

"My two brothers and mom knew about us almost from the start. Oh, the admiral, incurable romantic that she is, told me you got your own sub; is that right?"

"Yes and a promotion to captain."

"You made it to 0-6 as the admiral called it? I am so proud of you."

"Thank you, sweetheart. Oh, I was able to get some information on pre-burial and burial rights for Native American cultures."

"You mean that the chaplain with all of his hatred of us, actually was nice to you?"

"Yeah, can you believe it?"

"I'm suspicious of it is what I am. So when do you have to report to your new command and where is it?"

"The sub is at the Alameda Naval Shipyards and I have to report there by 1 April of this year."

"Sounds so cool. Can I see your new command?"

"After I report there. I might have to leave you here in Hawaii to pack up our stuff for shipment to the mainland. The sub is ultimately to be stationed out of Los Angeles."

"That's great, we could live in Venice Beach."

"Sounds good."

Andrew, after the funeral and burial, went back to Hawaii. Gary said he needed to help his mother and two brothers out. When Andrew arrived back aboard the SEASIDE HEIGHTS, Lou and Rob both met him. Lou handed him his new duty station orders. There was a quiet going away party for Andrew.

Andrew packed up his things and said good-bye to all of the officers and enlisted personnel that he had spent time with as the Weapons Officer. When he arrived on the quarterdeck, Lou and the Rob were standing there. They shook hands and saluted each other. As Andrew saluted the flag, Rob said something to the petty officer of the watch.

Gong, gong. Gong, gong, went the ship's electronic bells.

"SEASIDE HEIGHTS departing," gong went the single bell.

Andrew went home and found Gary there. He and Andrew spent the next few weeks packing up their stuff. They flew to Los Angeles where Andrew put Gary to work finding them a place in Venice Beach to live. Once they had found a place to stay at a local hotel, Andrew called the number on his duty orders; Captain Togant answered.

"Hello?" she asked.

"Captain Togant, this is Captain Hinton-Smith. I was told by my duty orders and Admiral Milton to call you when I got to Los Angeles."

"Excellent, Captain Hinton-Smith. My duty driver will pick you up and bring you up here to Alameda to see the sub."

"Sounds good. Has the ship been christened yet?"

"No. Since it is a 'Black Book' Project, only you can christen her. I have the bottle of champagne to do the job. Where are you staying?"

"The Palace Arms Hotel in room 717. Do you know where it is located?"

"Sure do and thank you. Oh, you can bring along your male better half to the christening ceremony as well."

"Will do."

Andrew hung up the phone and waited for the duty driver to show up. Andrew dressed into his captain's uniform. Gary was so excited that he went down to the hotel's souvenir shop to buy a disposable camera for the occasion. When the duty driver showed up, he took them both to the Alameda Naval Shipyards. When the duty driver had dropped them off at Captain Togant's office, she used her golf cart and drove them all down to dry-dock 62.

Along the way, Captain Togant was telling Andrew about the new sub, how excited everyone was to have been a part of her construction and other details. When they arrived at the dry-dock, Andrew saw the rundown outside. Leslie grabbed the champagne bottle.

"Don't worry Captain Hinton-Smith, it's VERY clean on the inside," said Leslie.

"Can I take pictures?" asked Gary, a little nervously.

"Sure. I handed the shipyard workers back their cameras a few days ago. If you will please get inside, we can start the ceremony."

Leslie opened the door. It was very dark inside. Leslie stepped over towards some large circuit breaker boxes. She flipped up six, large, red-handled circuit breakers as Gary shut the door. The lights started coming on one section at a time. The first set of lights illuminated the aft end of the sub.

Andrew saw the twin propellers with three rudders and the sight almost took his breath away. He walked very quickly to the edge of the dry-dock to get a better look. He saw the propellers were 7-bladed each. The rudders were even more impressive. He looked back at Leslie trying to catch his breath.

"She was built to your specifications, Captain Hinton-Smith," said Leslie.

"Can I touch her, Leslie?" asked Andrew almost crying.

"Sure."

Gary started taking pictures as he walked with Andrew along the dry-dock bottom from the aft end of the sub to the forward end of the sub. Andrew came out of the bottom of the dry-dock and ran his hands along the conning tower and upper hull. He could feel the SAM and RAM materials. That's when he saw all 140 shipyard workers standing at the front end of the dry-dock. There were cameras flashing and eager faces looking at Andrew. Andrew then saw the Navy News Camera Crew. Leslie came up to him and handed him the bottle of champagne.

"Everyone is waiting, Captain Hinton-Smith," she said, pointing to the small platform.

Andrew walked up to the top of the platform. There, hung from the rafters above, was a rope. Andrew tied the bottle of champagne to the rope. It was then that the Navy News personnel pointed their microphones and cameras at him. The Navy journalist first class petty officer pointed both his microphone and camera at Andrew.

"Do you have any words to say, Captain Hinton-Smith?" he asked.

"This is the proudest moment in any commanding officer's career, the christening and launching of his command," replied Andrew, choking on his tears of joy.

For Andrew, the next five minutes went by in slow motion. He stepped up to the microphone.

"I christen thee the USS DIAMONDBACK," said Andrew, grabbing the bottle. He then hurtled it towards the forward sonar dome. The bottle exploded on the hull.

Cheers went up all over. There was the clapping of hands, whistling and that's when Andrew saw Captain Henning, Vice Admiral Bonds, Vice Admiral Williams, Admiral Rosen and the Secretary of the Navy. They paraded by Andrew, shaking his hands and congratulating him. Andrew turned around when he heard an alarm going off with flashing lights. The dry-dock was being flooded. On the gangway, the sign was being dropped down to announce the ship's name: "USS DIAMONDBACK, SSN-75." Captain Henning came over to Andrew after everyone else had had cake, ice cream and soda.

"Well, Captain Hinton-Smith, congratulations. Whomever we sick you on, whoop their ass with that technological terror of yours," he said, smiling.

"Yes, sir. When do I get my crew?"

"Your crew is on their way. We've offered reenlistment bonuses and automatic rank advancements with back pay as incentives for being part of your crew."

"Sounds like you've thought of everything."

"You have to have her battle ready by September 15th, because we go to war on the 1st of November."

"Good."

"If any of these technological advancements don't work, you're dead."

"I understand, sir."

"The sub, when the dry-dock is completely flooded, will be dead sticked to pier 6."

"Okay. Who's going to be my XO?"

"Someone you know. He will be here in the morning. Get some sleep, you get underway at 0500 hours."

"Yes, sir."

The next morning, Andrew sent Gary back to Honolulu to meet the government movers. They said their good-byes the night before. When Andrew woke up, it was foggy and cold. He put on his uniform and his Eisenhower jacket, as it was called. Leslie had sent her duty driver to pick him up and take him to the sub. He stepped up the gangway, which was retracted after he arrived at the conning tower. He looked around from the conning tower as the dry-dock doors were opened.

A cold draft inundated the dry-dock. Andrew could see his breath. He heard a couple of blasts from the air horns from the tugboats. They effortlessly moved into the now flooded dry-dock and started tying up to the sub. Without her own power, the sub was being moved by a method known as dead sticking. Andrew could see all sorts of civilian personnel who had jumped off the tugboats to make sure the ropes were in their proper positions. Andrew noticed that one of the personnel made their way to the conning tower.

"Good morning skipper, my name is Paul and I will be your stevedore today. When we get the sub tied up to pier 6, we'll hook up all the shore connections. Sit back and enjoy the trip."

"Okay, Paul."

Paul pulled out a two-way radio. He started talking to the tugboats. In minutes, Andrew felt a slight jolt. The tugs all gunned their engines and the dry-dock started moving away. In another few minutes, the sub was free of the dry-dock. Andrew watched as the dry-dock doors closed and the gates locked. Andrew turned to Paul.

"How much does she weigh?"

"10,500 tons right now. With a full combat load, 11,300 tons and when she is submerged, 14,500 tons."

"I thought my XO was to be with me in the conning tower today," commented Andrew.

"He's here. He arrived at about 0330 hours this morning and is probably still asleep."

"I think I will let him sleep."

Andrew looked around him. He could see all the other dry-docks. Some were empty and some had ships in them. All the tugboats turned the sub around and headed her out to sea. When the final dry-dock had been passed by, the tugs started turning her towards pier 6. Andrew could see the pier personnel ready with the shore connections. Soon, the sub was moored to the pier and the connections were made. All the tugboats departed along with Paul.

Pier personnel connected another gangway to the conning tower. Andrew went down to the pier to meet some of his new crew. He ran into some officers and enlisted personnel whom he recognized from his previous commands.

Within an hour, he had met the Medical Officer Lieutenant Commander Earl Wise, the Communications Officer CWO2 Deborah Smith, the Diving Officer Lieutenant Junior Grade Andrea Walters and the 1st Lieutenant, Lieutenant Jon Eldorf. Andrew had served with Jon Eldorf when he was an enlisted man aboard CG-55, USS MONTEREY. He saluted Andrew.

"It is good to see you again and a privilege to serve under you, sir. I'll get the flags up and open the ship's official logbook," he said.

"Carry on."

Andrew remembered the rest of the enlisted crew from his other commands as well. Andrew continued to receive personnel for the rest of the day. Around lunchtime, Commander Bill Ellsworthy, the XO, woke up. He shaved, showered and had lunch in the wardroom. He had several cups of coffee before searching the sub for Andrew. The Chief of Boat, MACM (SS/SW/AW) Roy Steers, took Bill to the captain's cabin. Roy knocked on Andrew's door.

"Who is it?" asked Andrew.

"Chief of the Boat with the XO, sir."

"Send him in, master chief."

Roy opened the door and Bill walked inside. Andrew turned around to see Bill standing there with the new rank of commander. Andrew's jaw dropped open.

"Master chief, I need a current crew list and shut the door."

"Aye, sir."

Andrew looked at Bill.

"So you're my XO," said Andrew.

"Yes, sir. I was the last part of the great experiment. Captain Bonner's theory was that by putting a slightly younger, more attractive and muscular male in your presence, you would want to make some moves."

"Well, I think that part of Captain Bonner's theory went down in flames."

"I believe it did, sir. Permission to speak freely?"

"Granted."

"There were times when the wife and I were fighting pretty harshly. I was very full of testosterone. I wish you would have made some moves on me."

"You're a very attractive, straight male. You're happily married and have four kids; three boys, one girl. No, hands off."

"I appreciated that, sir. I think you will find that there are going to be a lot of familiar faces on this sub."

For the next few hours, they talked about the crew of the sub. The chief of the boat was the only interruption. Andrew looked over the list that Bill had brought with him. He made a call to Captain Henning requesting for a reactor officer as soon as possible. Mel said he would check on the location of the request at NMPC. Andrew said he needed a supply officer, a personnel officer and a chaplain as well. Mel asked Andrew to be patient and that handpicked personnel were on their way.

At dinnertime, Andrew and Bill had dinner in the wardroom along with the other officers. The weapons officer had just arrived as dinner was ending. Andrew had the Mess Management Specialist in charge of the wardroom, MS1 Darnel, keep some food out for the man.

The new weapons officer was Commander Adam Frost. He came back to the fleet after completing up his shore duty tour at Naval Weapons Systems Command. He was handed the weapons capabilities of the new sub and gladly volunteered. Bill showed him his bunk and went back to the wardroom.

Later that night, the ship's Personnel Officer, Ensign Mike Roads arrived. Andrew handed the man all of the current personnel records of those aboard. As the early evening turned into late evening, Andrew and Bill went down to the pier to look at the sub from a different angle. The sub was definitely wider and longer than the other fast attack subs that the navy currently had, but her new potentials outweighed her size problems. They went back aboard.

The next morning was chilly. Andrew put on his uniform and grabbed his Eisenhower jacket. After breakfast, Andrew toured the spaces and found the chief of the boat having an argument with someone in the forward torpedo room. Andrew walked a little closer to the argument and saw that the chief of the boat was having an argument with TM3 Bart Bradley. Mr. Bradley was not about to surrender his diving gear or spear gun.

"What's the problem, master chief?" asked Andrew.

"TM3 Bradley, here, won't surrender his diving gear or his weapon. He thinks that he owns the forward torpedo room, sir."

"Well, TM3 Bradley, it is good to see you again. Yes, master chief, TM3 Bradley owns the forward torpedo room as much as you own the brig. Mr. Bradley can store his diving gear here in this compartment. As for the weapon, I'll make sure that it is locked up."

"Yes, sir."

"Mr. Bradley, please bring your weapon with you and kindly follow me to the armory."

"Aye, sir."

Andrew walked with Bart to the sub's armory. It was already unlocked and when Andrew opened the door up, he found GMG2 Wendell Halt inside. Wendell was doing an inventory and saw Andrew looking at him. He put down the electronic clipboard and looked up at Andrew.

"Good morning, sir. What can I do for you?" he asked.

"Lock this up and make sure that it is included on your inventory list. I will let you know when to issue it to Mr. Bradley, here. Make sure that when it is issued, that it is logged in and out," said Andrew, handing the man the spear gun.

"Aye, sir," said Wendell, who looked the spear gun over, found a barcode on the side of it and scanned it. The device went beep and the information, when it was verified as correct by Wendell, was added to the inventory list.

"Any questions?"

"Only one, sir."

"What's that?"

"Why does the armory need three M-107's with three magazines each?"

"Good question, to which I will find you an answer. Return to your duties."

"Aye, sir."

# Chapter 17

Captain Henning drove up to the transient personnel barracks at the naval base outside of Los Angeles. The barracks housed officers on one side and enlisted on the other side. The enlisted and officer personnel at the barracks were waiting for either transfer back to the fleet or discharge. Mel stopped his car in front of the officer's portion of the barracks. He went inside and found an ensign sitting at the front desk and a senior chief petty officer standing to the ensign's left. The senior chief approached Mel, saluted him and shook Mel's left hand.

"Good morning, Captain Henning, what can I do for you?" asked Senior Chief Gotez.

"I was looking for Captain Neil Ott. Is he here?" asked Mel, while clutching his briefcase tightly.

"I believe Captain Ott just came back from breakfast. I'll go see if he's in his room."

The senior chief left and, a few minutes later, the senior chief returned.

"Captain Ott is on his way down, sir."

"Thank you, senior chief."

"Care for some coffee?"

"No, thank you."

About 20 minutes later, Captain Neil Ott arrived at the front desk. He saw Mel sitting there in the waiting room. Neil, with the assistance of his cane, walked over to Mel. Mel stood up, looking over Neil. Mel saw the cane and thought this was going to be a big mistake. Mel smiled and shook Neil's right hand and then Mel saluted Neil.

"Captain Henning. I must say this is a surprise. I kind of thought senior chief was joking when he told me you were here."

"Let's get down to business. How far can you walk without that cane?"

"About 20 yards. What does the Commanding Officer of Submarine Squadron 22 want with an old warhorse like me?"

"Twenty yards? Perfect. Let's take a walk," said Mel, ignoring Neil's question.

They walked out the door and into the small courtyard. Mel opened up his briefcase and took out the design plans for the propulsion plant for the USS DIAMONDBACK, SSN-75. As they walked around the courtyard, Mel struck up the conversation as he handed Neil the plans.

"Have any regrets about the nuclear navy?" asked Mel.

"None. I was proud to serve aboard all of my nuclear navy commands."

"I thought you might have regrets for the pain it is causing you," remarked Mel, pointing at the cane and Neil's stiff, right leg.

"No, that was my own fault. I should have watched my footing better in that storm. I lost my footing when the ship was hit with a large wave and simply cartwheeled all the way down into the number 1 reactor room. Hit my leg on the heat pump for the reactor. Snapped my right leg clean in half," said Neil as if he were reminiscing.

"Do you remember the command?"

"Sure do, it was the USS PASCAGULA, CGN-44."

"What do you know about an S9W?"

"The S9W is the most advanced, pressurized water reactor available to the submarine nuclear navy. It is manufactured by Babcock and Wilcox."

"When was the last time you saw the inside of a nuclear powered sub?"

"It's been awhile. I was the precommisioning reactor officer for the last OHIO Class SSBN."

"I need a reactor officer for a new, fast attack sub. Are you interested?" asked Mel as he handed the specifications sheets to Neil.

"Can I think about it?" asked Neil as he took the sheets.

"Sure, but call me before April 1."

Mel left Neil standing there in the courtyard. Mel stepped into his car and drove back to his office. He arrived at his desk and the phone was already ringing. He picked up the receiver.

"Hello, Captain Henning speaking."

"Mel, I'm in, when do I report?"

"I'll have my duty driver pick you up in an hour. Have a copy of your Fit for Duty certificate ready and try to lose the cane, if you can."

"Will do. Strangely enough, I just received my Fit for Duty certificate an hour ago. I'll start packing my bags."

Mel hung up the phone. He then called Captain Hinton-Smith.

"Andrew, I've got your reactor officer. He's on his way and try to overlook the fact that he walks with a limp and cane."

"Aye, sir. What's his name?"

"Neil Ott."

"Captain Neil Ott, sir?"

"Yes; good-bye," said Mel, hanging up the phone.

Andrew hung up his phone. Bill walked into the wardroom and stood to Andrew's left.

"XO, muster all of engineering department in main control."

"Aye, sir."

Twenty minutes later, all of engineering department was mustered in main control. Andrew stepped into the compartment and shut the door.

"I have received word that our reactor officer will be arriving this afternoon. Captain Henning told me that he is none other than Captain Neil Ott. Does anyone not know who he is?" asked Andrew.

No hands went up, so Andrew dismissed the crew. Andrew spoke privately to the senior machinists' mate before letting him go. Andrew turned to the XO.

"Bill, see if Ensign Roads will switch quarters to one of the empty ones nearer to his office. Put Captain Ott in Ensign Roads' quarters so that he is closer to the reactor control room."

"Aye, sir. We still don't have a chief engineer or the chaplain yet."

"We have quarters for them, right?"

"Aye, sir."

Andrew and Bill continued walking forward when they heard yelling and a fight going on. There was a terrible amount of blows and a scream. When Bill and Andrew arrived at the top of the ladder, the chaplain was choking out MA1 Grace Hinds. After she passed out, the chaplain dropped her on the deck; he looked down at her and then straightened up his uniform.

"I told you, bitch, to leave your hands off of me."

Andrew turned to Bill.

"That is either the chief engineer or the chaplain," said Andrew.

"Twenty dollars says it is the chaplain," said Bill, pulling out his wallet.

"You're on, XO," said Andrew, pulling out a $20.00 bill from his wallet.

"Excuse me, sir, are you the chaplain or the chief engineer?" asked Andrew, not wanting to get too close.

"The chaplain, Ensign Jeff Rohas. I've been briefed by Vice Admiral Bonds on everything. Sorry about MA1 Hinds here, but I hate women touching me," he replied, shaking their hands.

"So I see. XO, escort MA1 Hinds to the sickbay," said Andrew, handing Bill the $20.00 bill.

"Aye, sir."

"Well, welcome aboard Ensign Rohas. Let's get you a bunk and we will talk later," said Andrew.

Bill returned a short time later. Andrew and Bill walked around the rest of the sub. They had lunch in the wardroom. After lunch, Captain Ott arrived. Bill showed him where his bunk was located and Bill took Neil's service record to Ensign Roads. Bill then went back to see if he could help Neil unpack. Andrew had MS1 Darnel reserve a lunch for Captain Ott. After Neil had eaten lunch, he walked slowly down into the reactor control room.

The reactor control room was the reactor command center. Like the rest of the sub, all readouts were digitalized. Captain Ott sat down in his chair and took a good look around. Captain Ott was able to see into both reactor rooms at the same time. With the Closed Circuit Television Cameras, he could monitor both engine rooms. He glanced around at all the other controls and readouts. He was rubbing his eyes when MMCS Lou Matter walked into the control room.

"Excuse me, sir, I didn't mean to disturb you," said Lou.

"That's okay, senior chief. I never thought I would live long enough to see the inside of a dream reactor control room," replied Neil.

"It is a marvel of modern technology, isn't it, captain. I'm glad that we don't have to fill out any more paper logs."

"Yes. I believe all the logs are digitally recorded and off-loaded every 24 hours."

"That's right, sir."

"Do you know who the chief engineer is supposed to be?"

"Lieutenant Commander Sheila Waters, sir."

"We're fucked already and we haven't even left the dock."

Suddenly the ship's announcing system sounded. The bells were ringing fast.

"Fire! Fire! Fire! Class Charlie fire in the forward torpedo room; CO2 Fire Suppression System activated," said the petty officer of the watch.

About 45 seconds later, the announcing bells sounded again.

"Forward torpedo room C02 Fire Suppression System discharged."

The whole ship shuddered slightly as three, 50 pound/25-kilogram CO2 cylinders discharged their payloads into the forward torpedo room. The space was filled with about 9,000 cubic feet of CO2. When the fire party entered the forward torpedo room, they found TM3 Bradley lying on the deck.

He had his fingers in his ears and the breathing tube from his diving gear in his mouth. There was CO2 "snow" all over the compartment. Andrew and Bill arrived a few seconds later.

"Are you alright, Mr. Bradley?" asked Bill.

"Yes, sir. That CO2 is cold, sir."

"Yes, it is. What the hell happened in here?" asked Andrew.

"All three of the torpedo fire control boxes shorted out while I was testing them, sir. They caught fire and I was trapped in here before I could get out."

"Well, you're alive. XO, get the weapons officer and the reactor officer in here for inspection, report and repairs."

"Aye, sir."

The weapons officer, after one of the machinist's mates had electrically disabled the damaged fire control boxes, opened them up; the damage was extensive. There was a puddle of melted wires in each one of the boxes at the bottom of the box. As the weapons officer completed his inspection, the reactor officer hobbled into the compartment. He opened up the same boxes, looked around inside and then closed the boxes back up. He sat down with the weapons officer and reviewed his report. Captain Ott then added his observations and recommendations to the report.

The report was then sent to the shipyard and Captain Hinton-Smith. The boxes were replaced and the breakers were made larger in amperage. The cause of the fire would not be known for at least another week. The shipyard suspected a faulty or damaged circuit breaker caused the shorts and subsequent fires. Andrew, for the time being, had put Captain Ott in charge of both the reactors and engineering until the chief engineer arrived.

It was now three days before dock trials were to begin and the chief engineer still had not shown up. Shortly after breakfast, Andrew was summoned to the quarterdeck. There was an altercation on the quarterdeck with the officer of the deck, MMCS Lou Matter and a redheaded female dressed in civilian clothes. Andrew suspected that the person was the chief engineer Sheila Waters. The petty officer of the watch stopped Andrew. He turned around to see HM2 (SS/SW) Halie Queem standing there.

"I was the one who called, sir. I felt the senior chief could use all the help he could get," she said.

"Good thinking."

Andrew walked over to where he caught the last little bit of the conversation.

"Senior Chief Matter, when you get off of your watch, come see me in the Number 1 engine room for a one-on-one session," she said.

"Yes, ma'am."

"You must be the Chief Engineer," said Andrew, extending his left hand.

"Yes, sir. Lieutenant Commander Sheila Waters, sir," she yelled.

Bill arrived a few seconds later.

"Welcome aboard, commander. When you get unpacked and into a proper uniform, see the Reactor Officer, Captain Neil Ott, for a briefing."

"Yes, sir. This conversation isn't over with yet, senior chief," she said.

"Yes, ma'am."

She disappeared below decks with Bill. Andrew walked over to the senior chief.

"Think you can handle that Chief Engineer?" asked Andrew.

"I think so, sir. Red on top and fire in the hole!"

"Good luck."

Andrew went back down below decks. He went to the bridge where the Diving Officer was training BM3 Oliver Franz and BM2 Scott Orr on the new controls. Andrew continued aft to the chartroom where he found QM1 Traci Walker arranging several boxes of what appeared to be compact discs. She turned around to see Andrew.

"Good morning, sir," she said

"A good morning, QM1 Walker. So, what do you think of your electronic maps and charts?"

"This is going to take some getting used to, sir. I never thought the navy would go paperless. However, these compact discs take up a lot less space than the old paper charts."

"You're right. I, also, didn't think that the navy would go paperless, either. Someone, somewhere, along the way, determined that paperwork was a fire hazard and that it should be eliminated, if possible."

"So, it took the government 110 years to figure out paperwork was a fire hazard, sir?" she asked with an incredulous look on her face.

"Yep, have a good day, QM1."

Andrew returned to the wardroom. He found Bill and Sheila talking to some other officers who were getting coffee. Andrew got himself a cup of coffee and sat down at one of the tables. Bill came over and sat down with him. Andrew spoke first.

"Bill, all officers meeting in the wardroom in 15 minutes."

"Aye, sir."

Bill left the wardroom. In a few minutes the other officers started filing into the wardroom. The last officer into the wardroom, Ensign Roads, closed the door. They all sat down as Andrew stood up to address them.

"We begin dock trials in 48 hours. If all is successful, we will move to sea trials in mid-May in the north pacific. Shock trials will begin in mid-June or earlier if all other things go as planned. This sub needs to be battle ready by no later than mid-September."

"My engine rooms are ready, sir," said Sheila confidently.

"Good, continue with your work every one of you; dismissed."

The next two days went by fast for Andrew. Soon, it was Saturday morning, 1 April. The dock trials began in the cold and drizzle of the day. Andrew met with the inspectors. After meeting with the inspectors, Andrew met with the department heads. He told them to cooperate with the inspectors fully and, until the inspectors told them it was a drill, all personnel were to treat the orders as if they were real.

Steering checks were first. The rudders were moved to all the positions possible for real submerged or surface operations. The helm was given a satisfactory rating. Emergency drills were performed. Only the abandon ship drill was a complete disaster. Some of the crew couldn't find the right escape trunk. There were arguments between the crew and the inspectors. However, this was the least of Andrew's worries. Shortly after lunch, the diving drill went totally awry.

The helmsman at the time pushed the buttons for real. Air rushed out of the empty ballast tanks. The sub was submerging right at the pier. It was the quarterdeck watch who called Andrew on the bridge. QM1 Walker handed Andrew the phone.

"Yes EWC (SS/SW/AW) Krose, what can I do for you?" asked Andrew, not expecting the answer he received.

"Sir, I am currently standing knee deep in seawater and it's getting deeper. I am under the strong suspicion that we are sinking, sir."

"Sinking, right. Thank you for calling Chief Krose."

That's when Andrew looked at the ballast tank control panel. Water was indeed entering the ballast tanks. The sub was really sinking at the pier. But, because the sub wasn't moving, the water was entering slowly.

"Stop the drill! Emergency surface!" yelled Andrew.

The whole bridge erupted into a frenzy of personnel pushing buttons. The sub returned back to the surface when the last ballast tank had been emptied. Andrew was able to get emergency relief watches for those that had been on the quarterdeck so that they could go get some dry, warm clothes on. Everyone else was laughing after the inspectors had left. Andrew had dinner and was once again summoned to the quarterdeck by the command duty officer.

"Yes, Commander Frost, what can I do for you?" asked Andrew.

"Two things, sir. First, you have a visitor at the shipyard pass office and second, you have a conference call with Rear Admiral Upper Half Sandra Milton and Vice Admiral Bonds," he said, handing Andrew the receiver.

"Thank you. Yes, admirals, what can I do for you?"

"You sunk the sub at the pier, captain?" asked Vice Admiral Bonds, almost laughing hysterically.

"Yes, sir. I certainly did sink the sub. But, I thought that was what the difference between the surface fleet and the sub fleet was, sir. The sub fleet's ships sink on purpose."

"You know your actions might be considered improper hazarding of a vessel," he said, not being able to control himself any longer.

"Yes, sir that is correct. However, I can safely lay blame on your blue-eyed, red-haired, lieutenant junior grade jack off for giving my BM3 Franz the order to dive. By the way, she failed to tell him it was a drill, sir."

"Heard some people on the quarterdeck got their feet wet," commented Sandra.

"Yes, they did, Admiral Milton. I provided them emergency relief's so they could change into dry, warm clothes and I made sure that Lieutenant Commander Wise, my Medical Officer, gave them a clean bill of health before they returned to their watches."

"Well, sounds like you covered everything, Captain Hinton-Smith and we both warmly welcome you to the wonderful world of being the commanding officer of your first duty station; good-bye," said Sandra.

Andrew hung up the phone and turned towards Commander Frost.

"Commander, I'll go see who my visitor is. I'll return shortly."

"Aye, sir."

As Andrew stepped off the ship, the electronic bells sounded. Gong, gong. Gong, gong.

"DIAMONDBACK departing," gong.

Andrew walked to the end of the pier. He then turned left and walked to the shipyard pass office. He entered the pass office and saw Gary standing there.

"Hey, you're a sight for sore eyes," said Gary smiling.

"You, too. When did you get in?"

"A few hours ago. All of our stuff will arrive in a few weeks."

"You already found us a place to live?"

"Sure did. Called an old weightlifting friend of mine who owed me a favor. We are going to be living in Venice Beach, just like I said."

Andrew made a quick call on the command issued cell phone. He then went home with Gary. He returned the next morning early to the sub. Another day of inspections and meetings with the inspectors. Andrew knew today would be the other part of the engineering operations as well as reactor drills. He stepped aboard the sub and was greeted by FTC (SS/SW) Kyle Elliott.

"Request permission to come aboard, chief," said Andrew, saluting the chief and the flags.

"Permission granted, sir."

The sub's electronic bells sounded. Gong, gong. Gong, gong.

"DIAMONDBACK, arriving," gong.

Andrew went to his quarters and changed into his uniform for the day. He then went to the wardroom and had breakfast with Bill, Neil and Sheila. Andrew discussed his new battle plan for the week. As they were leaving the wardroom, Andrew ran into the first lieutenant Jon Eldorf.

"Jon, somehow we need to educate our shipboard personnel that there are three emergency escape trunks on this sub," said Andrew.

"Sir, I've been trying very hard to educate shipboard personnel on that issue. I can't seem to do anymore. There's pathway lighting to the escape trunks and the life rafts are all clearly labeled and fully functional as we just did the 60M-1R PMS check on them! What more do you want me to do, sir?!" he replied, rather exasperated.

Andrew looked up at Jon.

"Pathway lighting, you say? Shut off the lights," said Andrew sternly.

"Aye, sir."

When Jon shut off the lights in the passageway they were in, pathway lighting became visible. Red LED lights were clearly visible in the deck alongside the doors of the passageway. The lights were bright enough that you could see the tiny arrows someone had thoughtfully put into the system. Jon turned the lights back on and followed Andrew to the nearest escape trunk.

When they arrived at the aft escape trunk, Jon turned off the lights. There appeared a large, green LED circle. Green LED lights in the shape of an arrow illuminated the middle of the circle as well. The arrow pointed directly to the middle of the escape trunk and the hatch directly above.

"Jon, during the next abandon ship exercise, tell everyone to look down when the lights go out."

"Aye, sir."

Andrew arrived on the bridge to begin getting underway. He grabbed his underway check-off list and started going through the motions. In the reactor control room, everyone had taken their positions. The inspectors arrived and checked everyone's positions. The MMCM (SS/SW/AW) looked at the reactor officer.

"Lets get this sub underway," he said as he started grading everyone's performance.

"Aye, sir," said Neil as he reached for the phone.

"Reactor Control Room, Conn," said Neil.

Andrew reached up and grabbed the phone.

"Conn, aye," Andrew replied.

"Request permission to activate number 1 and 2 reactors."

"Permission granted."

One of the inspectors walked over to where MMFN Gallagher was standing. MMFN Gallagher was manning up the reactor controls for the number 1 reactor.

"Activate the reactor," said the MMC (SS/SW).

"Aye, sir," he replied.

MMFN Gallagher went through all of the steps to actually turning the reactor on. When he arrived at the point of really turning on the reactor, he looked back to see the MMC (SS/SW) staring at him sternly with a pen in one hand and paper in the other. MMFN Gallagher turned the reactor on.

"Captain Ott, we are at 10% output on the number 1 reactor. Please alert the number 1 engine room that they can activate a ship's service turbo generator in four minutes."

"Will do. Reactor Control Room, Number 1 Engine Room," said Neil into the phone.

"Number 1 Engine Room, aye," said Sheila.

"Place one SSTG on line in three minutes and 30 seconds."

"Aye, sir."

"Captain Ott, pressure and temperatures are holding steady. I'm going to take the number 1 reactor to 30% output. Have number 2 reactor placed into operation at this time. Please inform main control that they may put another SSTG online in a few minutes."

"Reactor Control Room, Conn."

"Conn, aye."

"I show one SSTG online, another one will be online in three minutes. The helm will be ready to answer all bells in nine minutes."

"Conn, aye."

"Very impressive, Captain Hinton-Smith. Light off to underway in 16 minutes," said one of the inspectors.

"Main Control, Conn."

"Conn, aye."

"We're ready to shift from shore power to ship's power now. I have four SSTG's online."

"Conn, aye. First lieutenant, pass the word to shift from shore power to ship's power in two minutes."

"Aye, sir," he said, grabbing the microphone at his station.

"Attention all hands, prepare to shift from shore power to ship's power in two minutes. Place all electrical and electronic gear in stand-by."

The shift was flawless. The lights on the sub flickered a little bit, which was normal. The sub was running on her own for the next eight hours. Andrew received a frantic phone call from Vice Admiral Williams. Vice Admiral

Williams was holding a satellite photo that showed two "hot spots" on the USS DIAMONDBACK.

"Are your reactors operational?"

"Aye, sir, they are. Is there some sort of problem with us running on our own power, sir?" asked Andrew, rather confused.

"No, nothing wrong with that at all, Captain Hinton-Smith. However, I don't want the enemy knowing she's ready yet. This is a direct order, shut down your reactors right now!" he said loudly and hung up the phone.

"Aye, sir."

Andrew hung up the phone. He then grabbed the bridge phone.

"Conn, Reactor Control Room."

"Reactor Control Room, aye."

"By orders of Vice Admiral Williams, you are to shutdown your reactors right now."

"Aye, sir."

The ship was quickly shifted from ship's power to shore power. The sub then went through the shutdown procedures. At the end of the shutdown, Captain Ott even went so far as to post shutdown watches in the reactor rooms. The inspectors left and Andrew was left to finishing off paperwork. While Andrew was finishing up his paperwork, the chaplain visited him on the bridge.

"Yes, Ensign Rohas, what can I do for you?" asked Andrew.

"Was that gorgeous, muscular hunk I saw you with last night your better half?"

"Yes."

"Fine man, sir. Very fine man, sir; good-night."

# Chapter 18

Andrew had to wait for four days before receiving the dock trials assessment. The assessment ranked the sub at better than 95% material readiness. All systems were a go for getting underway for sea trials. As Andrew looked over the report, he smiled at the final score, 96.4%. Andrew knew that a sub, or ship for that matter, only needed a 70% to get underway. Andrew had copies of the dock trials report made and distributed to all the departments. It was a Thursday afternoon and Andrew had called an all officers' meeting in the wardroom.

"Sea trials start on Monday morning. First Lieutenant?" asked Andrew.

"Yes, sir?" asked Lt. Eldorf.

"Have sea and anchor detail personnel on station at no later than 0645 hours. We get underway at the next high tide which is at or about 0715 hours."

"Aye, sir."

"Supply Officer, take on at least a 30 day supply of provisions and any necessary supplies."

"Aye, sir."

"Reactor Officer, you have permission this time to activate the reactors at 0400 hours on Monday morning if that is enough time."

"Aye, sir. I think that is too much time."

"Chief Engineer, be ready to get underway at 0715 hours."

"Aye, sir."

"The Operations, Weapons and Engineering inspectors will be aboard by 0600 hours on Monday morning to begin their grading; good-night."

Andrew went home for the weekend. He spent as much time as possible with Gary before leaving Monday morning. He told Gary that the sub would be in and out of port for the next month. Gary said good-bye to Andrew early Monday morning. Andrew arrived on the pier at 0400 hours. Andrew went to the conn and started going through the underway check-off list.

"Conn, Radio," said RM1 (SS/SW/AW) Joey Tonga.

Andrew reached up and grabbed the receiver.

"Conn, aye," he said.

"Radio communications have been established with the commanding officer of ASR-58."

"Conn, aye. Where is ASR-58 going to pick us up at?"

"On the other side of Treasure Island, sir."

"Conn, aye."

Andrew went back to the underway check-off list. He had the list filled in completely by 0600 hours. The Reactor Officer called him.

"Reactor Control Room, Conn," said Captain Ott.

"Conn, aye," said Andrew.

"Reactors are stable, request permission to parallel the reactors whenever main control is ready to do so."

"Conn, aye."

The Chief Engineer, Sheila Waters, who was sitting in main control, looked over the most recent reports from both engine rooms. The jacking gear had been engaged and lube oil samples were taken. She then looked at the final lube oil samples from both main engines. She pulled out her lube oil color chart and matched it up with the color in the test tubes. The color was light amber indicating excellent samples. She handed the samples and the chart to the engineering inspector. He looked it over carefully and nodded his head up and down.

"Shift from shore power to ship's power," said the MMCM inspector.

"Yes, sir."

She reached up, after verifying she had at least three SSTG's online, and grabbed the phone.

"Main Control, Conn," she said.

Andrew reached up to answer the call. All the while, he was being watched and graded by one of the Operations inspectors.

"Conn, aye," said Andrew.

"We are ready to shift from shore power to ship's power, sir."

"Conn, aye. Chief of the Boat!" yelled Andrew as he put the phone back up into its cradle.

"Aye, sir?" responded MACM (SS/SW/AW) Roy Steers.

"Pass the word to shift from shore power to ship's power in five minutes."

"Aye, sir."

The ship's electronic announcing bells sounded.

"This is the Chief of the Boat. Prepare to shift from shore power to ship's power in five minutes. Place all electronic and electrical gear in stand-by."

The lights flickered a little bit, but, again, that was expected. The switch over was complete. Main control called again. Andrew looked up at the clock, 0635 hours. Bill joined Andrew on the bridge. Bill gave Andrew a foul weather jacket, gloves and a foul weather hat with his rank on it only.

"Bad weather up there, sir," said Bill.

"Thank you, Bill. Tell the First Lieutenant to remove all shore connections."

"Aye, sir."

A few minutes later, all the shore connections had been removed from SSN-75. Only the mooring lines were keeping the sub connected to the pier. The First Lieutenant walked up to Andrew. Andrew looked up at the clock, 0645 hours.

"Shore connections have been removed, gangway removed and sea and anchor detail set, sir," he said.

"Thank you, Jon. Chief of the Boat, pass the word to set the complete sea and anchor detail."

"Aye, sir."

Andrew put on his foul weather gear and went up into the conning tower. Bill, a couple of the operations inspectors and the port and starboard side watches, soon joined him. A helmsman appeared to set up the splashguards and take over communications. He put on his sound powered telephone set and nodded his head at Andrew indicating he was ready for orders.

"Is Main Control ready to answer all bells?" asked Andrew.

"Conning Tower, Main Control," said BM3 Kylie Leans.

"Main Control, aye. Inform the captain that we have paralleled the reactors."

"Conning Tower, aye. Are you ready to answer all bells?"

"Ready to answer all bells."

"Conning Tower, aye. Captain, Main Control reports that the reactors have been paralleled and that they are ready to answer all bells."

"Very well. XO, single up all lines."

"Aye, sir."

The lines were reduced from eight down to four. Andrew looked at his watch, 0705 hours. He looked around for the tugs but didn't see any of them. Andrew turned to Bill.

"XO, if the tugs are not alongside in 15 minutes, we get underway without them."

"Aye, sir."

Another member of the officer crew joined them in the conning tower. He stood all the way at the back of the conning tower so he would be out of the way. Andrew turned around to see who it was and saw the Chaplain standing there. The Chaplain smiled at Andrew.

"I hope you don't mind, skipper. Some of the crew have finished singing and praying for us for our maiden voyage."

"Very well, I don't have any problems with that, Chaplain. What songs were the crew singing, if you don't mind me asking."

"Anchors Aweigh and Eternal Father for Submariners."

"Excellent choices."

Andrew looked down at his watch, 0716 hours. There were no tugs. Andrew looked at Bill.

"XO, pull in all lines on my command. Helmsman, reverse port engine one RPM for 15 seconds."

"Aye, sir."

The sub slowly pulled herself up to the pier enough to loosen the four remaining lines. Shipyard pier personnel removed the mooring lines and tossed them onto the sub. The First Lieutenant's personnel went to work making the mooring lines disappear into the sub. The sub started to float free of the pier and Andrew ordered an all stop on the engines.

"Rudder amidships, reverse engines 1/2."

"Aye, sir."

The sub started slowly pulling away from the pier. Once the sub was clear of the pier completely, Andrew looked around. There was a low cloudbank that had the consistency of fog. Drizzle and a slight breeze were hanging with the cloudbank. He waited until the sub was well out into the shipping channel before giving the next set of orders.

"Ten degree port rudder, come to new course 350."

"Aye, sir."

The helmsman relayed the orders. Andrew looked down at the compass in the conning tower. When the needle was pointing at about 350, he issued the next set of orders.

"All stop, rudder amidships."

"Aye, sir."

The sub coasted to a stop.

"Engines ahead 1/3 for 7 knots, maintain course 350."

"Aye, sir."

The ship glided effortlessly through the water. Andrew followed the center river channel out into San Francisco Bay. When the sub had passed Treasure

Island, California, Andrew saw ASR-58 join them. Both ships passed under the Golden Gate Bridge. Andrew decided to pick up speed.

"Engines ahead 1/2 for 12 knots, new course 275."

"Aye, sir."

After about an hour of this, Andrew increased his speed again.

"Engines ahead Standard for 15 knots, commence rudder checks."

"Aye, sir."

For the next four hours, the sub weaved a bizarre, snake like course in Open Ocean. Andrew looked down and saw that the water was turning clearer each minute. He looked aft and saw the whitewater trail behind the sub. He looked ahead and saw nothing but clear sky and water. The inspector turned to Andrew.

"Lets see what this sub is made of, skipper," the man said.

"Aye, sir. Engines ahead flank, maintain course 010."

"Aye, sir. Engines ahead to flank, maintain course 010."

The whole sub started to shudder as the new propulsion system was allowed to stretch its legs. Andrew looked forward and saw that the front of the sub was slightly higher than it had been earlier. He looked aft and saw that the stern end was equally lower in the water. Andrew turned to Bill.

"Bill, look aft," said Andrew.

"Sonar, Conn, sounding?" asked Andrew, as Bill turned back around with his eyes wide-open and mouth agape.

"Sonar, Conn, sounding 1,200 feet/400 meters, sir," said STS3 Jon Costillo.

"Conn, aye."

The ship stayed at flank speed for several hours before slowing back down to 10 knots. Then, the sub went in reverse for several hours. When this was completed, the inspector looked at Andrew as the sun was setting.

"How deep is it skipper?" the woman asked.

"Sonar, Conn, sounding?" asked Andrew.

"Conn, Sonar, sounding 1,800 feet/600 meters and getting deeper."

"Conn, aye. Sonar reports depth at 1,800 feet/600 meters and getting deeper."

"Good. Time to pressure test the hull, skipper; take her down to 600 feet/200 meters."

"Aye, sir. Clear the conning tower!" yelled Andrew.

The watches secured the splashguards and their equipment. They hurried down below. The inspector, the XO, the Chaplain and finally Andrew disappeared below. When Andrew arrived on the bridge, he took off his foul weather gear as one of the watches, BM1 Joe Smith, secured the conning tower hatch.

"Chief of the Boat, close all watertight doors, we're taking her down," said Andrew.

"Aye, sir," he said as he left the bridge.

A few minutes later, the Chief of the Boat returned to the bridge.

"All watertight doors are closed, sir."

"Very well. Begin the leak checks when we reach 600 feet/200 meters."

"Aye, sir."

"Diving Officer, maintain your course and speed. Make your depth 600 feet/200 meters."

"Aye, sir. Helm, 15-degree down angle on the diving planes, make your depth 600 feet/200 meters."

The air rushed out of the empty ballast tanks as seawater replaced the air. When the last ballast tank was filled, the conning tower disappeared. The depth gauge started showing more and more depth. The diving officer looked over at the captain.

"Depth at 150 feet/50 meters, sir."

"Very well."

A few minutes later, the depth gauge read 450 feet/150 meters. The hull was starting to moan and groan under the stress of the dive. The diving officer looked over at the captain.

"Depth at 450 feet/150 meters, sir."

"Very well, level off the dive."

"Aye, sir. Helm, zero bubble, bleed the tanks."

The hull moaned and groaned again. The diving officer looked back at the captain.

"Depth 600 feet/200 meters, sir. Course 010, speed flank."

"Come to new course 270, decrease speed to 10 knots."

"Aye, sir. Helm, come to new course 270, decrease speed to 10 knots."

"Yes, ma'am," said BM3 Franz.

When the diving gauge and other instruments had read a level ship for a few minutes, Andrew looked over at the Chief of the Boat.

"Chief of the Boat, begin leak checks. Report all leaks to main control," said Andrew.

"Aye, sir."

For the next two hours Andrew waited for leak reports. The Chief of the Boat was waiting on the Chief Engineer to report to him. As the hour hand on the clock ticked off another minute, main control called.

"Main Control, Conn," she said.

"Conn, aye," said Roy, the Chief of the Boat.

"Leak checks complete. No leaks were reported or found."

"Conn, aye. Captain, no leaks."

"That's good news. Chief of the Boat, open all watertight doors."

"Aye, sir."

The sub surfaced and dove down again to 600 feet/200 meters. The sub did this repeatedly until the inspectors were satisfied with the results. The sub then stayed submerged until daybreak when the inspectors decided to test the weapons systems. The sub fired water slugs to simulate the actual firing of the weapon ordered. When these tests were completed, the sub returned to the shipyards for a short period of time. Some of the inspectors left while others came aboard to replace them.

More supplies were taken on and some extra parts were brought aboard. Andrew called Gary. Gary was very happy to hear from Andrew. The sub was underway once again for more diving tests, anti-submarine warfare training and electronic countermeasure training. When the ship picked up ASR-58, the sub continued sailing out to sea. The sub submerged under the waves around lunchtime, while Andrew and the XO met with the inspectors in the wardroom.

"Okay skipper, make your depth 200 feet/67 meters and deploy your TOW array. Let's see who is out here with us," said the inspector.

"Aye, sir. Diving Officer, make your depth 200 feet/67 meters. Slow down to 3 knots and deploy the TOW array."

"Aye, sir."

The sub rose up out of the depths. When the sub reached the ordered depth and had slowed down to the ordered speed, the TOW array was deployed. STS3 Jon Costillo was in the South Center with the TOW array and the amidships sonar. He put on his headphones as the inspector entered the center. The inspector looked at Jon, pulled out his pen and evaluation forms and started asking questions of Jon.

"What do you hear, Mr. Costillo?" asked the inspector.

"Nothing right now, sir. Just background noise."

Several minutes went by before Jon picked up the propeller noises of ASR-58. He then transferred this noise over to the computer for a positive identification. He listened for a few more minutes before he was able to determine bearing, course and speed. Jon turned to the inspector.

"Senior chief, I have a surface target."

"Positive ID, yet?"

"No, senior chief, the computer is still chewing on the noise."

"Best guess, then."

"ASR-58."

"Make your report."

"Aye, sir."

Jon reached up and grabbed the receiver.

"Sonar, Conn."

Andrew reached up to grab his receiver.

"Conn, aye," replied Andrew as one of the inspectors looked at him and wrote things down on his paper.

"Surface target, sir. Designated Sierra 1."

"Conn, aye. What is Sierra 1's bearing and distance?"

"Bearing 165 at 25,500 yards/8,500 meters."

"Course and speed?"

"Course 345 at 12 knots."

"ID?"

"Unknown at this time. Best guess is ASR-58, sir."

"Conn, aye."

STS3 Paul Ortiz, who was on duty in the North Center, was listening to nothing but background noise until almost the end of his watch. His forward sensor picked up a low-power sonar pulse. He looked at the sonar pulse strength and determined it was coming from a ship at the outer limits of the sonar computer's range. He then, as the inspector evaluated him, turned his sonar sensor over to "SONAR INTERCEPT." He decided to let the computer chew on the noise for a short period of time.

"Mr. Ortiz, do you have a confirmed noise in the water?" asked the inspector.

"Yes, I do, senior chief."

"What is it?"

"Surface target, I have designated it Sierra 2. Sierra 2 is also emitting a low-power sonar pulse at regular intervals."

"Make your report."

He picked up his receiver.

"Sonar, Conn."

Andrew reached up for his receiver.

"Conn, aye," said Andrew, smiling at the inspector.

"Surface target. Designated as Sierra 2."

"Bearing and distance?"

"Bearing 005 at 60,000 yards/20,000 meters."

"Course and speed?"

"Both unknown at this time."

"Classification?"

"Unknown, but Sierra 2 is emitting low-power sonar pulses that the navy does not use, sir."

"Very well. Let me know when you have course, speed and definitive classification on Sierra 2."

"Aye, sir."

After 30 minutes, the computer had positively identified the sonar source. The sonar source was listed as: LARGE CIVILIAN CRUISE SHIP/LINER of the TITAN CLASS. Ortiz started listening closely to the faint propeller noise. The ship was on a course of 225 at a speed of 20 knots. He confirmed the sonar computer's identification of a cruise ship. He called Andrew.

"Sonar, Conn," he said.

"Conn, aye," said Andrew.

"Sierra 2 has been positively identified as a TITAN Class cruise ship."

"Thank you. Do you have a course, speed and correct distance?"

"Aye, sir. Sierra 2 is now at 50,000 yards/16,667 meters on a course of 225 at a speed of 20 knots."

"Very well."

During the night, Electronic Warfare and Countermeasures was tested. As dawn approached, the sub headed towards port again. When the sub arrived in port, all of the inspectors left. The sub was going to be shock tested over the next few weeks.

The sub was in and out of port for the next few weeks. Parts were replaced as well as any leaks or cracks that were found were fixed. Some equipment didn't survive the shock tests and ended up being replaced. More testing was done after each set of repairs. On the last trip to sea, Gary said good-bye to Andrew. As Gary waved good-bye to the sub, he went home and called Admiral Milton. He warned her that the sub wasn't going to be coming back.

That night, Gary woke up, sweating. He was breathing fast and heavy. A nightmare of epic proportions had woken him up. Gary could see Andrew slowly suffocating on the bottom of the North Pacific. He looked over at his clock, 0100 hours. As he put his head back against the pillow, he closed his eyes. Any more sleep was turning out to be almost as elusive as the night itself.

In the North Pacific depths, an injured sub was laying on its starboard side. The last explosion damaged something inside of the reactor control room. The systems shutdown and the sub went to the bottom in a large, helicopter like pattern. Smoke filled the bridge as well as most of the sub. Some of the crew were walking around with flashlights and battle lanterns. Andrew looked up as the XO helped him to his feet.

"Thank you, XO. Chief of the Boat, begin damage checks," said Andrew. He noticed that it was cold enough to see his breath.

"Aye, sir."

Andrew looked around and made his way to the chart room. He found QM2 Jill Peters looking over her charts. She had a battle lantern out and was trying to pick up her station. QMSN Carl Davids was there as well.

"Jill, where are we?"

"I don't know, sir. Just before the lights went out, our position was somewhere southeast of Adak, Alaska at some 800 nautical miles."

"Can we navigate?"

"Negative, sir. My equipment is too badly damaged. I wouldn't trust it, sir."

Andrew looked over at Mr. Davids watch. His watch was temporarily glowing in the dark. Andrew looked at the watch suspiciously.

"Mr. Davids, how long can your watch operate without a light source?"

"About six months, sir."

"Good. Keep it handy, we may need it, later."

"Aye, sir."

Andrew left there and followed the emergency lighting back to the bridge. He bumped into the Supply Officer, Lieutenant James Jones. The supply officer backed up and flashed his battle lantern into Andrew's face.

"Sorry, skipper," he said.

"That's okay. Do we have enough foul weather gear aboard, including the orange 'Mustang' suits, for the entire crew?"

"Yes, sir."

"Issue the foul weather gear. I will get the Chief of the Boat to assist you."

"Aye, sir."

When Andrew arrived on the bridge, he received the report from the XO. When the briefing was completed, Andrew looked around the bridge.

"Chief of the Boat, please assist the Supply Officer in issuing out the foul weather gear to the crew."

"Aye, sir," he said, leaving the bridge.

"Diving Officer, what is the ship's current status?"

"Just before the lights went out, the depth gauge read 3,125 feet/1,046 meters. Ballast tanks 3, 5, 11 and 13 were not emptied yet."

"So what you're telling me is, we may have some 5,400 gallons of seawater sitting in our starboard ballast tanks?"

"Yes, sir. That amount of seawater makes the weight about 24 tons."

"Get someone into the pressure hull area and check those valves."

"Aye, sir."

"Skipper, Mr. Bradley wants to talk to you in the forward torpedo room," said Bill.

"Very well. XO, please assist the Chief Engineer in anyway possible."

"Aye, sir."

There came a knock at the apartment door where Gary and Andrew lived. Gary walked over to the door and opened it up. He saw Rear Admiral Upper Half Milton, Captain Mel Henning and someone he didn't recognize. Gary looked down at the man's uniform; a gold cross was visible.

# Chapter 19

"Yes Admiral Milton and Captain Henning, what can I do for you?"

"May we come inside?" asked Sandra, pleasantly.

"Sure."

When everyone was inside, the man that Gary didn't recognize sat down.

"Gary, this is Captain Lee Stubbs. He is the Command Chaplain for Submarine Squadron 22," said Mel, pointing to his left where the man had sat down.

"It is my sad duty do inform you that the sub went down last night. We are searching for her at this time," said Lee.

"Any wreckage?" asked Gary as he tried to choke back tears.

"No. ASR-58 is conducting the search and rescue, right now," said Sandra as she reached out and touched Gary's left forearm.

"No bodies?"

"Not yet," said Mel.

"Gary, I should never have doubted you. I am so sorry," said Admiral Milton, almost ready to cry herself.

"It's okay, Sandra. Andrew always told me that if the unthinkable happened, the ocean floor would become his tomb," said Gary, crying this time.

Gary looked up at the Command Chaplain. The Chaplain spoke first as he handed Gary his business card. On the card were the Chaplain's main number to his office and his cell phone number.

"If there is anything I can do for you, please call. If you don't want to talk to the crew's families, please tell them to call me."

"Thank you, Captain Stubbs and I'm surprised that you're even talking to me."

"I know what you are, Gary. Twenty years ago, as a young lieutenant, this visit would have bothered me quite a bit. I've learned a lot in 20 years. Here's an information packet for you explaining what will happen if the Navy declares Andrew dead," he said, handing Gary a folder.

A few minutes later, Lee, Sandra and Mel left. Gary sat on the couch and cried. After about an hour of crying, he stood up and went about his daily routine. Andrew had told Gary that a routine would keep him from becoming too depressed. Gary went to his gym and began his workout.

On the bottom of the North Pacific, Andrew had noticed ice forming on the steel supports of the sub. Andrew, dressed for cold weather, looked at the Chief of the Boat, who was also bundled up against the cold.

"Chief, how long do you think we've been down here?" asked Andrew.

"About eight hours I think, sir. You know that at this depth, $CO_2$ becomes fatal faster than at, say, 600 feet/200 meters."

"Thank you for reminding me of that fact, master chief."

"Sorry, sir."

"Chief, I'm going to go talk to Mr. Bradley. I want an all officers meeting in the wardroom."

"Aye, sir."

Andrew made his way to the forward torpedo room. He found TM3 Bradley sitting in one of the empty torpedo racks. Bart stood up when Andrew entered. After Andrew had secured the hatch, Bart spoke.

"In sub school, sir, we were taught that suffocation was a most painful and horrible way to die because you can feel it until the very end."

"Yes, that is correct, Bart. That is especially true if you're awake for the ordeal."

"I have a special request, sir," he said, handing Andrew a special request form.

"What's the request?" asked Andrew taking the form.

"If we're going to die, sir, I wish to be euthanized."

"That decision takes a very brave person with a lot of spirit."

"I understand, sir."

"Do you have a light so that I can sign the form?" asked Andrew, pulling out a pen from his left, jacket pocket.

Bart grabbed his glow-in-the-dark diving compass/air tank pressure gauge. He handed this to Andrew. Andrew signed the form and gave everything back to Bart.

"Bart, does that glow-in-the-dark compass need a light source?"

"No, sir. It is powered by Tritium."

"Keep that compass handy, we may have a use for it."

"Aye, sir."

Andrew left the compartment and headed for the wardroom. He entered the wardroom and noticed that the Chief Engineer and the XO were not present. He decided to start the meeting without them.

"Medical Officer, how much longer do we have before the $CO_2$ levels in the sub become fatal?" asked Andrew.

"At this depth? $CO_2$ will become fatal at 5%. Right now, the $CO_2$ level is about 3.3% and rising. If the level continues to rise at its present rate, we have six hours, maybe less, before the end."

"Thank you. Please give me an inventory of on-hand Sodium Thiopental, Potassium Chloride and Pancuronium bromide."

"Aye, sir."

"Supply Officer, follow my orders if we get power restored."

"Aye, sir."

The door to the wardroom opened and the XO, the Chief Engineer and the Reactor Officer walked inside. Andrew turned towards the Reactor Officer.

"Why aren't the reactors operational?" asked Andrew.

"There's far too much damage to the automatic controls. The only way to put them online is to have two people inside of the reactor compartments to operate the controls manually. But, I am not going to do that maneuver, sir."

"I completely understand your professional opinion on the matter. If those reactors are not operational in six hours, this sub and the North Pacific Basin becomes our tomb."

"I understand where you're coming from, sir. But, if any of the seals on either reactor are compromised, those two people, when that reactor goes into operation, will be hit with a 350+ RAD per hour dose of radiation. They'll be dead before I can get them out."

"I appreciate your concern, Neil; find some volunteers. Did the radiation alarms go off before the reactors were shutdown?"

"No, sir."

"Do we have radiation suits available?"

"Yes, sir."

"Use them. You have your orders."

"Aye, sir," said Neil as he left the wardroom.

Andrew looked over at the XO and the Chief Engineer.

"Damage report?" asked Andrew.

"I've replaced all of the damaged circuit breakers, wiring assemblies and circuit card assemblies in the battery area. If everything goes right, we will have 48 hours of emergency lighting and other emergency equipment," said Sheila.

"Can we run the ballast tank heaters, the O2 generators and ventilation?"

"No to the ballast tank heaters, they pull too many amps. I can run the O2 generators for 12 hours. After that, without main power from the reactors, the batteries will be dead."

"Good. Let me know when you're ready to go online with the batteries."

"Aye, sir."

"Any damage to the propulsion systems?"

"Not that I can tell, sir. The Syntron seals are intact and the water levels in both shaft alleys have remained the same."

"Very well. Does anyone else have any questions for me?" asked Andrew to the rest of the officers in the wardroom.

"Yes, sir. Some of the crew would like to pray and sing somewhere, sir."

"Very well, Chaplain. Sheila, do you have any objections to using the Number 2 engine room as a temporary chapel?"

"No objections, sir."

"Dismissed."

Everyone left the wardroom and returned to their respective post. Andrew arrived on the bridge, putting on his sound powered telephone headset. All he could do was wait. He started listening to the various sub communications.

"Battery Room, Main Control," said Sheila.

"Battery Room, aye," replied MM1 Brad Mays.

"Close circuit breakers 1 Alpha, 2 Alpha and 3 Alpha."

"Battery Room, aye."

The lights came on dimly at first. As more batteries were added, the lights became brighter. A round of cheers went up around the sub. Andrew breathed a sigh of relief. He continued listening.

"Battery Room, Main Control," said Sheila.

"Battery Room, aye."

"Close circuit breakers 1 Bravo, 2 Bravo and 3 Bravo."

"Battery Room, aye."

A few minutes later, the Supply Officer reported that the next meal would be served hot. Andrew listened in as all the emergency circuit breakers were closed. After sitting on the bottom of the North Pacific for over 12 hours, it was nice to have the air being circulated once again. Andrew noticed that the crew's general morale went up several points when the ventilation systems were activated. The Medical Officer showed up and handed Andrew the drug inventory to Andrew. Andrew was having a hallucination that he was in Gary's warm, loving arms when the Medical Officer tapped Andrew on his left shoulder.

"I know what you were thinking captain and I can't blame you for requesting for the drug inventory. It was a very brave thing to do. I have enough of those drugs to have euthanized only about 20% of the crew. The rest of us would have to suffocate," said Earl.

"Thank you, Earl. Before the ventilation came back on, what were the CO2 levels?"

"4.88%, sir. We were literally only a few breaths away from suffocation."

"That would explain the headache and the hallucinations; dismissed. XO, lock this up in your safe," said Andrew handing the inventory to Bill.

"Aye, sir."

In the reactor control room, Captain Ott was reviewing the latest reports on the reactor controls. The machinist's mates had done their best to repair the most critical systems for reactor operation. He set the report down and looked up at the battery readouts. The batteries were being depleted faster than expected due to the cold water. Captain Ott picked up the phone.

"Main Control, Reactor Control Room," he said.

"Main Control, aye," said Sheila.

"I need power restored to the emergency hydraulic controls for the Number 1 reactor."

"You know that closing that circuit breaker will put an enormous pull on the batteries."

"Yes, I am aware of such a thing. But, you cannot run the propulsion plant on batteries anymore. Besides, if we are successful, I can recharge the batteries."

"True. Battery Room, Main Control," she said.

"Battery Room, aye."

"Close circuit breaker 11 Alpha."

"Battery Room, aye."

The lights dimmed and the ventilation ceased. The drain on the batteries was almost too much. Andrew looked up at the XO and the rest of the bridge officers. Captain Ott turned around in the reactor control room as the hatch opened. MMCS Lou Matter, MMFN Fred Gallagher and MM3 Dawn Ellis entered. Fred and Dawn were suited up in the yellow radiation suits. Their hoods were in their hands.

"Captain Ott, I found you two volunteers," said Lou.

"Thank you, Lou. You know that if the seals on the reactor are compromised, you're going to get cooked before you can get out of there," said Captain Ott.

"Yes, sir, we are aware of the dangers of this type of operation. But, we are also aware that this sub isn't the *K-19* or the *Kursk*, sir," said Fred confidently.

"You two have a lot of spirit. Take this grease pencil, when you get inside the reactor compartment, mark a spot on the bulkhead behind the large, brass wheel. Mark another spot on the wheel so that the two marks line up," said Neil handing Fred the grease pencil.

They put on their hoods and Lou escorted them to the outer door to the reactor compartment. Lou used one of the two keys he was carrying to open the large, high security lock. Lou opened the lock and opened the door. Lou looked at Fred and Dawn, pointing at the space into which they all entered. Lou looked at the gauges and dials; no radiation alarms, no power outputs, no nothing. Lou then unlocked the lock on the inner door, opened it up and pointed them into the reactor compartment.

"Good luck, you two. The Reactor Officer can talk to you, but you won't be able to talk to him," said Lou.

"We understand," said Dawn as they both entered the compartment.

Lou shut the door behind them and exited the compartment. He shut the outer door and returned to the reactor control room. Neil looked up as Lou entered. Lou saw MMC Henry Gold, HMCS (SS/SW/AW) Marne Toldst, HM2 (SS/SW) Chris Holder and the Medical Officer all standing in the reactor control room.

"They're in there, sir," said Lou.

"Thank you, senior chief. Main Control, Reactor Control Room," said Neil.

"Main Control, aye," said Sheila.

"Number 1 reactor is ready for manual operation. If everything is successful, we can get underway on main power. Align your systems."

"Main Control, aye. MM1 Karla St. John and MM1 Brad Mays, cross connect Number 1 and Number 2 engine rooms."

"Aye, ma'am," they said as they started opening certain valves and closing others.

They also went about aligning the ship's service turbo generators. The lights were almost out. The battle lanterns and flashlights were turned on. Everyone was holding their breath as Neil picked up the phone.

"Conn, Reactor Control Room," said Neil.

Andrew reached up for the receiver.

"Conn, aye," he said.

"We are ready for manual operation of the Number 1 reactor. If all goes right, I can get us underway at full power for 18 knots."

"Conn, aye and good luck."

"Reactor Control Room, aye," said Neil.

Neil switched channels so that he could talk to Fred and Dawn.

"Fred and Dawn, did you mark the bulkhead and wheel like I told you to do?"

They looked up at Neil and gave him the thumbs up signal.

"Good. Turn the large, brass wheel 20 turns."

They shook their heads up and down. They grabbed the wheel on opposite sides and began turning the wheel. It was very heavy at first to turn. They could soon feel their hearts pounding in their ears. After struggling for almost 30 minutes and counting the turns on the bulkhead, the 20th turn arrived.

Inside the reactor control room, Neil waited for the red indicator to turn to green. When it didn't turn green, he ordered another 10 turns of the wheel. The red indicator turned green. One by one, all the equipment was put back online. Soon, all four SSTG's were operational. With main power restored, the reactor control room could control the reactor.

"Senior chief, get those two out of that compartment," said Neil.

"With pleasure, sir."

On the bridge, everyone was getting ready to get underway. Andrew looked over at the Diving Officer.

"Activate the ballast tank heaters," said Andrew.

"Aye, sir."

After four hours of keeping the ballast tank heaters on, the starboard ballast tanks were emptied. A few minutes later, the sub began to float off the bottom.

"Diving Officer, make your depth 60 feet/20 meters, engines ahead standard."

"Aye, sir. Helm, 10-degree up angle on the diving planes. Make your depth 060 feet/20 meters, engines ahead standard."

"Helm, aye."

The sub began rising from the depths. As it passed up through the thermal layers, her twin-propeller noise was picked up by a SOSUS monitoring station in the North Pacific. The man at the SOSUS monitoring station immediately recognized the noise as belonging to SSN-75's propulsion plant. He called his supervisor only after the computer had positively identified the noise. He picked up the phone while looking over the report.

"Commander, this is NORPAC Station 26, Operator 38, come in please," the man said.

The Commanding Officer of NORPAC Station 26 picked up his phone.

"Go ahead, Operator 38, this is Commander Deering," he said

"I have positive confirmation on the location of the USS DIAMONDBACK."

"Where is she?!"

"About 775 nautical miles southwest of Adak, Alaska. I think she's on the surface doing a very noisy 18 knots."

"Course?"

"I don't know, sir. She's on the very outer edge of my SOSUS equipment."

"Very well."

The Commanding Officer of ASR-58 was not doing well. He hadn't slept very well in the last couple of days. He was dozing off on the bridge when Admiral Rosen called him. He was just hooking up with the USS MONONGAHELA AO-178 to take on fuel and provisions.

"Captain, the Secretary of the Navy has decided to call off the search and rescue," said Theodore.

"I'm not going to give up on the search and rescue of the sub. Andrew is my friend and I refuse to give up on him or the rest of the crew. They deserve to be found, sir."

"I understand, Captain. How much longer do they have?"

"They should have suffocated 12 hours ago, sir."

"I'll give you 12 more hours, Captain. If you haven't found them by then, you are ordered to report to port."

"Yes, sir."

On the surface, navigating without radar, sonar, ECW or radio, the USS DIAMONDBACK had surfaced into a thick fog bank. When the conning tower was manned up, no one could see anything. Then, slowly, icebergs appeared here and there. Andrew ordered the engines slowed down to 10 knots for safety reasons. It was QMSN Carl Davids who reported some good news.

"Captain, I used our GPS Locator because it was the only thing undamaged. I have our approximate location."

"Where are we?"

"We are in the middle of GPS Grid Square 2930. We are only about 50 nautical miles from the International Dateline."

"We can't navigate, skipper. What direction are we going?" asked the XO.

"I know what approximate direction we're going, XO. We are on an approximate course of 180," said Carl looking down at his watch.

Andrew just smiled.

"XO, rotate the watches every four hours. Use Mr. Davids watch compass during the day. Get Mr. Bradley up here with his diving compass. We will use it during the night because it glows in the dark," said Andrew.

"Aye, sir."

"Mr. Davids, have QM2 Peters plot me a course to San Francisco from here."

"Aye, sir."

The radio room aboard ASR-58 came to life once again. The captain had just eaten lunch and was taking a nap in his quarters, when the duty radioman began knocking frantically on his door. The captain woke up and put on his glasses before answering the door.

"Yes, RM1 Sanders, what is it?"

"We've received a priority radio call for you, sir. The person calling is a Commander Deering of NORPAC Station 26."

"NORPAC Station 26? That's a SOSUS station. Is he still on the line?"

"Yes, sir and he wants to talk to you personally."

The captain rushed into the radio room and put on a headset with an attached microphone.

"Commander Deering, this is the captain of ASR-58. What can I do for you?"

"I have some good news for you, Captain. Six hours ago, we picked up the propeller noise of SSN-75. I didn't want to contact you then because the computer had to confirm the noise."

"I understand, Commander Deering. Where is she?"

"We plotted her relative position in the middle of GPS Grid Square 2930. She's about 50 nautical miles southeast of the International Dateline. Since her propeller noise is getting weaker, the computer plotted her at 775 nautical miles southwest of Adak, Alaska."

"What's her course and speed?"

"I don't know her course, however, her speed was 18 knots."

"Thank you."

The captain left the radio room and headed to the chart room. He gave the information to the Navigational Officer. The Navigational Officer plotted the area and speed. He gave his report.

"Captain, if we maintain flank speed for five days, we will get there," she said.

"And we will have exhausted our fuel supplies as well."

"Correct, sir."

"Have the USS MONONGAHELIA follow us at a distance. She will need to refuel us in four days. Have her lookouts keep a sharp eye out for the USS DIAMONDBACK. Her radar systems will allow them to scan a larger area than what we could."

"Aye, sir."

"Make sure to get us on a probable, collision course with SSN-75."

"Aye, sir."

"Where's the closest medical facility to us?"

"I believe that the USS ABRAHAM LINCOLN, CVN-72, is out here on maneuvers with us. I think she is somewhere southeast of our current position at about 650 nautical miles."

"That's good. Ask her captain to prepare for an unknown number and type of causalities from SSN-75 and ask her to deploy her aircraft as the captain sees fit."

"Aye, sir. What makes you think we will find SSN-75?"

"I have a hunch that Andrew is going to be heading back to San Francisco."

"Aye, sir."

"Tell the USS ABRAHAM LINCOLN to assume that SSN-75 has inoperable radar, radio, ECW and sonar."

"Aye, sir."

The USS ABRAHAM LINCOLN, CVN-72, changed course and increased her speed. ASR-58 did the same and radioed Sandra about the findings. As nightfall approached, the Chaplain visited Gary once again. This time he brought good news. Gary felt much better that night and decided to sleep for as long as he could.

The USS DIAMONDBACK broke out of the fog bank and bobbing icebergs at dusk. Andrew immediately increased speed back up to 18 knots. He then ordered the distress flares fired every two hours during the night. Navigating with only a compass was a challenge to the quartermaster. Andrew joined the XO on the bridge the next morning.

"We need something that will reflect radar at great distances, XO," commented Andrew while drinking his cup of coffee.

"I've been thinking the same thing, however, what do we have available?"

"Good question, XO. Let me think about that for awhile."

It was while Mr. Davids' wristwatch was reflecting the sunlight that an idea came to Andrew. He finished off his cup of coffee as the morning wore on. When he had finally finished off the cup of coffee, he set the empty cup down on the splashguard.

"XO, I have a plan. Get me the Chief Engineer, the Supply Officer and the First Lieutenant up here."

"Aye, sir."

The First Lieutenant showed up in the conning tower first.

"Jon, do you have any wire or small diameter rope and Aluminum tape?" asked Andrew.

"Yes, sir."

"Good. I want you to string the wire or rope from the forward most VLS tube to the aft most VLS tube. Make sure to string the wire or rope over the conning tower to include ECW and Radar."

"Aye, sir."

"Before you string up the wire or rope, let me know."

"Aye, sir."

The Supply Officer showed up next.

"James, what are those cookie sheets in the galley made of?"

"300 series Stainless Steel, sir as required by health regulations."

"Good. Bring me 12 of them up here and two rolls of Aluminum Foil."

"Aye, sir," he said, disappearing below.

The Chief Engineer showed up next.

"Sheila, I want you to weld together, in the shape of a cone, the 12 cookie sheets that the Supply Officer went to get. I want you to place the cookie sheets over the top of the periscope after the First Lieutenant's people have covered them in Aluminum Foil."

"Aye, sir."

Within hours, the whole sub looked like a circus tent complete with streamers. The periscope was raised as high as it could go with the welded-together cookie sheets over the top of it. The cookie sheets spun freely in the slight breeze created by the sub's forward motion. The Aluminum tape and Aluminum Foil streamers were flapping in the breeze as well. The ECW/Radar unit, although it couldn't send/receive, still spun around. The Aluminum Foil streamers were flying around with it like a propeller.

"Skipper, someone would have to be blind not to see us on radar," commented Sheila.

"That's what I'm counting on, Sheila," said Andrew as he went down below to bed.

# Chapter 20

SSN-75 had been on the surface for over 48 hours. They had not seen another ship or even an aircraft. The cookie sheets were still rotating in the breeze created by the sub as it propelled itself through the water. The Aluminum Foil strings were flapping in the breeze as well. At 1000 hours, QM1 Walker ordered a change of course to 080. The XO joined Andrew and the watches in the conning tower. The early morning fog bank had finally worn off.

"Skipper, why haven't they found us yet?" asked Bill.

"I don't know, XO. I think it is odd that we haven't seen anyone or anything else out here. No military or civilian traffic of any kind."

Andrew picked up his sound powered telephone set.

"Conn, Navigation," said Andrew.

"Navigation, aye, QM1 Walker speaking."

"QM1 Walker, aren't we near any of the shipping lanes?" asked Andrew.

"Yes, sir. Cruise ships, ULCC's, VLCC's and freighters all use this area during certain times of the year."

"Conn, aye. XO, the conning tower is yours, I'm going below to get a cup of coffee."

"Aye, sir," said Bill as he raised his binoculars to his eyes.

Andrew poured himself a cup of coffee and was headed back to the conning tower when he ran into TM3 Bradley.

"Good morning, Bart."

"Good morning, sir. Since the weapons systems are inoperative, I was wondering if you could use another watch."

"Why, yes, Bart, I could use another watch. Thank you for volunteering.

Go see the First Lieutenant to get your gear and post yourself outside the forward escape trunk."

"Aye, sir. Sir, I won't be needing this," he said, handing Andrew the special request form.

"I'll dispose of this. In case you're wondering, I asked the Medical Officer to inventory the lethal cocktail meds. He had enough of the drugs to euthanized 20% of the crew. Your name was at the top of the list."

"Thank you, sir."

Andrew climbed back up into the conning tower. He looked around then tossed the form over the side. He then put on his sound powered telephones. Bill looked at him strangely.

"Skipper, how do you know we are at least 50 nautical miles from land in order to be able to dump trash and garbage?" asked Bill.

"If we were closer than 50 nautical miles from land, we would have been spotted already. There's a new watch being posted on the forward end of the ship."

"Aye, sir."

Bart opened the forward escape trunk hatch, put on his sound powered telephones and started scanning the horizon with his binoculars. An airborne early warning aircraft was flying on a north/northwest course of 299. The pilot was loosing faith in the air search for SSN-75. So far, since taking off from the carrier, they had chased down several icebergs, a VLCC and a cruise ship, but, no sub.

The radar operators were all watching their scopes. So far, nothing but empty ocean. In another hour, the plane would have to turn back to refuel. It was then that the ensign, who was monitoring the starboard side radar array detected SSN-75. The return was one large hit with numerous smaller hits. The ensign called the pilot.

"Another hit, sir. Bearing 305 at the outer edge of my scopes."

"What's the distance?" asked the co-pilot.

"120 nautical miles, sir."

"What does the radar computer say the hit is?"

"A large surface missile surrounded by a chaff charge."

Both the pilot and co-pilot looked at each other with bizarre looks on their faces. The pilot looked down at the fuel status; one pass. The pilot looked back over at the co-pilot.

"Steer new course 305 and take us down to 100 feet/33 meters above the water," said the pilot.

"Aye, sir," replied the co-pilot as they both pushed down on their yokes at the same time.

The plane dove down towards the surface of the North Pacific. It headed towards SSN-75 without knowing it directly. As the plane got closer to SSN-75, the radar operator was able to get a good fix on SSN-75.

"Sir, I have a speed of 18 knots on a course of 080 degrees."

"Then, it is not a cruise missile, sir," said the co-pilot.

"No. Keep your eyes peeled."

"Aye, sir."

It was Bart who spotted the plane first. He almost screamed into his sound powered telephones.

"Conn, Forward Watch. Plane coming in low over the horizon, bearing 080 degrees!"

"Conn, aye," said Andrew raising his binoculars to his eyes.

Andrew saw the large rotating dish first and knew it was an airborne early warning plane. Andrew then told everyone to start waving frantically. As the plane approached, they saw the streamers and the cookie sheets rotating on top of the radar unit. Both the pilot and co-pilot saw the decorations at the same time. The pilot banked the plane around SSN-75. He then "waved" the wings as he flew by just off their port side.

"Skipper, I think that plane means that there is an aircraft carrier in the area," said Bill excitedly.

"Don't get too excited, XO. That plane has at least a 300 nautical mile range which means that aircraft carrier could be anywhere."

"Sorry, skipper."

"That's okay. That plane will radio our location, though."

Aboard the plane, the pilot was able to get a good fix on SSN-75. He looked down at his fuel status; one pass then back to the carrier. He decided to do the last pass as low as possible. He called the navigator.

"Brad, I'm going to make one pass, very low. I want you to load the forward drop-bay with a floating ELM."

"Aye, sir."

The plane assumed an attack type posture and came in low towards SSN-75. At the last second, the plane dropped the floating ELM. It hit the water and came floating up close to the sub. Andrew had Bart grab it when it came by. Bart and few deck personnel hauled the ELM aboard and tied it off to the forward escape trunk. The ELM was already beeping. Andrew was able to get an estimated course only on the plane of 155 degrees. Andrew then went below to the chart room.

"QMSN Davids, show me on a course of 155 degrees from here to a point at 300 nautical miles," said Andrew.

"Aye, sir."

QMSN Davids pulled out his grease pencils and electronic charts. He then plotted the distance from SSN-75 to a point estimated at 300 nautical miles. If there was an aircraft carrier somewhere in the area, the ship was in the middle of GPS Grid Square 2935.

"Sir, assuming that 300 nautical miles is correct on a course of 155 degrees, that aircraft carrier should be somewhere here inside of GPS Grid Square 2935."

"Alright," said Andrew as he reached up for the sound powered telephones.

"XO, pass the word to the night lookouts that an aircraft carrier could appear on the horizon anytime after midnight."

"Aye, sir."

When Andrew had returned to the conning tower, Bill talked to him.

"Skipper, why not turn towards the aircraft carrier?"

"Too risky, XO. I have to assume three things at this time."

"Which are?"

"One, that the plane radioed our course, speed and location to the aircraft carrier. Two, the aircraft carrier is plotting an intercept course based on our current course, speed and location. Three, that the carrier will assume that we will maintain course and speed."

"You're right, Andy; sorry."

"That's okay, Bill."

Aboard the carrier, the information was given to the captain. The captain took the information to his chart room. The Quartermaster Senior Chief plotted an intercept course. The XO soon joined them in the chart room.

"At flank speed, sir, we can overtake them sometime after 2345 hours tonight on a course of 300."

"Excellent, senior chief. The pilot reported they had no active radar or radio, XO."

"But they do have the ELM that the pilot dropped."

"You're right on that point, XO. XO, notify the commanding officer of ASR-58 that we have located SSN-75. She is somewhere inside of GPS Grid Square 2918 on a course of 080 at 18 knots."

"Aye, sir," said the XO as he left the chart room.

"Senior Chief, how long before ASR-58 can intercept us?"

"Already plotted to include refueling time, intercept time is 39 hours."

"Thank you."

The captain went to the bridge. He had the helmsman change course and speed. Within an hour, all the planes in the search and rescue effort were aboard the carrier. For the captain, there were many ways of doing a rescue at sea and at sea at night. He looked up and called down to Main Control.

"Bridge, Main Control," said the captain.

"Main Control, aye," replied the chief engineer. A loud noise could be heard in the background.

"Can you give me any more speed?"

"Sorry, sir, I'm at maximum output right now; 48 knots is the best I can do."

"Bridge, aye."

The XO joined the captain on the bridge.

"Skipper, I called ASR-58. She says she is about 39 hours away and asked us if we could assist with any injuries or wounded until she arrives."

"Sure. Notify the sickbay to prepare for an unknown number of injured, submariners soon."

"Aye, sir."

"XO, after nightfall, no Dog Zebra. I want this ship as fully illuminated as possible."

"Aye, sir."

"Inform Colonel Danes that we will have need of his LCAC's and medical personnel."

"Aye, sir."

"XO, I'm going below to take a nap. Wake me up the minute SSN-75 is spotted," said the captain as he left the bridge.

"Aye, sir."

Aboard SSN-75, hope was beginning to fade. It was nightfall already and no more planes had been spotted. The aircraft carrier was nowhere in sight. Andrew had dinner and took a short nap before returning to the conning tower for watch duty. There was a full moon out and the seas were relatively calm. Andrew, as an afterthought to something else, had the running lights turned on. Two hours and 45 minutes from actually being able to see the SSN-75, the massive radar assembly was able to detect them.

"Bridge, Combat," said OS2 Smith.

"Bridge, aye," replied the XO, drinking some coffee.

"Surface target, sir. Bearing 305, speed 18 knots on a course of 080."

"Bridge, aye. Identify surface target as SSN-75."

"Combat, aye."

"Petty-officer-of-the-watch, wake up the captain."

"Aye, sir."

The XO picked up the phone.

"Colonel Danes, be ready to launch your LCAC's in 45 minutes."

"Yes, XO."

The XO changed channels.

"Hangar Deck Control, Bridge."

"Hangar Deck Control, aye."

"Hangar Deck Control, lower both flight deck elevators to the hangar deck for bay 3."

"Aye, sir."

The XO hung up the phone as the captain arrived on the bridge. The captain decided against using the helicopters because of nightfall. The XO informed the captain that Colonel Danes was prepared to launch the LCAC's at the top of the hour. The captain nodded in agreement with the XO's plan.

The starboard watch aboard SSN-75 spotted the carrier. The moonlit night allowed him to see the wall of whitewater being pushed ahead of the ship. He then moved his binoculars up to the flight deck where he saw lights. He alerted Andrew and Bill immediately.

"Captain, XO, large ship on the horizon, bearing 165!"

"What do you make of her?" asked Andrew.

"Aircraft carrier, by the way she's lit up, but I can't make out the number on the tower."

"Very well, maintain course and speed; fire flares."

The distress flares were launched. Even at that distance, the aircraft carrier's watches detected them. The captain ordered the ship to a stop. When all forward motion had ceased, the LCAC's were launched. The LCAC's turned on their powerful and bright lights, which allowed SSN-75 to detect them.

"Skipper, looks like small craft are approaching us," said Bill, pointing at the lights.

"I see them. XO, assemble the crew on the forward deck of the sub."

"Aye, sir."

A large, freight train-like noise could be heard. Within minutes, the LCAC's had passed SSN-75. They merely turned around and came towards the sub's aft end. Andrew prepared for them to tie up, but they didn't. The LCAC's merely coasted aboard the aft end of the sub. The doors opened up and Andrew recognized the Marine Corps uniforms. A person, with the rank of a Major, ran up to the conning tower. He saluted Andrew and Bill who returned his salute.

"Request permission to come aboard, Captain Hinton-Smith," he said.

"Permission granted, major," said Andrew.

"Thank you, sir."

The major entered the conning tower.

"Captain Hinton-Smith, I'm Major Moriarty with the 184th Marine Detachment aboard the USS ABRAHAM LINCOLN, CVN-72. We have been instructed to start taking your personnel back to the carrier in groups of 15 for medical exams."

"Sure thing, major. My executive officer will assist you."

"Aye, sir. Major, if you will follow me."

About 45 minutes later, the aircraft carrier was alongside. The crew of SSN-75, after complete medical exams, were returned to the sub. The carrier and her air wing stayed alongside until the following afternoon when ASR-58 arrived on scene. The carrier departed and ASR-58 guided SSN-75 back to port where a complete inspection of the sub was done.

The report showed that some systems were destroyed, necessitating a complete replacement. Captain Togant estimated that SSN-75 needed at least 90-days in the shipyards. Gary was just happy to have Andrew back alive. They talked after dinner.

"You know, the Chaplain was going to assist me with your funeral arrangements," said Gary, trying not to cry.

"The Command Chaplain is a good man."

"It was a very scary visit, Andy. Seeing Mel, Sandra and the Command Chaplain standing there in the doorway."

In Washington, D.C., the President was reviewing the estimated downtime of the USS DIAMONDBACK along with the repair bill from the shock trials. She was looking across the desktop at Admiral Rosen. When she was through reviewing the report, she set that one down and picked up another report on Iran. She saw that this intelligence report indicated no recent military type activity outside of the normal maneuvers for the last three months. She glared at Admiral Rosen.

"I'm not a happy woman, Admiral Rosen. That pet project of yours just cost the taxpayers another $815,000,000.00 including the $10,000.00 a day storage cost."

"A minor setback, madam President. I still have her scheduled for deployment with the USS CARL VINSON, CVN-70 and her battle group."

"I'll trust you on that one, Admiral Rosen. However, I want another battle group from Norfolk, Virginia ready for deployment one month after the last battle group gets underway from the West Coast. Who's on the list?"

"I believe the USS GEORGE WASHINGTON, CVN-73 is about ready."

"Good. I want the battle group to get underway with full combat loads and have them go to the Persian Gulf to keep an eye on Iran. They've been a little too quiet, recently."

"I understand, madam President. Is there anything else?"

"No; dismissed."

After the admiral had left, the President picked up the phone. She called her secretary.

"Yes, madam President?" asked the voice.

"Get me both the Israeli Prime Minister and the Iraqi Prime Minister on the phone and I don't care in what order."

"Yes, madam President."

A few minutes later, the Israeli Prime Minister, Yetsar Rafik, was on the phone.

"Yes, madam President, what can I do for you?"

"If the Iranians attack you, please wait to retaliate against them until I have called you first; okay?"

"Very well, madam President. I will resist the urge to nuke them. May I, at least, keep planes in the air?"

"Yes, that will be fine and I will make sure that you get some humanitarian aid as well from as many countries as I can get to cooperate."

"Thank you; is there anything else?"

"Yes, there is an intelligence report circulating around the Middle East that Ahmadenijad may have Alzheimer's."

"I see and you know, your predecessor said the same thing about Saddam Hussein as well," he said as he hung up the phone.

An hour later, the Iraqi Prime Minister, Al Ahamadijiki, was on the phone.

"Look, I know you don't like me very much because I am a woman and I'm currently running the United States, but that doesn't mean that we can't be diplomatic about a national security issue."

"What can I do for you, madam President?"

"I have a strong suspicion that Iran plans on attacking Israel. I want your country to start massing troops along your border with Iran from September 1st until October 15th."

"Then what do you want me to do?" he asked as he started writing things down on a small notepad that was attached to his desktop.

"Have your troops appear to be conducting battle maneuvers prior to an invasion. Then on October 16th, I want you to leave your troops in such a position that it would appear that you're going to invade."

"I don't think the Iranians are going to take to these maneuvers very nicely."

"That's the point, sir. I want the Iranians a little on edge so that maybe they won't attack Israel for a little while. Anyway, on October 31st at around, say, 0100 hours your time, I want you to open fire on the Iranian border. Don't directly target civilians, but do inflict some damage with rockets, missiles, etc."

"Let me see if I have this written down correctly. You want me to look like

I'm going to invade my neighbor. Then you want me to fire on my neighbor? You know they will shoot back."

"Precisely, sir. That will keep the Iranians busy for a few days trying to sort things out. On November 1ˢᵗ at, say, around 0500 hours your time, I want you to pull all of your troops away from the border."

"Then what?" he asked as he continued writing down what had been said.

"I'll arrange for a press conference at which time you will tell the world that a most unfortunate accidental weapons discharge into a neighboring country has occurred. I want you to profusely apologize to the Iranians."

"What do I tell the Iranians has happened?"

"Tell them something like an Iraqi troop member fell asleep at the missile launch controls of their respective missile launcher. They slumped forward against the fire button and poof!"

"I see. I will do as you ask and thank you for the call."

"Good-bye."

She pressed the receiver down and let it come back up again.

"Yes, madam President?" asked the voice.

"Get me General Orndorf on the line."

"Yes, madam President."

A few minutes later, General Orndorf was on the phone.

"Yes, madam President, what can I do for you?" he asked.

"How many of those Massive Ordnance Air Blast devices do we have in our arsenal?"

"100 all together, with some already deployed."

"How many are in the Middle Eastern theatre of operations?"

"25."

"Use all of them on Iranian military, high value targets, if I tell you to."

"Yes, madam President. Is there anything else?"

"Keep a couple of squadrons of fighters, bombers and cargo planes on alert in Italy. Tell the cargo planes to drop food, medical supplies, weapons and ammunition on those areas as may be designated by the Director of the CIA."

"Yes, madam President."

"Good-bye."

The USS DIAMONDBACK was getting repaired. She was able to get underway and made it to her new home at the Los Angeles Naval Base. There, minor repairs were completed and the training continued. Admiral Rosen was pleased to see a report on his desktop one morning in late September that the logistics fleet was underway three weeks earlier than planned.

Admiral Rosen then typed up the orders for the USS GEORGE

WASHINGTON and her battle group. He made sure that the orders included a requirement for the logistics fleet to be underway at least two weeks prior to the main battle group being deployed. The orders were sent out and received by USS GEORGE WASHINGTON's commanding officer. She read the orders and called a meeting of the department heads.

All NATO members were put on alert in September. Air Force bases in northern Italy, southern France, Greece and Turkey were placed on stand-by. The planes were fueled and armed. One could see rows and rows of NATO and U.S. fighters, bombers, cargo planes and attack craft of all types and shapes. Ordnance was prepared and pre-staged for an attack, if the orders came. The President hoped that Ahmadenijad was seeing the pictures.

Ahmadenijad turned off his TV and picked up the phone. He dialed a special number. When the phone was answered, they spoke Arabic to each other.

"We attack Israel on the 1st of November," said Ahmadenijad.

"Yes, sir."

"Make sure that our Hamas and Hezbollah Brothers are ready and know as well."

"Yes, sir. Allah will be proud of us," he said as he hung up the phone.

The President was in a secret meeting with the Director of the CIA. The meeting was short and to the point. The President did most of the talking.

"We've been arming and training the Iranian civilian population to overthrow their government, right?" she asked.

"Yes, that is correct. They have been secretly training for the last 40 years or so since Ahmadenijad came to power. They want to be a free, Democratic society, like us."

"If the Iranians attack Israel, they will have their chance. So that they have a better chance at success, I will soften up the Iranian military and some of their war machine; put the word out to those loyal people to take cover if Israel is attacked."

"Yes, madam President. Is there anything else?"

"No; good-bye."

# Chapter 21

At 0800 hours, Pacific Standard Time, on October 5, the Day of Reckoning had arrived. The President of the United States had called a press conference. She stepped up to the podium when she was told that they had live feed from the west coast. The picture shown was of Shelly Roth, KKLA TV-12, Los Angeles, California. She was on a hillside opposite the Golden Gate Bridge. The cameras panned passed her to the ships all leaving the various shipyards in the Bay area, as it was known. The man in charge of the video footage gave the President a thumbs up signal.

"Ladies and Gentlemen, the President of the United States," said the mechanical voice.

"Thank you. My fellow Americans, five carrier battle groups got underway today to fight an enemy to the United States with maximum force. 40,000 naval personnel are underway at this time. Their target is the drug-infested country of Somalia. We now go to some live footage," she said.

The press personnel suddenly saw Shelly Roth of KKLA TV-12. In the background there was an aircraft carrier with a large "74" painted on her bridge area and flight deck. Shelly was soon talking to Vice Admiral Bonds. The cameras turned to her and Vice Admiral Bonds.

"Vice Admiral Bonds, how many aircraft carrier battle groups are departing?" she asked.

"Five in all, along with their escorts and logistics ships. The USS NIMITZ, CVN-68, got underway about 0400 hours, Pacific Standard Time. The USS CARL VINSON, CVN-70, was underway yesterday at 0700 hours, Hawaii Standard Time. The USS ABRAHAM LINCOLN, CVN-72, was underway about 0630, Pacific Standard Time."

"I can see an aircraft carrier passing under the Golden Gate Bridge right now. Which aircraft carrier is that one?"

"That is the USS JOHN C. STENNIS, CVN-74. The USS RONALD REGAN, CVN-76, will get underway by 1000 hours, Pacific Standard Time."

"Are there any submarines assisting the carriers?"

"Yes. All fast attack subs from Submarine Squadrons 18, 20, 22 and 24 are already underway, including our latest fast attack sub, the USS DIAMONDBACK, SSN-75."

"Does the Navy plan on using any of its ballistic missile fleet?"

"No, not at this time. However, we have many new technologies that we want to test in combat to see how they work."

"Sounds good and thank you, Vice Admiral Bonds. Now, back to our studios in Los Angeles. This is Shelly Roth of KKLA TV-12 reporting to you, live, from San Francisco."

When the cameras were turned back towards the Golden Gate Bridge and Vice Admiral Bonds had seen the microphones turned off, he stopped Shelly.

"How would you and your camera crew like to tape the USS JOHN C. STENNIS, there, launching her part of the attack?" he asked.

"Are you kidding me, Vice Admiral Bonds?"

"Absolutely not. The U.S. Navy will fly you and your camera crew to the island of Diego Garcia. Then, the night before the attack, you'll be flown out to the carrier to video tape their part of the attack."

"You're on, Vice Admiral Bonds."

"I'll make the arrangements," he said, dialing numbers on his cell phone.

Since all the eyes of the world were on the deploying west coast ships, no one noticed the USS GEORGE WASHINGTON, CVN-73 and her battle group deploy to the Persian Gulf. Only a little snippet in the news gave any indication that the east coast had done anything. Before too many questions were asked, the battle group was many hours out to sea. All the ships were doing flank speed.

The Iranians were carefully watching the Iraqis. The Iraqi troops were doing exactly what their commanding general told them to do. The Iranian leader was getting apprehensive. He thought that maybe the Iraqis had figured out his plan and were trying to stop him. Ahmadenijad told his troops at the border to keep a close eye on the Iraqis.

During this time, the USS GEORGE WASHINGTON's logistics fleet safely transited the Strait of Hormuz without being detected. Now, precision timing would be of the essence to allow the aircraft carrier and her battle group to transit the Strait of Hormuz without being spotted as well.

Shelly and her camera crew landed aboard the USS JOHN C. STENNIS, CVN-74, a little after the "accident" had occurred. Since there was still intermittent artillery fire and missile exchanges, the USS GEORGE WASHINGTON, CVN-73 and her battle group were able to safely transit the Strait of Hormuz without being detected. In fact, the aircraft carrier simply slipped in between some VLCC's. Only a lone fishing vessel spotted the carrier.

After being shown to their quarters, Shelly and her camera crew were taken on a tour of the ship. When the tour was done, the guide, Commander Davis, the ship's Operations Officer, took them into the Combat Information Center, or CIC as it was called aboard the ship. Commander Davis turned to Shelly as her camera crew finished taking pictures and video footage.

"Do you have any questions?" asked Commander Davis.

"How many people are aboard this ship? Some people back home find it hard to fathom what a ship this size is really like."

"Fair enough. This ship currently has 6,900 personnel aboard."

"How big is this ship?" she asked, taking notes.

"126,666 tons with full combat load at this time. However, there are cruise ships that are bigger than we are."

"What's the length and width of this ship?" asked one of the camera operators.

"At the waterline, this ship is 1,110 feet long, 208 feet wide and the same height as a 28 story office building from bottom to top. At the flight deck here, this ship is 3.9 football fields long and 1.5 football fields wide. If you stood this ship upright, it would almost reach the top of the Sears Roebuck Tower in Chicago."

"That means this ship is almost 1,200 feet long at the flight deck and 425 feet wide at the flight deck?" commented Shelly.

"That's pretty close to a right guess. Now, in a few minutes, I will be taking you to the bridge. Unless spoken to, don't say a word."

"Yes, Commander Davis."

They left the Combat Information Center and headed towards the bridge. When they arrived, the Commanding Officer, Captain Janice Luge, looked over at them.

"Shelly, I heard you really liked the landing," she said with a smile.

"Yes, Captain Luge, the landing left me speechless."

"Good. You're really going to love the takeoff. I just received word that the first wave of cruise missiles are on their way to their targets," she said, pointing at the binoculars.

Shelly looked down and saw the spare binoculars. She picked them up and looked in the direction Captain Luge was looking. She could see them faintly at first, but as they got closer and closer to the ship, she was riveted to them. They kept getting closer and larger until they looked like they were going to hit the ship. At the last second, they went up and over the ship. There was hardly any noise from the cruise missiles. Shelly put down her binoculars. The look on her face was priceless.

"Since we are entering the official designated combat zone, all civilian personnel must leave the ship. It was a pleasure to have you aboard Shelly Roth; good-bye," said Janice.

Aboard the USS DIAMONDBACK, Andrew was looking over his battle board in the large communications center. He was in constant communication with all the forces in the area whether they were sea, air or land. The large communications center also had live satellite uplink and downloading capability. This allowed Andrew to see in minutes if enough damage was done to a target or not.

He was issuing orders to all the surface and submarine forces in the area. The Somalian navy was destroyed in the first part of the melee'. As ground forces prepared to move in, Andrew continued issuing orders to surface ships as well as the subs in the area. Andrew put on his headphones as he looked at the battle board, which was being updated every three minutes.

"USS CONNETICUT, fire on positions 2, 6, 17 and 19."

A few minutes later, after the cruise missiles had hit their targets, Andrew looked at the satellite images of the damage. The targets at positions 17 and 19 had not sustained enough damage.

"USS DENVER, fire on positions 17 and 19; not enough damage. Also, you may fire on positions 98, 121 and 149."

Andrew waited for the results before issuing more orders. After four days of attack, ground forces started moving into the country. They met little resistance. When some of the submarines had returned from being resupplied with more cruise missiles and HARPOON's, Andrew sat back and started listening to the ground forces reports. One report he listened in on sounded rather frantic. As Andrew looked over the reports of heavy incoming fire, he cut into the conversation.

"First Sergeant Faulkner, this is Captain Hinton-Smith of the USS DIAMONDBACK. Where is that incoming fire originating?" asked Andrew.

"Hill 9! Hill 9!, sir," he yelled. Andrew heard another set of explosions.

Andrew looked over his battle board. There was nothing available at sea to help the man. He looked at the flight groups next. Andrew found that a squadron of B-52H's was near the area.

"First Sergeant, remain calm, take cover and don't move from your current position until help arrives. Help will be arriving in five minutes."

"Yes, sir!"

Andrew snapped his finger at CW02 Smith to connect him to General Orndorf.

"Yes, Captain Hinton-Smith, what can I do for you?" asked the general.

"I just monitored a call for help from a ground unit that is coming under heavy fire from a position called Hill 9 inside of GPS Grid Square 3939."

"What do you want me to do?"

"I don't have any naval assets close enough to fire on that position. Could you please divert B-52H, number 354 to that area?"

"Will do."

Andrew watched on his battle board as the requested B-52H bomber suddenly turned toward the area. The bomber bombed the hillside and into the next valley with its payload. When the incoming fire had ceased, the ground units moved in. The deadly payload of 108, 500-lb./250-kilogram bombs had done a brutally efficient job of destroying the enemy stronghold. A solid line of troops was now headed towards the city of Mogadishu and the last stronghold of the last drug/warlord.

It was 1200 hours local in Israel when the Iranians, only slightly delayed by the Iraqi "accident" unleashed their attack. Only 500 of the incoming missiles could be shot down. Once the anti-missile defense systems were empty, the rest rained down destruction on Israeli cities, towns and military installations. The President of the United States called the Israeli Prime Minister after the attack had been completed.

"How many dead?" she asked.

"A rough estimate of 84,000. My general is chomping at the bit to launch on them."

"I know. I have a carrier battle group ready to launch an attack on them to soften them up before you retaliate. Move your JERICHO-IID and JERICHO-IIIB missiles into firing position and await my next call."

"What about help?"

"I am sending all the help I can at this time. Help from your neighbors and others will be arriving in the next few weeks."

"I will do as you ask. The Iraqis, that was no accident was it?"

"You're very perceptive, Mr. Prime Minister."

"Good-bye."

The Iranians were stunned to note that there was no return fire. The return fire came four days later after an attack led by the carrier GEORGE WASHINGTON had softened up the Iranians. The Israelis fired almost all of their missiles at Iran including those missiles with tactical nuclear warheads. Ahmadenijad and his top leaders were killed when one of the missiles, carrying a 250-kiloton, low yield, tactical nuclear warhead, ground impacted above his bunker.

After the civilians finished off what was left of the Republican Guard, the new civilian run government temporarily in place demanded for help to clean up the mess and in becoming a Democracy. The President of the United States was only too glad to assist with those requests. Foreign aid started pouring in from all over the world including the former Soviet Union nations.

SSN-75 was getting ready to return to port after the battles were completed. It was the holiday season and Andrew was looking over TM3 Bart Bradley's Enlisted Service Record. Bart had been lost at sea during a particularly heavy clash with the pirates. SSN-75 was trying to follow the pirates back to their lair to put them out of commission, but it backfired terribly.

Both SSN-75 and the pirates exchanged small arms fire and rocket propelled grenades. As Andrew looked down at the small service record, he closed it after reading the final page entry. The XO knocked on the door to Andrew's cabin. Andrew opened the door.

"Yes, XO, I know it is about time for the eulogy. XO, you're going to learn something one day when you have command of your own boat that the 'we regret to inform you' letter during the holiday season is one of the worst duties to perform."

"Are you going to tell his parents?" asked Bill.

"Not yet, XO. We won't be out of the official combat zone until after the first of the year. Naval Regulation 122 states that only official information can be transmitted outside of the combat zone. There are few exceptions."

"That is true, sir."

"Make sure that you and the master-at-arms inventory his personal effects. Cut any locks on his rack, foot locker, etc."

"Yes, sir. Is there anything else?"

"See if the personnel officer can place Mr. Bradley's service record in the MIA status. We never recovered a body," said Andrew, handing Bill the service record.

"Aye, sir."

After the XO had left, Andrew put on his cap and started walking down the passageway towards the bridge. When he arrived on the bridge, there was a solemn quiet about the place. The only noises were coming from cooling fans and some computers that were running. Normally, the bridge would be filled with lively conversations; today it was starkly quiet. Andrew turned to the Chief of the Boat.

"Chief of the Boat, pass the word that all crewmembers, not actually on watch, muster on the forward deck for the…," Andrew started to choke.

"I'll take care of it, sir."

"Thank you master chief."

"It's hard, sir, I know. On your way to the eulogy, TM1 (SS) Doenitz would like to see you, sir."

"Is she in the forward torpedo room?"

"Yes, sir."

"Very well."

As Andrew left the bridge, he hardly noticed the announcement made by the master chief. He knocked on the hatch to the forward torpedo room. TM1 (SS) Heather Doenitz stood up and opened the hatch. She spoke with a heavy, husky voice.

"You may enter, sir," she said sniffing.

"You wanted to speak to me?"

"Yes, sir. Bart and I had started to become very close, sir, on this voyage. You know that I really don't like males on an intimate level, but Bart was different. He treated me as an equal…," she said as she choked on tears.

"And that made you feel special, didn't it?"

"Yes, sir. I just can't believe he is gone, sir," she said, drying her eyes.

"Never give up hope, Heather. Remember, we never found a body and Bart is rather creative."

"Yes, sir. I just wish we could do something for him."

"I think something can be arranged. Load tube 1 with a water slug."

"Aye, sir."

Andrew left and returned to the bridge. He told the Chief of the Boat what he wanted to do. After delivering the eulogy and firing tube 1, Andrew returned to the bridge. He turned to Bill.

"XO, submerge the sub; secure all masts," said Andrew.

"Aye, sir."

SSN-75 slipped under the waves. As the sub leveled off at 200 feet/67 meters, everyone went back to their duties. That night, the Supply Officer approached Andrew about the waterproof bag that Bart had last been seen with on his last mission.

"Supply Officer, list that item as lost/missing," said Andrew, dryly.

"Aye, sir. The weapons officer needs to talk to you as well, sir."

"Send him in," replied Andrew.

"What do you want me to do with the .45 that he had been issued?"

"List it as lost/missing."

"Aye, sir."

"Did GMG1 get the weapons cleaned and ammunition inventoried?"

"Yes, sir. All in accordance with regulations; the bottom of the report has the on hand stores," said the weapons officer handing Andrew the report.

"Very well. Did he put all of the PMS checks that he did on the weapons on his PMS quarterly boards?"

"Yes, sir."

"Dismissed."

The next morning, the sonar crews were listening to the noises in the water on their headphones. The North Sound Center picked up high-pitched, sonar pulses. Jon Costillo was on watch in the sound center and began both a track on the noise as well as writing down the sound pulses. Jon recognized the sound pulses as Morse code, but since he wasn't familiar with Morse code anymore, he handed the pulses to the South Sound Center where Sam was on duty.

"Sam, you know Morse Code, right?" asked Jon as he talked into his headset.

"Yeah, Jon, what do you have?" he asked.

Jon walked into his center and handed him the piece of paper with the dots and dashes on it. Sam took the paper and was able to decipher it quickly. Sam handed the paper back to Jon who now had a better track on the noise. He picked up the phone.

"Sonar, Conn," said Jon.

"Conn, aye," replied Bill, who was serving as Officer of the Deck.

"XO, object in the water bearing 020 at 12,500 yards/4,167 meters, emitting our hull number in Morse Code pulses."

"Conn, aye. Diving officer, come to course 020."

"Aye, sir."

It was almost nightfall when Andrew went to his quarters. Bill was first watch and had the sub close in on the noise. Jon, in sonar, was able to get the sub within 500 yards/167 meters of the sound. Andrew gave permission to Bill to surface the sub. Bill and a couple of watch standers began looking around. The port watch stander spotted the bright yellow bag with the flashing strobe light. Bill had the bag fished out of the water.

Bill took the bag below as SSN-75 slipped under the waves. Bill opened up the bag at the same time he saw the left side of the bag; "SSN-75." Bill pulled out the sonar transmitter and found out why the bag felt so heavy. The transmitter was connected to a circuit board. The circuit board was wired to a 6-volt lantern type battery. Bill shut off the transmitter and found more objects inside.

There was Styrofoam packing, the .45 with all empty magazines, the diving equipment that included the compass, knife and GPS locator and Bart's diving watch. Bill dumped out all the remaining objects along with some seawater. Bill had the supply office and weapons officer report to the bridge. The next morning, the sub was buzzing with talk of the bag. Bill found

Andrew on the bridge shortly after breakfast. Andrew had just examined the knife and the .45.

"Make sure, XO, that Bart's recent personal effects are put in with his other personal effects," said Andrew.

"Aye, sir. Shouldn't we close out his service record now?"

"Not yet, XO. Still no body or body parts; by the way, did you know that the knife has blood on it?"

"No, sir, I was not aware of that issue."

"Did you know that the .45 has blood on it?"

"No, sir, I was not aware of that issue, either. He probably got eaten by something, sir."

"You may be correct, XO. However, until the military finds conclusive proof that he is dead, we must abide by Naval Regulation 206 and the rules governing POW's/MIA's."

"Aye, sir."

"Maintain our course and speed to Diego Garcia and if Heather asks about the bag, tell her all we know. That way, she can't accuse us of hiding information."

"Aye, sir."

As Andrew drank his cup of coffee, a thought hit him.

"XO, did you turn on his GPS locator?"

"No, sir."

"Turn it on."

"Aye, sir."

Bill turned on the device. The screen came on with a warning first, "LOW/DEAD BATT." The screen flickered a little then the device shut itself off.

"Dead batteries, sir. It won't stay on," said Bill.

"What type of batteries does it need?" asked Andrew.

"4 'AA's, sir."

Andrew removed his wallet from his back, right pocket and pulled out a $10 bill. He handed the money to Bill.

"Go buy some batteries, XO."

"Aye, sir."

When Bill had left, Andrew turned to the Chief of the Boat.

"Do you carry the Luminol® test kit aboard?"

"No, sir, I'm sorry I don't have that particular test kit aboard."

"Would Diego Garcia have one?"

"Yes, sir."

"When we get to Diego Garcia, take both the knife and the .45 to their lab. I want to know if this blood is human or not."

"Aye, sir," said the Chief of the Boat, taking the items with him to his office.

Bill returned with the batteries and put them into the unit. When the screen had lit up, he handed the unit back to Andrew. Andrew went directly to the last, locked GPS entry. Andrew saw the coordinates and turned the unit as he turned to face Bill.

"XO, I'm going to my quarters. I want you to stand by the phone and send the medical officer to my quarters," said Andrew as he left the bridge.

"Aye, sir."

Andrew arrived at his quarters and started looking through the GPS unit's memory. Andrew saw that the last, locked entry had been made 40 days earlier at 19:49 hours. This was at the same time the sub and the pirates were exchanging fire with each other. Andrew saw the coordinates were latitude and longitude and not GPS Grid Square. Andrew tore a piece of paper out of a small notebook that was on his desk and took a pen out of his left shirt pocket to write down the coordinates. He turned the unit off when the medical officer knocked on his door.

"Enter," said Andrew.

"You wanted to see me, sir?" he asked.

Andrew stood up from his desk and locked the door.

"How long can a human survive without food and water?"

"Seven days, sir. After that, the body simply shuts down."

"Thank you. Let's assume that I am stealing food and water and that I eat uncooked or perhaps half-cooked food and have unclean water to drink? Then how long could I survive?"

"You could survive at least a month or more. However, the unclean water and undercooked food would start to affect you."

"Thank you; dismissed and I am ordering you not to talk to anyone about our conversation."

"Aye, sir."

"One more question, what blood type is TM3 Bradley?"

"He's rare, sir. AB negative."

"Thank you; dismissed."

When the medical officer had left, Andrew locked up the GPS unit in his safe. Andrew left his quarters and headed to the chart room. When he entered the chart room, he locked both doors and put his hat over the only door with a window. QM1 Traci Walker looked up at Andrew.

"What the hell did I do to end up at the top of your shitlist, sir?" she asked, rather concerned.

"Nothing, I just don't want to be watched. Can you tell me where these latitude and longitude lines intersect?" asked Andrew, handing the paper to QM1.

"Sure, sir."

QM1 sat down at her computer. She typed the coordinates into the computer. The computer located the coordinates as being in the extreme northeast corner of GPS Grid Square 4145. She looked up the CD she would need, 38-25-95. She turned to Andrew as she opened up the CD tray on the chart table.

"Sir, located behind you is a CD labeled 38-25-95."

Andrew located the CD and handed it to her. She put it into the tray and it automatically closed. The image that came up of GPS Grid Square 4145 showed a peaceful fishing village with a remote cove to the northeast.

"Can you show me where we were at 40 days ago at 1949 hours?"

"Yes, sir."

She typed the time and date into the computer. The image that came up showed the sub just entering GPS Grid Square 4145. According to the log entries, the sub and the pirates had been shooting it out. It was also about the time that Bart was lost at sea. QM1 looked up at the captain.

"You don't think that Bart followed them back to their lair do you, sir?" she asked.

"That's exactly what I'm thinking. Is that cove accessible all day?"

"No, sir, just at the major high tides."

"Good. You're under orders not to discuss this meeting with anyone," said Andrew as QM1 shut off the computer.

"Aye, sir."

Three days later, the sub pulled into Diego Garcia.

On the evening of the first day in port at Diego Garcia, the radio room received its message traffic. The duty radio operator, RM3 (SS) Rick Stone, decoded all but one message. After routing all the messages to their respective departments, RM3 (SS) Stone looked at the last, coded, message. He looked at the message classification header and saw the bold letters of NATOSECRET. He called the command duty officer.

"This is RM3 (SS) Stone in radio. Is the captain still aboard?" he asked.

"Yes, I believe he is with the Chief of the Boat going over a report," replied the weapons officer, who was the CDO.

"Have him report to radio, I have a message for him."

"Will do."

A few minutes later, Andrew showed up in the radio room.

"You have a message for me?" asked Andrew as he yawned.

"Yes, sir. A NATOSECRET message according to the message classification header."

"Very well."

Andrew walked over to the computer and inputted his special password. The computer accepted the password and printed up the message. As a courtesy, RM3 (SS) Stone stepped out of the radio room and closed the door. Andrew read the message and then destroyed it in the paper shredder. He opened up the door.

"Where's the CDO?" asked Andrew.

"Quarterdeck, sir."

"Thank you."

Andrew went to the quarterdeck and found the CDO.

"Weapons officer, how many TLAM's do we have aboard with boosters?"

"Eight, sir."

"What's their maximum range with the boosters?"

"690 nautical miles, sir."

"Put TM1 (SS) Doenitz in charge of putting the boosters on those eight TLAM's. Tell her we are going hunting."

"Should I have her load the VLS or the tubes, sir?"

"Load tubes 1 through 8."

"Aye, sir. Do you have our coordinates?"

"Not yet, the message stated that those coordinates would follow in the next 24 hours."

"Aye, sir."

Andrew found Bill and the Chaplain. He quickly informed them of what was going on and some of the contents of the message that he had received. When SSN-75 was back underway, they fired on the coordinates that had been sent via TOPSECRET message to the ship.

The TLAM's, despite the tropical storm covering the pirates' base of operations; hit their target with devastating results. Once Andrew had seen the damage inflicted from the satellite shots, he made a copy for TM1 (SS) Doenitz. Andrew then went to see the Chaplain.

"Yes, captain what can I do for you?" he asked.

"At our next port of call, contact the Command Chaplain for our squadron. Tell him to make arrangements for Bart's parents to be flown to Vandenberg Air Force Base in Nevada. Also, do not talk about this conversation with anyone, you have been so ordered."

"Aye, sir."

"Also, check up on Heather regularly. Keep me informed of her spiritual and mental health."

"Aye, sir."

Eight weeks later, as SSN-75 was pulling into port at the Pearl Harbor

Submarine Base, Andrew called for Heather to come see him. He set her temporary duty assignment orders on his desktop. She knocked on his door as Bill showed her inside. After she saluted Andrew, she took off her cover.

"Wait outside, XO," said Andrew.

"Aye, sir," said Bill as he closed the door.

"I understand that the female bodybuilder from the Air Force keeps beating you year after year in the competitions; is that correct?" asked Andrew.

Andrew could tell by the look on her face that this question had caught her totally off guard.

"Yes, sir. I would like to beat her, sir; professionally, of course," replied Heather, stumbling over her words.

"I can understand that answer, Heather. Where is this female bodybuilder stationed?" asked Andrew, trying to keep her from finding out the reason for the questions.

"Vandenberg Air Force Base in Nevada, I believe, sir."

Andrew handed her temporary duty orders.

"When we have finishing docking, the XO will take you to the airstrip."

"Why, sir?" she asked suspiciously as she took the orders.

"It has been brought to my attention that you have been under a lot of stress recently. Perhaps a good workout with a fellow female bodybuilder will help relieve some of that stress."

"Ulterior motive, sir?"

"None that I am aware of, except, of course, that perhaps, with some tact, diplomacy and the workout, you might gain information that will be helpful in beating her at the next round of competitions."

"I suppose you're right, sir. I had better pack."

The XO escorted her out of officer's country so that she could pack. When the sub finally completed docking, the XO drove her to the airstrip in total silence. Eleven hours later, under the cover of darkness in the desert, the jet landed at Vandenberg Air Force Base.

Heather was picked up by a duty driver for the base and after passing through several checkpoints, she was escorted to the north wing of the hospital. When she opened the door to room 805, she almost fainted. There was Bart on the bed with his parents by his side and his right leg and left forearm in casts. He waited until Heather was seated by his left side before telling his story to her.